They came within three feet of him, then stopped.

He could see them better now. One was a man, the other a woman. His gaze was drawn to their faintly luminescent eyes, glowing with a sick green light.

He tried to get up, to run, but he couldn't. Something held him down. The weight of those eyes.

The woman knelt down and took his head in her hands. Slowly, almost gently, she tipped it back, as if she wanted to avoid hurting him. Then she leaned forward and put her lips lightly to his neck, and he noticed two things as her teeth entered him.

First, the fear was gone.

And second, absurdly, he had a hard-on.

I0688706

Copyright © 2008 James Viscosi
ISBN-13: 978-0-6151-9775-3
All Rights Reserved

Long Before Dawn

a novel

by James Viscosi

Prologue

The war never ended.

It could be a dazzling winter morning, the sun shining like it had just been born, glinting on the snow like a multitude of diamonds; and the war still smoldered like a buried ember, ready to catch the world on fire. It could be a languid summer afternoon, hot as hell's boiler room, bugs humming in the bushes; and the war still cast a chill into the humid air, a warning that the light would not last forever. And every evening, when the shadows joined together like drops of liquid darkness growing into an ocean, the sleeping beasts awoke, and the fighting began again.

Ken Fletcher knew the odds were bad, but that didn't stop him, any more than it stopped a gambler on the strip. With his wife Lauren and their friend George Follett, Ken had scored a few victories; these, like the war itself, passed unnoticed by most. They were minor wins anyway, against minor foes, the grunts, the shock troops, instead of the generals.

Today it would be different.

Today they had caught up with a general.

He cut the engine and it shuddered as it died. From the driver's seat, Ken stared across a field of shattered blacktop toward the decrepit building, the old warehouse. It was still in the shadow of the trees, but the small hill where he had stopped was catching the full morning sun; it was why he'd chosen this spot.

He and his two passengers disembarked from the vehicle. The

dewy grass showed dark lines behind the car, like bruises, marking their passage up the knoll. It sloped gently down to the remains of the parking lot. The blacktop had been reduced to a network of increasingly small plates separated by a spider web network of expanding cracks. Soon—not yet, but soon—there would be small trees and bushes growing where cars and trucks had once roamed. Nature was turning the macadam back into soil; there was no longer any clear demarcation where the grass ended and the pavement began. Toward its edges the lot was visible as necrotic patches of grey between spreading colonies of tough wide-leafed weeds and crabgrass, whereas in its interior the asphalt remained mostly free of vegetation.

Disuse had had its way with the building as well, each day leaving some mark of its passage on the structure. The sun and rain had warped and twisted the network of boards that had been nailed over the windows and doors of the place, so that now the building's interior darkness was visible through large gaps in the aged planking. A large oak had fallen against the right side of the warehouse, buckling the wall and smashing through the roof; rusty stains like dried blood spilled from the wound, running down the corrugated iron shell of the building. Ken could imagine, years and years ago, warehouse employees sheltering in the shade of the tree, hiding from the summer sun as they ate lunch from brown paper bags. Did something of the past still linger, ghostlike, in this place? Or was time the perfect solvent, erasing every trace of what once had been? Could those workers under the tree see, in the right circumstances, the wreck the place had become, see the three frightened people setting up outside, a traveling minstrel show whose music was violence, whose instruments were weapons?

If you can see us, Ken thought, pray for us; because desolation is where we dwell.

"Big building," George said, shading his eyes with his left hand. His right clutched the handle of a battered suitcase.

"Yeah, but it's early," Ken said. "We'll have time to search it."

"Krone will be up and about," George said.

"We know that." Lauren, Ken's wife, was impassive as she spoke, her gaze locked on the warehouse. "We've got a gun for Krone."

"Yeah. Yeah, we do." George stared at the warehouse a moment more, then turned and started walking back and forth, working out the kinks in his muscles. Despite his size—he was nearly as big as Krone, though nowhere near as strong, no one was—he insisted on riding in the tiny back seat of Ken's vehicle. He always told Ken a man should be next to his wife, and would not be persuaded otherwise.

After several minutes of walking and stretching, George crouched down and balanced the suitcase on his knees. With thick, slightly trembling fingers, he undid the locks and lifted the lid of the bedraggled case, revealing the tools of their unusual trade: Sharp wooden stakes and a mallets; holy symbols from five different religions; medical supplies; garlic cloves; a crowbar; three small flashlights; a gun, for Krone. Everything was securely buckled or belted or snapped into place, to keep the suitcase from rattling like a box full of rocks.

George took the gun, holding it up so the sun reflected dully on its dark barrel. It wasn't a very modern gun, but it fired large bullets without jamming, and that was the important thing. George snapped open the revolving chamber and began loading it. Meanwhile, Ken opened the trunk of the car and lifted a small steel gasoline can from its storage compartment. He carefully removed the cap from the can and replaced it with a nozzle.

"Think they know we're here?" Lauren asked.

"Don't they always," Ken said, not looking up.

"I wonder where they are." Lauren stared at the boarded-up windows. She tangled a finger in her long blonde hair and twirled it slowly. "I wonder where *he* is."

"I don't know about *him*, but Krone is probably watching us right now," Ken said. "Waiting for us, like last time."

Lauren stopped twirling her hair at the mention of Krone's name.

The chamber filled, George rotated it back into place and spun it. "Anybody for Russian Roulette?" he asked.

"Just going in there is Russian Roulette," Ken said. George nodded and closed the suitcase. When the time came, if they made it that far, Ken would call on him to open it again and take out the stakes and the mallets and the garlic. If they made it that far. If Krone didn't stop them this time.

They had a gun for Krone.

"Let's do it." Ken's knuckles were white on the handle of the gas can, but he kept any tremor out of his voice. He started toward the warehouse and the others fell in behind him. As the broken asphalt crunched under his feet, he unconsciously began to hum a hymn, *Adeste Fidelis*, a relic from his Catholic childhood. He saw Lauren glance at him and smile, and he realized he was doing it again; but he didn't stop. After all, what could happen when one of God's songs was in the air?

Soon the front door stood before them. It had once been shielded from the weather by a little awning, but this had collapsed into a jumbled heap of boards and nails and shingles. Like the windows, the door had planks nailed back and forth across it, but thanks to the vanished shelter, these boards had weathered the years better than most.

Ken set down the gasoline can as George opened the suitcase again and handed him the crowbar; then he clambered up onto the pile of debris and, perching himself precariously on a heap of shingles, set to work prying the boards loose. Below the two-by-fours was a layer of smaller boards; these were in almost perfect condition, the wood sturdy and the nail heads gleaming. Ken grunted and strained at them for a little while, then looked at George. The big man unsteadily scaled the collapsed porch and took the crowbar from Ken's hands. Ken returned to Lauren and the two of them stood close together, a last embrace before the battle started, waiting for George to finish. Lauren, her face against her husband's neck, murmured, "I love you, Ken."

"I love you too," he said, nuzzling her hair. It smelled like strawberries.

George ripped off the last board, paused a moment, and began to chuckle. He looked back at Lauren and Ken and then stepped aside so they could see the legend printed on the door in a circus marquee font.

Harris Bros. Caskets.

"They're coming."

Krone whispered the words, knowing that his Master would hear. He had been watching the hunters in their preparations, and when they began approaching the warehouse, had gone to warn his Master and the lady.   Krone couldn't see them; they were the same temperature as the rest of the room, and although he could see in the darkness, only patterns of hot and cold were visible to him. But he didn't need eyes to locate his Master; other, less sophisticated, feelings were enough to do that: A tingle on the skin, a tightening of the bowels.   Even he, Krone, the Master's servant, was not immune to fear of the beast; he knew it better than anyone else.

His words had received no reply, so he tried again. "Did you hear me, Master? I said—"

"I heard you."   The voice was soft but yawning, as if the words themselves could consume you, swallow you up like an open grave. "I've been expecting them."

"Should I kill them?" Krone asked, making two large fists.

"Have you been able to kill them in the past?"

Confused by the question, because the answer was obvious, Krone said: "No."

"That's right. Go and get the car ready."

"Get the car ready? Are we running away?"

"Do as I say, Krone."

"Yes, Master."   Surely the Master wasn't afraid? No, impossible; Martel did not know fear.   He had some plan in mind.   He must. Wondering what that plan might be, Krone turned and shambled out of the room.

"I hear something moving," George muttered.

"It's just us," Ken whispered.   "Our echoes."   They were in the main storage area, a huge, cavernous room that made their footsteps come back at them from tricky angles.   Boxes, crates, and old caskets abandoned by the Harris Brothers, whoever they had been, were piled all around; they had to thread their way through narrow, crowded aisles, staying alert for any enemy that might be hiding in the refuse.

"No," George said. "Stop a minute and listen."

They did.

Outside, a crow was cawing.

Somewhere, a beam was creaking.

And ahead of them, through the twists and turns of the maze, someone was walking. It was a heavy tread, first one footfall and then another, the second dragging slightly: *thud-scrape, thud-scrape, thud-scrape.*

"I hear it," Lauren whispered. "It's Krone."

George drew back the hammer of the revolver.

"Easy," Ken said. "We don't want that going off by accident."

"When Krone comes, we won't have much time. Remember what happened before."

"Well, he's not coming," Ken said. "He's going away." The footsteps were indeed receding, as Krone retreated to some distant part of the warehouse.

"Maybe he doesn't know we're here," Lauren said.

"Maybe." George's voice was doubtful as he slowly returned the hammer to its resting position. "Maybe."

"Come on," Ken said, creeping off into the darkness.

They moved more slowly after they heard Krone, more cautiously, keeping the flashlight beams low to the floor. Ken did not want to encounter him in these close quarters: Krone, who could tear metropolitan phone books in half, who could crush bricks with his hands, who could scoop out a man's insides the way a chef might gut a chicken. He could bury them under an avalanche of caskets and assorted shit without breaking a sweat, then rip them to pieces at his leisure.

A last turn brought them to the end of the maze. A stretch of open floor lay before them, offering nowhere to hide. Ken played his beam up and found a wall about twenty feet away. It was bare wood with a large picture window and a door beside it. "A half-dozen yards of open ground and then an office," Ken whispered, looking over his shoulder at the others.

"That's where they are."

"In the office?"

George nodded. "I feel them. I feel *her*."

Her referred to George's daughter, Elspeth. She was a casualty of the war, or a recruit of the other side, depending on how you looked at it. Ken called her a casualty. That she was, indeed, in the office was not in doubt; George was sensitive to his daughter's presence, he could *feel* when she was near. George refused to describe this *feeling*, clamming up whenever the subject was broached; Ken wondered sometimes why that was, but had never pressed him on it.

"Any way to get the sun in here?" George whispered.

Ken played the beam around quickly. "No windows nearby."

"Even if there were, he'd have them covered," Lauren said.

"*If* he had time to prepare," George said. "We don't know how long he's been here."

"Okay, if they're in the office, then that's where we have to go." Ken swallowed hard. Twice before they had caught up with this creature, and both times he had eluded them, leaving only a mocking taunt hanging in the air. But maybe they had been fortunate; although George had once sustained a concussion that had put him into the hospital for a week, and Ken and Lauren had both suffered cuts and bruises of varying severity, they hadn't suffered any lasting damage.

Would today be different?

"This time it ends," George said. "Let's go."

They went, keeping the beams on the floor in front of them, three dim shapes stealing through the darkness. George passed Ken and Lauren along the way and reached the office door first. He stood there, staring into the darkened office, as the others caught up. Hoping for a glimpse of Elspeth, Ken thought, Elspeth as she slept, looking like any other sleeping teenager, innocent and peaceful. Lauren went up to the picture window and carefully probed the office with her light. After three sweeps, she located female feet, small, wearing soiled leather moccasins, dirty grey soles, toes pointing at the ceiling. Lauren immediately pulled the beam back and looked at George. The man was staring through the doorway, his jaw working soundlessly. "You saw?" Lauren asked.

George nodded. "Elspeth," he whispered.

Lauren aimed her flashlight at the floor and waited.

"I'll do the gas." George reached out to Ken for the can. Ken exchanged it for the pistol.

"Do you want me to stake her?" Lauren asked.

"No!" The exclamation was loud, too loud for the circumstances, and George quickly lowered his voice. "No. I mean, no. I'll do it."

"You're doing the gasoline," Lauren said.

"I'll do the gas and then 5 then *I'll* stake her."

"If she wakes up?"

George's jaw was set. "Do what you have to do to keep her down, but *I* stake her, and that's that." Breaking off the conversation, he crept into the enemy's lair.

Ken came up close to his wife. "You stake her if you have to," he murmured, lips brushing her ear, a lover paying a compliment.

"You think I wouldn't?"

As they entered, Lauren flashed the light quickly around the walls and drew a sharp breath. "Windows. Painted."

"Painted?"

"George was right. He must not have had time to board them up."

"George!" Ken hissed. "George, wait." But George didn't seem to be listening; he was pouring the gasoline along the base of the wall and muttering to himself in a low, rhythmic voice.

"Let him be," Lauren said. "Just shoot out the window."

"Okay—keep the light on it." Ken raised the gun and pointed it, barrel trembling, at the thin barrier that kept out the cleansing power of the sun. The fear of the Master was in him like a snake, but he suppressed it, trying to keep the pistol steady. He would only get one shot. One shot, to wake the Master.

Ken squeezed the trigger.

In the garage, Krone heard the gunshot. He swung his massive head around and looked back toward the office. The hunters were there! They were shooting at his Master and the lady! He started to run back, but checked himself. The Master had said to get the car ready, and that meant they were going to *drive* the car, so ... so he would take the car to the Master!

Wouldn't Martel be pleased?

Grinning, Krone slid behind the wheel of the battered Lincoln.

Immediately after the gun's report came the sound of glass shattering, but the brilliant, cleansing sun did not appear; beyond the window was only more warehouse, dark and still. They had screwed up, failed to survey and understand the layout of the place before attacking. A stupid, stupid mistake. Ken heard Lauren say, "Oh no —" and then Martel, the Master, was in front of him. The vampire's pale skin was luminous in the flashlight beam, his eyes a luciferous green. He grabbed Ken's shirt and crotch, lifted him up overhead, and hurled him across the room as if he were a doll stuffed with

16

feathers. Ken smashed into the wall and tumbled down in a heap, lights dancing across his eyes, pain shooting down his back and into his legs.

"Ken!" George shouted from somewhere in the darkness. Then a match flared and fell, and a flame erupted at George's feet. It spread back along the wall, leaping higher with every second. In the flickering light all was revealed: The shattered glass, darkness beyond; the moldering desks; and the cocoons, plastered against the right-hand wall, gleaming like fresh cinnamon chewing gum, stuck in place with drooping tendrils of thick, jellied plasma. The cocoons reeked like corpses left out in the sun too long, shivered like gelatin with every vibration; even after all this time they were still the things that horrified Ken the most, these hideous nests made of half-digested human blood.

Elspeth was over near George, hissing at the fire, while the Master remained where he had been, clutching Lauren with a cold white hand and eyeing the flames warily. As a man, he must have been handsome; but now he was extraordinary. His features were pale and fine, his hair jet-black, his fingers long and clever; he exuded a sensual quality that was almost hypnotic. Ken had never understood why something cold and dead should have such a sexual power, but still he felt it, from Elspeth and the Master both, though there was no question whose pull was stronger. Ken tried to shake off the feeling, which came to him even now, as he lay there on the floor and his wife was still and quiet in Martel's cold hands.

"Fire?" Martel said. His eyes were shining. "You've not tried fire before. You must be getting desperate, to choose so undiscriminating a weapon."

"*Fuck you!*" George shouted.

Martel sighed, as if he longed for sharper repartee. "You are neither as eloquent nor as clever as some of my other foes; there have been many, over the long years, men better and braver than you and your pathetic band." Contempt frosted his voice. "I killed them all. Humans come and humans go, and still I remain, Martel the eternal." He turned to look at Lauren, his eyes boring into hers; she made no move to pull away. George took a step toward them and suddenly Elspeth was on his back, tearing at him with cracked and dirty nails, screeching inhumanly. Martel chuckled and did not look away from his golden prize.

Ken rolled over onto his stomach, his groan drawing the Master's attention. "Ah, Mr. Fletcher. Awake, are we? Good. I want you awake. She is pretty, your Lauren, with her flaxen hair and her fine body." Martel put his hand on the neckline of Lauren's blouse and ripped it down so that it hung like a tattered flag. He tore off her bra with powerful fingers, leaving a red mark up her chest and over her shoulders.

George toppled over, his daughter on his back, his blood on her fingers. She was sucking greedily at the base of his skull where her claws had torn through skin and flesh.

Ken stood shakily. His fingers still clutched the stake. His eyes flicked to George and the slurping, ravening Elspeth, and then back to Lauren and Martel.

"A dilemma, no?" Martel said. "Which to save? But do not trouble yourself; you cannot save either." He pulled back Lauren's head, exposing her neck. Two dozen tiny fangs glittered in his mouth, surrounding the four largest ones, the killers.

"No!" Ken shouted; but his cry was drowned out by a sudden crash from outside the office. Tires screeched, and seconds later the front end of a huge car smashed through the partition. The picture window shattered into a million tiny stars that cascaded down the hood of the car and spread out in a delta across the floor. Martel looked in shock at the automobile, and even Elspeth paused in her feeding to stare at this unexpected intrusion into the battle.

They gawked; Ken moved. He vaulted the desk over which he had been thrown, ignoring the pain in his side, and came down in a dead run. He was on Martel before the Master realized he was under attack, and holding the stake in both hands Ken shoved it into the beast's chest, pushing toward Martel's heart. But Martel was too fast; he grabbed Ken's wrists before the stake was firmly planted, and there had never been much chance of penetrating the breastbone by sheer force of muscle anyway, it was a desperation move, nothing more. Ken gasped as the Master wrenched his arms sideways, forcing him to let go of the weapon. As Ken lunged forward again, Martel kicked him hard in the stomach, sending him staggering backwards.

"Lauren," he moaned.

"She's mine," Martel said, yanking out the stake. No blood came from the wound; Martel had not been in his cocoon this night.

Martel had not been in his cocoon!

Yes, and neither had Elspeth. They had been waiting, not resting. Attacking Martel here had been a disastrous folly; everything about this lair favored the vampires, from the carefully chosen location in the middle of the warehouse to the disorienting maze of rubbish. Martel had known Ken and the others would come, had lain in wait for them, confident and patient as the minotaur in his labyrinth. Cursing himself for a fool, Ken retreated as Martel walked forward, in no particular hurry, holding the stake in the air like a knife. He spun Lauren away from him. She slumped against the wall and slid to the floor, hunched over, motionless. As the flames reached the ceiling Martel snarled and leapt at Ken. Ken attempted to twist out of the way but his foot slid in George's blood; he stumbled and Martel struck, stabbing him in the back near his left shoulder. The force of the blow drove him to his knees. Ken cried out and tried to strike at the vampire, but Martel easily cast him aside, sending him sliding across the floor and into a desk, leaving a slick of blood behind him.

Martel strode back to where Lauren leaned dazedly against the wall. He grabbed her arm and yanked her to his side, then spared a glance for Elspeth. She was standing, blood smearing her face and arms, grinning widely; George lay prone on the floor, the base of his skull opened up and oozing a clear watery fluid mingled with bright red blood.

"Idiot," Martel said. "Did you think you would take me asleep again? Did you think I didn't know you were coming?"

"B-b-ba—" Ken stumbled over the word. His head throbbed, pain speared out from his shoulder. His mind felt as dark and cluttered as the warehouse in which he would die.

"Spare me your small words," Martel said. "I am unimpressed."

Then, with a roar and a crash, the ceiling of the left half of the office collapsed. Elspeth had time to look up at the burning timbers, and she raised her arm over her head and shrieked; then she and George were buried beneath the inferno. Ken could only watch dumbly, pain and smoke forming tears in his eyes. From the car, Krone bellowed something. Martel seemed stunned, but only momentarily, and this time there was no assault by Ken, who lay broken and defeated on the floor.

"So," Martel said, glaring at Ken, "you rob me of my woman, even as I rob you of yours."

"No," Ken said. He got up on his hands and knees, but couldn't support himself and collapsed. Numbness radiated from his wound; there was no pain, not yet. There would be soon, he knew.

If he lived so long.

Martel glanced at the fire. It was spreading rapidly; soon the entire building would be engulfed. Still holding Lauren's elbow, he turned his back on Ken and strode over to the car. "Goodbye, Mr. Fletcher," he said. "But know this: You brought yourself to this fate. I do what I must to survive; you *chose* to follow me into the darkness. Now it claims you, as it so long ago claimed me."

"This isn't over," Ken said from where he lay. "I'll get you, you bastard."

"I rather doubt that, Mr. Fletcher," Martel said.

9:30 AM

"You are an imbecile, Krone," Martel said.

The Lincoln had left the burning warehouse behind and was now traveling north through the daylight, a moving refuge from the angry sun. Jet-black windows shielded the back seat from the destroying radiation; an opaque barrier separated it from Krone. Martel's words passed through a silver-slatted grate in the divider.

"I'm sorry, Master," Krone whined.

"The pests were defeated, and then you drove the car through the wall! You gave Fletcher the chance to drive his stake into my chest! No one has done that in over two centuries, Krone."

"I know, Master. I'm real sorry."

"How many times must I tell you that you're not intelligent enough to think for yourself?" Martel said.

The wretched Krone could only blubber.

"Turn on the police scanner and listen for news about the fire. I have things to attend to." Satisfied that the fool had been chastened, Martel turned his attention to Lauren, who lay against the car door as if asleep, her breasts bouncing with the bumps. He licked his lips. True, he had only taken her in spite against Fletcher; but she *was* beautiful, and he *had* lost Elspeth. Perhaps he would turn her, let her exist for a while, and then dispose of her when she became tiresome. After all, he mused, a vampire could not live on blood alone.

He leaned forward and took her in his arms, tilting her head back to expose her neck. He leaned over, his jaw opening as if it were hinged, his four huge canines sliding down from their sheaths; but as he bent for the bite they hit a large bump in the road, and Martel lost his balance and slid down into Lauren's lap.

"Krone!" he exploded.

The response was more blubbering.

"Be quiet, Krone. Pull over for a little while."

Martel waited until the motion of the car had stopped, and then he began again where he was. After all, it was not *necessary* that he bite her in the neck; that was just a matter of convenience, because of the large vein there. But there were veins in other places.

Legs, for instance.

He worked his teeth on her thigh, scissoring through her denim jeans until there was a large patch of bare skin. Then, taking his time, he began to nibble, not using his fangs. Lauren moaned softly. Martel slowly slid down the zipper of her jeans and began massaging her gently with his tongue. As she groaned and clutched at his hair, he suddenly switched his mouth back to her leg and dropped his lower jaw, again unhinging it and raising his canines. He sunk his teeth into the flesh of her inner thigh, sucking on the blood that welled out. Lauren gasped as the teeth entered her, a gasp of pleasure, and her hips bucked as her jeans grew wet. Then, moaning softly, she went limp.

Martel sucked and sucked to drain her dry; he was biting to kill, not simply to feed, not this time. It didn't take long. He could tell the exact moment she died; her taste changed, turned flat and sour, and he withdrew his fangs. Blood welled from four puncture wounds in her bare leg: Poisoned blood; dead blood. It quickly stopped oozing. He pulled himself back to a sitting position and examined Lauren. Soon she would awaken, and then she would be his.

He turned to the voice-grate. "Drive, Krone."

"Drive where, Master?"

"Wherever. North. We should be out of the state before nightfall. When the authorities find the bodies at the warehouse, there will be questions."

As the car began moving, Martel slumped back against the door. The wound in his chest troubled him slightly. He had almost forgotten what it felt like to be injured; it was more a memory of pain than pain itself, annoying but nothing more. It was the insult to his person that he found intolerable. Fletcher had joined an elite company, Martel thought: Those who had done him physical harm. He thought of the fire, and hoped it had consumed the man slowly, roasting him alive.

With that pleasurable image in his mind, Martel lost himself in a caricature of sleep; a deep, black, dreamless well filled with echoes of a life lost, and memories of the light.

1

5:30 PM

Roxanne Carmichael stared, horrified, at her boyfriend Christian Keems. He had promised to behave this evening, he had *promised*, but she should have known that like so many of Christian's promises, this one was subject to change or revocation without notice.

Facing Chris from about three paces away was the evening's hostess, Roxanne's friend Abby, construction company heiress and indirect target of the remark that had brought the congenial cocktail party screeching to an appalled halt.

"Abby, I'm sorry … I'm sure he didn't mean it," Roxanne said, although *she* wasn't the one who had just made a terrible, rude, boorish comment.

Abby said: "I am going to ask you—*you*, Chris, and not Roxanne—to apologize for insulting my family. Otherwise you'll be wearing this drink on your way home."

Please, apologize, Roxanne prayed, even though that was about as likely as the world suddenly ending and sparing her further humiliation. The other guests were utterly silent, waiting for the denouement. She half-expected Chris to take a bow for his ability to bring an enjoyable evening to the brink of social disaster and then, as its arms windmilled at the edge of the precipice, give it a good solid kick in the ass to push it off.

"Why should I apologize?" Chris said, smirking. "You don't really think anyone here believes your dad got this rich in construction without doing some deals with the Mob, do you?"

And the party, Christian's foot deeply planted in its backside, plummeted to its demise.

5:40 PM

"Your friend's really bitchy," Christian said.

Jerk, Roxanne thought.

"I mean, is she really so naive that—"

"If you don't shut up right now, I swear to God you can walk home."

He looked startled, then annoyed, but he shut up as requested. Too bad; she almost wished he would call her bluff, so she could demonstrate that she wasn't bluffing. Just like Abby hadn't been bluffing; Chris was going to have to pay to get his suit dry-cleaned. The remains of Abby's beverage were currently drying near the collar of the pale blue jacket, red as blood, as you would expect from a Bloody Mary.

She really shouldn't be driving right now, Roxanne knew. She was tired and she'd had a drink or two, not enough to get a buzz but still, you never knew, her reactions could be off, she might get in an accident. Her sporty little car, emphasis on *little*, wasn't really designed for withstanding impacts.

It also wasn't designed for running without gasoline, but that was what she was asking it to do: The needle was riding on empty. Luckily they were near Interstate 81, so there would be plenty of gas stations once they got off the private road that led to Abby's hilltop residence, financed, according to Chris, by kickbacks and drug money.

Abby's road took them to the bottom of a deep valley, depositing them on a bumpy little street that paralleled a frozen grey stream. The snow along the creekside was deep, white, and pure, with bulbous ice formations that glistened in the light of her headlamps.

"She asked for it, anyway," Chris muttered.

A few minutes later he was standing on the side of the road as Roxanne drove away, alone.

Not long after ejecting Chris from her car, Roxanne stopped at a Mom and Pop gas station, so rurally low-tech that the pumps didn't take credit cards and they didn't make you pay cash in advance, even after dark. The price per gallon, however, was all city. As she stood there holding the nozzle and marveling at how quickly the numbers in the price were going up, another car pulled in on the other side of the island. It was truly a tank, a big, battered Lincoln with deeply tinted rear windows, like a rich person's car that someone had stolen, taken off-roading, and never properly repaired.

The driver got out; he was the biggest guy she'd ever seen, seven feet tall at least, with muscles like a gorilla's and a head shaped like a turnip. The guy was wearing tight jeans and a muscle shirt despite the chill, and didn't appear to be the slightest bit cold. He didn't look like any chauffeur she had ever seen.

The nozzle clicked in her hand. She checked the pump to see the damages, then went into the gas station mini-market. She decided to pick up a snack to eat in the car, as Chris had gotten them kicked out before dinner. She was still eyeing the collection of rather sorry-looking candy bars and potato chips when the driver of the other car came in to pay for his gas. Big car like that, thought Roxanne, he probably put enough fuel in it to deplete a major oil field.

She finally spotted a single bag of trail mix hiding behind the cheese puffs. That might be slightly less toxic than the brilliant orange Styrofoam in front of it. She grabbed it and got in line behind the gorilla.

The Lincoln was still there when she came out of the store, running, belching white vapor from the exhaust. Now the rear window was down. Inside the car it was jet black, she couldn't see anything of the occupants; but she got the creepiest feeling that *they* could see *her*, and not only that, they were *studying* her. She felt invisible spiders crawling on her skin as she circled the back end of the big car and headed for her own. She resolutely ignored the Lincoln and whoever might be in it, and her step faltered only a little when she heard the window on the side nearer her open as she passed. She refused to give the creep the satisfaction of turning around, of letting him know he was bothering her; that only encouraged this sort of weirdo.

Oh, hell.

She stopped near her car, turned to the Lincoln, and said: "Can I help you with something?"

No response.

"I'm talking to you," she said. "Do you have a problem? Never seen a woman before? We're all over the place, you know."

Two small green lights appeared inside the Lincoln, eye-shaped, though of course they weren't really eyes, because they glowed. Maybe the guy was pointing a camcorder at her or something, capturing her for future viewing in the privacy of his own home. But the lights were so strange … almost hypnotic …

Suddenly disconcerted, because those lights almost seemed to be *doing* something to her, Roxanne looked away and got into her own car; and when she did, the Lincoln rolled away from the pump and out of the parking lot, heading for the Interstate. Good riddance to ugly freaks, Roxanne thought. Then someone tapped on her passenger side window and she gave a startled little shriek. She turned and looked. Chris was bent over next to her car, trying to look sheepish and shivering like a scared mouse.

Speaking of ugly freaks.

5:50 PM

"Jesus, that was weird," Roxanne said.

"What was weird?" Chris said. He had managed to weasel his way back into the car; the encounter with the spooky driver and his unseen passenger had made her reluctant to drive home alone. Besides, she couldn't *really* abandon him out here, rewarding as it might be.

"Back at the gas station. Before you came. There was this big ugly car and some weirdo in the back seat was staring at me." Roxanne shuddered. "It was creepy. And you should've seen the driver!"

"What about him?"

"Well for one thing he was huge. And he wasn't wearing any coat. And … what are you doing?"

As she'd been talking, he'd reached over and put his hand on her knee, squeezing it softly. "Relax, babe. You're tired, you've had a few drinks." Chris let his hand slide from Roxanne's knee to her thigh. "Maybe you'd like me to help you calm down?"

"I'm driving, Chris. I don't want us to end up wrapped around a tree."

"The road has guardrails," Chris said.

26

"I don't want us to bounce off a guardrail either. Just drop it, Chris, okay?"

Grumbling, Chris leaned back in his seat.

"Stop sulking," Roxanne said.

"I'm not sulking," Christian said.

"Yes you are."

"Anyway, why should I sulk?" Chris said. "I mean, it's not like you kicked me out of your car or anything."

"You were being an asshole."

"Oh, now I'm an asshole?"

"At times. This is one of them."

"Is this supposed to make me stop sulking?"

"I'm trying to explain why I don't like to be around you sometimes."

Chris frowned and looked thoughtful for a moment, then said: "Is it that time of the month again?"

Roxanne turned the radio up very, very high.

Just south of the New York state line, they passed an ostentatious, floodlit billboard: *The Pennsylvania Pilgrim Motel! Fifty Units, Open Year-Round. Satellite TV! Waterbeds! Reasonable Rates!* Roxanne had had enough driving for the evening, so she took the exit suggested by the sign. It deposited them practically in the motel's parking lot. Chris didn't offer to go get the room—he was still sulking—so she got out of the car and headed for the office. As she was about to enter the building, Chris stuck his head out the window and called, "Get a room with a hot tub!"

"Look at this place," she said. "Do you think they have rooms with hot tubs? Jesus Christ."

But she dutifully asked for one anyway.

And, surprise, they had them.

2

SUNDAY, JANUARY 10

1:45 AM

"The cows are acting strange," JoBeth McMillan said.

Her husband, Rex, didn't respond, so she shook him again, and this time he groaned and mumbled, "Why are you shaking me

"The cows are acting strange," JoBeth said. Rex sat up and, rubbing his eyes with the backs of his hands, listened. A cacophony of lowing drifted in through the half-opened window of the house, like a cow rock concert.

"They're being noisy," Rex conceded.

"Go and see what's wrong. Maybe there's a coy-dog in the barn again."

"Rex Junior would be barking if it was a coy-dog."

"You *have* to go and see!"

Grumbling, Rex stood and scratched his stomach. He cast about the room for his robe and found it wadded up on the Adirondack chair that stood between the dresser and the phone stand. He slipped it on over his ragged underwear, slid his feet into a pair of slippers, and headed out of the bedroom.

A few minutes later, Rex pushed open the outside door and descended the concrete steps to the path that ran from the side of the house to the driveway, and from the driveway to the barn. He had traded his slippers for a pair of boots, and wore a down coat over his robe; in his hands he carried a shotgun, loaded, safety off. Whatever was in his barn, it would learn how a McMillan dealt with trespassers.

He trudged along the frozen mud of the path, but when he reached the driveway he stopped. It felt like someone was watching him, watching and sizing him up like ... like the way he appraised his male cows when he was deciding how much they would fetch at the slaughterhouse.

He heard a window open behind him. "Go on, Rex!" his wife shouted from the second-story bedroom. Her voice seemed to ring in the night, an announcement that he, Rex McMillan, was outside in the darkness, woefully unprotected except by a noisy little stick.

The clamor of the cows brought him back to reality. What the hell was he thinking about? He was acting like a kid on Halloween, the dumb one everybody likes to scare.

His wife watching, Rex walked slowly up to the barn. He reached the milking room and, after fumbling for a few seconds with his keys, unlocked the door and pushed his way inside, switching on the light as he entered. He circled the stainless steel milk vat, heading for the entrance to the barn proper. Light from the milking room spilled through the open doorway, making the depths of the cowshed seem even darker by comparison.

Rex paused. Where was the low-level lighting? Had all the bulbs burned out at the same time? Unlikely. Maybe there'd been a short in the line. That was a possibility: There'd been a short, and it had made a spark, which had frightened the cows.

Rex groped for the master light switch of the barn. Before he found it there was a *click*, and the light in the milking room winked out. He suddenly felt sandwiched between two massive weights, as if the darkness in the barn and the darkness in the milk room were physical entities pushing on him from both sides.

Where the hell was the light switch?

Now he heard something coming from behind him, a faint whiskery sound like fabric brushing against concrete, something being dragged lightly along the floor. But what could it be? There had been nobody in there when he entered; he would have seen an intruder, there was nowhere to hide. The irrational fear came back stronger than ever, hitting him like a physical blow. His hand that scrabbled for the light switch began to shake, even as he tried to convince himself that what he heard was a rat scampering across the barn.

Somebody snatched the shotgun from his left hand. Rex cried out and stumbled forward into the barn, tripping over a bucket. It bounced noisily along the floor. The cows bellowed even louder, drowning out the clanging of the pail.

Rex recovered his balance and started to run. There was another door nearby, a door to the outside. He would get out of here, go back to the house, call the police. His foot caught on something soft but heavy and he tripped again, this time going headlong into a damp metal pipe that carried water to the cows. It caught him in the midriff and he spun over it, landing heavily on his back, cracking his head against the concrete floor. He blinked, trying to ignore the pain in his skull, and saw two shapes approaching him, silhouetted against the windows. They were people, he thought; but even in this barn that housed sixty cows he could *smell* them: A faint odor of blood, a breath of decay.

How could he tell it came from them?

The figures came to within three feet of him and then stopped. He could see them better now. One was a man, the other a woman. His gaze was drawn to their faintly luminescent eyes, glowing with a sick green light. Rex had read somewhere that dead things glowed as they decayed; if that were true, he thought, they'd glow the same way as those eyes.

He tried to get up, to run some more, but he couldn't. Something held him down. The weight of those eyes.

The woman knelt down and took McMillan's head in her hands. Slowly, almost gently, she tipped it back, as if she wanted to avoid hurting him. Then she leaned forward and put her lips lightly to his neck, and Rex noticed two things as her teeth entered him: First, the fear was gone; and second, absurdly, he had a hard-on.

7:25 AM

Dawn. The endless show began with the crescent of the sun appearing over the hills in the east, narrow at first, widening as the fiery eye rose higher. Fingers of light stole along the ground, groping westward, caressing the earth like a fickle mistress. He watched them near the far bank of the river, stared as they dipped into the cool water and shivered toward him.

As the gently rippling water caught a sparkle from the morning sun, the boughs of the trees began to creak in a wind off the mountains. He could tell the wind was cold by the way it made his eyes feel, hard and sort of glassy. From where he hid, there at the water's edge, Martel watched the tide of day wash slowly forward, the forbidden country opening before him. For a moment he toyed with the idea of just staying there, where he was; yes, stay in the open to watch the sunrise, as was any man's prerogative. It had been so, so long; and it would end everything, wouldn't it? No more darkness. No more death.

The light crept closer. He stared at it, even though it hurt his eyes. Across the river the small town hugged the bank, clustered around a dirty grey factory jutting out on ancient weathered pilings over the water, leaching thin blue smoke from two tall, sooty towers. Houses were jumbled together left and right of the factory, as if they were rotten teeth in a wide, wet mouth, the factory a diseased grey tongue. Sleeping town; sleeping people. Most of them probably worked in that hideous factory, and dwelled in hovels, and would die of drink or industrial misadventure; they lived like maggots in a carcass. And he envied them. *He envied them!* And so he hated them. Yes, all of them, and every inhabitant of every stinking town he'd ever been in, every night, since before Columbus had sailed. Since the forest. He closed his eyes, thinking of the forest. His wife. His children. And the goat. The price of his life, one goat.

The sunlight was coming closer. He knew he wasn't going to wait for it; this was an old game he played, the oldest. Turning away from the low slumbering houses and the factory that leaked smoke, he fled through the forest. A few hardy birds were starting to sing, celebrating the warmth of the dawn. The world lightened around him and he thought: Faster, faster! He'd stayed at the bank too long! He forced himself to slip the tug of the earth, to fly in defiance of nature; his very existence was a defiance of nature. Tree trunks were a muddy blur to him as he flew, quiet as the wind rustling through the woods.

He burst out of the forest wall and onto the hard dirt road, bringing small branches and twigs in his wake. They spilled out across the old rutted track as he swung a hard right. He felt a tingling in his skin, a burning prickle, as the lightening world abjured him, tried to vomit him out like a stomach rejecting a rotten piece of meat. He saw a chain link fence ahead and soared over it; and beyond was shelter: The large dark car, hidden away from wandering eyes. He leapt over its roof, slid on his belly down the windshield toward the hood. He forced his body to release its cohesion, his very molecules to pull apart; in his haste he very nearly pushed it too far, taking himself to the edge of disintegration. This, the apotheosis of his power—that he could force his own flesh to betray the laws of nature —was not to be done in such a panic. He managed to halt the discorporation, and instead disbursed himself down the air intakes. Sunrays glanced obliquely off the hood of the car, probing fingers snatching at one who defied them; but, again, too late.

Thick mist flowed into the car through the vents, shooting past the snoring Krone and through the slotted metal grate in the barrier between day and night.

"There you are," Lauren Fletcher said, as Martel slowly materialized beside her. "I thought you'd been caught by the daylight."

"Almost," Martel gasped. "Almost." This brush with the sun had been the closest he could remember; his near-dissolution had left him drained and trembling. It would be some time before he would recover fully, days, perhaps even a week. He thought again of Ken Fletcher and the wound he had inflicted, which was as nothing compared to this brief exposure to the day. How puny humans were next to the order of nature! How puny he was, himself!

Martel slumped against the door, staring at the black window that showed him nothing of the outside world. What he would give to feel the sun on his face, just one more time.

Roxanne awoke to the sun on her face. At first she tried to blink away the annoyance, but soon she realized it was hopeless and opened her eyes. The light had found its way between the olive-drab curtains, forming a line of brilliance shot through with floating dust particles. She sat up and the beam transferred its affections to the pillow.

She glanced over at Christian. He was a lump beneath the covers; he had even pulled the pillow over his head. She frowned; he was usually an open-air sleeper. Then she noticed that the television was still on, so maybe he had gone under the pillow to avoid the light and sound of it. That made her look at the hot tub in the corner, barely used. Last night, Chris had filled it up, gotten in, and tried to convince her to join him; she'd just been wavering on the edge of doing so when he'd suddenly gotten all pale and trembling. She thought he might be having a heart attack; he insisted he was fine. But he had climbed out of the hot tub, into bed, turned on the television, and not spoken for the rest of the night.

Well, if he was dead under there, it served him right.

Roxanne rose and walked through the sunbeam, feeling its warmth along her body. She yawned and stretched, hearing her spine crack. Then she leaned forward, put her hands on the edge of the bed, and slowly slid her feet toward the window, stretching her back until it cracked again. The sunbeam tickled her thighs … and then it was gone. A cloud, no doubt. She went into the bathroom, and froze.

Someone was outside the bathroom window.

A dark shape stood on the other side of the rippled surface, leaning in, trying to see through. She could almost make out his face as he pressed it against the glass, shading his eyes with his hands. She could make out the shape of his head.

It might be the guy from the gas station last night.

Roxanne retreated from the bathroom, slamming the door shut. She jumped onto the bed, and onto Chris. He gasped and started thrashing around, trying to get away from her, shoving her with his hands. "Chris!" she yelled, ripping the pillow off his head and throwing it aside.

He stopped thrashing and looked at her with unfocused eyes. "Roxie?"

"Of course," she said. "Who else would it be?"

"Sorry, babe," he mumbled. "I was having bad dreams. I thought you were part of them."

"Thanks a lot," she said, rolling away and putting her eyes toward the television. "You're really showing me how much you care this weekend."

Christian rubbed his eyes with his hands and said nothing.

"Somebody was outside the hotel room," Roxanne said, still watching the TV. It was some local morning show, and they were talking about some farm somewhere. "He was looking at me."

"What?"

"I said there was somebody outside the room looking at me."

"Are you sure?"

"Christ, I'm sure."

"Oh … well, what do you want to do about it?" Chris's voice was thick and raspy, like he was coming down with something.

"Complain to the management, I guess."

Chris yawned and rubbed his eyes again. "God, I'm so tired," he moaned. "I feel like I didn't get any rest at all."

"You tossed and turned all night."

"Bad dreams, babe," he groaned. Then he peered at the television. "What's going on?"

"What?"

"On the TV. Aren't you watching it?"

"I wasn't paying attention," she said.

"Looks like a murder."

Was he trying to avoid talking about the peeping Tom? She focused on the news. They were showing jerky footage of some men carrying a black body bag out of a barn. Behind them, another man carried a smaller bag slung over his shoulder like he was Santa Claus. An off-camera reporter was explaining something about how a farmer's wife had found her husband in the barn with his head blown clean off with his own rifle, right next to the body of their dead dog. The police suspected some sort of satanic cult, because of the bloodletting that had taken place before the man was killed. The blood must have been collected in some sort of container, because there had been very little at the murder site, certainly less than one would expect given the dead man's injuries.

"Very nice," Roxanne said.

Chris said: "I swear to God, if there were as many Satanists running around as these tabloid reporters claim—"

Roxanne shut off the television.

"I was watching that," Chris said.

Roxanne said: "Let's try to focus. Shower. Dress. Report peeping Tom to management. Okay?"

"Okay," Chris said. He turned the TV back on. "You go first."

* * *

9:30 AM

The day man at the motel seemed unimpressed with their complaint. "Peeping Tom, huh?" he said lazily, eyeing first Roxanne and then Christian.

"Yes, a peeping Tom," Roxanne said. She got the impression that in addition to an obvious reluctance to tear himself away from the television set behind the counter, the young man (whose name tag identified him as Mark S.) couldn't care less that someone had been spying on her. She could've walked in and announced that cockroaches had eaten her boyfriend and this man would have said, in the same bored and condescending tone, *Cockroaches, huh?*

"So did you see him?" he asked.

"No. I mean yes, but I couldn't see any details through the bathroom glass."

There was a pause as Mark S. fidgeted with a pen on his desk. "Well," he said finally, "to be honest, we've never had a complaint like this before, and I'm not sure what you expect me to do about it."

Roxanne glanced at Christian, who stood off to one side, studying his fingernails. Then, looking back at Mark S., she said, "Don't you have a security guard or something? To send door to door? Whoever it was is probably staying here."

Mark S. looked at her like she had suddenly sprouted antlers.

She sighed. "Can you at least call the police and tell them there's a voyeur in the area?"

"They're busy with that McMillan thing right now," the day man said. "I'll call them this afternoon."

Roxanne raised an eyebrow. "Are you saying that every police officer in the area is at that farm?"

"More than likely."

"Never mind, I'll call them myself." She got out her cell phone. No signal. "Shit!" She put the phone away again.

"There's no call for bad language," Mark S. said.

"You want to hear bad language?" Roxanne said. "Get ready, because here it comes."

10:15 AM

Roxanne's little black sports car had rejoined the northward traffic on the interstate, skimming along the cold pavement and gradually leaving the hills of Pennsylvania behind. They drove in silence for a long time, the snow-covered scenery whizzing by. Roxanne stared straight ahead, ignoring Chris's decreasingly subtle attempts to get her to acknowledge his existence. Finally he made the mistake of speaking: "What," he asked, "is the matter with you?"

"What's the matter with me?" She turned to look at him. "What's the matter with *me?*"

"Yes, what's the matter with you?"

"God! Are you *trying* to piss me off?"

"What'd I do?"

"Most recently, you stood there like a wooden Indian while I complained to that idiot at the motel."

"Considering the circumstances I thought he was being reasonable. Anyway you're lucky he didn't kick you out when you started swearing at him. You sounded like a sailor."

"That little dweeb acted like it was a perfectly harmless pastime, going around looking at women through windows!"

Chris chuckled. "Well, it can be fun."

She smacked him in the shoulder; but then she laughed. "I did freak him out a little, didn't I?"

"I'm sure he never heard such language from such a pretty girl," Chris said. "I thought his ears were going to fall off."

"Yeah, this has been one hell of a weekend," Roxanne said. "What'll we do for an encore?"

"I'm thinking a multi-state armed robbery spree," Chris said. "I'll drive the getaway car, you knock over the banks and liquor stores. When they catch us, you can tell them Mark S. drove you to a life of crime."

"And what'll your excuse be?"

"Shit," Chris said. "Once the cops get a look at you during the strip search, they won't even have to ask."

3:25 PM

Officer Barry Brennan, patrolman with the White Bluff police department, sat on the hard grey bench in the locker room staring at the piece of paper in his hands. He was half-changed into his civvies —the lower part of his body wearing jeans and sneakers, the upper part wearing a dark-blue shirt, badge, peaked hat, black tie, and various small silver baubles—but he made no move to finish his temporary transition from cop to ordinary citizen.

An older man entered the locker room, his not-inconsiderable paunch pressing tightly against the front of his own uniform. He walked along the end of the lockers, habitually glancing down each row as he went to the one containing his own. He passed Barry, glanced down, and kept going, only to reappear a moment later, looking at the younger officer with some concern.

"Barry?"

Barry looked up and noticed his colleague. "Oh, hi, Jerry."

Jerome Klein walked down and plopped his wide fanny on the narrow wooden bench, which creaked in protest. "You okay?"

"Yeah," Barry said, looking back at the piece of paper. It was dense with typewriter characters, and bore an official seal.

"What you got there?"

"Oh, just notification that my divorce is final."

"Oh, is that all?"

"Yep. I'm a free man."

"Great. So when are you going to ask Monica out?"

"Don't start," Barry said. He put down the letter, finally, and began unbuttoning his shirt.

"Monica likes you—"

"Monica likes everyone. No offense. Look, Mr. Fix-Em-Up, I'll date when I find someone I want to date, all right?"

"You've been separated three years, and you haven't found anyone you want to date yet?"

"What are you, my bubbie? Don't make me shoot you."

"Okay, okay," Jerome said. He stood up. "You're off next weekend, right?"

"Yep."

"Great. I heard about this singles ski trip to Vermont—" He broke off as Barry reached for his gun. "Are you gonna shoot me now?"

"No," Barry said. "I'm gonna shoot myself."

4:40 PM

They had arrived in the little town earlier in the day, shortly before noon. After trailing the woman in the sports car to her home and noting the location, Krone had set about finding a hiding place for his Master and the Master's new lady.   There were plenty of abandoned buildings here, including one in a marsh that had looked especially promising, but after closer inspection he had deemed it too risky. The structure proved lopsided and rickety, as if a good winter storm might blow it down. And what if he chose a building that was scheduled for demolition on Monday? The Master would have his head.

So, in an unusual stretch for him, Krone had done a bit of detective work.

Noticing that there were a number of railroad tracks running through the area, Krone found a library and started rummaging through maps of the county. At six-foot-five, with a pointy, gourd-shaped head and bulging muscles, pale watery eyes, and sparse black hair that grew in tufts, wearing soiled jeans and a blue muscle shirt that didn't quite fit, he presented a memorable picture as he bent over the maps like some medieval navigator; but he ignored the inevitable stares he received, and after a few hours' work, he found what he was looking for: A defunct railroad with a tunnel. He rolled up the map and trotted out of the library with it, defeating with a snarl the security guard who accosted him with a tentative "Excuse me, sir, but that's library property."

He'd spent the rest of the day driving around trying to find the tunnel; the map was rather old, and many of the current streets didn't exist when it had been drawn. Now, though, he thought he was finally on the right track. He'd turned from a main road onto a narrower, blacktop side road; and from there he turned onto a poorly-maintained dirt road that climbed sharply up the south side of the valley. A few hundred yards after diverging from the blacktop, the road suddenly dipped and became nothing more than a wide path, probably grassy in summertime but now a foot deep in snow. To the left a steep hill rose, thick with trees and scrub; to the right was a ridge, a sharp downward slope, and then houses, their windows yellow squares in the twilight.

Just as he began to fear that he'd taken another wrong turn, he came to a break in the slope to his left. A low wooden fence, in extreme disrepair, formed a halfhearted attempt to keep trespassers out. The old rail bed continued off to the right, toward the houses, forming a ravine cut into the hillside. He wasn't surprised it had been abandoned; it was pretty steep for a train. They'd probably rerouted it around the hill.

He turned left, into the defile. The fence was even weaker than it looked and broke easily. Now they were in the rail bed, churning through deep, half-frozen snow. Krone could feel the periodic *thump* of an old railroad tie that had not yet given way to rot. The walls here were of rock, still showing the scars of the blasting that had created the pass.

He soon reached the tunnel, around a slight bend to the right. It was about fifteen feet wide and twenty-five high, a massive concrete mouth that was beginning to show the wear of the years; here and there the masonry had sloughed away to reveal rippled iron bars within. At the apex of the arch was a weathered stone; an inscription was still visible on it, just barely. It said *1899*. Krone tried and failed to recall what he and the Master had been doing in 1899. Were they out in California then?

Oh well. He had enough trouble remembering what had happened last month, let alone nearly a hundred years ago. Turning his attention back to the present, Krone guided the Lincoln into the tunnel.

5:00 PM

Martel was pleased. "This is perfect, Krone," he said, looking around, running a pale hand along the masonry wall. "Very well done."

Krone, excited beyond words that the Master thought his choice of abodes worthy, merely whined like a dog.

"It's horrid," Lauren said. "Cold and dark and dreadful."

"And what do *you* think would be appropriate?"

"We should have a mansion! We should have the greatest mansion in the world, and the light-dwellers should come and worship us and bring us offerings!"

Martel stared at her. "The *light-dwellers*? Is that what we call humans now?" Lauren started to speak but Martel cut her off. "Mrs. Fletcher, please, spare us your theatrics."

She looked at him as if he had slapped her; after a moment she turned her gaze to the floor and said, softly, "Don't call me that."

"Why?" Martel asked. "Is that not your name?" He watched her a moment, then switched his attention back to Krone. "Did you find the woman's home?"

"Why are you so interested in her?" Lauren said, looking up sharply. "You're mine."

"No." Martel pointed at the former Mrs. Fletcher. "*You* are *mine*. Remember that."

"I ..." Lauren seemed to lose her voice under his glare. Finally she looked away, at some point over Martel's shoulder. "I'm sorry, Master."

Martel eyed her carefully for a few more seconds, then turned back to Krone. "Well?"

"Yes, Master. I followed her all the way home."

"And where does she live, Krone?"

The big man was trembling with excitement. "A little town called Mapledale," he said, "in a little house in the woods."

It was rather pathetic, Martel thought, Krone's eagerness to please him, like a dog that had been kicked and kicked until it thought that *not* being kicked was a sign of affection. But since he had been the one doing the kicking, he supposed it was rather hypocritical of him to disdain Krone's behavior now. Martel turned away, looking at the wall of the tunnel. "In the woods, you say?"

"Yes, Master. Up a really long street, on a hill with a cliff that goes down to a river. It's called, um ..." He trailed off. Martel waited, knowing that shouting at Krone would only make him nervous and more forgetful; and finally Krone exclaimed, "It's called Summit Park Drive!"

"How many houses?"

"Not many, two or three others nearby, and they're all separated by lots of trees. Really *thick* trees, Master!"

Martel looked toward the mouth of the tunnel. There was only the dimmest hint of light coming from it, and even as Martel watched, it faded to black; and when it did his night-sight came up, presenting a finely detailed picture of the tunnel and the ravine beyond, illuminated in shades of grey. Lauren, looking sullen, stood off to one side with her arms folded, leaning against the cold stone wall. "I even learned her last name," Krone said. "I read it on her mailbox."

"And what is her last name?"

Krone grinned. "Carmichael!"

"Carmichael," Martel said. "I knew a Carmichael once."

"A stupid name," Lauren Fletcher muttered.

"Did I ask you to speak?"

"I suppose you want to go there tonight."

"No," Martel said. "Not tonight. Tonight we will explore, become acquainted with the local geography. It is prudent to learn our way around, should there be trouble."

"Trouble?" She laughed. "From the humans?"

"Yes, from the humans," he said. "You and your cohorts caused *me* no end of trouble. Or have you forgotten?" She opened her mouth to answer but he cut her off. "Oh, just be quiet, and do as I say. Tonight we explore. Tomorrow ..." He smiled and his coldly burning eyes took on a faraway look.

"Tomorrow what?"

He smiled. "Tomorrow we hunt."

3

MONDAY, JANUARY 11

10:15 AM

"You should dump him," Ryan said.

"You've been telling me that for six months," Roxanne said.

"And do you listen? Of course not." Ryan took a cautious sip of coffee. Scrunching up her face, she proclaimed it too hot, and returned it to the table. The coffee had come from the machine in the cafeteria of the Central New York Insurance Company, a small firm that administered health benefits for a number of employers in the region.

"He was okay on the way home. Once we left the motel, I mean. He was funny and charming."

"But where was he when it counted? Irving would've charged right out the door of that motel and he would've found the guy who was spying on you and he would've beaten the shit out of him. Pardon my French."

"Who would've beaten the shit out of who?"

"Whom."

"What?"

"My point is that Irving would've done *something*, instead of lying there like a lump."

"Chris is a lump?"

"I hate to be the one to tell you, but yes. Chris is a lump."

"He's not that lumpy."

Ryan smacked her.

"So I need a lumpectomy."

"Yes."

"But then I would be lumpless."

Ryan took a sip of her coffee.

"Not for long," she said.

5:40 PM

Roxanne looked over at the flashing light on her answering machine. Three flashes meant three calls, and they were probably all from Christian.

She sighed and pushed the front door closed with her foot. Ignoring the machine, she went into the kitchen to deposit the two grocery bags she was carrying. She began sorting the items, reciting what she was doing in an effort to keep herself from thinking about Chris. Eggs in the fridge, milk in the fridge, chicken in the freezer ...

The phone rang. She looked at it, then down at the large bundle of broccoli in her hands.

Ring.

Broccoli in the vegetable crisper, bacon in the fridge, cereal in the cupboard ...

The answering machine clicked on. "Hi, this is Roxanne. I can't come to the phone right now, but if you'll leave your name and number I'll get back to you. If this is Christian, Ryan says you're a lump."

Roxanne smiled, hearing that; after lunch, she'd called the machine from work and changed her message. Wasn't technology wonderful?

"Roxie, it's Chris. Are you monitoring?"

Yes, Roxanne thought.

"Tell Ryan I'm not a lump. I've met her husband, and if anybody's a lump, it's him. Call me, huh? Maybe we can get a pizza tonight. Bye."

A pizza? Not likely. He still hadn't properly apologized for ruining her weekend; after all, it was his fault that they'd gotten kicked out of Abby's house, and so by extension it was also his fault she'd run into those weirdos at the gas station, his fault she'd gotten spied on at the motel. She'd probably lost a friend over it too; her calls to Abby had gone unanswered and unreturned. Chris, meanwhile, was probably telling all his buddies that his girlfriend had a bad case of **PMS**.

Roxanne put the last of the groceries away and then went into the living room, where the machine was now reproachfully flashing four times, accusing her of neglecting her personal affairs. "In a minute," she told it, kicking off her shoes and plopping down into the chair beside the phone. She pushed the recall button and, as she removed her stockings, the machine told her who had called.

Beep! "Hi Roxie, it's Chris. Look, I'm sorry about this weekend. Give me a call, we'll get together tonight and I'll make it up to you."

Roxanne cocked her head. Did that constitute an apology? Was apologizing to the machine acceptable? She didn't think so, but it was a start. On the other hand, *making it up to her* was likely to involve sex, which, while fun, wasn't exactly the sort of contrition she was looking for.

Beep! "What? I'm a lump? Roxie, I don't like you having that message on your machine so everyone who calls you hears it. Call me, okay? And change your message!"

Everyone who calls. That was a good one. Nobody called her except him and Ryan and the occasional telemarketer.

Beep!

Silence.

"I want you," the machine said in an unfamiliar voice, "and I'm going to have you. I'm going to make you mine. I'm going to—"

And then she was scrabbling at the machine, stabbing at the button, trying to make it stop talking. She knocked it off the table, the phone with it, sending them clattering to the floor.

Feeling suddenly hot and foolish, she retrieved her equipment and put it back on the table. Why had she done that? It was probably just Chris playing games with her. Trying out a new sexy voice. If she had let the message play, he would no doubt have gone into explicit detail as to what he planned to do to her once he had made her his. That didn't constitute an apology either; but she *did* kind of like the new sexy voice. Maybe she would make him talk like that all the time from now on.

A relaxing shower sounded like a good idea; then she would decide what to do about Christian. She wandered toward the bathroom, shedding clothes as if she were leaving a trail of breadcrumbs: First her skirt, down around her ankles and left on the living room floor; then her slip in the hallway; then her blouse just outside the bathroom. Her bra ended up hanging from the doorknob. Nearly naked, she switched on the exhaust fan and the overhead light.

As she slid out of her panties, Roxanne glanced up at the skylight, but all she saw was her own reflection. The plastic dome was crusted with snow and ice; the light it admitted during the day was diffused through this wintry rime. At night, it was merely opaque.

Maybe, as a condition of forgiveness, she would make Chris go up on the roof and scrape the skylight clear. And then as his reward, he could watch her through it.

Chuckling, she turned on the shower.

5:50 PM

Martel moved through the forest, his feet dangling just above the snow as he glided among the trees. He left behind no physical traces as he flew, nothing for a tracker to follow, however keen his eye. In the past, when men had been more superstitious than in the modern age, this had served him well; those who sought to track him like the hunter tracks the fox found their animals worse than useless. Any dog that managed to catch his scent would howl and flee as if it had found the trail of the Devil himself.

Now, of course, the humans had their *technology*. Their cellular phones, their radios, their cameras, their Internet. Information traveled much too quickly these days. No mortal, over a lifespan of a few measly decades, could match wits with a being who had existed half a millennium; but thanks to their machines and their computers, the gulf of accumulated knowledge had narrowed. It made secrecy all the more important; but still, there were some things he just could not give up, even in the face of changing times.

The thrill of stalking a beautiful woman, for instance.

And so Martel drifted through people's yards, floated over their rooftops and past their windows; and their dogs whined and cowered, and their cats hissed from beneath the couch, and they themselves suddenly felt frail and mortal and they turned up their televisions and pulled closer to their spouse or lover or, if alone, hunkered into their own arms for comfort. His mere presence unnerved the living, even when they did not know he was near; if he concentrated, he could fill them with a cold, sickening dread, of the sort that would grip a man who stepped into a thicket and heard the telltale sound of a rattlesnake, felt the fatal bite. He'd lingered outside the Carmichael woman's motel room, that night in Pennsylvania, and had unleashed this power against her male companion; he had watched through the window as all amorous thoughts fled the man's mind, and Krone had confirmed that the fellow woke up the next morning haggard and unrested.

Ah, simple pleasures.

He found the woman's house easily enough; Krone's description of the neighborhood had been accurate, and as it turned out, she lived only a few miles from the tunnel. The roads did not run there directly, but Martel took an easier route, floating from one side of the valley to the other, high in the sky like a witch on her broom.

He wondered if she had listened to his message yet. He probably shouldn't have done that, but it gave him a certain voyeuristic thrill for her to know of his pursuit; it made the final conquest more pleasurable. As he made love to her, he would tell her: *You see? This was inevitable. You knew all along that I was coming, and you could not stop me.*

Roxanne Carmichael, that was her name; he had found her in the phone book, one of mankind's more useful innovations. He thought back to when he'd first seen her, refueling her vehicle, wearing a low-cut evening gown slit up to her thigh, her hair shining like a sunset in the glare of the lights. She had spirit as well as beauty; she had challenged him, she had resisted the lure of his gaze. To conquer her resolve and overcome her resistance would be a welcome challenge, a diversion from the endless nights of hunting and feeding. Martel was used to dwelling in the dark, to walking with ghosts, but still he sometimes longed for that which he had once known. And, since life was irretrievably lost to him, the closest he could ever come to it again was to pursue it, haunt it, seduce it.

And then destroy it; destroy it, to make it his.

The lights were on in her house, and her little black vehicle was nestled under the carport. He didn't need the car to know she was in there, though; he could *feel* her. She was thinking about him, though she did not yet know him; but she *would* know soon enough.

He glided into the air, circling the house, looking, listening. He heard the sound of a shower running but saw no bathroom; it must be internal to the house, windowless. He headed for the roof. Moisture billowed from a ventilation pipe like breath in the cold.

The pipe was near a skylight. He went to it, allowed his nails to grow, used them to scrape away the snow and ice. Now he could see into the bathroom. He waited, suspended over the skylight, for her to finish her shower and emerge, hot and naked for his inspection. He was soon rewarded; the rain-like sound of water ended, the shower door slid open, and the woman emerged onto her bath mat. Martel licked his lips as he drank her in. Her auburn hair was black with moisture, plastered to her head and shoulders; her waist was trim, her hips and buttocks generous, her legs smooth and shapely. She hadn't shown him her breasts yet.

Ah, to be human again, and young.

She took a towel from the rack and began drying herself, rubbing it first across her shoulders, then across her chest. As she did so she stepped away from the tub and under the skylight, where she immediately froze, giving Martel an excellent view straight down at her; and, he concluded, her breasts were superb.

The relaxation Roxanne had derived from her long hot shower fled in an instant, leaving an odd tension in its place, sort of the way your muscles contracted when you first stepped outside on a bitterly cold day. A chill seemed to be settling over her, as if the frigid winter air were pouring down from the skylight. She tried to lift her head to look up at the glass, but her muscles didn't want to obey, as if some external pressure was preventing her from raising her gaze, or some primitive backwater of her brain knew something was up there that she wouldn't want to see. But when she did manage to look, there was nothing; just the night sky, black above her roof.

The night sky? Hadn't there been snow up there? Hadn't she seen it, just fifteen minutes ago, when she first stepped into the shower?

"Oh my God," she whispered, thinking about the message on her answering machine. It wasn't from Chris; and really, she'd known that all along, hadn't she? She scrambled into her soft yellow robe, hurriedly secured it around her body. She went down the hallway, into the living room, to the front door. Loaded down with groceries, she hadn't turned the deadbolt when she came in; now she gave it a hard twist. The *click* of the steel going into the door frame was reassuring, but a deadbolt wouldn't stop someone from coming in through a window or, for that matter, through the French doors in her bedroom.

She picked up the phone. Dead.

Oh, no. She pushed down the receiver button, held it a few seconds, let it go. No dial tone. She slowly cradled the receiver. Where was her cell phone? Had she brought it in, or left it in her car? Not that it mattered; she never got a signal up here anyway. She looked for her purse, her eyes straying across a window; and there was a face, pale and distorted, peering at her and licking its grey lips. And there were hands, two of them, lily-white, long fingers splayed on the window, absurdly reminding her of the way a gecko's feet stuck to the glass of its terrarium at the pet store. She shrieked and the face vanished like a movie when the projector was suddenly switched off.

Trembling, she stood, and her bare foot came down on something cold and hard and sharp-cornered: The plastic end of the telephone wire, the part that was supposed to go into the receiver. It must have come loose when she'd knocked everything to the floor. She snatched it like a lifeline and, with fumbling fingers, reinserted it into the telephone; and then, picking up the headset, she heard the annoying, familiar, comforting sound of a dial tone. She almost cried in relief as she dialed 911.

... Ring ...

There was a noise from the front door, like someone scraping the wood with a knife.

"Come on," Roxanne whispered, willing someone to answer her call.

... Ring ...

Scratch-scratch-scratch.

"Go away!" Roxanne shouted.

The phone said: "911, what's your emergency?"

"There's someone trying to break into my house!"

"Okay, I can help you with that," the man said. "I'm showing that you're calling from 11930 Summit Park Drive, can you confirm that for me?"

"Yes!" The scratching at her door had abated; as she spoke, she looked from window to wall to window, wondering where her mysterious stalker would turn up next.

"Okay," the man said, "I'll contact the police and get a car up there as soon as possible."

"Thank you," she said; but he had already hung up. She decided that she should stay on the phone, stay *connected* to somebody, just in case this stalker came crashing in. She thought momentarily, and only one number presented itself to her mind; she dialed and got an answer after a ring or two. "Hello?"

"Hi, Chris," she said. "It's me."

Christian Keems looked at the telephone in surprise. He hadn't been expecting a call from Roxanne; he figured she'd stay mad at him for a at least a day or two. Shuffling back a few feet, he peered out the door of the kitchen at the living room. The off-duty lady cop he'd picked up at the video store along with a movie—Monica, that was her name—sat on the couch, sipping a glass of wine and waiting for him to come back. She looked his way and smiled; he smiled back, and waved.

"Chris?" Roxanne said.

He moved away from the door. "What's up?"

"Oh, God, Chris, there's somebody outside my house!"

"What?"

"I *saw* him! He was looking at me through a window!"

"Did you call the police?"

"Yes."

Pause.

"Did you … want me to come over?"

"Would you?"

Shit, of all the crummy timing. "Okay, sure. I'll be there as soon as I can." Christian looked at Monica, doing some quick mental calculations. Did he have enough time to fool around a bit with Monica and still get over to Roxanne's in a reasonable time frame?

Roxanne said something he didn't catch. "I'm sorry, what?"

"I said thanks."

"No problem."

"Chris—" He cut her off by hanging up, then ambled out into the living room, trying to put an expression of grave concern on his face. He must have succeeded, because Monica looked at him expectantly, then frowned and asked what was wrong.

"That was my mom," he said. "Somebody broke into her house.

She wants me to come over."

"That's terrible!" she said. Then: "Do you want me to come with you? I have a gun in my purse."

Hmm, he wondered if she had handcuffs in there too. The thought distracted him for a second. Then he spent another second wondering if there was any possibility of a threesome with her and Roxanne if he brought her along. Probably not. Finally he said: "No, that's okay. She already called 911."

He went to the closet and returned with their coats. As he helped Monica into hers, she said: "I have handcuffs in my purse, too."

Good Lord. This could well be the perfect woman.

"Well," he said, "maybe next time, you can arrest me."

6:38 PM

Barry Brennan turned right onto Summit Park Drive, heading up the side of the valley and into the woods. He'd been called to respond to a report of a prowler. He wasn't looking forward to this stop; it was probably some eighty-year-old woman, half-senile, who'd seen a raccoon on her windowsill and taken it for a masked marauder. Barry envisioned himself shouting at the woman (because she would be three-quarters deaf in addition to being half-senile), having to answer six or seven thousand questions, and being sworn to park in front of her house every night for the next six months. But that was the sort of thing you did when you were a cop.

In between the car chases and the shootouts, of course.

Roxanne realized that a flashing blue, red, and white light had arrived outside her house. She stood, hurried to the door, and looked through the peephole. There was the police car. She undid the bolt and threw open the door, startling the cop, who had just been reaching to knock. She'd vaguely been expecting some Barney Fife type, but he was youngish—early thirties, she guessed—with a broad build and soft brown eyes that seemed more appropriate for a puppy than a policeman.

"Hi, I'm Officer Brennan," he said, showing her his ID. "You called for assistance? You're Ms. Carmichael? Somebody tried to break in to your house?"

She nodded vigorously, feeling her still-damp hair bounce against her neck. "Yes, I saw him!"

He looked at her for a long moment before responding, then cleared his throat a bit sheepishly and said, in a voice that seemed deeper than it had been earlier, "Okay, ma'am, I'll take a look around." He produced a flashlight from somewhere, switched it on, and played the beam around the base of the wall.

"I saw him right through that window over there," Roxanne said, pointing at the window in question. "He also scratched at my front door. It sounded like he was using a knife."

The policeman frowned. "I don't see any footprints in the snow there, Ms. Carmichael."

"What?"

"I said there aren't any footprints. Are you sure it was this window?"

"I'm positive!" Roxanne pushed open the door and stepped onto the snowy landing. She looked at the pool of light beneath the window; the snow there was undisturbed, a pristine blanket of white that lapped against the wall like a frozen wave.

"Ms. Carmichael, I don't think you're really dressed for this," Officer Brennan said, eyeing her robe and bare feet.

"He was right there!"

"Okay, ma'am, I'll take a look all around the house. Meanwhile I'd suggest you return to your home and put on some slippers."

That sounded like a good idea. "Okay," she said, stepping back inside, kicking snow off her feet, which had already turned red from the cold. By the time she had retrieved her slippers and come back to the living room, the policeman was out of sight, probably circling the house looking for bad guys.

Suddenly she had a thought: What if that creep got the drop on the policeman and killed him? Then he would have a gun, on top of the knife or whatever it was he'd scratched at the door with. Worried that even now her stalker might be slitting the cop's throat, she went from window to window looking for some sign of him. She saw the officer's tracks in the snow, big boot prints heading around the side of the house, but no sign of the man himself. She went into the kitchen, peered through the window over the sink. From here she couldn't even see his tracks. Next she went to the master bedroom at the rear of the house, a big room with a shaggy rug and a set of French doors that gave access to the deck. It overlooked the valley and the flood plain below. In summer, the view was full of life and greenery; in winter it was stark and almost terrible, but still beautiful, with the frozen landscape and the houses that thrust up from the snow and trailed steam into the sky. First she checked the windows; no sign of the cop. The curtains were drawn across the French doors. She parted them and peered out.

The pale face she had seen before hovered just outside, staring at her, eye to eye.

Roxanne shrieked and fell back, away from the doors. She stumbled out of the bedroom, down the hallway. The interior living room door was still open. She saw a figure standing in the doorway, silhouetted against the glare of the police car's lights. She froze, helpless, as the man opened the storm door and stepped inside.

Chris.

"Oh, thank God," she said.

"Now that's what I call a greeting." He grinned at her for a moment, then looked around. "Where's the cop?"

"He went to have a look around. I don't know where he is. I'm worried that the guy got him."

"It's okay, I'm fine." They both turned as the policeman entered the living room. "I took a walk around the house and into the woods a little ways." He eyed Chris. "I'm Officer Brennan. Are you a friend of Ms. Carmichael?"

"Yes, this is Chris," Roxanne said.

"Roxanne's boyfriend," Chris added.

"Did you find anything?"

"I'm afraid not, ma'am," Officer Brennan said. "There are no footprints anywhere, except for bunny and deer tracks, and of course mine now."

"But I *saw* him!" she said. "He was outside that window. And I saw him again just now outside the doors in my bedroom."

"Okay, let's go take a look."

She led him down the hallway to the bedroom, pointed at the French doors. "Right outside there," she said. Officer Brennan approached the doors warily, keeping off to the side. "You have to unlock them from the top and bottom." He nodded and undid the locks, paused a moment, and then pulled open the door. Cold air rushed in, bringing a swirl of snow that quickly began to melt on the warm floor.

No one was there; the snow was pristine, unmarred by human feet.

Officer Brennan stood there for a second, his big frame taking up most of the door; then he closed it, locked it again, and turned, leaning up against the glass. "Whoever it was appears to be gone, ma'am," he said.

She went up next to him, peered out at the snow, at the night. The wind kicked up, pelting the glass with hard white pellets. Powdery ice crystals drifted through the trees down the slope, almost like a patch of fog slinking away from the house. "I don't understand. I saw him. He was right here."

"I know he was," Officer Brennan said, "but whoever it was, we probably scared him off, what with me and your friend both being here."

"Hear that?" Chris said. "I scared him off. Guess I'd better stay the night." He winked at her. "It's a sacrifice I'm willing to make."

"If you'd like, I could check in with you tomorrow—"

"I don't think that'll be necessary," Chris said. "I'll take care of her from here on out."

"Good enough. Have a pleasant evening, folks."

Roxanne showed Officer Brennan out, thanking him for his time. Impulsively, she offered him a cup of coffee; she thought he was going to accept, but then Chris came out of the bedroom. The policeman's gaze flicked to Chris, who said: "Roxie, it's pretty late, and I'm sure Officer Brennan has other people he has to help."

"I'm afraid your friend is right," Officer Brennan said. "But thanks for the offer, ma'am." He gave her a little smile, then exited, pulling the door shut behind him.

Roxanne rotated the deadbolt, then turned and pressed her back up against the door. Chris stood near the entrance of the hallway smirking at her. "Boy, was that guy hitting on you or what?"

"What?"

In a falsetto, Chris said: *"Do you want me to check on you tomorrow?"* Then, in a normal tone: "I bet he doesn't offer to check up on fat lowlife trash from the trailer park. You offering him coffee didn't help."

"I was just being polite. Anyway he said no."

"Yeah," Chris said, "but he *wanted* to say yes. Poor guy will probably have a hard-on the rest of the night. Luckily he's a cop; he probably knows where all the best hookers work."

"Christian!" Roxanne laughed. "You're awful."

"I may be awful, but I'll keep the boogeyman away." He waved his arms and made *ooga-booga* noises.

She stopped laughing. "I didn't imagine this."

"I'm not saying you did," Chris said.

It sounded like he had more to say. "But?"

"But that cop didn't find a thing. No footprints, no disturbed snow. He doesn't think there was anybody outside. He was just humoring you, babe."

"You don't think there was anybody here either, do you?"

"I think you might still be a little bit shaken up from what happened in Pennsylvania, is all. You might be overreacting to things."

"Really." Suddenly, Roxanne realized she'd been an idiot. "You think I'm imagining things? Listen to this." She strode across to her answering machine and pressed the recall button. She fast-forwarded through Chris's messages, going directly to the Mystery Caller. She watched Chris's reaction to the smooth, dark, well-oiled voice whose words flowed from her machine; she thought he turned a shade paler.

"Who *was* that?" he asked, when the tape had stopped.

"If I knew that, I'd tell the police," Roxanne said.

"You should've played it for that cop."

"I was so rattled I forgot all about it. But you see? I'm not imagining things. Somebody *is* harassing me."

"I'm sorry. I should've believed you." He crossed the room and took her in his arms, almost like he meant it. After a few seconds he started getting an erection; she could feel it against her stomach. He was no doubt going to want something in exchange for spending the night. Well, that was Christian for you. "You should call the cops in the morning and tell them about that message. It's evidence."

"I want to know who's doing it!" Roxanne pulled away, turned and slammed her fist against the wall. "I feel so damn *helpless*!"

"Don't worry, we'll get it straightened out," Chris said. "We'll find out who he is and send him to jail where he belongs."

Roxanne turned and took his hand. "Let's go inside," she said, nodding her head at the hallway. She led him to the master bedroom, then let go of him, heading for the French doors. She had seen the policeman lock them, but still, she wanted to be sure. The top and bottom bolts were both thrown, and the knob was locked as well.

When she turned, Chris was sitting on the bed, pulling off his socks. His shirt and trousers hung neatly over the back of a chair. He noticed her watching and made a show of removing his underwear, standing up and doing a half-turn so she could get his profile. She looked him over: his light blonde hair that ran down over smallish ears, bright blue eyes, narrow shoulders, waist that was just beginning to expand a little bit, and—she smiled and turned away. Christian was clearly hatching some nefarious plan to seduce her, if conditions just below his waist were any indication.

Then he was behind her, his hands on her shoulders; and they slowly slid down her arms and then to her waist. He took the knot of her belt and undid it, sliding the robe away from her body; she shrugged out of it and let it fall to the floor soundlessly, landing in a little yellow heap between them. Then he was up against her, pressing his hands against her breasts and his crotch against her backside.

His hands began kneading, and despite herself Roxanne began to get interested in what Christian had in mind; so as his right hand slid down to her stomach and beyond, she did nothing but inhale and enjoy it.

Peering through the bedroom window from his perch in a nearby tree, his unearthly vision piercing the light, gauzy curtains, Martel enjoyed it too.

4

TUESDAY, JANUARY 12

3:05 AM

   She was in a dark place, stumbling over unseen obstacles, feeling her way along a rough wall slimy with moss.   Icy, trickling water gathered in pools, splashed beneath her feet.   The echoes of her passage surrounded her as she ran, footfalls bouncing back at her from every direction; she heard her own breath coming fast and hard as she ran toward the light, a little luminous speck in the distance. She didn't know how she had gotten here or where she had come from; all she could remember was this tunnel and a piercing, shapeless fear that drove her onward like the wind.   She had been stumbling forever through a nightmare that never changed; she'd fallen from her mother's womb and hit the floor running and hadn't stopped since.

   Something tripped her, a chunk of moldy, half-rotted wood.   She tried to brace herself with her hands but they shot away on a cushion of frozen slime and she landed heavily.   The chill dampness of the floor infected her immediately, settling into her bones for a long, long stay.   She lay there for a moment, panting, before realizing that somewhere behind her the echoes of footfalls and splashes were still coming.

   Someone was in here with her.

   She didn't know why, but Roxanne immediately assumed that the other occupant of the tunnel was a threat, not a fellow lost soul. She fumbled in the dark until her hands closed on the wood that had tripped her. It felt slick and spongy, but remained heavy and solid in its core. She raised it above her head, moved up against the wall, and waited.

The splashing got closer, closer, until it was almost upon her, but still she saw nothing. Closing her eyes, she tried to *hear* the location of the runner, and when she thought the moment was right she brought the tie crashing down. There was a dull *thud* and the wood splintered in her grip. Then a hand grabbed her shoulder tightly. She shrieked, but the fingers quickly loosened and slid down her arm, releasing her at the elbow; then there was a groan and a splash.

"I got you!" she screamed. "I got you, you son of a bitch!"

A light flared across the dark place and a man was there, looking at her with glittering eyes. He was about six feet tall, dark and handsome, his shoulders broad and strong. In his right hand he held a cigarette lighter, the small flame like a sun in the darkness, surrounding him in a cocoon of light.

"Who are you?" she gasped.

"I am the darkness," he said.

She looked down at her feet now, and saw the man lying there, his skull fractured, blood pooling around his head. She knelt down and with a trembling hand reached out to lift his head; and she saw the blood-streaked face of Christian Keems.

"Oh, God," she whispered, cradling the battered head in her arms. She stroked his bloody hair, making her hands red and sticky.

Then Chris's eyes snapped open like a doll's, and he looked up at her with wide, white eyes. Blood flowed into them, staining them red. "Hi babe," Christian said, showing huge bloody canines.

Twisting, he sank them into her stomach.

And Roxanne sat up in bed, drenched in sweat, a scream dying on her lips. Then she collapsed forward, folding herself almost in half, holding her head in her hands and sobbing. She'd had nightmares before, but not like this, not so violent, not so *real*. Dreams about being naked in public or failing to study for the final exam, those were more her speed.

A warm hand slid over her back and a hot forehead leaned up against her shoulder. "Are you all right?" Christian said.

She whirled and was on him, squashing him in a bear hug. "Oh, Chris!" she exclaimed. "I had the worst nightmare!"

"Okay, babe, okay … take it easy … it was just a dream."

Roxanne squeezed him tighter.

"Roxie … I can't breathe."

She relaxed her grip a bit, then let go completely, falling back down against her pillow. The sheets were damp where she had been lying, and in the winter night had quickly grown cold. She turned and looked with bleary eyes at her alarm clock; it was three in the morning.

"Try to get some more sleep, babe," Chris said, rolling over onto his side and facing away from her.

5:59 AM

Roxanne tried to blink away the grainy feeling in her eyes but it didn't work; they still felt like raw, peeled onions rolled in ground-up glass.

The clock changed and the radio came to life in the middle of some dark, moody song with mournful guitars and a rough-voiced vocalist. She switched off the alarm and rolled over onto her back, staring at the ceiling. Since three o'clock she had been focusing on whatever she could to avoid going back to sleep. For twenty minutes, she had stared at the red light of the clock; then she concentrated on the feeling of Christian's foot against her leg. She had listened to herself breathe, listened to Christian breathe, and even listened to the wind outside; but that had reminded her that *someone was out there* and then the wind started to sound like muttering. She had been unable to bring herself to get up and walk to the living room to watch television; she hadn't even been able to muster the will to go get a book or an old magazine to read. Her bed, her warm covers and pillow, were a shield, a camouflage, protection from the eyes of the night; if she left them they would see, they would know, they would carry to her unseen stalker the news that she had dared to stir.

But now the alarm had gone off, it was morning, and she had to rise. She could feel the lack of sleep in her head; it was like a buzz, an unpleasant one, the sort you got from drinking cheap wine all night. She hoped a shower would make her feel a little better, but the only real treatment was going to be lots and lots of coffee.

She located her robe at the foot of the curtains, and after slipping into it she found herself pushing open the blue velvet to look out through the French doors. It wasn't long before dawn; the sky was lightening from black to navy, and the snow shone blue. The demarcation between the hills across the valley and the dark cloudy sky had become visible, the barren, skeletal trees along the crest of the ridge standing like polyps against the lightening horizon. The approaching sun improved her spirits somewhat. She turned and walked quietly out of the bedroom. In the hallway she stopped to gather up her scattered clothes, feeling a momentary flush of embarrassment; had Officer Brennan seen them lying around? What must he think?

Eh, why should she care what he thought? She had no reason to impress him, would probably never see him again; and besides, he had no doubt encountered much worse things than a few scraps of dirty clothing left lying about. She got her laundry together and carried it into the bathroom, stuffing it into the hamper; then she deliberately stood under the skylight for a few minutes, looking up at it. A fresh skin of snow had blown across it, rendering it once again opaque. Sighing, she reached into the tub and began fiddling with the faucets.

Twenty minutes later she emerged from the bathroom, toweling off her hair. Her yellow robe stuck to her moist body. She went to the front door to collect her morning paper, noticing as she did that Christian's car was gone. She wasn't surprised; he taught an eight o'clock class on Tuesdays and Thursdays, because he was the new man on the faculty and thus got the least-desirable assignments. But if he hadn't at least left a note, she would be forced to kill him. As it was, she was semi-ashamed of herself for sleeping with him without even getting a real apology; but she had been pretty stressed out last night, and it had been nice to wake up from that dream and have someone there with her.

Sighing, she took the paper into the kitchen.

She found a dirty cereal bowl in the sink, but she didn't find a note.

7:30 AM

Roxanne came out of the house, her coat wrapped closely around her. The morning felt arctic; she could almost see the individual ice crystals in the cloud of her breath, glittering in the pale early light. Predicting cold in January in upstate New York was not unlike predicting that the sun would rise in the morning; there was a chance you would be wrong, but it wasn't particularly likely.

The locks on her car were frozen. She took a tube of deicer out of her coat pocket and, inserting the little nozzle into the lock, dispensed a squirt of liquid. Once didn't do the trick, but twice did.

How very sexual, she thought.

The engine turned over on the third try, and while it idled she waded through the steam cloud of exhaust, scraping frost off the windows. It was twenty to eight when she rolled out of her driveway and turned left onto Summit Park Drive. It didn't take long for her lack of sleep to lead to a pounding headache. With dulled senses she drove down the hill and out onto the streets of Mapledale proper: Johnson Avenue, Holt Street, Route 71. She made a right onto what passed for a highway and headed toward White Bluff, the small city where she worked.

About a mile out of Mapledale the road narrowed and climbed the side of a high, steep bluff. Local folklore held that when the area had first been explored, the bluff had been thick with snow, much as it was today; it had been dubbed White Bluff and the name had stuck.

Speaking of being stuck, she was behind an old jalopy that was moseying along at fifteen miles below the speed limit. She signaled a lane change and glanced in her rear-view mirror; a little green Ford was right behind her, and a big silver Lincoln was behind that.

Oh, God. That looked like the Lincoln from the gas station down in Pennsylvania. And the driver; there was no mistaking him! She could see him through the window, larger than life and twice as ugly: Huge and broad, with a twisted mouth, splotchy skin, tufted hair, and large, mirrored sunglasses that made his appearance even more horrible. Wearing those glasses, he seemed insectoid, robotic.

She told herself to calm down. Just because the car was here didn't mean they had followed her. After all, hadn't they left the gas station first? And hadn't she driven all the way home, in broad daylight, without seeing them again? It was possible that the freakish driver and his unseen employer just happened to live in the area.

Yeah, right. And there just *happened* to be somebody sneaking around her house peeping through her windows, leaving her messages on her machine, and—fuck, she had forgotten to call the police this morning and tell them about the tape. Not that it would help; they couldn't arrest a voice.

She pulled out and quickly passed the little beater in front of her, then stepped on the accelerator and pulled away from the pack. She glanced in her mirror. The Lincoln was passing too, but so was the Ford so that didn't really prove anything.

She came down out of the bluffs. There was a little gas station on the right. She veered into the parking lot and stopped next to the mini-mart. She twisted in her seat and watched the road. The Ford drove on by, followed by the Lincoln. She waited until it was out of sight, then slowly backed out of the lot and rejoined traffic.

Ten minutes later, Roxanne was third back from a red light, drumming her fingers absently on the steering wheel. She missed her music, but she had discovered that playing the stereo at this particular time made her headache go ballistic, so she was doing without. Thick snow fell from the iron sky in huge, moist flakes, spattering and melting on her windshield. It was almost hypnotic, watching their slow, silent progress, so soft and peaceful and serene …

Suddenly she felt a sense of constriction, of eyes wandering over her and caging her. She twisted around in her seat and looked out the rear window; two cars back, in the other lane, she spotted the Lincoln. The driver was facing straight ahead, but those damn glasses hid his eyes; they could be aimed right at her. Quickly she turned to face forward, just as the light turned green. The cars ahead of her were intolerably slow in starting.

The Lincoln nudged closer.

As if they had suddenly developed their own volition, Roxanne's foot stomped on the gas and her hands twisted the wheel left. Then she was out in the center turn lane, passing the cars that had been in front of her. One of the other drivers was flipping her the bird but she ignored him. As she cleared the second of the slow cars a van pulled into the center lane, its turn signal flashing. She jerked the wheel hard to the left as the driver of the van gawked at her. She missed it by a foot or so, then saw the headlights of oncoming vehicles and realized she was racing head-on into a pack of cars that had been released from another light farther up. She quickly cut back into the middle lane, then slipped all the way over to the right. She was free of traffic, all alone; the Lincoln was behind her, stuck behind the other cars. He couldn't scoot through small gaps like she did.

The speed limit on this stretch of road was forty-five miles per hour. She took her car to sixty and kept it there. The other cars began dropping back as she gained on the traffic in front of her. Suddenly the sound of a siren pierced the air, and a black and white pulled out onto the street behind, lights flashing. Roxanne immediately pulled off into a parking lot, the patrol car behind her.

She flung her car into park, threw open the door, and jumped out, hurrying over to the police car. The officer inside, looking rather nonplussed, opened his door a crack and shouted, "Return to your vehicle!"

"Somebody's chasing me!" she exclaimed.

"Ma'am, return to your vehicle!"

"I'm being followed!" Roxanne looked at the road; the Lincoln was just easing into view, going slowly past the parking lot. "That's him!" she cried, pointing at Krone. The officer looked, and suddenly the Lincoln accelerated and shot away, vanishing in the flow of traffic.

The cop looked at her, then at the street, apparently trying to decide whether or not she was crazy. She suddenly had an idea and said: "Do you know Officer Brennan? He came out to my house yesterday because I had a prowler."

"Yeah, I know him," the cop said. "Ma'am, for the last time, return to your vehicle."

She finally went back to her car, settling into the driver's seat. A few minutes later the cop was there, tapping on the window. She rolled it down and he said: "Do you want to come to the police station and file a report?"

"You bet," Roxanne said. "Can I ride with you?"

"Sure, what the hell. Put your car in a proper parking space first."

The cop stood by as she parked, studying her vehicle; when she came over, he opened the rear door of the patrol car for her and closed it behind her. The back seat was quite comfortable; it was almost like being chauffeured. The cop eyed Roxanne for a few seconds, then pulled out into traffic.

"What's your name?" he asked.

"Roxanne Carmichael. What's yours?"

"I'm Marty."

"Nice to meet you."

"You were pulling some interesting driving stunts back there, Ms. Carmichael."

"I was scared. I saw that guy in Pennsylvania on Sunday, and now he's here, following me."

"You sure it was the same guy?"

"Positive. He's hard to mistake."

"Old boyfriend?"

"Are you kidding?" She shook her head. "I never even saw him before."

"Pennsylvania to New York ... that's a long way to follow somebody you don't even know."

Roxanne got the uncomfortable impression that Marty didn't quite believe her; he probably heard all kinds of bullshit from people trying to get out of tickets. Christian had told a whopper or two in his day, like the time he'd tried to get her to moan and clutch her stomach and pretend she had appendicitis; when she had refused he'd thought up some other disease with no symptoms (he'd called it gastrofibrulitis or some such nonsense), and, of course, had gotten a ticket anyway.

Well, it didn't matter. She was safe now, in the back seat of a police car; no one could hurt her here. She leaned back, slumped up against the door, and quietly fell asleep.

8:20 AM

The chair at the police station wasn't particularly welcoming. It was made of some sort of molded plastic that had once been a rather putrid yellow but was now streaked with brown and black, no doubt the result of countless less than sparkling-clean occupants shifting and sliding as they tried to get comfortable. Also, it had no arms, and Roxanne had difficulty deciding where to put her hands; finally she folded them in her lap, crossed her legs, and sat there primly as if on a job interview.

The detective behind the desk, a fellow named Jack Davidson, had been taking her statement when his phone rang; even now he was continuing a discussion with some unknown person, presumably an informant.

"I told you fifty dollars," Davidson said.

Roxanne glanced at the clock. She was very late for work. Ryan would be having fits.

"No, *fifty*," Davidson said.

She knotted her purse strap in her hands.

"A *hundred?* Dream on," Davidson said. "Wait a sec." He covered up the mouthpiece with a big, long-fingered hand. Looking at Roxanne, he said, "Sorry about this, Ms. Carmichael. My friend, he's a little edgy, he needs some encouragement, you know?"

"That's all right." She glanced at the clock again. "Can I make a phone call?"

Davidson waved her away, then returned his attention to the phone. "What?" he said. "*What?* You can't do that! Listen, you *cannot* do that!"

Roxanne wandered off. She had left her cell phone in the glove compartment of her car, so she headed for a pay phone she had noticed in the lobby. When she got there, however, it was occupied by a greasy-looking young man who stood facing the wall, slouching forward, propping himself up with one arm. His face was downcast and he was muttering "Aw, c'mon, Alice," as if it were a mantra. She stood there for a few minutes watching him feed quarters into the slot like a disheartened gambler, then moved over to the front desk. The officer working there looked at her expectantly.

"Do you have a phone I could use?" she asked.

"Local call?"

"Yes."

He produced a massive black rotary telephone from somewhere out of sight. "Keep it short," he said.

"Thank you," she said. The receiver seemed to weigh several pounds in her hand; the dial rattled loudly as it spun. Very retro, she thought.

After half a ring, a voice said: "Ryan Sloane."

"Hi, Ryan, it's—"

"Roxanne!" she exclaimed. "Where on *earth* have you been? I called your house, I called Christian at work—you *slept* with him, are you nuts?—and I was getting ready to call the police—"

"You should've started with the police," Roxanne said. "That's where I am."

"You're with the *police?* Are you in trouble?"

"Somebody was following me on the way to work, and—did Chris tell you about the man who was outside my house last night?"

"He said you *thought* somebody was peeping on you again. That's how he said it, *thought*, as in *thought being the operative word here*. Hey, that's also how he got on the subject of sleeping with you. Are you nuts? He didn't even wait for you to get out of the shower, what a—"

"I know, and he didn't leave a note, either. Listen, Ryan—"

"He doesn't believe you, you know, about the man."

"*What?* But I played the message for him! Does he think I recorded it myself?"

"He said the police came and couldn't find any footprints. He said the cop was hitting on you. He said—"

"I know all that. I was *there*, Ryan, remember?" Then she noticed the desk sergeant tapping his watch. "Uh, listen, Ryan, I have to go. I just called to tell you I'll be late today. Actually I don't even know what time I'll be in."

"Don't worry about that, Roxie. Don't even come in. Go home and try to relax. Watch the home shopping channel, that's what I do when I'm stressed. I'll stop by after work. You should've called *me*, Roxanne, not Chris, for God's sake—"

"Sorry, they need the phone back. See you later." Roxanne handed the phone back to the officer behind the desk, who was grinning widely.

"He's a real talker, huh?" the man said as he hung up the phone for her.

"Ryan's a she," Roxanne said absently. "And yes, she's definitely a talker. Thanks for the phone."

"No problem."

Chewing on her lower lip, Roxanne cast a last glance toward the guy at pay phone ("Aw, c'mon, Alice") and returned to Davidson's desk. He was still on the phone, but his demeanor suggested he was speaking to someone else now. As Roxanne approached she heard him say, "Hang on, she's coming back." He put the receiver down on his desk and looked at her as she sat. "Phone call go okay?"

"Fine."

"I'm talking to a friend of yours," Davidson said. "Officer Brennan. Remember him?"

"Of course. I told Marty about him. He came to my house last night."

"Yeah. Right. He confirms that you reported a prowler, but there was no evidence of trespass—no footprints, vehicle tracks, no perpetrator."

Roxanne got the impression that she was about to be dismissed. "That's right," she said, "but there was definitely somebody there. He called and left a message on my machine."

"Did he?" Davidson seemed mildly surprised. "You didn't mention that to Officer Brennan."

"I know, it slipped my mind, but I played it for my friend Chris."

Davidson picked up the receiver again. "She says he left a message on her machine." He listened for a moment and then nodded. "Okay. See you in a few." Then he hung up.

"What did he say?"

"He's coming out to get you. He'll take you to your car and thence to your home and listen to that message of yours." He grinned. "He's not on duty yet but he said he'll be here as soon as possible. Guess he sort of likes you, Miss Carmichael." She flushed. Davidson began chewing on the eraser of his pencil and was all business again. "After that, we'll see. Oh, Marty stopped by and said to give this to you." He opened a drawer, fished around in it for a few seconds, pulled out a slip of paper, and handed it to Roxanne.

It was a traffic summons.

9:00 AM

On the stoop of her house, Roxanne fumbled with the keys, as if she had never opened the door before. Beside her, stamping the snow off his feet, Officer Brennan waited. The stoop was barely big enough for them both, and his close proximity was making Roxanne flustered; she had realized, riding in his car, that she found Officer Brennan rather cute, with his short brown hair, brown eyes, narrow nose, and ears that stuck out just a little too far. She would've expected him to be annoyed at being called at home to come and collect her, but he didn't seem too unhappy about the situation.

She found the front door key, and promptly dropped the entire ring into the snow.

"I'll get it," he said, kneeling down and feeling around in the puffy accumulation. He quickly located the keys and picked them up by the house key. "This one, right?"

"Yes." He stuck it in the lock and turned it, and they went inside.

"Just put your coat anywhere," Roxanne said, hanging hers in the closet.

"I can't stay long," he said, not removing his parka.

"No? I was hoping you'd stay for coffee."

"Sorry, Miss Carmichael. I've got a haircut at eleven."

"Call me Roxanne." She was eyeing his hair, trying to figure out where it could possibly be so long that it needed to be cut.

"All right. Then you can call me Barry."

"Okay, Barry." She smiled at him, or to herself, she wasn't sure which. "Would you like a cup of coffee?" Idiot! She had already asked him that! He was going to think she was a babbling fool.

The smile never faltered. He said, as if the exact same words hadn't come out of his mouth ten seconds earlier, "Sorry, I can't; I have a haircut at eleven." This time he added: "I *am* kind of interested in hearing that telephone call that you mentioned to detective Davidson."

"Right." She walked over to the answering machine, feeling vaguely disappointed and furiously embarrassed. It wasn't her fault, she told herself; she sounded like an imbecile because she hadn't gotten any sleep. And if Barry wasn't attracted to her—if this was just business to him, a standard cop and civilian interaction—well, that was his loss.

But Davidson had said Barry liked her; maybe he considered her taken because of Chris.

Taken? My God. She shook her head and told herself to stop thinking like a teenager. She reached the machine. Three messages. She pushed the recall button and glanced at Barry. "I, um, I rewound the tape … it might have gotten recorded over."

Barry raised an eyebrow. "Your machine still uses tapes?"

"Yeah," she said, as the messages started. "Isn't it quaint? Hey, your phone at the station has a rotary dial, so don't get all high and mighty with me."

Beep! "Roxanne, it's Ryan. Where are you? Call me at work. Oh, it's quarter after eight. Are you okay? Please, call me!"

Beep! "Roxie, it's Chris. Ryan just called and said you weren't at work. Is something wrong? Did the bogeyman get you? Call me if there's a phone in his cave. Bye."

Oh, that was marvelous. Barry would think she was dating

somebody just as developmentally-arrested as she was.

Beep! "Roxanne, it's Ryan again. I called all the hospitals, so I know you're not there, and I called Chris, so I know you're not there, so ... where are you? Are you sick? Hello? Roxanne? Call me. It's quarter to nine."

Feeling extremely foolish, Roxanne turned to Barry. He was watching her with something that resembled amusement, and she immediately channeled her embarrassment into anger. "Don't look at me like that!" she snapped. "Chris heard the message, he'll tell you so!"

"I'm sorry," Barry said. "I'm sure he will. But really, Miss Carmichael, the message is not so important. The description of the car and the driver that you gave to detective Davidson will be more helpful in finding this person than the message would had been. That's probably why he sent me out here instead of coming himself."

"Oh, he sent you, huh? I thought you volunteered."

Barry grinned. "Well, to be honest, ma'am, he didn't have to work very hard to persuade me."

She gave him what was probably a goofy smile, then said: "Take off your coat, stay a while."

"I'm afraid I really should get going. Do you have someone who can stay with you for a while?"

"My friend Ryan is coming over after work."

"Good. You shouldn't be alone. Is there anybody you could call before that?"

She shook her head.

"No brothers or sisters? No parents?"

"No."

Barry said: "Well, I guess I could postpone my haircut then." Before she could answer, the doorbell rang. He looked at the door, then at Roxanne. "Expecting company?"

She shook her head.

"I'll get it." Barry went to the door and squinted through the peephole. Turning to Roxanne, who stood in the middle of the room with her hands clasped, he said: "Guess I can keep that appointment after all."

He pulled the door wide, revealing a huge bouquet of flowers and, behind that, Christian Keems.

* * *

"I called your office and they told me you weren't going to be in, so I canceled my classes for the rest of the day," Chris said, sitting at the kitchen table. "God knows the students won't mind."

Roxanne had arranged the flowers in a vase, the explosion of yellow, blue, red, and purple adding a welcome splash of color to the white kitchen. She should keep flowers in here all the time, she thought, if only she could get Chris to buy them again. She would probably have to get murdered to get another bouquet.

She wondered what sort of flowers Barry might have brought if he were her boyfriend.

"Thanks for the flowers," she said. "They're beautiful."

"Yeah. I thought you'd like them." He paused, and Roxanne knew something was coming that would wreck the convivial atmosphere that had prevailed for, what, ten minutes now. "So," Chris said, "what was Officer Aryan doing here?"

"Chris, don't call him that! He just drove me back to my car from the police station, then came up to hear the message, that's all. And he's very nice."

"Very nice, huh?" Chris gestured at the bouquet. "Did *he* bring you these lovely flowers?"

"Is *he* my boyfriend?"

"He'd better not be."

"Christian, you can be such a ... a ..." She trailed off, trying to think of just the right name to call him.

He jumped into the silence. "Listen, babe, let's not start fighting, okay?" She glared at him. "*Okay?*"

"*You* started it."

"Whatever. Anyway, listen, I think we should get away this weekend. You need to relax."

"We got away last weekend and it didn't relax me."

"This'll be different. We'll go to the Adirondacks and do some skiing." He flashed his best smile. "Do some hot-tubbing, too, while we're at it."

She considered this proposition. It *would* be nice to get away for the weekend and not have the whole experience go to shit. Unless the stalker followed her ... then she would need protection. Police protection. A really big policeman to guard her body ...

"Roxie?"

"What?" she said, looking at him, her eyes wide, her mind on something else entirely. She was wondering if Barry skied.

"I love you."

She looked at him blankly, not quite grasping this unexpected development. "You what?"

"I said I love you."

She stared at him.

"Do you have anything you want to tell me?"

"Um …" God, what the hell had brought *this* on? He couldn't possibly be sincere, but what was his angle? He was watching her, waiting for her to say it, too, but it wouldn't be any more true than when he had. "Look, Chris, we've had fun, but …"

"But what?"

"Come on, Chris. You don't love me."

"Why would I say it if I didn't mean it?"

"I don't know, but you don't. You like to have me on your arm at parties and you sure like to fuck me, but you don't love me."

Now it was his turn to stare at her. "That's not true at all," he said. "You're projecting your feelings onto me."

Great, now they were moving on to psychoanalysis. "Look, Chris, you and I both know that—what are you doing?"

He had jumped to his feet so fast that his chair tipped over. Picking up the vase, he smashed it on the floor. The glass shattered like a soda bottle dropped from a great height; little glistening shards danced across the floor, followed quickly by spreading water that carried broken flowers in its wake.

"What the hell did you do that for?" Roxanne said. "Is that supposed to prove that you love me?"

"I'm tired of your shit," he said. "You hear me? You're losing it, you really are, thinking people are following you, mooning over that stupid cop. I'm the one who's always there for you. When you're in trouble, who do you call? You call me! I'm the only one you can rely on and you treat me like crap!"

Where had this outburst come from? "Listen, Chris—"

He came up to her, grabbed her by the shoulders, shook her. "No, *you* listen. You're going to stop this nonsense, or—"

"Chris—"

He slapped her then, not hard, striking the back of his hand against her cheek; it didn't even really sting. "Shut up until I'm finished," he said, not angrily, but more like he was talking to a dim child who had disappointed him. "Another thing. You're going to stop hanging out with Ryan. I know you two talk about me behind my b—"

She gathered her strength and shoved him away, hard. Looking shocked, he stumbled back a pace and stopped, staring at her.

"Get the fuck out of here," she said. "And If you *ever* touch me again, I'll kick you in the balls so hard it'll make your father sterile."

After a moment, he said: "You're telling me to leave?"

"No, I'm *ordering* you to leave."

"You're crazy," he said. "I can get any woman I want, you know. Any woman!"

"You'd better hurry, then," she said. Her voice quivered as she strained to keep her composure. "Before she sobers up."

Chris glared at her a second longer, then turned and walked out across the broken glass, not failing to tread on every flower in his path. The front door slammed behind him.

Roxanne sagged against the kitchen counter, put her head in her hands, and dissolved into a swarm of something that might have been sobbing, or laughter, or both.

10:30 AM

A snowball sailed silently through the cold air, splattering against the black fabric of Ronald Dinkins's coat.

"Nailed! Right through the heart!" After gasping out his last words Ronald went into a death-stagger, then miraculously recovered and, laughing, scooped up snow to form his own projectile. Too late: The next projectile targeting him was already in flight. As Ronald stood to throw, the frosty missile smacked into his face, sending snow down his shirt and behind his glasses. The cold shot through him, stunning him, and for a few seconds he couldn't breathe; then he gasped and started wiping slush from his skin. He took off his glasses and wiped them on his plaid yarn mitten, removing the snow but smearing water across them, so that when he put them back on it was like looking through a wave.

Ronald's friend Jeff Tracey was approaching, his face split by a wide grin. "Tip number one," Jeff said, "never turn your back on your enemy."

Ronald spluttered.

"Whassamatter? Did you get dain bramage?"

"Face shots are against the rules."

"Rules? What rules? There aren't any rules."

"Well there should be, and face shots should be against them."

"If you can't take the cold, move to Florida, you old lady. Besides, that wasn't a face shot until you put your face in front of it."

They stood there for a few seconds, facing each other, their breath coming in clouds. Finally Ronald grinned. "I'll get you for that one later."

"You wish," Jeff said.

"Now where's that tunnel you were talking about?"

"C'mon, I'll show you." Jeff resumed walking up the snowy road. As he passed by Ronald, Ronald stuck out his foot and hooked it around Jeff's ankle. With a surprised shout Jeff went down face-first into the snow.

"You dweeb!" Jeff cried, lifting his snow-crusted face. Ronald looked at him and fell over backwards, rolling around in the snow and squealing with laughter. Jeff stood, brushing off his coat, his pants, and his face, then brushed the snow out the tight black curls of his hair.

When Jeff had gotten himself cleaned up, he turned and glared down at Ronald. "If you can't stand the cold move to F-F-Florida!" Ronald said.

"I'll get *you* for *this*."

"Ooooooh," Ronald said.

"Let's go," Jeff said. He started trudging up the road. Ronald scrambled to his feet and hurried after him.

It was Tuesday, and normally the two boys would be in school; but it was Teacher Conference Day, when strange and mysterious things were discussed behind the closed doors and brown bricks of their school. So today the great grey halls of School were closed; today they were free.

"Is it safe?" Ronald asked. He had at first been intrigued by Jeff's description of the old railroad tunnel, with its walls of brick and its arched ceiling of concrete, and the rotted ties that littered the broken stone floor; but as they got closer, he began to imagine himself buried beneath a cave-in of cement and rock, or perhaps eaten by a pack of feral dogs.

"Of course it's safe," Jeff said. "Steel bars in the walls and ceiling. After a hundred years, it's not going to collapse now."

"How do you know it's got steel bars?"

"Because you can see them in a few places where the concrete fell off."

"The concrete's fallen off!"

"Just little pieces," Jeff said. "Don't be such a wimp."

"I'm not a wimp."

"Yes you are. You're a big wimpy wimp."

"Am not!"

"All the other wimps beat you up."

"No they don't."

"Yes they do. All the other wimps say you're their bitch."

"No they don't."

"Yes they do."

They were still debating the point when, fifteen minutes later, they reached the ravine which had been cut long ago, when their great-grandfathers had been young men. Here they stopped momentarily. "Yes they do," Jeff said, but without enthusiasm; now that they were here, he felt a strange trepidation, a reluctance to actually enter the gap. He didn't know why; nothing had changed, except the fence was down. It was so old and rotten, though, it had probably just fallen over from the wind or the weight of the snow.

"You look scared," Ronald said, with evident delight.

"I'm not scared."

"But you *look* scared."

"Something's not right," Jeff said. "Something's different."

"Yeah, you turned chicken."

"I'm serious. I think somebody's *in* there."

"Big brave Jeff, scared of an empty tunnel," Ronald said. "You've been here lots of times, you said. You went all the through to the other side, you said."

Jeff tried to ignore the gibes, thinking that neither of them should venture down the narrow ravine, where the sun didn't touch the floor.

Not today. Something bad was in there; worse than bad, something *unholy*. Its presence billowed out like fog between the walls of the cut.

Jeff knew all about unholy things. He'd seen *The Exorcist* on television. Twice.

"We should go home and tell my mom somebody's up here. She'll call the police to come and check it out."

"Oh ho! You want to run home to *mommy*?" Ronald folded his arms and began flapping them at his side like wings, while strutting around making clucking sounds.

"You look stupid doing that," Jeff said, attempting to ignore the implication of Ronald's little dance.

"B-*kawk!*"

"I'm not chicken!"

"B-*kawk* kawk!"

"Stop it!"

Ronald didn't even speak this time; he was busy strutting around, scratching at the snow and looking for invisible nuggets of corn.

"Fine!" Jeff was getting angry, overwhelming the sense of danger he had felt. "I'll go!" He turned and stomped up the ravine, leaving his footprints in the snow to show where he had been.

Ronald continued to do the rooster strut, clucking and occasionally crowing, to help Jeff maintain his resolve; as a friend, he couldn't very well allow Jeff to humiliate himself through his cowardice, right? He kept up the act until Jeff vanished from sight into the darkness of the tunnel; then he straightened up, sighed, and smiled with the satisfaction of an unpleasant job done well.

Suddenly he looked around. He thought he had heard something, or maybe he felt it more than head it: A summons, a whispered voice that did not come through the air like other voices, but along some ethereal string directly into his mind. *Come into my tunnel, little boy*, the voice seemed to say, soft and sibilant and compelling. His crotch began to tingle the way it did when he saw women in bathing suits on television, and he actually took a staggering pace forward before halting and shaking his head.

Suddenly Ronald realized he was alone.

Alone.

What was that feeling crawling over his skin like tattered spider webs? What was that flutter in the bottom of his stomach? Jeff had said somebody was watching them, and now Ronald felt it too: Eyes looking him over, sizing him up the way a butcher might evaluate a piece of meat, trying to entice him into its lair.

And he had sent Jeff right to it.

Ronald shuddered and took a step away from the ravine, then another, and soon he was running back down the road, heedless of his friend and what might have become of him, in fact hoping—the terrible part, actually *hoping*—that whatever lay in wait up there would be satisfied with Jeff and would leave him alone. He never looked back, fearing that if he did he would see some terrible *thing* running hard at his heels, reaching out with bloody hands that were scant inches from his back.

He didn't stop until he reached his own front yard, panting, hot with exertion and shame. He had left Jeff behind, abandoned him, thrown him to the wolves. He should tell his parents, tell them where Jeff had gone; but if he did they would get mad at him, they would think he was a coward for running away and leaving his friend. They might even go up to the tunnel themselves, and then whatever was hiding there would get them too.

He went inside, tracking snow across the living room floor and into his bedroom, where he kicked off his sodden boots and shed his wet clothes and crawled beneath the covers, trying to will himself into invisibility.

Jeff would never come back, he thought; something was watching, up there in those hills.

Something was waiting.

The gaping black mouth of the tunnel swallowed Jeff up. He stopped momentarily just inside the opening as a strange sensation swept over him, like a swarm of ants crawling on his skin. The thought of going back to Ronald suddenly seized him, but the ribbing he would get would be merciless, especially in light of his earlier bravado; and the next day it would be all over school, and people would laugh at him for being scared of the dark. If he backed out and turned around, he would be labeled a chicken, and it would take him weeks—or months, maybe even until next year—to live it down.

He swallowed and proceeded into the tunnel. Cold, fetid air rolled over him. Jeff wondered why he couldn't see the speck of light that usually marked the other end. He fumbled in his pocket for the small flashlight he had brought, feeling the metal, cold even through his mitten. He took it out, snapped it on, and aimed the beam straight down the tunnel's throat. Ten feet in it hit a wall of fog and stopped, the beam forming a bright circle in the mist.

"Oh, cool," Jeff said. He had never seen such thick fog in here before. Somehow, it reassured him; that was why he couldn't see the other side, because it was blocked by fog. It wasn't like something had come and *changed* the tunnel, made it longer, made it stretch out into an endless nightmare corridor. And it was perfectly natural that there would be fog in here; the air was colder than it was above ground, so when the outside air came in it turned into fog. Nothing to it, right?

On the basis of this meteorological theorizing, Jeff walked boldly forward. The temperature plunged as he moved farther in; it was like walking into a freezer or, he mused, a meat locker. As soon as that thought entered his mind he realized that there *was* sort of a meaty smell to the air, an odor of decaying flesh and stale blood. Perhaps some animal had died in here?

He was starting to get nervous again. Glancing over his shoulder, he saw that he had come well into the darkness; the mouth of the tunnel was a good distance behind him, white and dazzling with reflected light. He could still walk out of here and back to Ronald, to tell his friend to go to hell and then just go home; after all, he'd done what he said he would do. He'd come into the tunnel. Maybe it was time to cut and run.

He heard a noise from the fog, a faint rustle, like clothes brushing against the rock. He paused, listening, and was soon rewarded with another sound: A low, female moan. Jeff was only thirteen, but he'd seen enough movies (mostly at Ronald's house, on the forbidden cable channels available there) to know a sigh of pleasure when he heard one.

Someone was down here, in the freezing cold and dark, *doing it*!

She moaned again, a little louder, and then she gasped. Jeff cut the flashlight and, sticking close to the side of the tunnel, crept forward into the mist. He was barely conscious of moving, as if someone else were issuing commands to his legs; he was intent on the sounds, all of his concentration spent on hearing. He didn't notice that the mist was cold as ice, or that it smelled like spoiled meat, or even that it didn't completely fill the tunnel as his bullshit theory would have suggested; it was merely a wall of fog ten feet wide, and beyond it was empty, vacant darkness.

He could hear heavy breathing now, still female, the breaths coming sharp and fast. He was getting closer, and he began moving faster, being less careful of where he put his feet. He paid for that as he kicked something large and hard and went down on his face. The breath knocked out of him, he lay there for a few seconds before scrambling back to his feet. His forehead felt warm. He pulled off his right mitten and rubbed his fingers up there, and then winced as the salt on his skin stung the gash in his head. His fingers came away damp and sticky. He could feel blood dripping down his face and around his nose like warm, thick tears.

"Come to me," a woman's voice said. Jeff, in the act of putting his mitten back on, froze. Was she talking to him? Did she know he was here? He stood as if made of stone, saying nothing.

"I said come to me," she repeated. "I want you. You there. Turn on your flashlight."

She *had* to be talking to him. In a daze he raised his flashlight and clicked it on, shining its beam toward the voice. And there she was, standing there on the icy floor, feet apart, naked from head to toe. Jeff's eyes took her in. He had seen naked women, of course, but only in the movies or in purloined magazines, never in person; and now here was one in the flesh, walking slowly toward him, seductive intent implicit in her every move. She ran her hands up her body, tracing a path from her stomach up to her breasts, stretching her arms up to catch her long, fine, yellow hair in her fingers.

"I want you," she said again, and she was right in front of him even though he hadn't noticed her cover the distance. Her eyes bore into his. He clutched the flashlight with nerveless digits, shining the beam up at her face and upper body. Her breasts cast a shadow on her shoulders, and her facial features took on a weird, sinister look. She smiled and her teeth were small white points that protruded from her lips. She reached out and slipped her hand down into Jeff's snowmobile pants, easily forcing it through the tied-off string. "Well, what have we here?" she asked, stroking what she found. Jeff shuddered; this was beyond anything in his experience. Things like this didn't happen to him or, for that matter, to anyone he knew.

"I want you," she said one more time. "I want to eat you up!" She leaned forward and began licking the blood off Jeff's face.

As if a spell had been broken, Jeff suddenly realized that things were very wrong here in this dark place beneath the earth. There should be no naked woman down here, no strange wall of fog; and what was that smell? Blood? His blood, or someone else's? He tried to pull away from the woman, but her grip tightened on him like a vise. "Oh, no. You're not leaving," she whispered. "I'm not through with you yet. Not yet. Hold still or I'll squash it like a banana."

Jeff ignored her words, still struggling to pull away; unless he escaped, she would do something much worse than squash his privates like a banana. She grabbed his hair and jerked his head back. The flashlight fell from his hand and rolled across the floor, casting its beam crazily around the tunnel. "Don't," Jeff said, beginning to cry.

"Beg me," she murmured, leaning in close to his neck. "Beg for the bite."

The flashlight came to rest in the middle of the tunnel, its beam a spotlight on the wall. A moment later, a man stepped into the spotlight. He was pale in the flashlight beam, his hair dark and shiny, his features masked in shadow.

He said: "Stop!"

The woman, her teeth poised and pricking Jeff's skin, paused. She lifted her head from Jeff's neck and turned her gaze toward the man. "I want him," she said, almost plaintively. "I'm hungry."

"No."

"Why not?" It was a pout. She slid her hand out of his pants, and Jeff almost cried out for her to put it back; but then she grabbed him by the neck and slammed him up against the wall, and the seductive spell was shattered once again.

The man ignored her, instead addressing Jeff. "Are you alone?"

"N-n-no."

"Who are you with?"

"M-my friend Ronald. He's outside."

"You see?" The man looked at his companion. "His friend would tell. They would come here looking for him."

"So we'll kill him, too."

"You'll brave the sunlight to bring him here, then?"

The grip on Jeff's neck loosened. "I thought—"

"You did not think. You never think. You are not invulnerable, and neither am I. You would have brought the locals crashing down on our heads." The man looked around. "Where is Krone?"

"I don't know and I don't care." She casually tossed Jeff across the tunnel, sending him rolling and sliding in the darkness until he banged up against the far wall. "Krone's a simpleton."

Jeff got unsteadily to his feet. He was disoriented, and his head throbbed in two places, and he could see nothing in the darkness; but he somehow knew that if he could run and escape through the mist, he would be safe. He stumbled along the wall blindly, hoping he had chosen the right direction. Behind him, the two *things* were still arguing.

"Krone has served me for centuries," the man said. "You have already proven yourself more stupid than he."

"Why do we have to stay around this stinking little town, anyway? I hate it here. Let's go to New York City."

"We will go when and where *I* say we go."

"You just want that woman."

"That's right. And I will have her. And—where did the boy go?"

Jeff heard that and stepped up his pace, heedless of the rocks and protrusions that bruised his feet, slipping and sliding but always moving away from the things ... hell, the vampires. Honest to God bloodsucking vampires. Un-*fucking*-believable.

Ronald would shit a brick.

The tunnel was getting lighter, and Jeff knew he was near the end. He saw the mist in front of him, pale and ghostly, the barrier between the world of night and the world of day. If only he could reach it, pass through it—

His hand touched something cold and sticky, some gelatinous festering mass gobbed onto the wall like a gigantic wad of mucous. His fingers sank partway into it and he jerked his hand back with a strangled cry. The stench—*unbelievable*! Goo was all over his hand, his fingers were webbed with it! Unnerved he shook his hand and felt gunk flying off it, shooting like snot-missiles from his fingers.

Then he was plucked off his feet by a powerful hand at his neck.

He felt the world spin as he was whirled around and slammed up against the hard stone wall. A piece of cement came loose and clattered to the floor. Jeff closed his eyes, shutting out the darkness behind a darkness of his own creation.

"Open your eyes."

"No," Jeff said.

"Open. Your. Eyes." The voice teased his mind, slithered through his brain like a cold snake. It stroked him, caressed him, cajoled him; and his eyes opened. To his right was the ghostly, shifting wall of mist. He had almost made it. A pale arm came out of the darkness and held him by the shirt, keeping him up in the air, his back pressed against the wall. The end of the arm was hidden in shadow, but where the eyes should have been Jeff could see two almond-shaped pale green glows. Farther off down the tunnel, another pair of luminescent eyes burned, pointed straight at him.

"Look at me."

Jeff reluctantly turned his head and looked at the eyes.

The voice said: "Sleep."

12:30 PM

Roxanne was just arranging her new flowers in her new vase when the doorbell rang again. She glanced at the clock; too soon by far for Ryan. Maybe it was Chris, coming back to again profess his undying love, this time by keying her car and slashing her tires. But no, it was Officer Brennan there on the stoop, taking up most of the doorway. "You're back," she said, unlocking the storm door so he could enter.

"I'm back," Barry agreed. He looked around. "I noticed Mr. Keems's car is gone. Did he leave?"

"You might say that."

"Is he coming back?"

"Doubtful," she said. "Mr. Keems and I have parted on less than amicable terms." He didn't need to know about the hitting, she decided; that would only complicate things.

"Oh, I'm sorry to hear that." He didn't sound sorry. After a moment he added: "Actually, I just stopped by to let you know I talked to Marty and took care of that summons."

"You did? Thanks!" She grinned at him. "You could've called and told me that, of course."

"I don't have your number."

"It's listed," she said.

"Listed?"

"In the phone book? You may have had occasion to use one at some point in your life. Maybe to track down bad guys?"

"Bad guys tend to move around a lot."

"Do they move around a lot because they're bad, or are they bad because they move around a lot?"

He laughed. "I would have to go with that first one."

"So did you get your haircut?" Roxanne asked, examining his head critically.

"Yes I did, ma'am, high and tight," he said.

He looked pretty much the same. "Looks good," she lied.

"Thanks." He looked around the room. "Well, I guess I should be on my—"

"Just shut up, take off your coat, and have a cup of coffee. Or do you have to run off and polish your gun?"

"I'd love a cup of coffee," he said.

5:20 PM

"... and when Chris said he loved me, well, I knew he didn't mean it," Roxanne said. "He wanted me to say it too, but I couldn't. And I told him he didn't really love me. Naturally, he didn't take that too well."

"So that was my day. Very eventful, huh?"

"I would say so," Ryan said. "And you didn't tell your new boyfriend that your old one hit you?"

"Barry's not my new boyfriend."

"Uh-huh."

"Anyway, it was just a ... a tap."

"Uh-huh."

"He was upset."

"Uh-huh."

"Look, I dealt with it. I don't want him to get arrested for something that wasn't really much of anything."

"Uh-huh. I'm sure that's what abused women tell themselves all the time."

Desperate to change the subject, Roxanne said: "At least my

stalker friend hasn't turned up again."

"Mmm. Probably because your new boyfriend is a cop."

"He's *not* my new boyfriend."

"It took him three hours to finish one cup of coffee."

"So?"

"So?" Ryan said, all huge ingenuous eyes and exaggerated innocence.

"He just got divorced."

"Rebound?"

"I don't think so. He's been separated a long time."

"Well, after Chris, I think all your dates should be approved by a committee, but …" Ryan trailed off and shrugged. "What's his name again?"

"Barry Brennan."

"Too many Bs," Ryan said.

"My God! You're right! I'll never see him again!"

"Mmm." Ryan sighed and leaned back against the soft white cushions of Roxanne's couch. She gazed around the living room. "I'm not sure what I think of your new décor." Everything was white or off-white, like a hospital, or maybe some mundane section of the afterlife. The couch and easy chair were both white; the shag carpet was white; the walls were white, as was the ceiling; even the mantel around the fireplace had been painted white. A white plaster column, made to look Grecian, in one corner, supporting a large bowl containing a fat blue fish with feathery fins.

"White goes with everything," Roxanne said.

"That doesn't mean everything has to be white."

"It's not." Roxanne started pointing around the room. "Ecru, linen, snow, eggshell …"

"It all looks white to me."

"Well, now you just sound like a guy." Then: "It matches the season. It's like walking in a winter wonderland."

Ryan looked at her and arched an eyebrow.

"Well, except for the big blue betta blowing bubbles in a bowl," Roxanne said, "and the fragrant flurry of fresh flowers."

"Oh, for God's sake," Ryan said. "What's a betta, anyway?"

"That's my fish. His name is Aristotle."

"Isn't he lonely all by himself? In that tiny little bowl?"

"The guy at the store said that in the wild they live in footprints full of water. You put two males in the same bowl and they fight to the death. I guess he'd like a girlfriend though. Hey, you know what the only bad thing about breaking up with Chris is?"

"The knowledge that you wasted six months on him?"

"Okay, the other bad thing."

"Knowing that now he's going to inflict himself on some other poor unsuspecting woman?"

"That's not funny."

"Sorry."

"It's just, he was talking about going skiing this weekend, and I was kind of looking forward to it. To getting away for the weekend and not having it turn into a fiasco."

Ryan looked thoughtful. "We should do it," she said. "We'll all go together. You, me, Irving, maybe Priscilla ..."

"I don't know—"

"It'll be fun! We can leave after work on Friday. That way we'll have all weekend. Do you suppose that Barry character would want to come?"

"*That Barry character?* It's not like I met him on skid row, Ryan. Anyway it's too soon for me to be inviting him away for the weekend."

"Well, of course it is. I just thought you'd want to travel with your new bodyguard."

Roxanne sighed. "Okay, let's go back to calling him my new boyfriend," she said.

9:00 PM

"Ronnie! Telephone!"

Ronald was still lying in his bed, but he had recovered sufficiently to get out from under the covers and start reading a comic book, although it wasn't really holding his interest, he was just looking at the pictures. The shades were drawn on all his windows, blocking out the night and, he hoped, the eyes of the *thing* that he was sure lurked up at the old tunnel. Did it know where he lived? Did it know his name?

"Ronnie!"

Ronald forced himself out of bed and went out into the hallway. It was dark, and he hurried along it, soon emerging into the living room. His mother was there by the fireplace, reading a book by the light of a floor lamp. Ronald padded across the shiny wooden floor to her. "Where's Dad?" he asked.

"Shoveling the driveway. It's been snowing all evening."

Ronald glanced out the living room window, but the light of the floor lamp turned the glass into a mirror, reflecting only himself, small, pale, and still frightened. He knew, though, that the window was only an illusion of a mirror; anybody outside could see in, see him, know where he was and what he was doing. Like the thing from the ravine.

"Aren't you going to answer the phone, honey?"

"Huh?"

Brenda Dinkins indicated the receiver with her thumb. "The telephone. Jeff wants to talk to you."

"Jeff!" Ronald grabbed the phone. "Jeff?"

"Yes, Jeff." His friend's voice sounded slightly distorted by its passage through the wires. "Took you long enough to get to the phone. Were you hiding in the basement or something?"

"Where are you?"

"I'm home, where else would I be? Jeez, don't be so dumb. And anyway, the question is not where am I, but where were you, numbnuts? You bailed and left me there all alone."

"I know, I'm sorry. I ... I got scared."

"Scared." Jeff sounded disgusted. "Dork. There's nothing to be scared of up in that old tunnel."

"Yeah, then why did *you* look so scared, huh?"

"I was just trying to make *you* scared."

"Well, I wasn't scared."

"You just said you were."

"Why are you two always trying to *scare* each other?" Brenda asked, looking up from her book. She shook her head. "Boys."

"Well, we'll talk more at school. Chicken!"

"I'm not a chicken!"

"Bawk-bawk-b-*kawk*!"

"Take that back!"

"See you tomorrow, Ronald McDonald." The line went dead.

As Ronald hung up the phone, his mother said: "Where have you and Jeff been creeping around this time?"

He went to the window, leaned forward, and shielded his eyes from the light. The glass was like a sheet of ice against his nose. Out there in the dim illumination of the porch lamp, he saw the dark figure of his father scooping up snow with the shovel and hurling it back over his shoulder, where it spread like a frozen cloud and then fell to earth in the yard.

"Ronald, I asked you a question."

"Huh?" Whenever she used his full name, he knew it was time to pay attention. "Oh, um, just out in the woods."

"The woods."

"Uh-huh."

"Well that doesn't sound so scary," she said, going back to her book. "You two and your imaginations, I'm surprised you don't give each other nightmares."

"Yeah," Ronald said. "Me too."

5

WEDNESDAY, JANUARY 13

2:00 AM

Roxanne rolled over and looked blearily at the red lights of her digital alarm clock. Two in the morning. Groaning, she rolled onto her stomach and buried her face in the pillow. She had gone to bed at about eight-thirty, shortly after Ryan left, and had slept maybe two hours since then. It seemed like every five minutes she woke up shaking from some bad dream. She wished someone were there with her. She closed her eyes and thought about her new friend, the police officer ... his big, strong arms ... his broad chest ... in her mind, he was wearing nothing but blue underwear with a badge on the crotch, and he was twirling a pair of handcuffs lazily around his finger ...

And then she woke up. Two-thirty. She had slept for a whole half-hour that time. Not bad, she thought; maybe she'd make it through an entire hour by next month. She jerked around, trying to get comfortable, eventually flopping over onto her side and facing the French doors, the sheet wound around her waist, the air cold on her shoulders and back.

As she closed her eyes, she heard a faint noise from the doors, a light scrabbling at the knob. She opened her eyes wide, staring at the curtains that looked black in the dim light. They were drawn tightly together, leaving no gap between them for probing eyes to penetrate, but still, she felt someone staring at her. She pulled the blanket up to her neck and stayed rigid, waiting for the noise to go away, but it didn't. Instead it moved to the window beside her bed, a faint scratch that sounded like someone dragging a nail across the glass. She tilted her head back to get a look up at the window, but here, too, the gauzy curtains blocked her view.

And did she really want to see?

Martel, whose vision penetrated the sheer material of the curtains, watched Roxanne greedily, hungrily. When she moved her head back, exposing the length of her neck, he had to fight the urge to smash through the window and take her immediately. He didn't want to turn her yet; the stalking was too enjoyable, and he wanted to have her at least once while she was still warm and human. It had been too long since he had had warm flesh. Twenty years? Twenty-five? Her name had been Marilyn, a girl from a farm in Oklahoma. She had gone out into the wheat field one night, alone and unprotected; Martel had found her and had taken her body, then her life. Feeling benevolent, he'd left her her soul, to journey through death to whatever God she favored.

Martel didn't know anything about the Oklahoma girl beyond her name; the lives of humans were clay for him to shape as he would, the humans dust, to be dispersed with a single puff of breath. That was the price they paid, to walk in the light of day; they must pay *something* for that right, that glorious right they all took for granted, and it was he who collected the toll.

When he came out of his reverie, Roxanne was gone.

The alarm clock came on, softly, waking Ronald up. He had set it to go off last evening, after the phone call from Jeff. Even then, he had been formulating a plan to reclaim his dignity, his manhood. He would have to be out of bed and into the shower by seven; that left plenty of time for him to prove, to himself at least, that he had no yellow stripe down his back. He rolled out of bed and started casting about for his boots.

Ten minutes later he was slowly pulling the front door closed. The lock caught quietly, and Ronald was outside in the night.

In the dark.

Alone.

The cold air tickled his face, probed the defenses of his coat. Ronald paused a moment to consider what he was doing. Wandering up into the hills to go exploring a railroad tunnel in the dead of night? Probably not the smartest idea he'd ever had. But it would settle the chicken issue decisively in his favor Jeff would never dare go to the tunnel at night, alone, and even if he did, Ronald would have done it first. And to prove it, Ronald was going to take pictures. He would drop the film off at the drug store on his way to school, pick it up in the afternoon on his way home, and show the pictures to his awestruck friends. He would be a Major Dude, and then they would see who was whose bitch!

The fact that he was carrying a can of pepper spray, filched from his mother's purse, was no reflection on his bravery; it was a simple precaution. Besides, taking the thing was in itself an act of courage, because he wasn't supposed to know it even existed and he'd get in real trouble if his mom found out he had swiped it.

He shined his flashlight at his watch. Two-fifty-five. He could be back by four, and no one would be the wiser.

Ronald jumped off the patio and hurried off into the night.

From her hiding place behind the shrubbery of a bowling alley, Lauren Fletcher watched cars stop and go at a red light. She had quickly learned that this particular intersection saw a lot of traffic, even at night, and so it had become one of her favored hunting grounds. She had no idea where Martel got his nourishment from; he was always going over to the Carmichael woman's house, peeking through her windows like some little pervert, leaving Lauren to her own devices. It disgusted her, such a foolish weakness; what was this nonsense about stalking, about the thrill of terrorizing? If he wanted the woman, he should just take her.

Then again, if he *did* take her, what would become of Lauren? For some reason, Martel obviously favored that little red-haired bitch. Would he keep both of them around once he turned the other woman? Lauren suspected not. When they'd been chasing him, he had never traveled with more than one companion. Which meant he was probably planning to leave her in a ditch somewhere once he was done with her.

Unless she struck first …

Lauren shook her head. This wasn't the first time she'd had such a thought, and it always made her mind go all fuzzy and her concentration went to shit. She struggled for clarity, but her brain was full of soap bubbles. Screeching, she punched the brick wall with her fist, a fierce but glancing blow that deeply scraped her knuckles. Mesmerized, she looked at her hand, at the torn skin hanging in shreds, the grey flesh and gleaming bones revealed by this misadventure. There was pain, of a sort, but it was more nuisance than agony, like an annoying sound that she couldn't quite tune out. She knew that her kind regenerated quickly; it would be interesting to see how long the wound took to heal.

She noticed a yellow sports car pull up to the light. The driver was alone in the car; the street was otherwise deserted. Perfect. She forced gravity to release its hold on her and half-leapt, half-flew at the car, the ground rolling by beneath her. She glided over the roof and landed lightly on the passenger side. She yanked open the door, breaking the lock, and started to climb in, only to realize that the passenger seat was occupied; there was a car seat strapped into the passenger's chair, and in it was a baby, a baby that had been dozing but now stirred and looked around blearily, its face annoyed. The driver, a woman, stared at Lauren, a stunned expression on her face. She looked to be in her late twenties, her face painted with too much makeup inexpertly applied, her long brown hair teased and sprayed into a tangled mess. The makeup was running a bit, as if she had been crying earlier but had since stopped.

Lauren hesitated, floating there with one hand on the door and the other on the roof, staring at the child. *A baby!* Horror spread through her guts like fungus. A baby, a baby! "No!" Lauren shrieked, reaching into the car and grabbing the car seat. The child screamed as Lauren pulled the basketlike apparatus out of the car; it wasn't secured, not even with a seat belt. She hurled the seat off into the snowy night, sending it spinning end over end, the child's ululating wail continuing until the seat smashed into the front wall of the bowling alley and clattered to the snow.

Shaking with revulsion at what she'd done—no, with *exhilaration*—Lauren slid into the seat the child had recently occupied. She was above human, beyond human, she could do whatever she wanted. The driver of the car was panicking, thrashing in her seat, fumbling with the buckle of her belt, sobbing. Lauren thought *sex* at her; her struggling slowed, then ceased, and she turned to look at Lauren with naked desire. Then her face faltered, and she looked away, back toward where her baby lay in the snow. Lauren reached out and slowly turned the woman's face back to hers. It was flushed scarlet; but her eyes were shining.

"Really," Lauren said, "what sort of a mother just puts the car seat in *front*? You're lucky I came along before the police stopped you." She put her hand on the other woman's breast. "Now take me somewhere we can be alone, and I'll show you things you never even dreamed of."

A moment later the car roared through the red light and into the darkness.

Ronald shined his flashlight at his wrist and discovered that it was nearly three-forty. He had been standing at the mouth of the ravine for several minutes, debating whether or not to go in, getting colder every second. Finally, as heavy flakes began peppering the older snow, he decided that he was being ridiculous. All he had to do was go inside the tunnel, take a few pictures, and run home. Jeff had gone inside and come out again, and nothing had happened to him.

He strolled into the gully, kicking up little clouds of snow around his feet. Soon he was around the bend, and then he was there, facing the mouth of the tunnel. The yawning maw swallowed up his flashlight beam like a black hole. Taking slow, measured steps, Ronald approached the opening and went inside. He crept along, swinging the beam back and forth. Finally, after thirty feet, he stopped. This was far enough. It was time for photographs.

He tucked the flashlight away in a spacious coat pocket, and from another took his small camera. He snapped open the flash, aimed the lens into the darkness, and took a picture. The flash popped, and for a second brilliant light flooded the tunnel; then all was dark again. Ronald lowered the camera. In the momentary light of the flash, he thought he had seen something up ahead. He hadn't come here to go exploring, but still … he would have more stories to regale his friends with. He walked cautiously forward, the flashlight back in his hand, and he quickly found the thing he had seen. It was some sort of vile, malodorous cocoon, a huge mass of reddish-brown putrescence slapped against the tunnel wall, stuck with brownish-red tendrils that clung to the brick like gluey tentacles. It was shiny and looked soft. What *was* it? He briefly flirted with the idea of touching it, but it was just too gross. Instead he snapped a picture. He circled around to get it from another angle. He raised the camera, took a picture.

Now he saw something else, a great big automobile a little farther in. With one last glance at the cocoon, he approached the sedan. He knew that sometimes people ditched their old cars in the woods; last summer he and Jeff had found the remains of a boxy, rust-red station wagon mouldering in the depths of an old sand quarry, and had taken any number of imaginary road trips in it, until the rotting upholstery had become home to a nest of raccoons who didn't want to share.

Still, driving a vehicle this far into a railroad tunnel … that was pretty extreme abandonment. Why would somebody go to the trouble?

Creeping up on the passenger side, he covered the flashlight with his fingers to dim it, then raised it up. The rear windows of the car were completely blacked out, but through the front ones, he saw a massive shape inside, lying across the bench seats: An enormous man, like one of those wrestlers from television. It didn't look like the guy even had a blanket. Was he dead? Had whoever killed him left the car here?

What if they came back?

Deciding that now would be a good time to go, Ronald clicked off the flashlight, turned, and hurried back up the tunnel. He didn't pause by the weird cocoon, just casting a sideways glance at it as he passed by. It quivered a little bit, reminding him of the vibration of a web that let the spider know an insect had blundered into it. For some reason this thought frightened him even more than the guy in the car had, and he quickened his pace; but, not looking where he was going, he ran into something immobile as a wall: Another man, clad all in black, like a burglar or a ninja. Before Ronald could react, a hand grabbed his arm, another his throat. The ground fell away beneath him as he was lifted up into the air; his feet kicked uselessly at nothing. His captor looked at Ronald with flickering green eyes. "Another little explorer," he said, licking his teeth and lips.

Ronald reached into his pocket with his free hand; his fingers closed on the can of pepper spray. He yanked it out and directed a prolonged blast directly into his captor's face. The effect was to make the man sneeze a few times, nothing more.

Oh, fuck.

As if carrying a loaf of bread, the man whirled and strode deeper into the tunnel, holding Ronald at arm's length, too far for his wildly swinging legs to connect.

Double-fuck!

"Krone!" Martel bellowed.

After a moment, the car door opened and the big man unfolded himself from where he'd been sleeping. "Master?"

"Take this," Martel said, tossing the boy into Krone's chest. "Be careful, he is armed with ... something." He sneezed again. Krone's big arms enfolded the boy in a crushing grip, his hands closing over the child's arm and mouth. Martel turned away, looking out at the sky. "Out a little late, aren't you?" he asked. "And carrying such a nasty weapon. Were I human, I suspect I would now be incapacitated."

The response was a muffled noise.

"Release his mouth," Martel said. Krone removed his hand, and the child immediately began screaming. Martel watched with an expression of detached amusement, then reached out and pushed the boy's mouth closed, holding his chin. In that position, he turned to Krone and said, "The child was just leaving the tunnel when I came in. He saw everything, but you would have let him escape."

"I'm sorry," Krone said.

"What has happened to you, Krone?" Martel asked. "You used to be so reliable. But this afternoon ..." Martel's voice hardened. "This afternoon, Krone, you left me here alone, undefended. Where were you?"

"I—" Krone licked his lips. "I was out."

"I know you were out. Where were you?"

"I ... Lauren Fletcher sent me on an errand—"

"Don't lie to me, fool. She has no errands, and no use for the likes of you."

"I went to ... I went to look at ... the red-haired lady."

"You *what*?" Martel bellowed. "Did she see you?"

Krone hung his head.

"You ass! Imbecile!" Martel cried. "What if she tells the police about you? What if she describes my car? Feh!" He turned away in disgust. "You are not to leave the tunnel during the day, Krone, unless *I* send you somewhere. Is that understood?"

"Yes, Master," he murmured, not raising his eyes.

"You are not to go near Roxanne Carmichael, or any other human, unless *I* tell you to."

"Yes, Master."

Martel stood there for several minutes, his back to his servant and his prisoner. He could hear Krone shifting from one foot to the other and back again, and finally the big man said: "What are we going to do with the little boy?"

"What are we going to do?" Martel turned and strode over to Krone. The boy hung limply, apparently having fainted, but Martel slapped him a few times and he groggily awakened. "Child," Martel said, "what is your name?"

The boy stared at him stupidly.

"Your name!"

"R-Ronald."

"Are you here alone?" he said, holding Ronald's head gently in his hands, gazing steadily into his eyes. Slowly Ronald nodded. "No one knows you came here?" Ronald nodded again. Martel looked up at Krone and raised an eyebrow. Krone pulled Ronald's head back. Martel's eyes glowed brighter; his mouth split open like a rotten orange bursting; his teeth grew into daggers.

Ronald tried to scream, but Martel was already sinking those fangs into his throat, and all that came out was a whimper.

11:00 AM

Roxanne scanned the doctor's bill, following the procedures and charges with the fingers of one hand and entering them into the computer with the other hand. Normally at three in the afternoon she would have a pile of entered claims several inches thick, but today her stack was far smaller. She couldn't concentrate; she entered prices wrong, or typed the wrong code, or hit two keys at once. Coffee at break and coffee at lunch hadn't helped her productivity at all; in fact, since she had had to run several times to the bathroom, the caffeine had only hindered her performance.

"You look like hell."

Roxanne jumped at Ryan's voice, then said: "Thanks."

Ryan folded her arms and leaned up against the cold plastic wall of Roxanne's cubicle. "Another night of no sleep? But you felt so good yesterday afternoon."

"Yeah." She tried to smile. "I got over it."

"You look like death warmed over."

"I slept in the basement last night."

"The basement?"

"Uh-huh. I piled up some old quilts and slept in the laundry room."

"Why?"

"Because there aren't any windows there."

"Wasn't it cold?"

"It was freezing."

"Poor baby! Listen, I was talking to Irving about your problem, and he had a good idea. Why don't you get a dog?"

Roxanne cocked her head. "A ... dog?"

"Yes, a dog. You know, one of those furry animals that goes *bow-wow* and eats burglars."

"I never had a dog. I don't know anything about them."

"You feed them, you pet them, they love you forever. It's not that complicated. In fact, my neighbor's German shepherd had puppies a few months ago. I think there's one left."

After a moment, Roxanne said: "You already got one for me, didn't you?"

"Yeah," Ryan said. "She's in my office. Come say hello."

5:45 PM

"Good girl, Bernice," Barry said. "Sit up!"

The shepherd puppy tilted its head and looked at Barry as if the man had antlers and a light bulb nose and was shackled to a sleigh.

"Real smart dog you got there, Roxanne," Barry said, leaning back in the chair. Bernice looked at Barry for a few seconds, then whined and rolled over on her back, legs waving in the air.

"Dog's aren't born knowing what *sit up* means, you big goof.

Anyhow, Ryan thinks she'll help keep the peeper away."

"Hmm. If this perp is as large as you described, he could pick her up by the tail and throw her out the window."

Roxanne, sitting on the couch, shrugged. On the end table beside her were an untouched cup of coffee (she had only made coffee to have a pretext for inviting Barry over) and a doughnut. Barry had brought a box of them from some place she had never heard of, but he assured her they were the best in town. She had refrained from making the obvious jokes, mostly because she was just too tired.

"You really look like beat," Barry said.

"Thank you *so* much. It's nice that everyone thinks I have enough self-esteem to hear that over and over again."

"Sorry," he said.

Bernice had apparently decided that her tummy wasn't going to be scratched, so she rolled back over onto her feet and started barking at Barry's feet, tail wagging furiously. Then she raced off, her bark echoing throughout the house.

"What have you been feeding that thing, speed?"

"She's a puppy. The book says they have a lot of energy." *The book* was a reference tome she had acquired from the library that purported to tell you all you needed to know about raising puppies. It was several inches thick. Roxanne had been shocked; she had thought a puppy was basically like a grown-up dog, only smaller. Apparently she had been wrong.

"Why'd you call her Bernice?"

"Why not?"

"It's a person's name."

"So is Rex. Or Max. Or Buddy."

"Dogs shouldn't have people names."

She stared at him. "You have some weird rules, Officer Brennan. Are you going to charge me with fraud?"

"Fraud?"

"For giving her a people name. Maybe I'm trying to pass her off as a dependent, claim a tax deduction." She winked at him.

Barry stared at her for a second, then grinned. "I suppose I could place you under arrest," he said.

Roxanne said: "Got your handcuffs with you?"

Before he could answer, there was a noise from the front entrance, as if someone had opened the storm door and let it fall closed again. Barry looked at it for a second, then got to his feet and warily approached the entrance. Roxanne watched in quiet amusement as the police officer checked the peephole, peered out the side window, and finally jerked the door open.

A copy of the evening paper fell over onto his feet.

"My hero," Roxanne said.

Barry picked up the paper and brought it over to the couch, kicking the door closed with the back of his foot. He settled down on the floor and unfolded the bundle, pointing at the headline. "I knew this would make the front page," he said.

"What?"

"A kid was murdered last night." Roxanne twisted around for a better look. "He was found down by the canal. His head was cut off. It doesn't say in the paper, but I happen to know that his heart had been removed." Barry pointed to a line that spoke of some unspecified mutilation. "This is all that's been released to the press at the moment."

"Ugh. That's horrible."

"Yeah." He closed the paper and tossed it aside. Suddenly Bernice reappeared and began sniffing around the edges of the newspaper. Before Roxanne could react, the puppy was squatting and urinating, front paws on the paper, back end on the carpet.

"My rug!" Roxanne cried.

"Somehow, I don't think white carpeting goes well with a puppy," Barry said.

11:58 PM

After the dog's performance with the newspaper, Roxanne had banished her to the hall bathroom for the evening, lining the floor with papers. This didn't sit well with Bernice, who apparently intended to stay up all night if necessary, whining and scratching and snuffling, until someone let her out.

Barry, attempting to sleep on the couch, found himself listening attentively to every little sound the dog produced. It was like water torture, waiting for the next noise from the bathroom. How had he gotten roped into spending the night on a narrow little sofa that couldn't even accommodate him, anyway? All he remembered was a lot of smiling, a few hugs, a quivery voice, and those great big blue eyes. When had he turned into such a pushover?

Bernice whined again. Roxanne was obviously unprepared for a puppy; she needed a crate, she needed a dog bed, she needed some more books on training. The one she had gotten from the library was about fifteen years old; surely someone had come up with new theories in the last decade. He was pretty sure locking the dog in the bathroom was not the right way to handle this situation. Maybe he would go let her out, bring her back to the couch, and see if she would quiet down.

But as he was getting up, the dog really started wailing.

Arr-Rooooooooo!

Bernice's howl jolted her awake. Roxanne stumbled out of bed and landed face down on the floor, muttering. Then she felt it: a cold breeze that blew through her soul, a breeze that pulled instead of pushed, pulled her toward the French doors; but first she had to do something. She went to the bedroom door, nudged it closed, locked it; Barry's heavy footsteps were coming down the hall, and she didn't want him disturbing her. That done, she turned and shuffled toward the French doors. The curtains were drawn, they were obscuring something she wanted to see. They needed to be opened.

Arr-Rooooooooo!

She heard Barry say, "For God's sake, dog, what's the matter with you?" The sound came to her ears muffled, as if her ears were stuffed with cotton. Now she stood in front of the curtains. With trembling hands, she reached forward and opened them. *He* was standing there, pressed close against the glass, his pale face staring at her. It was the same face she had seen two nights ago, peering through her windows, but how could she have failed to realize how beautiful it was? And the eyes, the eyes that glowed and burned themselves into the back of her skull; what pleasures they promised, what secrets they knew! With every step she took, she became more aroused, until she was standing a foot away from the glass and trembling with the excitement of the eyes. The man outside the window was watching her insolently, running his thick tongue over his gleaming teeth, and she shuddered at the thought of his rubbing that tongue on her. She reached out and put her hands on the door handles, turning them, unaware of the cold radiating from the glass.

He smiled.   His teeth glimmered in the dim light.   His eyes flickered, candles in the darkness.

She pulled on the handles.

6

THURSDAY, JANUARY 14

MIDNIGHT

When Barry opened the bathroom door, the little dog moved like a
missile, shooting between his legs, trying and failing to execute a turn,
crashing into the wall. Her feet scrabbled on the tile as she got back
up and bolted into the living room, tripping Barry up as he tried to
turn and see what the hell was going on. He grabbed for the
doorway but missed, falling against the large mirror that hung in the
hallway, which pulled loose and shattered against the floor. The
hallway around him was now littered with broken glass, each one
reflecting a different, dizzying angle of himself.

Great, seven more years of bad luck.

He looked down the hallway to Roxanne's room. The door was
closed. When he had gone to sleep, it was open. Had she decided he
might try to pay her a visit in the middle of the night? Feeling
vaguely affronted—why ask him to stay if she didn't trust him?—he
went to it and knocked softly. "Roxanne?"

Through the door he heard faint clicking noises, like someone
fumbling with a latch.

Louder this time: "Hey, Roxanne!" No answer. He jiggled the
knob but it wouldn't turn. Closed *and* locked? Had her boyfriend
sneaked in through those security nightmares, the French doors? He
backed up a step, staring at the door, and then he charged at it,
leading with his shoulder. The door frame gave easily, leaving him
with more than enough momentum to carry him into the bedroom.

There he saw Roxanne on her hands and knees fumbling with the bottom lock on the French door, and for an instant he saw something else, some dim shape, waiting in the darkness beyond; then the impression was gone, and all he saw was the sky.

He bounded to Roxanne's side. "Roxanne, what the hell are you doing?"

"He wants to come in," she said, not looking up, uncoordinated fingers still attempting to undo the bolt.

"Who wants to come in?"

"*Him.*"

"Roxanne ..." Barry looked through the window; the yard was empty. He bent over, grabbed her under the shoulders, hauled her to her feet. "Roxanne, there's nobody out there," he said.

"What?" She was looking at him with wide eyes and enormous pupils. Then, wildly, she turned her head and looked out into the night. Turning back, eyes narrowed, she said: "You made him leave!"

"Made *who* leave?"

"Made ..." She faltered, looked in confusion back out the door. "You made ..."

"Come and lie down." Barry half-dragged her to the bed and tucked her in beneath the comforter. Then he sat down cross-legged beside her. "Now, what are you talking about?"

"He was ... he was out there," she said. "Outside the French doors. I tried to let him in, but I forgot they were locked."

"You *tried to let him in*?"

"He ... he was telling me to."

"Roxanne ..." Barry trailed off, looking at her. She was all flushed, sweat beading on her forehead and her neck, her eyes bright and feverish. She finally looked at him as if she could actually see him. She pushed herself up onto her shoulder, staring at him.

"You're bleeding," she said.

"What?"

"Your leg."

"Huh." Barry inspected himself. "So it is. A piece of the mirror must have gotten me."

"Mirror?"

"Yeah. I broke your mirror. Sorry."

"That's okay. I've got band-aids in the bathroom." She started to get up, but he forestalled her with a raised hand.

"No, stay put, it's just a scratch. It'll be fine. There's broken glass everywhere, though. I'll clean it up." He cocked his head at her. "Will you be all right while I'm doing that?"

She nodded.

"Where do you keep your vacuum?"

"Hall closet."

"Okay." He stood and headed for the hallway. She called his name; he stopped and looked back at her.

"Come back in here after you're done," she said.

Alone in the dark bedroom, Roxanne looked at the French doors. Barry had closed the curtains, but she knew that beyond the dark blue cotton, the night was beating on her walls like a pounding sea, demanding admittance.

Why had she tried to open the doors? Was she completely insane? She tried to recall what she had thought, what she had felt, but everything was fuzzy, blurred, fragmented, like a half-remembered dream. She knew she had been turned on, but she didn't know why; why had she been in such a frenzy to get the doors open?

Maybe she should buy a house with no windows.

She had hoped her secret admirer would stay away if Barry was in the house, but obviously he didn't care if she had a man sleeping on her couch. He must be crazy, obsessed; or was he a figment of her imagination?

No. He was real. He had left a message on her machine; Christian had listened to it.

Hell. Maybe she'd been right the first time, and Chris had left the message himself, to spook her into calling him. She wouldn't put it past him. She'd have Barry check the patio, she decided; see if there were any sign that someone had been there.

And if not?

Well, she might be crazy, but—as Ryan had suggested—at least she had acquired a nifty bodyguard.

When Barry came back into the room, Roxanne said: "He was outside, Barry. Will you ... will you just look and make sure he's gone? Please?"

Barry nodded and went to the curtains, pushing them open enough to admit his head. He looked out into the night. A light snow was falling, peppering the trees as their branches rocked in the wind. In the dim light he saw the little iron railing that bordered Roxanne's patio. Here was a lump of snow, a pot buried by winter, out of which a little evergreen sprouted like a miniature Christmas tree; here were four deck chairs, their individual bars glistening white with ice like some strange frozen skeleton; but there was no sign of an intruder, no trace in the snow. Barry frowned; he thought he had seen someone standing there, if only for an instant, but apparently it had been a trick of the light. No one could've disappeared that quickly, and even if it were possible the perpetrator would have left footprints.

He shut the curtains and walked over to the bed. "There's nobody out there," he said. "Everything's undisturbed."

"Nobody was out there, huh? No footprints? Just like before?"

"Just like before."

"Am I crazy?"

"Maybe it was a nightmare," Barry said. "You should go back to sleep."

"I don't want to."

"You'll have better dreams this time, Roxanne. I promise."

"Call me Roxie."

"Everybody named Roxanne is called Roxie," Barry said. "I'll call you Annie instead."

"Annie." Roxanne smiled sleepily. "I like that."

Barry sat there watching her until her breathing became deep and regular, then he stood, circled around to the other side, and lay down beside her. Her hair splashed over the pillow, black in the dim light.

Looking up at the ceiling, he lay there for some time, and he didn't even notice when he fell asleep.

7:17 AM

"Sorry about your door," Barry said.

"Hm?" Roxanne looked up from the floor, where she was busily scratching Bernice's ears.

"Your bedroom door."

"Oh," Roxanne said. "It's okay. I'll get it fixed." Then, giving the dog's head a vigorous scratching: "You is a scaredy-dog. Yes you is!" And, in a quieter tone: "I'm glad you were worried enough about me to bust it down, actually."

It took Barry a moment to register that comment. "That's good," he said. "I was afraid you would think I was a psycho."

"After Chris, you'd have to do a lot more than that before I'd think you were a psycho." Then, to the dog: "Is you a good girl?"

"I'll never understand," Barry said, carrying the coffee pot over to the table, "why people make baby-talk at dogs."

"Why not?"

"The dog doesn't understand it."

"Neither does a baby."

"Babies learn how to talk eventually."

"So will Bernice." Roxanne bent down and cradled the dog's head in her hands, looking into her big, soft, vacant brown eyes. "Won't you? Yes you will. Is she a googirl? Googoogirl?" She stood up, ran a hand through her mussed hair, and then plopped down into the seat across from Barry.

"You don't look so tired this morning," he said.

"I got a decent night's sleep, for a change. Thanks to you."

"Aw, shucks," Barry said, putting on a goofy voice. Then: "Do you like hockey? There's a game tonight. I have season tickets."

"Hockey? Brr, cold. Fighting. Yelling. Bad food."

"So that's a no. Do you feel up for a movie, then?"

"A movie where?"

"At a theatre."

"Don't you work tonight?"

"I traded shifts with somebody. If I was working tonight, I wouldn't be trying to ask you out."

"You haven't asked me out. You asked me if I liked hockey, and then you asked me if I felt up for a movie."

"You are a strange and mischievous woman," Barry said. "Would you like to see a movie with me tonight?"

She looked him over, smiled, and said: "Which one?"

1:35 PM

"He asked you to see a movie?"

"Uh-huh," Roxanne said, busily typing.

Ryan leaned against the wall of Roxanne's cubicle and folded her arms. "What time?"

"Eight-thirty."

"You'll be out after dark, then."

"Good. *He* can't spy on me if I'm not home, right?"

"I suppose," Ryan said, though she clearly didn't suppose.

"I thought you liked Barry."

"I've never met him."

"Well, the *idea* of Barry, then."

"What makes you think I don't like him?"

"Well, for one thing, you're grilling me like a common criminal."

"I am not."

"Yes you are."

"Did he say anything about this weekend?"

"No. What do you … You mean about the skiing?"

Ryan was mute.

"How would he even know about it?"

"I … may have mentioned it."

Roxanne cocked her head. "May have."

"Yeah." Pause. "Also, I may have invited him to come along."

"Ryan!"

"Well, I called the police station and asked to talk to him—I wanted to see what he was like—and it sort of slipped out. And besides, it's not as if … what's so funny?"

"I invited him myself this morning."

Ryan raised an eyebrow. "This morning?"

"Oops." Roxanne clammed up and turned to pretend to concentrate on her work.

"Roxanne Carmichael, did he spend the night with you?"

"He just slept at my house, that's all. To keep the bogeymen away."

"And did he?"

Roxanne thought about the night before, about the man outside her house, and frowned. Her mind seemed to suddenly shoot off into darkness, traveling along sunless paths to catch another glimpse of the intruder, longing for a second chance to open the French doors instead of forgetting to undo the locks right away.

"*Roxanne!*" Ryan snapped her fingers in Roxanne's face.

Coming back to the present, she said: "What?"

"You just spaced right out. I said your name three times."

"Sorry. I didn't hear you."

"I guess you didn't."

"I've been really, uh, preoccupied lately."

"Yeah, I know."

She still sounded miffed, Roxanne thought. "Listen, why don't you and Irving come over for dinner tonight? I'll invite Barry, and you can get to know each other."

"I thought you were going to the movies."

"You can come along."

"Ha. You know what Irving thinks of Hollywood. Anyway, Barry isn't going to want to hang around with your friends on your first date. I can't believe *you* want to."

"It'll be fun."

"Fun. Right." Ryan looked at her for several long seconds, then said: "Well, if you're sure."

"I'm sure. I want you to meet him. In person, I mean."

"Okay. Just dinner, though. For the movie, you're on your own."

"We can handle that."

"Mm. I'll be judging him, of course."

"Of course. Why do you think I want you to meet him?"

Jeff shuffled down the hallway at school, head down, clutching a backpack filled with books in his right hand. He hadn't slept much the last few nights, and when he did doze off he had nightmares that sent him screaming back to wakefulness. Ronald's murder had done nothing to make his dreams more pleasant.

The other students were avoiding him at the moment. It was well known that he and Ronald were best friends, and no one seemed to be quite sure what they should say to Jeff. Should they should give him an encouraging pat on the shoulder? Should they offer their apologies? Should they just pretend Ronald had never existed?

Unsure of what to do, most of them seemed to be pretending that *Jeff* didn't exist, thereby avoiding the whole problem.

There had been an assembly yesterday, with a policeman and the school psychologist. The policeman had assured them that the authorities were on the case, that the killer would be caught, that the children were safe; and the psychologist had tried to get together a school-wide "rap session," as she called it, to air their feelings about Ronald's death. This had resulted in a few comments and a lot of shifting around in the chairs, after which the psychologist had retreated with a few comments about the place of grief in the human life.

As it happened, Jeff was currently shuffling past the psychologist's office. She was waiting for him, standing in the doorway, and she collared him as he passed. "Jeffrey," she called, stepping out into the hall.

He stopped and looked up at her with dull, tired eyes.

"Come into my office," she said, steering him into the tiny, windowless room. She closed the door behind him. Jeffrey had never been in the psychologist's office before, and he looked around at everything: The small wooden desk, the spindly potted plant in the corner, the diploma on the wall declaring that Ellen Wozniak had a degree in child psychology. His gaze lingered on a large, cartoonish drawing of a group of people standing together as if in a graduating class. They were doing all sorts of strange things; one was giving another donkey-ears, two were holding some sort of keg, one stood proudly in polka-dotted underwear with his skinny, hairy legs and knobby knees displayed for all the world to see.

"Do you like that picture? It's supposed to be funny."

"What's funny about it?"

"Well, it's a bunch of really famous psychologists. The man reading the children's magazine is Freud, for instance. The man giving him donkey-ears is Jung. Over there, the fellow without pants is Carl Rogers. The man with the bucket of fried chicken is Erik Erikson." She paused. "You'll learn about these people, if you go into psychology."

"Oh," Jeff said, losing interest in the whole matter. The only one he had heard of was Freud, and all he knew about Freud was that he made people sit on couches and talk about their mothers.

"Jeffrey, your mom called me yesterday. She said you've been having nightmares, been waking up screaming, been talking in your sleep. You talk about your friend Ronald, she said, and about some woman."

Jeff looked at the floor and said nothing.

"If something is bothering you, it might help if you talk about it.

If somebody touched you in an inappropriate way—"

"Nothing's bothering me," Jeff said, not looking up. "Nobody touched me."

"Ronald's death doesn't bother you?"

Jeff shook his head.

"I think it *does* bother you," she said. "It's okay to admit it. You don't have to hold it inside."

He shrugged.

"Jeffrey, look at me." He slowly raised his head. His tired brown eyes met her bright green ones. Ellen Wozniak's natural eye color was a muddy mix of blue and brown, but she wore colored contacts that made her eyes a fiercer green than was strictly natural for a human. Jeff saw those green eyes, and suffered a sudden flashback to the things in the tunnel, the things whose eyes glowed green, the woman who licked the blood off his forehead and the man who hurled him against the wall. The smell of them suddenly filled his nostrils again, the scent of decay and old blood curdling in the darkness, and that gunky shit all over his hand.

"Jeffrey?" Ellen said, her voice suddenly concerned, almost frightened; but he heard it as if from far away, faint and muffled, and he paid no attention. He was spiraling down through darkness, and all around him was the beating of heavy wings, and cold hard fingers clutched his ankles, his arms, his throat. The darkness came up and swallowed him, chasing away the phantoms that pursued him.

Jeff Tracey, his eyes wide and reflecting the blankness inside, slid from his chair and sprawled limply on the floor.

7:15 PM

"Now, take this kid, who got his throat cut," Irving Sloane said, making a slashing motion with his fork, spilling teriyaki rice onto Roxanne's tabletop. "Oops, sorry," he said, brushing it onto the floor, where Bernice bounded over and started licking it up.

"Don't worry about it," Roxanne said.

"Where was I?" Irving said.

"You were holding forth about the kid who got his throat cut," Barry said. Upon learning that Barry was a police officer, a fact that Ryan had apparently neglected to mention, Irving had launched into a jeremiad, still ongoing, about the escalating crime rate in the White

Bluff area.

"Right. The kid. Now, that's not just a crime, that's an *offense*—against nature, against divine law, whatever you want to call it. What's a thirteen-year-old boy done to deserve to die like that?"

"What could *anyone* do to deserve that?" Ryan said, apparently forgetting that she had once suggested that the governor of the state should suffer a similar fate.

"Well, that's a whole nother topic," Irving said. "Maybe later we'll talk about that. But anyway, you know what it is?" Here he leaned forward over the table and went for the conspiratorial whisper. "Two things: The prisons, and the drugs."

"Hmm," Barry said, obviously humoring the man. Roxanne felt herself getting more and more flushed. Ryan had been right, this was a bad idea; it felt as if Barry was meeting her family, and they were embarrassing her something fierce.

"You got the prisons bringing in the criminals' families, and you got the families bringing in the drugs. You see? And they get the local kids hooked, and *bang!*" He gestured with his fork, sending a piece of beef bouncing across the table. It left a trail of thick brown sauce behind it before skidding off the surface between Roxanne and Barry and landing wetly on the floor. Bernice snatched it up; Irving didn't seem to notice. "They get involved in these drug wars and gangs, and they end up getting their throats slit."

"I don't think White Bluff has *that* much of a gang problem."

"It's *hushed up*, that's all. Bad for the city's image. People have got to take a stand against this sort of thing, not sweep it under the rug the way the politicians do."

"I'm pretty sure that if there were gangs in White Bluff engaged in open warfare, I would know about it."

"You're a Mapledale cop, not a White Bluff cop. You're not involved in the conspiracy of silence."

Even Ryan was starting to look embarrassed now.

"But I *am* a White Bluff cop. White Bluff cops patrol the suburbs, too, ever since the county voted to consolidate police departments. Budget cuts. I'm sure you remember."

Irving gave Barry a long, searching look, as if trying to read the marks of conspiracy on his face. After a moment he said, "Ryan tells me, Roxie, that someone's been spying on you. Sneaking up to your windows and whatnot. You know why those young kids do stuff like that these days?"

Against her better judgment, Roxanne said: "Why?"

"The Internet!"

"Your friend's husband is quite a character," Barry said. They were at the mall, standing in line for tickets to the movie, which would be starting in ten minutes.

"Oh, my God," Roxanne said. "If I had known … I mean, I *knew*, but I never saw him go that far around the bend before. I didn't … that is, I … help me out here, for God's sake."

"It's okay. He's …" Barry looked thoughtful for a moment. "He's seeing things deteriorate and he's trying to understand it, I think, but he can't; so he looks for something to blame. Drugs, television, the Internet, terrorism, whatever."

"Was it?"

"Was what?"

"Drug-related?"

"The kid? Nobody knows. He was supposed to be home in bed, but there he was all dressed up for being outside. His parents don't know why he left the house. As far as we know, he had never used drugs; they're running tests now. There wasn't a lot of blood left in the body, so they're working on some tissue samples—"

"All right, all right," Roxanne said, putting her hand on his arm. "Don't go into the gory details."

"Sorry."

"Anyway, Irving is coming on the ski trip with us this weekend. I hope you don't mind."

"It'll be fine. We'll be too busy breaking our legs on the slopes to talk about the rising crime rate among black bears in the Adirondacks."

"I sure hope so," Roxanne said.

The windows of her house were dark, but she was not in her bed; she must be out. Perhaps she'd found a place to hide, thought Martel, where she hoped to sleep in safety. Well, he would find her; he had his hooks in her, had planted the seeds of desire in her last night. He could track her now, should he want to, wherever she ran. And he did want to; he wanted her, wanted to feel her warm flesh beneath him, surrounding him and enfolding him. He wanted to torture her with pleasure until she begged him for release, which he would, in his benevolence, grant.

He paused by the kitchen window, listening to the stupid little dog howl and whine. He gently scratched his nails along the glass the howling stopped, reduced to a whimper, as the dog sought shelter behind the toilet or under the couch.

Not a very brave dog, that one.

As he took to the sky, Martel was vaguely disappointed. He'd gotten rather fond of his nightly voyeurisms. Oh, well; tonight he would feed, and tomorrow he would deliver the first bite to Roxanne Carmichael.

With that pleasurable thought, he took to the sky, leaving the house and its whimpering occupant far behind.

7

FRIDAY, JANUARY 15

7:30 AM

Jeff Tracey awakened with a start, feeling a sudden cold wind blow across his exposed feet. He was lying on a hard mattress, beneath a thin sheet that did little to protect even the parts of him it covered. He opened his eyes to an unfamiliar room, with dark paneled walls and a thick red rug and vaguely disturbing paintings that seemed to be just out of focus. Inexplicably, a nearby window was wide open to the winter chill; snow had accumulated on the sill and floor beneath it, the curtains flapped wildly, and the white chandelier above the bed creaked back and forth like a pendulum counting out the hours.

Jeff hauled himself into an upright position, from which he could get a better view of his surroundings. It was certainly nowhere he had ever been before. Although it had the appearance of opulence, Jeff could sense some sort of rot seething, just waiting for a chance to shatter the brittle illusion and make itself known.

The furnishings in the room were deceiving. Cunningly carved or painted, it was only when he inspected them closely that their character was revealed. Were the dark wooden knobs of the bed large pineapples, or were they human heads with the skulls split open to reveal the brains within? Was that a portrait of a pair of lovers, or was the man strangling the woman? Was the chandelier made of human bones?

He didn't know why he was in this room, but he didn't intend to stay here a moment longer. He threw back the covers. A blast of cold air rushed through the window, raising goosebumps on his bare skin. He swung himself around, deciding that the first thing he would do was close the window, and jumped off the bed.

The carpet was soggy and slick; his feet shot out from under him and he landed heavily on his ass. The thick, spongy fibers of the carpet squished revoltingly beneath him. Carefully, he pulled himself to his feet. As he walked to the window, he realized that his legs and hands were sticky; he was smeared with blood where he had touched the carpet. The bottoms of his feet were coated in the stuff, slick, red, icy cold. He slipped and stumbled to the window, put his head out, and retched into the night. But there was no ground outside; beneath him was only floor after floor of windows, finally vanishing beyond his sight. He watched his pathetic burst of vomit grow smaller and smaller until it was swallowed by the distance.

Suddenly something struck him head-on, knocking him back into the room. He skidded across the slick carpet, coming to rest against the paneling across the room. His impact jarred loose a picture, and it crashed to the floor beside him. The frame cracked when it hit. Involuntarily he glanced at it, and saw a photo of himself and Ronald when they were small, making a sand castle at the lake, and rising from the water behind them was the decrepit, decaying form of a long-drowned girl in a bulging pink swimsuit.

Movement drew his eyes from the picture. The woman he had met in the tunnel was gliding in through the window feet first, settling delicately on the squishy carpet. She walked slowly toward him. Jeff tried to stand, but pain shot through his back and with a grunt he slumped back down.

"Don't worry," the woman said, drawing up close. "You won't need to move for what I have in mind." She bent down, her golden hair tickling his legs, one hand grasping each ankle. Her touch was cold as the night outside, and dry as paper.

She looked up at him, her eyes leaping with green fire, her mouth split wide and her jagged teeth gleaming. She lunged forward, sinking her huge fangs into his crotch.

Screaming, Jeff awoke to a sunbeam on his face.

He sat up in bed, looking around, minutely examining every aspect of the room. It looked like a bedroom in a nice house, certainly nicer than his own, with a four-poster bed, portraits on the wall, shag carpet, paneling.   Still, it was suspiciously similar to the bedroom from his dream.   He leaned over and tested the rug with his hand before climbing out from under the sheets.   Then he started going around from picture to picture, looking at each one before going on to the next.   Finally he went to the window and tried to open it. Locked.   The sun was shining brightly outside, hanging low in the clear, cold sky, glaring off the white snow that covered the dead world. Jeff could see that he was in a building on a hill, with a large yard that sloped in gentle waves down to a street several hundred yards away.   The road was a black gash in the otherwise-unbroken whiteness, like a cut that had become infected.

A sudden creak sent him jumping back into bed.   His hands fumbled for the blankets, to pull them up and hide himself under them, but then he recognized the familiar shape of his mother entering the room.   "Mom!" he cried, holding out his arms.   She crossed the room in seconds and then she was on her knees beside the bed, crushing him in a bear hug, the sort he had not permitted since he was ten. "How are you, baby?"

"Don't call me that, Mom," he said.   "Where am I?"

There was a momentary silence.   "In a hospital," she said.

"This doesn't look like a hospital."   He was glancing around, trying to see through the charade.   His eyes stopped briefly on the large mirror that dominated the wall to his right.   "That's a window, isn't it?"   His mother nodded.   "And there's probably doctors behind it watching us."

"Just one doctor," she said.   "His name is Dr. Kinney.   He wants you to get better, just like I do."

Realization dawned on Jeff like a cold winter morning.   "This is a *mental* hospital!"

Silence.

"I'm not crazy."

"I know you're not crazy," Annette said.   "But these doctors can help get rid of your dreams—"

"*I'm not crazy!*"

"I know," she said, putting her hands on his shoulders and squaring him to herself, looking into his eyes.   "But you can't sleep through the night, and when you do sleep you wake up screaming and shaking, just like you did this morning.   You were so exhausted that you fainted at school yesterday afternoon. The doctor can find out why. He can help you."

Jeff sank back against the soft pillow and closed his eyes to shut out the room, the window, his mother. He heard her babble on, trying to reassure him. The doctors would take care of him; they would stop the dreams, or at least make him sleep without dreams; the insurance company would pay for it; soon he could go back to school. He heard her words, but they only fluttered around his head like sonic butterflies that he couldn't, or wouldn't, take hold of. Finally his mother stopped. He could hear her breathing, could feel her watching; then she took his small, hot hand in her cool ones. She pressed it tight between her palms, and kissed it, and told it that Jeff would soon be all better. He yanked his hand away and buried it under the blankets.

A moment passed, or an hour; Jeff couldn't tell. He was residing in some hazy world just below waking but just above sleep, in a place where the twin horrors of his nightmares and this new reality couldn't reach him. But then he heard the door open, and soft footfalls across the rug. Someone, a man, mumbled something to his mother. "No!" she exclaimed. "No, I won't leave!"

"Come on, Mrs. Tracey. Let him rest. Dr. Kinney wants to talk to you."

Jeff heard his mother get up, and he was suddenly seized by the desire for her to stay, to hold his hand, to babble whatever soothing nonsense she wanted to hear. He reached out his hands and grasped the empty air, but too late; the door clicked shut.

12:05 PM

"Are you looking forward to tonight?"

Roxanne, her mouth full of pizza, nodded.

Ryan smiled. "Good. Have I told you all the details yet?"

"Details?"

"Everyone who's coming, I mean."

This ski trip had taken on a life of its own since Ryan had thought it up. "Somebody else besides the four of us?"

"Well, Priscilla heard me talking to the lodge and she wanted to come, with her new boyfriend."

"Another one?"

"Yeah. His name's Waldo."

After a moment, Roxanne said: "As in *Where's?*"

"I understand he's kind of sensitive about that whole thing."

"I'll take it under advisement. Anyway if it's like last time, we'll never see Pris or her boy-toy."

"How'd you sleep last night?"

"Fine," Roxanne said.

Ryan cocked her head. "What's that grin for?"

"What grin?"

"The grin on your face."

"I'm grinning?"

"Yes. Some might call it a shit-eating grin, but I would never be so crude." Ryan drummed her fingers for a few seconds, then said: "You slept at Barry's place!"

"I admit nothing," Roxanne said.

"Did you—you know?"

"Nope. Just slept."

"Why didn't you—you know?"

"I hardly know the man," Roxanne said.

"Oh, yes," Ryan said. "You hardly know him and he's not your boyfriend." Roxanne grinned, winked, and then slid her chair back from the table. "Where are you going?" Ryan demanded. "I want more details!"

"Sorry," Roxanne said, tapping her watch. "Lunch is over."

5:45 PM

"So how do you like my tiny little vehicle?" Roxanne said.

Barry laughed. "I feel like the clown who drives around the big top in a car the size of a shoe. Could be worse, though. I could be on Waldo's bike."

Apparently Waldo was a motorcycle enthusiast; he was piloting some massive contraption with big, gleaming pipes and a proliferation of chrome plating that, in Roxanne's opinion, made the thing look more like some weird bathroom fixture than a vehicle. Priscilla, bundled up like an Arctic explorer against the winter cold, sat behind Waldo with her arms in a death-grip around him; Waldo was just wearing a helmet, leather jacket, gloves, and jeans. Roxanne didn't know of anyone else who would drive a motorcycle into the

Adirondacks in the dead of winter, and had decided that both of them were crazy.

The motorcycle brought up the rear in their little caravan; Roxanne and Barry were in the middle, while Irving and Ryan were in Irving's sedan up in front. They hadn't carpooled because Roxanne wanted to run home over the weekend to spend some time with Bernice. She felt vaguely guilty about leaving the puppy, even though she'd hired a dog sitter, somebody Ryan's friend had recommended, to come in twice a day.

As they crested a hill and started down the other side, the radio station they had been listening to dissolved into fuzz and static, with only an occasional snatch of music. She flipped through the presets but found nothing that was both interesting and clear, so she switched it to the CD. To her chagrin, it quickly became apparent that she had last been listening to the new release from the latest boy band on the scene. She quickly hit the changer button, hoping that the next CD was something less embarrassing, but it turned out to be even worse: The barely twenty-year-old nymph who was, if the tabloids were to be believed, virginally dating the lead singer of the very same boy band whose CD had just been shuffled off the player.

Beside her, she heard Barry trying to suppress a laugh. "Oh, and what do *you* listen to, Officer Brennan?" she said.

He did laugh then, and said: "Just turn it off, and we'll talk."

She had to fight the urge to goggle at her passenger. Did he just say to turn off the stereo and they would talk?

That was it. She was going to marry him.

10:50 PM

"Hey Barry!"

At the top of the ski run, Barry turned and looked at Roxanne, putting his face directly in the path of a snowball. It exploded against his face with a wet, white pop. He spluttered and wiped the melting snow from his face, then poled his way towards her. "I'm gonna give you such a noogie!"

"Gotta catch me first!" she cried, thrusting herself forward to the hill. Then she was gone in a little puff of snow, a dark figure schussing back and forth beneath the yellowish glare of the lights. Barry watched her go, debating what to do. She was a much better skier than he was; if he chased her, she would get back on the ski lift before he could catch her. Maybe he would wait here and intercept her when she came back up. He glanced to his left, at one of the massive poles that supported the chairlift high in the air. It was green, but in the half-darkness it looked black; and Barry could clearly see, gleaming like the white belly of a fish, someone's head and hands. The person was standing behind the pole, holding onto it with his arms. He was looking down the slope, his head slowly tracking some moving object.

Roxanne.

"Hey!" Barry called. "Hey, you! Behind the pole!"

The face that turned his way looked dead white, but its eyes seemed to flicker with a sickly green luminescence. For a moment their gazes met, and Barry felt a chill that cut through the January night, lanced through his layers of insulating clothing and settled somewhere just below his heart. Or maybe it was the other way around; maybe those eyes were sucking the warmth right out of his body. Maybe they would leave him cold and dead.

The man opened his mouth; Barry could see the little black circle. Now it was the size of a ping-pong ball; now a baseball; now a softball. He heard a thin, high laugh as the man raised his arm and pointed down the slope with a long, slender finger. "The woman is mine," he said.

Motherfucker! Barry kicked off his skis and dropped one pole. Holding the other like a bat, he charged at the ski-lift tower. The white face and hands vanished behind the support. When Barry rounded the pole, there was no one there, and no sign that anyone ever had been. The snow was undisturbed, except where Barry's own feet stepped. He stood there in confusion, hearing the gentle creak and whir of the lift cable as it traveled on its endless journey to nowhere.

What the hell was going on?

Nine feet above Barry's head, Martel clung to the cold steel support, shielded by the darkness and the human's natural inclination not to look up when seeking what he thought was a fleeing member of his own species. The man didn't know, of course, about the earth's reluctance to hold Martel to itself; that with a little effort, it could be persuaded to let him slip away, to glide silently through the night air.

So many things they did not know.

He could kill this human now, Martel thought, as the fellow looked left and right in confusion. He lifted one hand off the pole, considering it; but then the man muttered a curse and started back to the ski slope, and Martel returned his grip to the tower.

Just as well. He had no real reason to slay this person; he was no threat, and murdering him, while perhaps amusing, would only distract him from his real purpose here tonight.

She would be coming up the chair lift soon. Perhaps he would pluck her from her seat and carry her away. That would confuse them, wouldn't it?

Chuckling, Martel let go of the tower and drifted off into the darkness.

Roxanne was waiting at the bottom of the hill, scanning the slope for Barry, when she started to feel like she was being watched. She looked around nervously, but everywhere people were going about their business and paying her little or no attention. She must be getting paranoid, she thought, as she shielded her eyes from the glare of the lights and tried to see into the night beyond.

Suddenly she heard a woman cry, "Look out!" She turned, but it was too late; another skier plowed into her and they went down in a tangle of limbs and skis, with Roxanne on the bottom eating snow.

"Shit, I'm sorry," the skier said, untangling herself and standing up. "I lost control." She reached down with a mittened hand and pulled Roxanne to her feet, helping to dust her off, swatting the snow from her body.

"That's okay," Roxanne said. "It happens."

"Are you all right?" The skier pulled her wool cap off, allowing a cascade of shimmering hair to tumble down around her shoulders. She was wearing dark glasses to help offset the glare of the harsh lights along the run.

"I'm fine. Just a little shaky." Roxanne grinned uncertainly. "How about you?"

"Me? Never been better." The woman smiled, showing brilliant, white, even teeth. "My name is Lauren. What's yours?"

* * *

Barry returned to his skis. They were lying across each other at right angles, like an "X". No, thought Barry as he got closer. One ski was close to the top of the other. It was more like a cross.

He straightened them out and set about snapping his boots back into them, acutely conscious of the black wall of trees behind him. He felt a thousand eyes on his back, the eyes of the night, as if every star were a baleful orb watching him with quiet contempt.

At last his fumbling hands completed the job. Picking up his second pole, he launched himself down the mountainside.

"Have you been skiing long?" Lauren asked as they positioned themselves at the edge of the slope. To their right was a field of trees; the ones that directly bordered the run were marked with reflectors to warn skiers of their presence, just in case their dark, looming shapes were not sufficient.

"For a while," Roxanne said. "I took lessons a few years ago but I don't get to come very often."

"This is only my third time," Lauren said, looking down at the snow. The crowd on the slope was starting to thin out as the skiers retired to the lodge for coffee or stronger drinks; and most of them were toward the middle of the run. Roxanne had been skiing there, too, but Lauren had somehow persuaded her to come over here, to the edge of the trees, where, she said, the skiing was more exciting.

"I think this'll be my last run for tonight," Roxanne said. Lauren was standing very close to her, and it was making her a bit uncomfortable.

"Good idea." Lauren was practically whispering in her ear. "There are other things to do here besides ski."

Roxanne shifted herself a few inches, moving away from Lauren's lips. How had she ended up here, alone on top of a mountain with a woman she didn't even know? Lauren had just talked and talked and suggested they ride up together, and Roxanne hadn't said no. Now, as Lauren made what looked an awful lot like a pass at her, she began to think she had made a mistake. This could be awkward.

"I'm going to shove off," Roxanne said; but Lauren caught her hand in a grip of iron. Roxanne could feel the woman's fingers, even through Lauren's thick mittens and her own snowsuit. Lauren dragged her around sideways so they were face to face, but the dark glasses made Lauren's visage unreadable and mysterious. A smile was playing at her lips.

"Am I making you nervous?" Lauren asked.

"Let go of me," Roxanne said, trying and failing to pull free. She flailed with her free arm, which Lauren promptly caught and held as well.

"Now I've got you," Lauren said, slowly pulling Roxanne towards her. The snow crunched beneath Roxanne's skis. Lauren's skis didn't budge, as if they were nailed to the snow.

"Please let go of me."

Lauren released Roxanne's hands, but caught her around the waist with her right arm and held her tight, pressing their bodies together. Roxanne felt the other woman's breasts against hers, felt an unexpected tingle in her groin as Lauren's left hand traveled slowly up Roxanne's side, stopping at her cheek. The wool mitten was prickly on Roxanne's skin. Slowly Lauren tilted Roxanne's head back, until she was looking up at the heavens. The stars were bright and clear.

"I don't understand why he's so interested in you," Lauren said. "You're not prettier than me. You don't seem very smart. What do you have to offer?"

Lauren opened her mouth and caught Roxanne's scarf in her teeth. She easily pulled it loose, leaving Roxanne's throat exposed to the cold. Then she leaned in close and put her lips against Roxanne's neck. "I've been thinking," she murmured, "that he must want you because you're human. So if I take you before *he* does, he'll lose interest." Roxanne felt Lauren's teeth pricking her neck, sharp as needles. A cry tried to force itself out of her mouth, but it died before reaching her lips.

"Beg for it," Lauren whispered. "Beg for the bite."

Roxanne pleaded silently with the stars, praying for them to send her some sort of deliverance; and suddenly there was a cold rush of wind that caught her hat and set it fluttering down to the snow. Strong hands grabbed her under the shoulders and lifted her up, sending her sprawling beside her hat. At the same time, a hard, icy voice shouted, "No!"

Lauren cried, "I won't let you cast me aside like I'm nothing!"

"Cow!" The voice was contemptuous. "You *are* nothing. I do what

I please. You do not *let* me do anything!"

Roxanne didn't know what was going on or who had rescued her, and she didn't care. She felt weak from fear and cold, her body trembling uncontrollably as she raised herself up on her hands and knees.

"Why did I ever come with you?" Lauren said, sobbing. "All the things you promised me——"

"I promised you nothing."

"Your *eyes* promised everything! But it's all a lie, everything. I hate this life! I hate it!"

"Whatever promises you saw in my eyes," the man said, "you put in them yourself. And if you hate this existence, then let me end it for you."

Roxanne knew that voice; it was the voice from her answering machine. She found one of her ski poles close at hand and, gripping it, slowly straightened up. Her skis were unsteady on the powdery snow.

"I sent your husband to the grave," the man said. "It's time you joined him!"

Roxanne didn't hear Lauren's reply. She was looking down the slope, staring at the lights of the lodge. There was warmth there, people, safety.

Barry was there.

She pushed off with her pole and the world began to blur as she shot down the nearly deserted slope. She told herself she wasn't scared; told herself she'd make it to the lodge, safe and sound. She tried to ignore the horrible feeling that there was something right behind her, reaching out for her ... but of course she couldn't, and when she turned to look there was Lauren, flying——*flying!*——above the snow, her mouth twisted into a vicious sneer, her eyes glowing like small green suns. Absurdly, as she reached out toward her with a clawed hand, Roxanne wondered what had become of Lauren's sunglasses.

"Bitch!" Lauren shrieked.

Roxanne turned and plunged her pole into the snow, pushing herself to the left, toward the brightly lit section of the slope. But Lauren had anticipated the move and she was there with both arms waiting. As Roxanne cut right she saw a dark shape, the mysterious stalker who had become her savior, plow into Lauren. Then Roxanne shot over a mogul and, airborne, flew among the trees. One second she was in the empty night, and the next she was weaving desperately amid a maze of dark boles. The snow was black with pine needles. After a few seconds in the shadowy forest, Roxanne completely lost her bearings; she was cut off from the light of the slope by the obscuring evergreens. Her arms ached from the effort of steering with one pole.

What the hell were those ... those things? They weren't people. Lauren wasn't a person. People couldn't do that, couldn't *fly*, weren't that strong. People's eyes didn't glow, they didn't have fangs.

A word rose in her mind, unbidden: *Vampires*.

Suddenly the massive trunk of an ancient maple appeared before her, and with a desperate effort she shoved herself left. Her pole jammed between two rocks hidden in the snow, and her right ski wedged itself beneath the hump of a root. Roxanne saw herself lose her balance before she felt it; the darkling world spun, the snow turning to become a sky from which trees grew downward. Then the back of her head smashed into something hard, and an explosion of lights in her head was followed by restful oblivion.

The subject fell asleep at 11:27, Scott Gerber wrote, *despite efforts to stay awake.* Scott closed his notebook and took another swallow of the coffee produced by the hospital vending machine. He hated that machine; the liquid it dispensed was weak and watery and burnt-tasting, and too hot for the thin paper cup in which it was served.

"How's our boy?"

"Jesus!" Scott bent down and retrieved his notebook, which he had just dropped in shock. Then, looking at the door, he growled, "You know I hate it when you do that."

The woman there pushed her way on inside, grinning merrily. "You keep rewarding me. That's why the behavior continues." She came to Scott's chair, bent over, and planted a light kiss on his pale lips. He pulled her back for another one. After the kiss, Melinda Robinson settled down on the table next to his notebook, putting one of her feet in his lap. "So what's old man Kinney got you doing now?"

"I have to observe the kid. All. Fucking. Night. Kinney's such an asshole. He treats me like his slave."

"You *are* his slave."

"I'm his graduate assistant."

"Same thing." Melinda smiled. "Too bad you couldn't have gotten somebody good, like Dr. Reichert. She's awesome."

"Yeah, yeah, yeah," Scott said. "All hail the glorious Dr. Reichert." He shook his head. "Kinney's such a freaking Luddite. Somebody ought to explain to him that they have these things called video cameras now that can record all a patient's behaviors without having to have some poor schlub watch them all night."

"So how's the kid doing?" Scott held up the notebook. After a moment, Melinda said: "You've been here four hours and you've written one line?"

"Duh," Scott said, flipping back a page. The paper was covered with his garbled scrawl.

"Can you translate this into English?"

Scott grabbed the notebook away from her. "First he played video games," he said, pointing at a portable television stand with a console and a stack of titles. "Then he started to get sleepy. He was almost falling over before he shut off the TV. He checked the window five times to make sure it wouldn't open, even though nobody has been in to unlock it, and then he finally went to bed and fell asleep two minutes ago." Scott closed the notebook. "Fascinating stuff, isn't it?"

"Why did he check the window so many times? He's on the third floor."

"How the hell do I know?" Scott said. "I'm just a goddamn tool who has to sit here and watch the little ankle-biter sleep."

"*Ankle-biter* is a term generally reserved for children much younger than this one."

"Oh, I'm sorry, I didn't realize you had switched majors to linguistics."

She punched him with a small fist, then said: "I wonder what he's so afraid of."

"Kinney thinks he's having a delayed reaction to his father getting blown up in a car wreck," Scott said. "And of course the kid's friend was decapitated a couple days ago." He paused, looked thoughtful. "Kid's got bad karma, I think. Did something awful in a past life. Probably best to avoid a lot of contact with him."

"You know what I like about you?" Melinda said. "You're so compassionate."

"That's why I went into psychology," Scott said. "I love to laugh at the mentally ill; it makes me feel better about myself."

"My future husband, ladies and gentlemen," Melinda said, standing up. "Isn't he great?"

The first thing Roxanne felt was the cold. It had clawed through her snowsuit and consumed her feet and hands. Mumbling, she tried to find her blanket, then remembered she was not in bed; she was out in the forest in the middle of the night, lying in the snow. She opened her eyes and found herself sighting up the trunk of an evergreen. She had apparently slid under the low-hanging branches and was now sheltered beneath the canopy of needles.

Her head throbbed. She tried to sit up, but her hair seemed to be caught on something. Grunting, she tried again, and this time pulled free with a faint snap. Pain shot down her neck and into her spine. Turning, she saw a lump of half-frozen blood and a good amount of hair stuck to the base of the tree. Her scalp was feeling warm and she realized that, having torn herself loose from the bark, she was bleeding again.

"Christ." Her head pulsed and her shoulder throbbed. One ski was missing and the other was broken, sheared off a few inches beyond her toes. Apparently she'd done some tumbling.

Rolling over onto her hands and knees, Roxanne crawled out from under the tree. The needle-bound limbs grabbed at her head and back, scratching painfully at her wound. Then she was out, the other trees opening up around her, and the forest that before had seemed close and claustrophobic now seemed wide open and exposed. Looking around, she tried to figure out where the lodge was, which direction she should go, but they all looked the same. Downhill was probably a good bet though. She circled the tree and found her trail in the snow. She had plowed her way down the mountain, end-over-end, rolling between the trees like a pinball. She was lucky that she hadn't been killed, snapped her neck on one of those unyielding trunks. Somebody was looking out for her.

No, somebody was looking *at* her.

Roxanne glanced around. The moonlight was pale and sickly

through a wispy cover of clouds, but the trees were in such sharp contrast to the glimmering snow that she could see them in decent detail. Was that a shape she saw darting from one to the next? She tried to focus on it, but when she did there was nothing extraordinary, just trunks and powder. She kicked off her remaining ski. Turning, she struck off under the forest, leaving behind the broken fragment of her ski.

She stumbled on through the forest in the dark, looking for the twinkling lights of the lodge, glimmering through the trees like the distant stars above. She thought she had seen them at one point, but then had lost them and hadn't been able to find them again. She hoped she was getting closer.

From time to time she thought she saw someone following her, but whenever she turned to look, she never saw anything besides barren maples and bristly evergreens. Maybe she was imagining it; maybe the blow to her head had damaged her somehow, made her hallucinate. She tried to remember exactly how she had ended up there, under the tree. Someone had been chasing her, but she couldn't remember who; the evening's events were vague in her memory, like something she had seen on television a long time ago.

Roxanne came upon something in the snow, knelt down, picked it up. It was a section of ski. Her ski.

She was walking in circles.

Exhausted, desperate, lost, and frightened, she started to cry. Her knees gave out and she began to sink to the ground, but then fingers grabbed her elbow, lifted her up, and spun her around to face the man who had stood outside her French doors that night. He was tall and slender, with dark hair that had been churned and tousled by the wind. And pale; he was so pale, almost like the blind cave fish Roxanne had seen in the store when she bought her betta. But there was something beautiful in his features, something oddly delicate. He was looking down at her with eyes that glowed and flickered with an internal light. Roxanne squinted into those eyes and found herself lost in their depths, like sinking into the warm sea, going down and down, while around her the water swirled in luminescent currents.

Down she went, down and down, floating through the promises in his eyes. Promises of knowledge, of secrets, of pain, of pleasure … the green currents swirled around her, over her, tickling her sensitive areas: Caressing her breasts like lips, caressing her stomach like feathers, inserting themselves into—

Roxanne gasped, and her knees buckled. Oh, those eyes; the promise of those eyes!

As she sank to the snow Martel's hands shot out and caught her shoulders. He held her upright, kept her eyes on his, kept her down beneath the pressure of his will.

And still the currents swept through her brain. She saw herself with this man, them both naked, his hardness in her mouth, spurting fluid down her throat; or clutched in her hand as she stroked it; between her breasts or between her legs, cold and stiff, like …

Like a corpse.

"No," she murmured. She was about to lose herself in there, down in this strange pleasurable, dangerous sea; when had pleasure ever been so cold? She averted her gaze, looked past the man to the snow beyond.

There were no footprints except her own.

"Impressive," the man said. Even dazed and disoriented, she discerned an accent beneath his English. His voice was beautiful, haunting, thrillingly frightening.

"What?" Roxanne did not, *could not*, meet his gaze again.

"That even now, after such a night, you still have the will to resist me."

"I have to go," Roxanne said. "My head hurts." The sheer absurdity of standing out here in the night, freezing, talking to a strange man who had appeared as if from nowhere, made her think this might be just her imagination. But those eyes … the promise of those eyes.

"You cannot go. Not yet."

"I'm cold."

"So am I." He reached up and touched her chin with hands as icy as the snow around them. "That is why I need you."

Roxanne shuddered at his touch. She felt a little twinge as he caressed her.

Then he lifted her face to look up at his, and he smiled, and his teeth were daggers in the moonlight.

8

SATURDAY, JANUARY 16

12:10 AM

When they found her, she was lying curled up in the snow, her knees drawn up to her chest. Barry's flashlight beam touched her first, and he was the first to reach her; he held her head in his lap as the lodge's paramedics readied the stretcher and the Ski Patrol covered her up. "Oh, God," Barry said, feeling the cold, rubbery skin of her cheek. "Oh, God."

Roxanne's eyes opened and she looked up at him blankly. She struggled against his arms, but he only closed them tighter around her.

One of the Ski Patrol paramedics took her feet. "Help me lift her up," he said to Barry. Soon Roxanne was secured in the stretcher, under several layers of warm blankets. The paramedics strapped the stretcher onto their snowmobile, and then they were gone, the buzz of their engine disappearing down the hill, leaving Barry alone with the last searcher.

"Hop on, let's go," the man said, revving his machine.

Barry stared at the depression in the snow where Roxanne had been. Ragged footsteps led up to that spot, half-filled by blowing sheets of powder. The evergreens loomed around them like dark sentinels. What had the trees seen?

"Dude, let's go! It's too cold to stand around out here!"

"Yeah," Barry said. "Yeah." He climbed on the back of the snowmobile. They circled around, and started back toward the lodge, leaving behind a mystery, and a broken fragment of ski.

"This weekend isn't going at all like I planned," Ryan said. She, Irving, and Barry sat in the stiff, uncomfortable chairs of the waiting room of the lodge's small medical annex; the doctor on call, one Heinrich Smith, was developing X-rays in the other room. The place was well equipped to handle damaged skiers, Barry had to give them that.

"It's not your fault," Irving said.

"I know, but poor Roxanne! She had such a shitty week, pardon my French, and I was hoping this trip would make up for it, you know?"

"We should take her to a hospital," Irving said.

"The nearest trauma unit is forty miles away," Barry said. "That's why they have a clinic here."

"A head injury's not like a broken leg," Irving said. "You can't just put a cast on it and hope it heals right." He sighed. "I don't trust that doctor. He'll be more worried about looking out for the lodge than taking care of Roxie."

Irving meant well, but it seemed to Barry that he'd be more comfortable on a survivalist compound than in contemporary society. "Dr. Smith is all right," Barry said. "Anyway he was fawning over her like she was his own daughter."

"That's so she won't sue." Irving shook his head. "They need better security on the slope. You're not even safe in the wilderness anymore."

"You think somebody attacked her?" Ryan said.

"What else would she have been doing out in the woods? Somebody must have dragged her there."

"I think she just ran into a tree and got disoriented," Barry said. "I doubt there was any human mischief involved."

"Well, we'll see about that," Irving said.

Roxanne lay beneath an electric blanket, wrapped in a loose flannel nightgown that Dr. Smith had found somewhere. She was quite warm now, and relishing the heat far too much to think about turning off the blanket. The back of her head still hurt somewhat, but the doctor had given her an injection before stitching her up and that was keeping a lid on the pain. Her shoulder was sore and, she'd been told, covered with a huge purple bruise, but the cut on her head wasn't really that bad, it had just bled like crazy.

The door opened and Smith came in. He was in his sixties and looked every bit the kindly small-town doctor, lacking only the small spectacles and little black bag to complete the picture. "How are we feeling?" he asked.

"Better," Roxanne said, snuggling down.

"Here are the X-rays." Smith waggled a manila envelope. "Like I thought, nothing is broken. Also, none of the frostbiting. You probably have the minor concussions, given your disorientation and the slight memory loss."

"A ... concussion?"

"Now, don't look frightened, it is not as serious as all that. Nearly always the concussions get better on their own, and yours is mild. You can walk, you can talk, you know the day and the year. So none of the worries, yes?"

"Um, all right."

"Good. We don't want the worries, we want the relaxing."

He had a clipped accent, German, she thought. She wondered if his name was really Schmidt, or Schmitt, if he had Americanized it. For some reason, the idea made her a little bit sad. "So I'm going to be okay?"

"Oh, yes, yes. The lost bloods from the head always look worse than they are. The cut, it is really not that big. And the concussions, we just watch for a few days. I give you a paper, it tells you what to look for."

"Okay."

"Good. And even if you feel better, no more skiing this weekend! Your lift ticket is canceled. The lodge will give the refund, of course."

"Don't worry, the last thing I want to do right now is ski."

"Yes, yes, of course." Smith reached into his pocket and pulled out a piece of paper. He unfolded it and handed it to her. "This is guidelines for head injuries. If you notice any of these symptoms within the next 48 hours, call your doctor immediately! Or call the desk if you are still at the lodge. You will do that, yes?" She took it, looked it over, nodded at him. He smiled. "Good. Now then, there are people here anxious to see you. Shall I let them in?"

"Okay."

Dr. Smith grinned and left the room. Roxanne settled back in bed, carefully keeping her stitches off the pillow. Now that she was safe and warm, this part of the experience was almost pleasant. It was like being a child again, with mommy and daddy there to take care of her, to tuck her in and read her a story.

Her parents. The last time she'd talked to them had been when they called her from the Atlanta airport, where they switched planes while flying up from Florida. And then she had waited for them at Hancock International in Syracuse, waiting for a flight that never arrived, holding a big fruit basket that had never been eaten. It had sat on Roxanne's kitchen table, still wrapped in pink plastic, the fruit slowly turning brown and black and developing the sickly-sweet smell of decay before Roxanne had finally thrown it away.

Roxanne blinked. Why was she thinking about this? It always depressed her. It was a death thing. Whenever someone died, whenever she read about a train wreck or a plane crash, that was what she thought of, that fruit basket, and the cloying smell of apples and oranges rotting on her counter.

"Here they are!" Smith said, coming back with the gang in tow. Barry sat on the bed next to her and took her hand; Irving and Ryan stood back a bit. Ryan had obviously been crying; her cheeks showed the remains of her always-so-careful makeup, which must have run down and then been wiped up with some cloth or paper towel that wasn't quite up to the task.

"How are you doing, kiddo?" Irving said.

"Okay. I have a headache."

"You gave us quite a scare, disappearing like that," Barry said. "The lodge sent out the Ski Patrol to find you. I went with them. Do you remember when we found you?"

She shook her head.

"Do you remember what happened?"

"I ..." Roxanne closed her eyes. She saw vague images, heard indistinct voices, caught fragmented thoughts from the night on the slope. "I slipped and went down the wrong way," she said uncertainly. "I think I hit my head on a tree. I was under ... under an evergreen for a while."

"You don't sound too sure," Barry said.

"Well, the important thing is that she's okay," Ryan said.

Roxanne opened her eyes. "I'm okay," she said. "Where are the others?"

"Pris was, um, drinking heavily before your accident," Ryan said. "I think she's passed out in her room. Waldo's there with her. He's probably taking advantage of her in various ways."

Roxanne yawned; Pris drinking heavily and being taken advantage of was hardly newsworthy. "What time is it?" she asked, her eyes closed once again.

"Time for you to rest," Dr. Smith said. "Everybody out!"

The little doctor hustled Ryan and Irving out of the room, but left Barry at the bedside. Then he came back and put his hand on Barry's shoulder. "You are the ... husband?"

"I'm not quite sure what I am, yet," Barry said. "What happened to her out there?"

"Well, I guess just what she said, hmm? She hit the tree, whack. The sleeping will do her good. Help her regenerate the bloods and such."

Barry looked at Roxanne. Her eyes were closed and her chest rose and fell slowly. Her light freckles stood out sharply against her skin. "She's so pale," he said. "We don't have to keep her awake, then?"

"Oh, no, no. We must wake her twice during the night, though, make sure she can be roused, can walk around the room, can be coherent talking. You are the policeman, yes?"

"Yes," Barry said. *The Policeman.* The way Smith said it, it sounded like a superhero, or possibly the title of a dime novel.

"So you are used to telling people *stand up, walk over here, touch your nose, name the President!*" His accent got more pronounced, more German, as he issued the mock commands. It made him a little scary, almost. "Of course this means you must sleep in the room with her. She should have no sleeping alone for forty-eight hours. Can I trust you to be the heavy guy who does the tough job?"

"You can count on me," Barry said.

9:53 AM

"Lemme alone," Roxanne said, her voice slurred.

Barry opened his eyes.

"Go away!" she said.

She wasn't talking to him, Barry realized, unless he was a character in the nightmare she was having. He considered waking her up, then decided to let her sleep; he'd performed the prescribed two awakenings last night, and both times she'd been coherent and cranky. She deserved to snooze a little longer. Besides, maybe she would say something that would give him a clue what had happened to her; despite what he had told the others last night, he was not at all sure that there hadn't bccn some other agent involved in her misadventure. Even if she didn't remember what had happened, it might surface in her dream.

"I don't want to," she said. "I don't want to!"

She fell quiet, but began whimpering softly, and then she slowly tilted her head to expose her neck, showing two neat, round blemishes right along the blue shadow of her vein. Were they birthmarks? He didn't remember them, but then again he wasn't that familiar with the territory of Roxanne's neck. Yet.

If they weren't birthmarks, what were they?

Suddenly she began to whine, a soft, shrill whistle of abject terror. Enough was enough. "Annie, wake up," he said, giving her a gentle shake. Her eyes snapped open and she looked blankly at the ceiling; then she blinked and started sobbing, her entire body shaking.

"Oh, God," she said. She turned, found Barry, and crushed him in a bear hug. Her face was up against his neck, her nose beneath his chin. He could feel her crying.

"It's okay," he said softly, stroking her tangled hair, feeling like a total ass. He should have awakened her as soon as he realized she was having a nightmare, and what had he done? Eavesdropped on her subconscious. And what had he learned? Nothing. He gently disengaged her hands and pushed her back so he could look at her. "What were you dreaming about?"

"I don't remember," she said, "but it was horrible."

"Annie—"

"*I don't remember!*" Then she blinked, and said: "I'm sorry. I didn't mean to yell."

"It's okay. Forget I asked. Forget about what you dreamed, too." He gathered her up for a quick hug, but this time she flinched when he got too close to her shoulder and he let go. "Still hurts, huh?"

"Look at this." She turned her back on him and started undoing the buttons on her flannel top. Barry began to get an uncomfortably tight feeling in his groin. He told himself to behave as Roxanne shrugged partially out of the nightshirt and bared her back nearly all the way to the bottom. It was a nice back, curvy, smoothly muscled, but marred by a huge purple scar that started at the shoulder blade and spread out like an oil slick to cover the entire upper right quadrant of her back. "Does it look as bad as it feels?"

"Um, it depends. How bad does it feel?"

"It's down to a dull roar."

"In that case it looks worse. How's your head?"

"Not too bad at the moment." She put her shirt back on as footsteps echoed in the hallway; Dr. Smith entered just in time to miss the show.

"I am in my office thinking I hear voices," he said, "so I come to see. You two like to sleep, for sure." Barry glanced at his watch, which he had forgotten to remove the night before; it was about ten. "Of course, you both had rough nights, yes? And how is our lovely patient this morning?"

"I'm fine," Barry said.

"Well, so glad I am to hear that," the doctor said. "And our *other* lovely patient?"

"My shoulder hurts. My head hurts. My wrist hurts."

"But no dizziness, nausea, vomiting?"

"No, no, and you'd smell it."

The doctor chuckled. "Yes, I suppose I would. And mister Officer Brennan would probably be sitting in the hallway, yes? And we did the two waking-ups?"

"Yes, he did," Roxanne said, shooting Barry a look of mock disgruntlement. At least, he hoped it was mock.

"Ha ha, very good. Let me just do a bit of the poking and prodding and checking the stitches, yes?"

Barry heaved himself out of the way as the doctor set about examining Roxanne, heading to the window. He peered out through the blinds. Outside it was bright and cold, with a new layer of snow glistening over the old. The sky was clear and blue, with only a few wispy clouds spray-painted on it. And there was the sun, creeping along overhead.

How long did they have until dark? Seven hours?

How could he be thinking what he was thinking?

"Tell me about your father."

Jeff Tracey looked around the room. It was decorated like a study, with wooden paneling, shelves stuffed with books, even a fireplace. The floor was shiny hardwood, with a few throw rugs here and there. It even had a blue velvet couch, on which Jeff was sitting. In front of the couch was a mahogany coffee table, and sitting in a chair on the other side of the table was Randall Kinney.

"Jeff?"

Jeff stopped studying the room and looked at Dr. Kinney. "Huh?"

"Tell me about your father."

Jeff stared a moment, then shrugged. "He's dead."

"I know that."

"Is this really a hospital? It doesn't look like one."

"Yes, this is really a hospital, and I'm really a doctor, despite what some people may suggest." He paused. "Jeff, do you think about your father much?"

"Not any more. I mean, I think about him when I see other kids with their dads, you know? Like Ronald—" He broke off.

"What about Ronald?"

"Nothing."

"How do you feel about Ronald's death?"

"He was my best friend. How do you *think* I feel?" Jeff said, sitting forward on the couch.

"I have no idea."

Jeff leaned back and fixed a critical eye on the doctor. "You're not a very good psychologist, then," he said.

A muffled snort echoed from behind a nearby bookshelf. Jeff thought it sounded like somebody trying not to laugh. "What was that?" he said, craning his neck to peer around the doctor at the suspect wall unit.

"Um, nothing," Kinney said, although he looked annoyed and scribbled fiercely in the margin of his notebook. "Why do you say I'm not a very good psychologist?"

"Aren't you supposed to know how people feel?"

"I'm not a mind reader, Jeff. If I were, things would go a lot faster.

For instance, I could figure out right away what your dreams are all about."

"I can't remember my dreams."

"Your mother says you wake up screaming every night. You can't remember why?"

Jeff said nothing.

Dr. Kinney watched him for a few minutes, then smiled and said: "I think that's enough for now. I'll have Jonah take you back to your room." Jonah was one of the guys who worked at the hospital; he wore a white uniform and smelled like some sort of hand cream. He came in without being called and stood off to the side as Jeff slowly rose and turned, then fell in next to him as he headed for the door.

As it closed behind him, he heard Dr. Kinney start yelling at somebody named Scott.

Barry stood outside the front doors of Saint Elizabeth's Church. He wanted to go in there and ask the priest a few questions, but when he started up the steps he thought about exactly how absurd those questions would be. And why did he even need to ask them? He knew what he'd seen; what difference would a priest's opinion make? Was he hoping for some sort of magic prayer to make the problem go away?

Sighing, he turned and sat on the steps, looking out across the street. Beyond the road was a sparse copse of pine trees, browning at the tops and looking scraggly all the way down. Acid rain? Through the scaly brown trunks he could see the white surface of one of the area's many lakes, the water locked beneath the snow and ice.

Behind him the door clicked open. He heard footsteps on the stairs, but did not turn to look until a man plopped down next to him on the chilly concrete. Then he turned and saw a priest next to him, wearing a dark overcoat, earmuffs, and a hat to protect his balding skull from the wind. His face and eyes were kind and seemed ready to laugh, unlike the stern and threatening demeanor of the fire-and-brimstone preacher Barry remembered from the church his parents used to drag him to.

"Hello," the priest said. "I'm Father John. I saw you out here trying to decide whether to come in."

Barry was nonplussed at this development. "Um, hi."

"Is there something you want to talk about?"

"I have a question that's going to sound ... strange."

"Don't be so sure." Father John leaned over and said, in a conspiratorial whisper, "I used to be a priest in Brooklyn. I've heard everything."

Barry looked at the dark snow by the side of the road. A car whizzed by, adding its own imperceptible layer of dirt to the darkening roadside snow. Father John studied Barry for a second, then said: "Would you like to go inside?"

"Do you think God would allow vampires to exist?"

"Do I think ..." Now Father John looked thoughtful, and wary. "Are you sincere, or are you just amusing yourself?"

"Sincere."

"Hm. No one has ever asked me that before; I was wrong, I haven't heard everything. God forgive me for my arrogance." Pause. "Well. God allows evil to exist, because it is part of His design. If we understand a vampire as an embodiment of evil, then, yes, I suppose such a creature could exist. I should caution you, though, that this is not a subject I've considered before, and my thoughts on it are hardly authoritative. Am I to understand that you're suggesting there's a vampire on the loose in Brown Bear?"

"No. I mean, it's not *strictly* a theoretical question, but ..." He trailed off. "Do you think I'm crazy?"

"I don't know you. You don't *seem* crazy. But I would like to know what led you to ask this question."

"Circumstances. A man's been stalking someone I know, but he never leaves any trace that he's been there. She's seen him twice outside her house, but there weren't footprints in the snow either time. And last night, on the ski slope, I saw somebody behind the ski lift pole. He looked at me and ... and I could've sworn his eyes were glowing. So I went over, but when I got there, there wasn't anybody around, and the snow there wasn't even disturbed. And then my friend disappeared, and when we found her, she had these two marks on her neck, and—" He cut himself off, realizing that he had started babbling; it felt so good to tell somebody, he had just spewed everything. Father John was looking at him curiously. "So, um, what do you think?"

"Wait here a moment." Father John stood and hopped up the

stairs, vanishing into the church. Maybe he was going to call the guys in white coats to come take Barry away.

By the time he returned, carrying something dark and gleaming, Barry had stood and was stamping his feet to shake off the cold. "Here," the priest said, handing Barry a wooden crucifix with a shiny little gold figure of Jesus attached, arms spread, tiny nails protruding from his wrists.

"Thank you, but I couldn't—"

Father John waved a hand. "It's not as if that's my only one; I have them by the crateful in the basement." Then, when Barry continued to hesitate: "Please. Take it. For your peace of mind."

"Um, okay. Thanks."

"God moves in mysterious ways," the priest said.

"I want you to have this," Barry said, handing the crucifix to Roxanne. She was still in bed, but at least she was back in her own room, where the mattress was a lot better than the cot they'd had her on down in the infirmary.

"This is a cross," she said, examining it.

"Yes. A crucifix, actually."

"Po-ta-to, po-tah-to." She dropped it on the covers. "Why are you giving this to me? You're not a holy roller, are you?"

Barry picked up the cross. The smooth, dark wood was cool to the touch, and the metallic figurine was actually cold. Wasn't the deepest layer of hell supposed to be ice or something? "No, of course not. I would just … feel better if you kept it with you."

"Well, um, thanks, but I'm not comfortable with the whole religious iconography scene, okay?" Pause. "Can you put it away? I don't want to see it."

Dismayed, he took the crucifix and put it in the pocket of his coat. He would have to find out from Ryan if Roxanne had always had an aversion to such things. "How do you feel now?"

"Shoulder hurts, head hurts, back hurts—"

"How about your neck?"

"My neck is fine. A little stiff, that's all."

Barry sat down on the bed, but instead of looking at Roxanne he looked out the window. The sun was already on its way to the far end of the sky, the shadows stretching out to the east. He searched his mind for a way to tell Roxanne about his suspicions, but his imagination failed him. This was harder than talking to a strange priest; she would think he was crazy, and that mattered a lot more than what Father John thought.

"Barry?"

But why did she say she didn't want to look at the cross? Did she have something against religious icons in general, or was something more sinister at work? If only he knew her better ...

"Barry, look at me."

He turned away from the window. Roxanne was lying there, looking very tired. Her hair was still tangled and matted from the previous night's adventure, but her color had returned and she looked much healthier. "Look, I'm sorry. I'm sure it's a very nice crucifix. I just ... don't want to see it right now."

"Why?"

"It reminds me of being a little kid in church with the priest glaring at me," she said. "It makes me feel guilty."

"Like you're going to burn in hell for your sins?"

"What? Barry, you're freaking me out. Did you get religion while you were gone? I thought you were just going to check on my stalker situation, not become an evangelical."

"Yeah. Nothing to report on the stalker. I don't think Davidson's given it a thought since you left his desk. Sorry."

She grunted. "Can't say I'm surprised. Everybody thinks I'm imagining it."

"I don't." He went back to the bed, leaned over, and kissed her on the lips. She seemed startled but pleased, and returned the kiss enthusiastically, darting her tongue across his lips. When they broke the kiss she was smiling at him, her eyes shining, her cheeks flushed.

"Care to add a few more sins to my list?" she said.

11:45 PM

Roxanne was asleep with her head on his chest. Barry looked out the window at the night and wondered where the strange man from the ski slope was, what he was doing. Was he outside the lodge, creeping about in the darkness, scratching at the windows with his long, slender fingers? Or was he taking the night off?

Barry looked down at the mass of red hair that billowed out from

Roxanne's head. Her intriguingly sinful offer had been interrupted by a visit from Dr. Smith and a representative of the lodge, the latter bearing coupons and a small gift basket. The rep had left fairly soon, but Dr. Smith had hung around making small talk; then Roxanne had asked about washing her hair. Barry offered to do it for her, under Dr. Smith's careful supervision, which mainly consisted of saying *Don't touch the stitches* at frequent intervals. Roxanne had a lot of hair, so that ate up the rest of the afternoon.

Tomorrow they would leave for White Bluff, and Barry wouldn't get another weekend off until God only knew when; Roxanne would be all alone at night, except for that stupid little dog.

He twirled his fingers in her hair and continued staring out the window, where the snow fell softly, as it had for millennia.

9

SUNDAY, JANUARY 17

11:30 AM

"Today, you go home," Dr. Smith said, as he shone a pencil-sized flashlight into Roxanne's left eye. "But in a couple of days I want you to go see your own doctor for evaluation of your condition, yes?"

"Okay," Roxanne said.

The doctor moved to the light to her right eye. "Good. You should not drive home I think. Not good to be operating a motor vehicle for a long period of time just yet."

Roxanne looked at the doctor, then at Barry. Smith made a clucking noise and, reaching out with one small hand, gently rotated her head back to him. "He has to drive me home?"

"Yes."

"Doctor's orders?"

"Yes."

She turned to look at Barry; Dr. Smith clucked his tongue and turned her head back toward himself. "Dent my car and I'll hurt you," she said.

"Understood," Barry said.

"I'll hurt you *bad*."

"Please not to talk so much," Dr. Smith said.

"Sorry," Roxanne said.

"When can we leave?" Barry asked.

"Whenever you wish," the doctor said. "As soon as we're done here, if you like."

"Oh, let's not leave yet, Barry," Roxanne said.

Dr. Smith clucked his tongue.

"Sorry." Then, after a moment's silence, she continued talking anyway. "If we leave, Ryan and Irving will insist on leaving, too. Let's let them finish up their weekend. We can all go home together tonight."

"What will we do while they're having their good time?"

"I'm sure you and I can think of something."

Barry had to admit that this sounded like a good idea.

The doctor chuckled and said: "The check out is at noon. I hope that does not interfere with whatever it is you were planning."

"Rats," Roxanne said.

Smith clicked off the light and waggled his finger at Roxanne. "You don't listen so good when you start to feel better!"

"Oh, you're such an ogre," Roxanne said. She stood and kissed the short German on his balding forehead. Dr. Smith flushed bright scarlet, grinned, and mumbled something about his wife.

"Don't worry," Barry said. "We won't tell her a thing."

8:20 PM

Barry and Roxanne followed the Sloanes home, once again trailing behind Irving's sedan. Far ahead, the taillight of Waldo's motorcycle was a small red dot, getting smaller, finally lost among the curves of Route 28 as it wound southward through the Adirondacks. The sky was troubled with clouds, no stars, only the moon struggling free now and again to grace them with its light. In the gargantuan wilderness, with no large cities for dozens of miles, Roxanne thought, the night must be as black as it had been hundreds of years earlier, before electric lights had turned the sky grey. For a moment she felt the weight of time on her shoulders, and a sudden sense that despite it all, all the progress, the science, the electric lights, the night remained the same as it had ever been: The refuge of things that lurked beyond the ken of humanity's limited understanding and its small, pathetic, artificial illumination.

But if there were no cities ahead, why did she see a small glow showing over the crest of the next hill?

"Hello, what's this?" Barry said, as the source of the light came into view. Down below, a thousand feet or so ahead, the inky night was lit up with an inferno of swirling red police lights. About six prowl cars were there, three on one side of the road, two on the other, and one in the middle. Waldo's bike was stopped in the harsh glare of a spotlight as he spoke with a husky police officer in a thick blue coat. As they watched, the cop waved Waldo on, and the bike sputtered off into the distance.

Where's Waldo? Ditching his companions, she thought. "Maybe it's a drunk check."

"Yeah," Barry said. "Maybe." He took his foot off the gas and they coasted down the hill toward the roadblock. The trees pressed thick against the highway here, as they did along most roads in the Adirondack park, and Barry could see bright lights about twenty yards off the road to the right. It appeared that a section of the woods had been cordoned off; shapes moved in the forest, walking quickly through clouds of their own breath.

They rolled to a stop just before the roadblock. The cop there was quizzing Irving, who was behind the wheel, while another shone his flashlight into the windows to examine Ryan. Roxanne saw ID being displayed, heard snatches of questions being answered; then they waved Irving on through. He rolled past the roadblock, flicked on the flashers, and pulled over as Barry pulled up to the cop. "We're together," he told the officer. "That's why they're stopping."

"Uh-huh. As long as they stay in the vehicle, I don't care. ID please." Barry wriggled around in his seat trying to get at his wallet, while Roxanne opened her purse. The other officer shined his light into her face and she winced. Then he knocked on her window. She rolled it down.

"What happened to you?" the cop asked.

"Skiing accident," she said. "I hit a tree."

Barry showed his wallet to the officer, not coincidentally displaying the mini-badge pinned inside. The patrolman gave him a closer look. "What force?"

"White Bluff."

"Be glad you don't work up here." He stepped back, waved them on, and turned back to the empty road, waiting for another car to come along.

As they rolled up their windows and continued down the road,

Roxanne said: "What was *that* all about? What did he mean, be glad you don't work here?"

"I don't know," Barry said. Ryan pulled back onto the road and they resumed their southward progress. "That wasn't a drunk check, though. Did you notice the Volvo in with the patrol cars on the right?"

"No."

"It looked like they were turning it over for evidence. They wouldn't have that many cops for a routine traffic stop, I'll tell you that much."

After a long straightaway they rounded a curve, and the lights of the investigation faded into the darkness behind them. Roxanne said: "I got the shivers back there."

"You did?"

"Yeah. All those cops ... the bright lights ..."

"The lights are to give them an advantage; they can see everything about you, but you can't—*Jesus!*" Barry slammed on the brakes as something flew out of the woods by the side of the road. The thing came from the top of a huge rock just off the shoulder, flopped to the ground in front of Irving's car like dead-weight; in the instant before Irving ran over it, Barry knew it was a body.

The little Honda's tires skittered on icy snow and it half-turned sideways; the Ford's taillights blazed and its tires locked as Irving slammed on his brakes, but there was never any real possibility that he'd avoid hitting the person.

Barry spun the wheel hard to the left and got the car pointed straight again, but then it began to fishtail. His foot on the brakes, he watched the world weave back and forth ... and then he realized that they had stopped. The other car was ten feet or so ahead, turned slightly to the left, humming in the snow. Ryan and Irving were getting out of the car; Irving's face was grim, while Ryan looked like she was going to throw up.

Turning to Roxanne, Barry said: "Stay here."

"Don't have to tell me twice."

Ryan, Irving, and Barry gathered around the body in the road, a twisted mess just behind the Taurus's rear fender. Barry noted the important characteristics: Caucasian male, late forties, six foot something. The body's weight was tricky to determine, as it was bundled up in a heavy, expensive-looking coat. Ryan stared at the corpse, her face white as the snow that swirled around them; Irving kept muttering, over and over again, "Oh, God."

Barry knelt beside the man's corpse. The Honda's lights lit him up in brutal detail, down to the snowflakes which fell to pepper his upturned face. His face ... the snow was sticking, not melting, not even a little. The body was already as cold as the night air, which had to mean the man had been dead long before Irving hit him; which in turn meant that somebody had thrown him off that rock.

Unless ...

"Guys," Barry said, "get back in your car."

But before they could move, the dead man opened his eyes and started screaming.

Christian Keems parked his Corvette under a streetlight and activated the alarm with a button on his key chain. The car made a happy burbling noise and all the lights flashed at once. Satisfied that his baby was thus protected, Chris trotted around the car and down the stairs that gave access to the Ace of Hearts, a nightclub and bar, and Chris's favorite place for finding women. Nearly everyone he'd dated, or simply fucked, in the last two years had come from this place.

Nearly everyone; but not Roxanne. He'd picked *her* up at the bookstore in the mall. That would teach him to go outside his usual watering hole when cutting females from the herd. He liked that image, and thought of it often: Himself as the sleek, powerful predator, stalking slow-witted women who didn't realize he was coming for them until it was too late.

He wondered who his victim would be tonight.

She saw him come in, saw the slight wrinkling of his nose at the smell of cigarettes and cheap beer; obviously he wasn't here for the ambiance. He was wearing expensive clothes, silk probably, and a tie. A few others in the Ace of Hearts had ties, but they wore jeans with theirs. The newcomer was clearly trying to make some sort of statement, standing out in the crowd like that. Obviously insecure about something.

She knew who he was: Roxanne Carmichael's boyfriend. She'd

seen him once or twice in the last few days, when she'd followed Martel on his little voyeuristic escapades. But even if she hadn't known his face, she would have recognized him anyway; she'd been close enough to him to pick up on his thoughts, and their pattern was distinct as a fingerprint. Despite the face he presented to the world, on the inside, this was a very angry fellow.

A perfect recruit.

Lauren Fletcher crushed out the cigarette she had bummed from a man with a moustache and moved off toward the new arrival. She felt the mustachioed fellow watch her go, and put a little extra wiggle in her walk.

After all, it never hurt to leave a good impression behind.

Chris had taken up a position at the end of the bar, where he could look over any new arrivals as they entered; but he'd only been there for a few minutes when a woman slid onto the stool next to him. "Hi," she said. "I'm Lauren."

"Chris."

"Pleased to meet you." She shook his hand. Her skin was cool and dry. He tried not to be too obvious as he looked her over. She was blonde, attractively pale, with a trim body effectively showcased by a tight blue dress. The straps over her shoulders were little more than strings, and he thought they would require minimal effort to remove. He was surprised to discover that he was already developing an erection, like he was some horny fifteen-year-old; sure, Lauren was sexy as hell, but usually he had better control than this.

"Do you, um, do you live in White Bluff?" he asked.

"No. I don't really live anywhere."

"Funny. You don't look like homeless person."

"Actually I'm just back from a ski trip."

"Oh, you ski?"

"Not really." She tilted her head forward. Silky golden hair fell down in front of her eyes, but they shone through anyway, green and lively. "I just like to play with poles."

She loved the Corvette; she loved driving fast on the highway; she thought Christian Keems was the funniest, cutest, smartest man she had ever met. At least, that was what she let him think she thought.

And she laughed a lot, in a vacant way she could tell Chris liked, and she kept her hand on his thigh (or thereabouts), and told him how it was unbelievable that any woman could have been dumb enough to dump him.

Ah, he corrected, *he* had done the dumping.

She smiled, enjoying herself. Wouldn't Martel be surprised when he returned and discovered that he was no longer the only Master in town? After events on the mountain, she had taken refuge in a small cave in the woods, a crypt-like opening beneath a pile of rocks deposited by some ancient glacier, as if even then someone had known she would need shelter from the sun. Come nightfall, she'd taken to the air and left the Master, Krone, and that bitch Roxanne Carmichael behind. She had stopped along the way for a bit of fun; she was sure it would be in the news tomorrow. It was intended as a gauntlet thrown to the Master, a declaration that his rule and his rules were both overthrown. Then she had returned to White Bluff, had found herself a new hiding place, and begun feeling her own power. She could make vampires too, even though the Master—no, not the Master, she had no master, he was just Martel—had ordered her not to do so.

Why should *he* be the Master? She was as strong as he; or at least, she would be, soon enough.

"Are we going to your place?" she asked.

"Sure, if you want to."

"Yeah." She slid her hand farther up Chris's leg, to show him what she would do at his apartment. His foot came down on the accelerator and they burned through the intersection where he had been waiting for the light to change.

He was certainly enthusiastic, she thought. Like Ken had been, when they first—

She shut that thought out immediately. Thinking about Ken gave her a strange, empty ache inside; a sort of nostalgia, a longing for something precious that she'd lost. She pushed the image of his face away. It was a stupid, sentimental notion, anyway, love and all that human bullshit; none of it meant anything in the end. One year or seventy, however long it lasted, eventually everything human turned to dust. But not her. She would keep going, on and on, long after everyone she had ever known was dead and rotted and returned to the soil.

"Hey, are you okay?"

Christian's question drew her out of her reverie and back to the present. She shook her head to clear it, and smiled at him. "Sure I'm okay," she said.

"You sure? You look ... sad."

Sad? Sad? The word meant nothing. Instead of answering, she slid her hand up to his crotch and said, softly, "Let me help you shift."

The not-so-dead man flung Barry to the ground and climbed on top of him. He looked up at Ryan and Irving, eyes burning with green fire, fangs like the wicked tusks of a mad boar. "Get out!" he roared. Ryan screamed; Irving grabbed her and half-dragged her back toward the front door of their car.

The creature looked down at Barry, ran his tongue over his twisted teeth. Slaver dripped from his lower lip and spattered Barry's down jacket, the waterproof material beading it into tiny blood-flecked drops that caught the glitter of Roxanne's headlights. Barry stared up at the thing, his thoughts like a disorderly classroom full of hyperactive children, until finally one shouted down the rest: The crucifix was in his coat pocket.

But the vampire was on top of him, holding him down, and he couldn't move his arms enough to get at the cross. He heard tires spinning on snow. Ryan and Irving, abandoning him? No, it was the front tires of Roxanne's car. What on earth was she doing? For a second he thought they would find no traction, that they would just spin there; but then the car lurched forward. The dead man's head swung to his left, spittle trailing in the air, hanging for a second like a string of crystal pearls. He raised his left hand as if to protect himself from the oncoming vehicle, planted his right on Irving's bumper. That freed Barry's arm; he reached into his coat, hunting for the crucifix.

Roxanne's car drove into the vampire's open palm, and simply stopped. The tires spun on the slick road, not getting enough traction to overcome the resistance.

This monster was powerful enough to stop a car.

The thing looked down at Barry, his lips twisting into a crafty smile; then he slowly began to release the tension in his arms, letting the

Honda inch forward. The bumper crumpled under his fingers as he guided the car to the side, aiming the spinning wheel at Barry's head. "Roxanne!" Barry shouted, his voice cracking like a teenager's. "Lay off the gas!" But she didn't hear, or was too panicked to respond; the tire didn't stop.

The pocket with the cross in it was zippered shut. He managed to work it open one-handed; his fingers closed on the object within. He felt the Jesus figure, cold beneath his fingers. Grabbing hold, he pulled it out, grabbed a fistful of the dead man's mail-order-catalog ballistic nylon winter coat to steady himself, and shoved the cross right into the thing's face. The monstrous parody of a man howled and pulled back, actually *flying* into the air, pulling Barry along for the ride. The ground spun beneath him but he kept his grip, shoving the cross between the vampire's jaws and then, with a crunch, through the roof his mouth and into the cavity above.

They landed hard by the side of the road, Barry on top, the creature writhing beneath him. Smoke rose from the it's mouth, acrid with the smell of burning flesh. It had stopped screaming. Then, with a final body-wide spasm, it lay still.

Barry stood up, staring down at it, at the black blood welling from its mouth and running down its cheeks. The cross itself seemed completely undamaged, Jesus not tarnished in the slightest, even though it had burned an image of itself into the man's face from his chin to the bridge of his nose. Unthinkingly, Barry returned the crucifix to his soiled jacket.

Roxanne emerged from the car, her face pale, eyes wide. She whispered, "God. Oh God. Did you *see* that?"

"Yeah," Barry said. "Yeah, I saw that. Felt it. Smelled it."

Roxanne came a pace closer, stared down at the not-dead thing. "Did you kill it?"

"I think so," Barry said. "The crucifix killed it."

"Jesus God in heaven," she said.

"Oh yeah," Barry said. "Go back to the roadblock. Get some cops. They'll want to see this."

"I don't want to leave you here alone out here with this thing," she said, her voice small and frightened.

"Ryan and Irving will ..." He trailed off, realizing with a start that the other car was gone; he and Roxanne were quite alone. Looking around, he said: "Where—"

"They took off while you were … flying through the air. Barry, I'm sorry, I freaked out, I thought I could ram him off you but instead I almost ran you over—"

"It's okay. I'm fine." Her car had some minor front-end damage, in addition to what the vampire had done to the bumper; she must have rear-ended Irving's car. Maybe that had jolted him into fleeing the scene. "Listen, we can't leave the body alone, and I don't want you here if it wakes up again. Go on back to the roadblock, get help. Be careful."

She hesitated a moment, then kissed his cold lips before hurrying back to her car. Barry stared after her, conscious of the corpse—the vampire—there at his feet.

This thing was what Roxanne could become.

And he had not a blessed clue what to do about it.

Lauren threw Chris down on the bed, attacking him hungrily, kissing his face, his ears, his neck. She nibbled lightly, making him squirm. "Bite me," he moaned.

"Soon," Lauren said.

She worked her way down now, removing his tie and unbuttoning his shirt. She rained kisses on his chest, licking and nibbling when the urge took her. But Chris was impatient; he took her head in his hands and guided her lower. She unzipped his pants and pulled them off, tossing them into the corner, then tore off his underwear. Soon she was hard at work, her head bobbing.

Chris closed his eyes and concentrated on the sensations as she slid him up and down in her mouth. In short order he came, his hips jumping, barely containing a cry that would have certainly awakened the neighbors. Lauren swallowed it, and more.

He opened his eyes and saw Lauren sitting on the edge of the bed, wiping her chin. "Can I use your bathroom?" she asked.

"Huh?" Chris wasn't thinking too clearly at the moment.

"Your bathroom."

"Oh. It's over there." He pointed at a darkened doorway in the bedroom wall. Lauren rose, smiled, and headed for it. She had slipped out of her dress at some point, and her body was every bit as good as Chris had expected.

She stopped at the doorway and looked back over her shoulder. She snapped on the bathroom light and paused there, silhouetted between light and darkness, every curve of her body done in outline; and those eyes, those lively green eyes, were *glowing*. "You might want to clean yourself up," she said; and then she laughed and went into the bathroom. The door clicked shut behind her.

Chris looked at the lower half of his body, which, he suddenly realized, had gone numb.

And then he saw the blood.

Lauren heard him scream once, heard him try to stand, heard him topple to the floor; after that, he was still. She looked at herself in the mirror, at the thin crimson line trickling from the corner of her mouth, and smiled. She was what she was; and now Chris was what she was, too. And why stop there? She could have a whole legion under her control. She could show Martel a thing or two about power. He was afraid of the government, afraid of being discovered by the living. She was not.

After all, what did she have to lose?

She smiled at herself, saw her stained, red teeth, stopped smiling. She wiped the blood from her mouth with her palm. That wasn't her in the mirror, was it? It was the face of a ghoul. Eyes of fire, fangs dripping gore. That wasn't her. It couldn't be her.

But, of course, it was.

Fear. She wrote it in Chris's blood on Chris's mirror.

There it was.

She struck out with her hand and the glass splintered beneath the word. Leaving her fear behind, she turned and walked out of the bathroom, to wait on the bed for Chris to wake up.

They sat shivering on the rear bumper of a police car as photographers took pictures of the corpse from a dozen different angles. Up on the rock, policemen prowled for clues, but in the rapidly falling snow there was little real hope of finding anything; and Barry's gut instinct was that, snow or no snow, there would be nothing to find there. Nothing at all.

"So the body fell down in front of your friends' car." The officer in charge of the scene, who had identified himself as Derek Mahoney, leaned on the hood of Roxanne's car, eating what looked like an egg salad sandwich as he spoke to them.

"That's right," Barry said.

"He ran over it, then you hit it."

"Yes. We both hit it."

"You're looking kind of bloodied up yourself," Derek said. "What happened?"

"I attempted CPR," Barry said.

"You tried CPR on *that*?"

"My instructor said it was always worth a try."

"Maybe so, but … *Jesus.*" Derek shook his head. The photographers concluded their task and others descended on the scene. "You're a better man than me."

"I think he was already dead when we hit him," Barry said. "The body was cold."

"Yeah, that's what the medical examiner suggested as well." Derek rubbed his hands together, breathed into the space between them. "You think somebody tossed him into the road? Or was he balanced on the rock, waiting to fall, and just happened to drop in on you guys?"

"I couldn't say," Barry said.

But he *could* say; that thing had been perched on that rock, watching, waiting. If it had just wanted a victim, Waldo and Priscilla would have been far easier targets. Swoop, snatch, done, dinner. Someone had told that dime-store Dracula what to look for. What car; what people.

No, not *people*.

What *person*.

Roxanne shivered and looked up at the sky. She was hating this conversation, hating the night, the cold, the clouds in the sky. She hated every second they spent near that *thing* that had attacked Barry. It was horrid, repulsive, ungodly; and its existence suggested something which she did not, *really* did not, want to think about.

"Found his wallet," one of the investigators announced, a short woman in a warm-looking ankle-length coat.

Derek snapped his fingers. "Bring it." She swished over with the leather billfold. He took it, flipped it open, and after a second said:

"Damn."

"What's wrong?" Barry asked.

Derek looked at him, started to speak, stopped, started again. "Aw, hell," he said. "We've got a whole family dead in the forest back there. Throats torn open, hearts ripped out. One's got his head crushed with a rock. Family's last name, from the mom's ID, was Barron." He flipped around the wallet. In the harsh glare of three floodlights, a picture of a clean-cut sandy-haired man smiled at them. "The guy you ran over is Carl Barron, Episcopalian minister and dear old dad." He gave a sad look at the body, now being transferred to a black plastic sack. "Well, there goes my primary suspect."

"Maybe he offed himself," the female investigator said.

Derek brightened visibly at the prospect. "Yeah, that's a possibility. I hope there's enough left of him to find out."

A patrol car, lights flashing, appeared from the south. It pulled up next to Roxanne's car and the driver got out and came over. Roxanne could see two figures in the back of the vehicle. Ryan and Irving, no doubt. She still couldn't believe they had just run off like that, after all the gung-ho get-involved take-a-stand speeches Irving had given over the years.

Derek said, "What have you got for me, Wiggins?"

"We caught up with the other vehicle involved. We have the driver and a passenger. They're both pretty hysterical, not making a lot of sense. I thought it best not to let them come back under their own power."

He sighed, then winked at Barry and Roxanne and said, "Joy and merriment is sure to follow." He clapped Wiggins on the shoulder. "I have to go talk to your friends. Don't go anywhere, okay?"

"We'll be right here," Barry said.

Once they were alone again, Barry turned to Roxanne and said: "How are you holding up?"

"I think I'm in shock."

"You and me both." Barry leaned in so his lips were near to her ear. "Vampires."

"Barry, I think … the guy who's been following me—"

"Yeah."

"No, you don't understand … I think he *bit* me."

After a moment, Barry said: "Yeah. I think so too."

"So what does that mean?" The corpse had by now been loaded into an ambulance, and that's where she looked. "How long before … ?"

"I don't think you're going to die from being bitten. You're not even sick. He got you, what, two days ago, probably when you were up on the slopes—"

"Barry, please. I don't want to think about it. Not now. Even if I wanted to, I can't remember what happened."

"I know a hypnotist who does work for the department. I could call him, he could put you under. We could find out for sure."

Roxanne looked up at the sky. It went on forever. "I'm scared, Barry," she whispered.

"I know, honey." Barry glanced over at the car where Derek was berating Ryan and Irving for driving away. "Leaving the scene of an accident," Barry said. "Well, under the circumstances, maybe they won't press charges."

"He killed that whole family, didn't he?" Still looking at the sky. She didn't want to look around them any more.

"Yeah, I guess he did."

"Why did he do such awful things to their bodies?"

"I don't know."

"I wonder what it'll be like to be a vampire. What will I see when I look at a person—just meat? What'll blood taste like? Will I miss the sun?"

"Don't talk like that. We'll save you."

"How? I've got his poison inside me. God, now that I know about it, I can *feel* it working in there. You think I'm not sick? I am. I'm the woman who has metastatic breast cancer and doesn't even know it."

"We'll save you. We will. We'll get a book—"

"A *book*? Barry, vampire books are fairy tales. They're fiction. This is real. How can we believe what they say in a book?"

"A book of legends. The real legends."

"Legends." She kicked a clod of snow across the road.

"What else can we do? Wait for Van Helsing to show up? There's nobody coming to save our bacon, Annie. It's just you and me, nobody else. Unless you think we can count on Ryan and Irving over there."

"We could tell Officer Mahoney."

"*Not* a good idea."

She turned away. "I want to go home."

"They'll let us go home when they're good and ready. For now, come sit in the car where it's warm." They walked together to her little Honda, through the drifting clouds of exhaust steam lit up with flashing red and blue; and the snow fell silently down.

11:57 PM

Roxanne lay in Barry's bed, her arms locked around a pillow. Sleep had eluded her, but rage had come in its place: Rage that this *thing* thought it was its right to pursue her, terrorize her, *violate* her. She wanted to scream and beat the walls; she wanted to stand on the rooftop and scream her anger at every passer-by; she wanted to go to court and get this vampire sentenced to Hell. Or was that a sentence he was already serving?

She rolled over. Barry had a twin bed, but since he was away at work she had more than enough room. She felt better here in his apartment, safer than she did in her house, especially with the crucifix there by his bedside. They had used it to kill one vampire, so it could kill more. It could kill the one who had attacked her at the ski slope, who had spied on her and followed her and scared her half to death.

She didn't expect to need the crucifix tonight, though. She knew, in a vague sort of way, that a vampire couldn't enter a home unless invited by the rightful owner. Barry wasn't here, so unless her mysterious stalker could entice her to leave the apartment—which she had no intention of doing—she should be safe, right?

The air seemed to be getting colder. Had the heater quit? She shivered and pulled up the blanket, and looked around the apartment with frightened eyes. Her neck tingled where the bites were. Was it the cold? Or something else? She looked at the window. A mist had arisen outside, and now it frothed behind the pane of glass, and seeped in through tiny cracks, flowing thick and viscous ... mist that faintly glowed ... for a second she almost drifted into a strange semi-sleep, but then she snapped fully awake; and, with a sudden shocking fear, she *knew*.

Someone was in the room with her.

It was *him*.

10

MONDAY, JANUARY 18

MIDNIGHT

Oh, God. He was here, in the room; and she was alone, vulnerable, defenseless ...

No, not defenseless. Her hand slid across the cool sheet to Barry's nightstand, and closed around the crucifix there.

Her neck tingled, as if with kisses.

"Go away!" she screamed at the darkness. Before the echo of her voice died away, she saw a white shape standing in the corner, a construction of snow and moonlight and imagination.

"Go away?" it mused, stepping forward, resolving itself into the man from the ski slope. "Go away? Is that what you want?" He stopped at the side of Barry's bed and stood there looking down at her, his gaze seeming to pierce the blankets under which she lay. He came closer, knelt beside the bed. "Are you so upset to see me?" She whipped the crucifix around, aiming for his face, but he caught her wrist easily in one cold, dry hand. He examined the cross, then gently unwound her fingers and took it away from her. "Poor workmanship," he said, tossing it across the room.

Astonished, she said: "But—"

"The Nazarene does not impress me." He reached out and put his hand on the top of the blanket, gathering it up in his grip. "I took you on the slopes that night," he murmured. "I drank of your blood. Now we will drink of each other in a different way."

"No," Roxanne said, but her voice was small and weak. She didn't resist as he slowly pulled the blankets off her body. The chill raised goosebumps on her flesh, sent shivers up her legs and down her spine. She was wearing her most grandmotherly nightshirt, all flannel and fasteners, but she found herself removing it, undoing one button, then another, then another, until she slipped the garment off and dropped it beside the bed. He came up to her, pushed her onto her back; he put one hand on her breast and squeezed it gently, his touch cool and dry. His other hand slowly went to work on himself. She stared at it, up and down, up and down, wondering what vampire ejaculate might look like.

"You will be my bride," he told her, kissing her on the neck.

"Please stop," she whispered, as his mouth slid down from her neck, down between her breasts, down to her stomach and beyond. "Please—" But then her breath was driven out of her by a stab of pleasure that seemed to shoot straight up her spine and into her brain like a spear made of ice. She gasped and her hands went to his head, pushing him against her.

She told herself this was wrong, screamed it silently, this—

"Oh, God!" she cried, arching her back.

—was wrong. So, so, so terribly wrong. What was he doing to—

"Uh!" she gasped.

—her? No, this wasn't right, this—

She ground herself against him as the world exploded around her. Sweat broke out all across her body. Her guts, her muscles, all turned to jelly, to water, to fire. He reached up with long arms and squeezed her breasts with slender fingers. Then, when her gasping had subsided, he pushed himself up. She could feel him against her leg, up to her thigh, inches away from her. She put her hands on his buttocks to hurry him along. And then—

—and then she remembered the dead man lying bloody in the snow, not so dead after all. She seized on that, clutched it as if it were her last possession, and when his face came close to hers she threw it at him.

"Why did you do it?" she asked, her voice absurdly weak.

Martel paused. She could feel the tip of him touching her, and she grabbed the mattress with both hands to keep from shoving him inside. "I do what I must to survive, and to stay sane," he said.

It sounded like a stock answer, rote and trite. "You ... had to kill a whole *family* to survive and … and stay sane?" Her breathing was shallow and ragged as the echoes of that incredible orgasm resonated inside of her; but she was getting herself under control, regaining possession of her faculties.

"What are you speaking of?" he said, his tone sharpening.

"You know what." She seemed to be coming out of the spell that had held her, coming back to herself, her voice growing stronger even though she felt like she had just run a marathon up a mountain with bricks tied to her feet. "In the Adirondacks. The Barrons. You butchered them and left the father a monster, like you."

His luminous eyes flickered like distant candle flames. "Is this some sort of ruse?"

"No. Read tomorrow's paper, and you'll see."

He retreated, actually climbed off her, stood beside the bed looking at her with those glittering, glowing eyes. There! She grabbed the sheets and pulled them up to cover herself. The vampire made no move to stop her, just stood there staring down at her, his expression unreadable, his fabulous body glowing in the moonlight. "I committed no such act. I would not behave with such … flamboyance." Then: "But I know who would."

"Who?"

"I regret that our union must be postponed, but this reveals something that I must deal with quickly. We will continue our liaison another time. I leave you with the memory of my kisses."

"Who killed them, if it wasn't you? Answer me, damn it!"

But he didn't answer; he was already melting, his features running like wax as mist rose up around him. Then he was gone, and in his place was a viscous cloud that smelled faintly of blood and corpses. It slurped across the floor and under the door, leaving no trace of its passage.

Blood and corpses. She would remember that odor the next time he came to her, the next time he tried to put his mouth on her or his tongue inside her. That was the smell of death to her now. Fruit, rotting under plastic—hah! That was wholesome compared to this.

She leapt out of bed and ran to the door. The floor was cold on her feet, the air icy on her naked body. She got down on her hands and knees and looked at the crack through which he'd gone. It was a quarter-inch high, maybe. How did he *do* that?

Shaking with relief, she collapsed on her side, right there on the cold wooden floor. Would she ever be able to forgive herself for what she had allowed him to do to her?

But no, it was wrong to think that way. She hadn't *allowed* it to happen. He had forced himself on her, and would have done worse than that if she had not chanced on the words to stop him. Remember that, she told herself; it could have been worse. Because after he had fucked her, she knew, the vampire would have killed her, and made her like him.

After a few minutes, she crawled to the corner and retrieved the crucifix from where he had thrown it. There was a dent in the wood, and Jesus' head was bent downward slightly, but other than that it appeared undamaged. How had he been able to touch it, examine it, and then discard it? But it had worked on the other vampire, so she would keep it near anyway, just in case. She carried it quickly to the bed and deposited it on the nightstand; and then she put her nightgown back on and climbed back under the covers to await Barry's return.

Krone's uneasy slumber was interrupted by a gentle tapping on the window of the car. He grunted and refused to wake up. The tapping continued, and was followed by the opening of the car door. His feet, which had been propped up against it, flopped down and dangled out of the front seat of the Lincoln. That woke him. In the glow of the dome light he saw golden hair, pale skin, green eyes that glimmered and shone.

"Hello, Krone," Lauren Fletcher said.

He stared at her.

"Poor Krone," she said, tracing his leg with her finger. "Out here all alone in the cold and the dark. Martel won't even let you leave the lair anymore, will he?"

He tried to say something, but his brain couldn't seem to form words. Her eyes held him like magnets.

"Poor Krone," she said. Her finger-tracing had moved to his crotch. "It must be lonely. Mustn't it?"

Krone's mind seemed to be working even more slowly than usual. Hadn't the Master said Lauren was no longer their friend? What was she doing here? Why was she speaking nicely to him? Usually she just ignored him, except when she was being insulting.

"You like me, don't you, Krone?" she asked. She was massaging his crotch now. The sensations this generated stirred vague feelings, feelings and memories ... from before ...

"You like to look at me. I've seen you doing it. And you like to look at Roxanne. That's why you followed her, spied on her. Isn't it?"

"The Master got mad at me for that."

"He's always angry with you for something, Krone. But I'm not." Her fingers found the zipper of his too-small jeans and slowly pulled it down. "You like to look at women. It's only natural. Poor Krone, you just want a woman of your own, don't you?"

Did he? He tried to remember if he did or he didn't. What did one do with a woman, anyway?

She undid the button of his pants and he popped out of them like a jack-in-the-box. "Well, Krone," she said, taking him in her hand. Then she slowly shifted herself around, slid up her skirt, guided his hardness into herself.

Krone made a gasping noise. He continued to make it as she rocked back and forth, up and down, side to side. Krone's beefy hands clutched at the seats, clutched at the door handle, clutched at her with enough force to leave bruises on her breasts and buttocks. Then he groaned and fountained like a geyser inside her.

When it was over—when his gasps had subsided to whimpers, when his massive erection had gone flaccid—she leaned forward and tickled his ears with her voice. "You liked that, didn't you, Krone?"

He whined.

"I could come back tomorrow night and do it again," she said. "Would you like that?"

He managed a nod. Yes, yes he would. He would like that very much.

"But, Krone," she said, her voice sharper now, sharp as her teeth, "if Martel finds out I was here, he'll stop me from coming back. You want me to come back, don't you, Krone?"

He nodded again.

"So if Martel asks you anything about me—if he asks you if I was here, if you've seen me, if you know where I might be—you have to tell him no. You don't know anything. Okay?"

"Okay."

She smiled at him. "Ah, Krone," she said. "We'll have such fun tomorrow night. Remember, tell Martel nothing."

"Nothing," he repeated.

She stayed there a moment longer, then pulled herself off him and slipped out of the car, vanishing in the darkness of the tunnel.

Krone cleaned himself up by rolling in the snow. The cold made his skin red, but the rough, icy crystals erased the lingering vestiges of Lauren Fletcher's visit. She was right; if the Master knew she'd been there, he would forbid Krone to see her, maybe even tell him to kill her. And then, of course, he would have to do it. But what the Master didn't know, he couldn't give orders about.

Krone was still sweeping up the snow, using a tree branch to erase the signs of disturbance, when the Master arrived, dropping out of the sky like a stricken raven. His eyes glowed brilliantly; obviously he was furious about something. Did he already know what Lauren Fletcher had done?

"Krone!" he roared.

"I'm right here, Master."

"Come with me," Martel said. Krone tossed the tree branch aside and fell in behind the Master as he strode into the tunnel. Martel stopped beside the Lincoln, striking it so hard that he dented the metal. "Krone, that damnable Fletcher woman slaughtered an entire family up in those mountains."

"She did?"

"Yes. Damn her to hell! It was nothing less than wholesale butchery!"

Krone didn't understand why the Master found this upsetting. "So what?"

"You know perfectly well so what. This is a direct challenge to me. She will have left no footprints in the snow, no traces, nothing. The police will be suspicious. Those with ... open minds may begin to wonder."

"Nobody believes in us," Krone said, a bit sullenly.

"Are you *defending* her?" Martel roared. "Nobody believes in us because we *conceal* ourselves. But *she* advertises her presence in letters nine feet high! And what's worse, she created another like herself. Like ... me."

"There's no one else like you, Master."

"Hm. I wonder." He shook his head. "I never should have taken her. I've been a fool this past week, Krone. I've revealed myself to more than one human, thinking it was safe, enjoying the game. And now this ..." He gestured out into the night, at Lauren, wherever she was. "This ... this *psychopath* conducts a slaughter that would blanch the most hardened killer. All the rules are broken."

Krone thought about all the people he and Martel and his various lady-friends had killed in the years he'd been with them. Hundreds, if not thousands. He didn't see why it was such a big deal that Lauren had killed a few more tonight. It was true, of course, that Martel didn't let his ladies make their own spawn; but really, what difference did it make? There was still only one Master.

Oops. Martel was still talking, and Krone had stopped listening. He started again. "... let me know at once," Martel said.

Krone nodded and said, "Yes, Master." He didn't know what Martel had just said, which was good, because it had probably related to Lauren Fletcher; and if he didn't know the Master's orders, he could hardly be blamed for not carrying them out.

He was surprised he'd thought of that. Perhaps he was getting smarter.

"Feh." The Master sounded disgusted. "Rarely have I seen such behavior from one of my kind. I should have known that only the most reckless of women would have persisted in hunting me for so long. I should have guessed what she would become." He walked to the cocoon he had placed on the tunnel wall. He dug his fingers into the nest of jellied blood, ripping an opening for himself. The thick, viscous goo slid from Martel's cold dry skin like water from a freshly waxed car. "Ah, Krone, the change has unhinged her mind. I hope I can stop her before she brings the entire world of humans down on our heads. I must think, rest, refresh myself. This is going to be difficult."

He clambered into the cocoon and disappeared.

Krone sighed in relief. He had successfully bluffed the Master, but the exertion had given him a headache. He crawled back into the Lincoln, shut the door, and drifted into a sleep filled with dreams of Lauren Fletcher.

* * *

Roxanne was still awake when the front door opened and Barry entered. She watched him look her way, then go into the bathroom and close the door. A few minutes later he came out and approached the bed. He sat down next to her and stroked her hair; she grabbed his hand and kissed it.

"Hey there," he said.

"He was here."

"*What?*"

"He was here. In this apartment."

"Are you all right? What did he do to you?"

"I'm okay." She opened her mouth. "See? No fangs."

"How did he get in? What about the cross?"

"I showed him the cross. He just took it and threw it away. He said he wasn't impressed." She gave Barry a second to digest this, then continued. "He tried to rape me—"

"I'll kill the motherfucker," Barry said.

"Shhh." She put her finger on his lips. "I know. I know you will. But he didn't do it; I stopped him."

He stared at her for a long moment, and she realized with a start that he was deciding whether or not to believe her. Finally he said: "How did you stop him?"

"I asked him about the family he killed. He says he didn't do it. He didn't know anything about it. He got upset and left."

"That's it? He just … left?"

She nodded.

"And he says he didn't do it? Then who did? Who else would leave a bloodsucking father of four running around?"

"Why would he lie?" The only answer she had.

"God knows why he does anything. I'm sure he doesn't think like you or me." Barry stroked her hair for a few more minutes. "Do you … will he … be back tonight?"

"No," she said. "I mean, I don't think so."

"How did he get in?"

"Under … under the door. Like … fog."

"He can turn into fog?"

"I guess so."

"Jesus. Well, so much for the theory that you have to invite them in, I guess. How do we keep fog out?"

"Run a dehumidifier?"

They looked at each other for a second, and then Barry cracked a smile that turned into a chuckle. He made as if to stand, but she pulled him back down. "Where do you think you're going?"

"To sleep on the couch?"

"The hell you are," she said.

"Roxanne, the bed is barely big enough for me, let alone the two of us."

She sat up and took his hands. The sheets fell away from the top half of her body and Barry's eyes traveled there. "We'll have room," she said, pulling him down.

He started to say something, but she blocked his mouth with hers. Her hands left his and went to his shoulders, then traveled down the sides of his body to his waist, fingers hooking into his belt. Breaking the kiss, she said: "Care to arrest me, officer?"

"How's your head?"

Oh, for the love of God. "It's fine. Really."

"I think," he said, gently removing her hands from his body, "that you need to rest."

Rest. She didn't want to rest. She had awakened from her semi-sleep feeling charged, hyped up, full of fire and vinegar. She grabbed him and pulled him close and kissed him furiously; he responded for a moment, then disengaged. "Listen, Annie, you had a good knock on your head. I don't want to hurt you. Just rest and take it easy for a few more days, okay?"

She stared at him, disbelieving. The vampire wanted to rape her, and the human wouldn't touch her. "Do you … do you think I'm … dirty or something? Because of what happened to me?"

"What? Jesus Christ, no, of course not. Look, don't think that I don't want to make love to you—after this I'll probably be disappearing into the bathroom to work through my fantasies—but I'm willing to wait until you're healed a little bit more. I'm *going* to wait." He sounded almost like he was telling himself that. "Okay? It's got nothing to do with what did or did not happen to you. In a few days, I promise, you won't be able to keep me from attacking you." Pause. "Okay, *attacking* is probably a bad word choice, but you get the idea."

"Wow," she said. "That was some speech."

"Thank you. I've been practicing it."

"Barry?"

"What?" he asked, stroking her hair some more.

"You don't have to disappear into the bathroom."

It was dark in the basement of the old plant at the edge of the marsh, but Chris could still see. He had gone out feeding tonight, his first time, and the blood was still warm in his stomach.

He knew what he had to do now. He had to make a nest.

He selected a spot in the corner. He stood there staring at his chosen site, shaking slightly; then he opened his mouth and vomited a stream of thick, steaming gore at the wall. Tonight's meal, becoming his bed. It splashed against the wall, congealing into a gelatinous mass, an enormous bloody cocoon. He closed his mouth, cutting off the stream, inspecting his quivering handiwork. Not big enough. He concentrated, willing his stomach to produce more of the stuff that changed blood into this quasi-solid goo; he felt it in his stomach like a lake of acid, vile and bilious, and after a moment he belched up another ropy spurt of slime.

He closed his mouth and once again appraised his new abode. It looked like he could fit inside it if he assumed the fetal position. It would have to do; he was out of blood. He'd enlarge it after his next meal, tomorrow night. He crawled inside the cocoon, curled himself up inside its warm, dark, wet confines. He felt its soothing, nourishing substance soaking into his skin, like pond water to a frog.

His clothes were tucked away in a garbage bag to keep them clean and presentable; he no longer needed them, except to keep up appearances when he cruised his bars and nightclubs, looking for victims. It would be much harder to get young single ladies to leave with him if he showed up naked and bloody.

Chris shifted around to get more comfortable in the soft, slick cocoon. It seemed as natural as his own mattress had been. Or Roxanne's mattress. He smiled at the thought of her. Ah, Roxanne. She should be back from her weekend in the mountains. She should be home. Home, the place she thought was her little fortress.

Soon, he would show her just how strong a fortress had to be to keep *him* out.

* * *

7:25 AM

Roxanne tiptoed around Barry's apartment, getting ready to go to work. She'd showered, keeping her stitches dry as per Dr. Smith's instructions, and had changed into one of the outfits she'd brought for the weekend and then failed to wear. With her suitcase plus the clothes she'd brought over earlier, it seemed like she was going to need drawer space here soon. She wondered if that would freak Barry out. Somehow, she didn't think so.

Before leaving, she kissed Barry gently on his sleeping eyes. He groaned and rolled over, exposing a length of neck, and she kissed him there too. She didn't nibble; she just kissed.

Then she was out the door and down the stairs and on her way.

He had been driving for hours, running on coffee and pain. His right arm, the good one, was sore from holding the wheel, and his right foot was roaring its disapproval of his overuse of it on the pedals. But he had finally tracked *it* down, and he had to go where *it* was, try to stop *it* one last time.

His rented piece-of-shit Ford was red like blood. It wasn't supposed to leave the state of North Carolina, but his quarry had fled north and he would pursue it. Because this was war, war between man and the inhuman *thing* that preyed on man, war between light and darkness; and he was the only soldier left. In war, the normal rules didn't apply. In war, you could kill, and you could die, and you could lose your wife and your friends and everything you ever cared about, and who gave a shit if you pissed off some cheap-ass rental car company?

On the seat beside him, stained with spilled coffee and the remains of a jelly doughnut, was a crumpled copy of a newspaper; on the front page, with a grainy black-and-white photograph of a pale body with the dark brand of a cross seared into its face, was a screaming headline: *Ritual Slaughter in New York.*

Ken Fletcher yawned, and the road blurred briefly in his vision. He would have to find a motel soon, and get a bit of sleep, or he would begin nodding off at the wheel and wreck the car. Then who would be left to stop the beast? He blinked away his sleepiness and squinted at the road signs as they came into view. One advertised a motel called The Pennsylvania Pilgrim; being a bit of a pilgrim himself, a wanderer, a stranger, he would stop there, and endure a few hours in the vast charnel house of his dreams. In the afternoon he would resume his journey north, to New York.

And then, one way or another, there would be an end to it.

3:05 PM

Roxanne knew the cops up north had let the Sloanes off with a warning, so there was no reason for Ryan not to be at work; but she wasn't. She didn't answer her phone at home, either, and her answering machine didn't pick up. They didn't have a cell phone; Ryan thought they were a fad that wouldn't catch on, and Irving didn't trust them, believing them to be a way for the government to keep track of people's whereabouts.

The unexplained absence worried Roxanne, but for a different reason than her co-workers. They suspected an upcoming wave of layoffs; she had visions of Ryan and Irving lying pale and bloodless in their bed, on the floor, in the back yard. Finally it had become too much for her, and on her two o'clock break she had called Barry, waking him out of a nap, and asked him to check on them. He agreed; she gave him the address, and afterwards she felt better.

Then she got The Claim.

It was a bill from a psychologist who was treating a little boy with bad dreams. As usual, copies of the doctor's notes were attached, and they caught her eye. *The patient manifests increasing anxiety as dusk approaches*, they said. *He checks and rechecks his window to ensure that it is locked. During REM sleep he evidences extreme agitation and often awakens screaming, but cannot remember his dreams.* They went on to describe the treatment he had received, but Roxanne didn't read further. She slowly lowered the paper and stared unseeingly at the computer screen.

Bad dreams. Afraid of the dark. Checking his window.

This little boy *knew*.

Not necessarily. Lots of kids were afraid of the dark. She looked at the notes again, scanning them for something else, some more evidence that the boy, Jeff Tracey, was afraid of something specific. Something with fangs. Something deadly. Something with eyes green as emeralds, bright as fire.

She found it.

Possible delayed reaction to his father's death in an auto accident, exacerbated by the murder of his friend Ronald Dinkins [see attached news clipping].

She saw the attached newspaper clipping. Ronald Dinkins was the boy who had been found mutilated by the canal, his head cut off, his heart removed. You could kill a vampire that way, right? Cut off its head, cut out its heart? So it stood to reason—insofar as *reason* applied to anything anymore—that the same things would prevent a vampire from rising in the first place. If, for instance, you didn't want your victim coming back as one of the undead.

Ronald Dinkins had been killed by a vampire; and, at some level, Jeff Tracey knew it.

What was in his dreams?

Barry had said he knew a hypnotist who did work for the police; she would find a way to bring this boy and the hypnotist together. She scribbled down the patient's address and phone number on a piece of paper, and the doctor's name and number as well. Making sure no one was nearby, she folded the paper into a tiny square and tucked it into her purse. Then, because Ryan wasn't there to approve her going home early, she just got up and left.

If she were caught taking patient information out of the office, she would certainly get fired; but if she didn't follow up on this ... well, the consequences were likely to go far beyond her job, weren't they?

Roxanne knew something was strange as soon as she pulled into her driveway. She couldn't place it exactly, but a sense of wrongness clung to her house like a bad smell. She parked her car under the awning, got out, went around to the front door, and suddenly stopped. Retreating to the end of the driveway, she took a close look at her house.

The dome of her skylight was missing. It stuck up several feet, and she could see it from the driveway; but today it wasn't there, and its absence had registered on her subconscious before she had actually realized it was missing. Unsure of what this meant, she hurried back up the drive and on into the house, opening the front door a crack and peering around the interior.

Fist-sized holes had been punched all around the living room, in the walls, in the ceiling, in the hardwood floors. The stuffing had been pulled out of her sofa and its pillows and scattered around like feathers at a cockfight. The marble column in the corner had been smashed, the fish bowl nowhere to be seen.

And where was her dog?

"Bernice?" she called. There was no answering yip, no scurry of puppy feet on tile or carpet.

Roxanne backed off from the door, hesitating on the step. No way was this simple burglary. She looked at the sky. The sun was still fairly high; with the big windows throughout her house, she should be safe enough, for a while. She couldn't think of any pockets of shadow where *he* could hide, except in the basement, so she certainly wouldn't be going down there. She was lucky she hadn't come home to this in the dark.

She flung the front door wide, took a step into the living room. No shrieking ghouls descended upon her. Walking carefully through the wreckage of her life, she headed into the kitchen, from which a grotesque stench of burned flesh and roasted hair emanated. The smell made her want to retch, but she fought it down and instead followed it to its source: Her oven.

Oh, God.

She grasped the handle that would open the stove's door, but she didn't pull it. She knew what was in there; did she really want to see it?

No. Roxanne turned away from the stove and went back to the living room, over to the phone. It had not been touched. She saw that there were three messages flashing on the machine; she had the feeling one of them would be from her unwanted suitor. She drew several gulps of breath, and then pushed the button. The tape rewound, and then the messages began to play.

Beep! "Hi, Roxanne, it's Chris. Sorry I missed you." She frowned; his voice sounded strange, deep and throaty, not at all like him. Perhaps he had a cold. "I thought maybe we could get together soon. We'll talk more later." Pause. "Count on it."

Beep! Barry's voice: "Annie, I went out to Ryan's and Irving's and they're not there. The place is deserted. I think maybe they left town. I suppose under the circumstances that's a sensible thing to do, but ... well, I'll call you later. Bye."

Beep! "Hello, is this Roxanne Carmichael? My name is Ken Fletcher. If you're monitoring, please pick up. This is very important." Pause. "Okay, you're not monitoring. Call me as soon as you get in. I'm staying at the Sleepytime Motel, in room 112. This is *urgent*, Ms. Carmichael. Call me. Room 112." He gave a number, which she didn't write down.

Who the hell was Ken Fletcher? Whoever he was, he'd have to wait. Her first call was to the cops. She got them on the third ring, gave them her name and address, and told them about her living room and her kitchen. They said, "Did you say you were Roxanne Carmichael?"

"Yes," she said.

"Barry's friend?"

"Yes."

"We'll send someone right over. Stay where you are. Don't explore the house until the officer arrives. In fact I would suggest returning to your vehicle and locking all the doors."

"Okay," she said, and hung up.

Her next call was to Barry, but he wasn't home. She tried his cell phone but he didn't answer that either, and when she tried to leave voice mail, it told her his mailbox wasn't initialized, so she hung up. "Join the twentieth century, Barry," she told the uncooperative receiver.

She wasn't about to call Christian back, so the next order of business was this Ken Fletcher person. He had certainly sounded serious when he told her his business was urgent. She wondered what it was about. Maybe he wanted to sell her aluminum siding.

Oh, what the hell. What could he do to her over the phone? She played the message again, wrote down the number this time, dialed it, and asked for room 112. A bored voice told her to wait a minute, and after a few clicks the phone began ringing again. One ring, two, three; she was about to hang up when a hoarse voice said: "Hello?"

"Hello. This is Roxanne Carmichael. Who are you and what do you want?"

"Ms. Carmichael." It sounded like he was dragging himself out of a deep sleep, even though it wasn't even four o'clock yet. "Yes. You got my message?"

"I did. How did you get my number? Why are you calling me?"

"I got your name from the newspaper. I got your number from the phone book."

"My name was in the paper?"

"No. But some people at the paper knew you were involved in what happened up in the mountains. They—"

"I was told our names would be kept out of it."

"You can get information if you ask the right questions of the right people. It's called social engineering. Will you talk to me about what you saw that night?"

"Why don't you call the police and ask them?"

"The police aren't talking, certainly not to the likes of me. *Please*, Ms. Carmichael. I've tried everyone else who was there and you're the only one to call me back."

She frowned at the phone. He had a Southern accent, not strong, but definitely noticeable. A transplant from Dixie? Usually Northerners went down there, not the other way around, especially in the dead of winter. "Are you a reporter or something?"

He laughed, the sound eighty percent bitter, twenty percent demented, and zero percent amused. "No, my interest in this is not journalistic in nature. You might find this hard to believe, but you may be in some danger, Ms. Carmichael."

Now it was her turn to laugh. "I *may* be in danger?" she said. "Thanks for the news flash. What would *you* know about it, Mr. Fletcher?"

For a moment, all she heard was his breathing, coming down the line from the Sleepytime Motel; then he said: "I know its name. I know where it came from."

She took the phone away from her mouth and looked at it, as if that would give her some information about this mysterious voice that claimed to know things. Then, bringing it back to her mouth: "What?"

"This may sound crazy, but hear me out—"

"Don't bother with the *it sounds crazy but it's true* speech. You said you knew his name. What is it?"

There was a very long pause, and then Fletcher said: "Martel."

So. The monster had a name. "Martel," she said, trying it out, seeing how it sounded. Like a winery, she thought, or a purveyor of flooring products.

There was another lengthy silence from Fletcher's side of the phone. "I'm getting the impression that you're more heavily involved in this than I suspected."

"You might say that." Outside her window, blue lights were flashing: The cavalry had arrived.

"I'd like to get together with you and the other witnesses," he said. "If we can—"

"I'm sorry, Mr. Fletcher. The police are here. My house was broken into while I was away and some ... some things were damaged. I'll call you back as soon as I can."

"But—"

"Wait for me to call," she said, and hung up just as the cop rang her doorbell.

Apparently somebody at the station had gotten hold of Barry, because he arrived while the other cop—Jerome Klein, an older officer with an expansive paunch and a receding hairline—was still surveying the living room. Upon entering, Barry's reaction was fundamentally similar to Officer Klein's; he looked around and said, "Jesus Christ."

"Hey, Barry," Jerome said.

"Hi Jerry. What hit this place?"

Officer Klein pointed at the remains of the marble column that had once supported Aristotle's bowl. "I think the perp used that as a battering ram, until it broke, anyway. Excuse me." He wandered into the kitchen. Once he was out of the room, Roxanne flung herself at Barry and crushed him in her arms.

"Oh, God. I'm so glad you're here."

Barry hugged her, then whispered: "*Him?*"

"I don't think so. This sort of thing would be ... beneath him."

"Why, because of what he said in my apartment? You can't believe anything he tells you."

"You didn't talk to him," she said. "He was so ... I don't know, so *urbane*. Like someone at a dinner party where everybody is more sophisticated than you are."

"A dinner party where *you're* the dinner."

She heard the oven door open, followed by a strangled expletive. A few seconds later, Officer Klein emerged from the kitchen. "This is one sick fuck," he said. "Who would do that to a dog?"

"What happened to the dog?" Barry said.

"Whoever it was baked Bernice," she said, looking at the floor. When she looked up, her eyes were bright and hard, her cheeks flushed with anger. "I'm so sick of this, Barry. I'm sick of it!"

"We need to check the rest of the house," Officer Klein said. "I'll take the upstairs. Barry, can you do the basement?"

"I'm on it. Annie, you stay here."

She nodded, and mouthed: *Be careful.*

As Barry headed for the kitchen, Officer Klein went down the hall toward the bedrooms. He paused at the bathroom door, looking at the ceiling inside. "Looks like they came in through your skylight," he said.

At the basement door, Barry paused, his hand on the knob. His gaze met Roxanne's. "That's impossible," he said.

"Well, it's here on the floor, and I don't see any other signs of forced entry. Looks like they pried it off with a crowbar or something; the flashing and nails are still attached."

"Check the master bedroom," Barry said, coming back into the living room. "It has French doors. He might've gotten in that way."

"French doors, really," Officer Klein said. "You talk like a man who's seen this part of the house before."

Roxanne felt herself blush, then realized that Barry, too, was flushing crimson from his neck to the roots of his hair. For some reason, that made her feel a little better. Listening to the floorboards creak under Officer Klein's feet, she crossed the room to where Barry stood. "Listen," she whispered, "I got a phone call today from a guy named Ken Fletcher. He says he has something vitally important to talk to us about. He claims to be familiar with … with our friend. Says his name is Martel."

"Really." He sounded skeptical; he was probably used to hearing from all kinds of crackpots. "How'd he come by this familiarity?"

"No idea. I only talked to him for a few minutes. He wants to get together to discuss it."

"I don't think I like that idea. It could be a trap."

Officer Klein's voice drifted from the bedroom: "Miss Carmichael, I need you to come here and see something."

Barry and Roxanne exchanged a glance, then walked down to her bedroom. It proved undamaged and mostly untouched, the French doors intact; but on the bed, someone had arranged two anatomically correct inflatable dolls, one male and one female, fucking in the doggy-style position. A bright red stringy-haired clown wig hung down from the woman's head, but they were otherwise unadorned. She stared at the red wig and fingered her own coppery locks. "Chris," she said, stunned.

"Chris?" Officer Klein was taking notes.

"You think *Chris* did this?" Barry said.

"Can I have this gentleman's full name?"

"Chri—Christian Keems."

"How do you know him?"

"He was my boyfriend. We broke up recently, after he …" She trailed off, glanced sidelong at Barry. "After he hit me." The look she got back from him suggested they would be discussing this later. "Oh, God, I don't believe it. There's a message from him on my machine."

"I'd like to hear this message."

"Okay. Okay." Still twirling her hair around her finger, she turned and led them back to the living room. Her mind seemed to be on autopilot, and the autopilot was broken. Chris had done this, not a vampire. She imagined him up on the roof in the snow, working the skylight loose, dropping into the bathroom *Mission: Impossible* style, proceeding to trash the place before letting himself out the front door. The weird thing was, she actually felt relieved. She didn't need crosses and stakes and Ken Fletcher to deal with Chris; he could be arrested, put on trial, sent to prison.

She went to the machine and pressed the button. Chris's message played, and then she pressed the button again, stopping the tape.

"Interesting," Officer Klein said. "I'd appreciate this gentleman's address and phone number."

She gave it to him.

"I'd also like to take the tape."

"Okay," she said, popping it out and handing it over. "There's personal stuff on there too. Personal messages."

"Don't worry, you can trust me," Officer Klein said. "I'm with the police. This is the only message from your … friend?"

She nodded, feeling her curls bounce. The sex doll's red wig was curly too. Chris had always liked to do it doggy-style. "The others are from Barry and a … a reporter, I guess, who wanted to talk about the murders in the Adirondacks."

"Noted. Barry, are you done checking the cellar?"

"Um, that would be negatory."

"Let's go have a look, then, shall we?"

"Okay. The door is in the kitchen."

"Again with knowing the layout," Officer Klein said, giving Barry a wink and a clap on the shoulder. "Lead the way."

She drifted to the edge of the kitchen, but didn't go in, as their footsteps clumped down the stairs into the basement. Maybe Barry was right, and nobody was down there, just an empty cellar, boxes and old furniture and dirty laundry.

She could hear them moving around down there, their murmuring voices, though she couldn't make out any words. Officer Klein was probably giving Barry the business, teasing him about her; or maybe he was getting information about Chris. Or maybe they were discussing the weather.

Had someone said her name? She moved a little closer to the cellar door.

Suddenly she heard Officer Klein's voice, a barked order to freeze, a grunt, an abbreviated scream, a horrible wet tearing noise. Barry, shouting. Gunshots, one, two, three.

High, pealing laughter. A man, a woman. Giggling.

Suddenly she knew, with a sick cold feeling in her stomach, that she had only been half-right before; or rather, she had been right twice. Chris had done this, *and* a vampire had done this; Chris was one of *them* now, they had sought him out and taken him, probably because of his connection with her.

A heavy tread came pounding up the stairs. Oh, God, who was it? Chris? She retreated to a patch of weak sunlight, but the daylight was failing, how had it gotten so late? Where was the crucifix? Had she left it in the car?

Barry stumbled out of the cellar, into the kitchen, bloodied, long scratches on his cheek. Something like a big rock flew after him, slammed into the small of his back, sending him sprawling to the floor. The thing spun away, leaving crimson swirls across her white floor. Officer Klein's head.

Roxanne covered her hand with her mouth and stared at the head, making little choking noises deep in her throat. The head stared back, mouth open as if in shock; it hadn't come off cleanly, bits of muscle and gristle trailed after it like small, obscene tentacles, and the blood that remained in it was draining out onto the tile.

Barry staggered to his feet, half-bent, like a man with stones in both kidneys. She hurried to help him but he waved her back, back, stay in the light. He stumbled to the sink and rinsed the cuts on his cheek. The were shallow but ragged, nail scrapes, she thought, not a bite.

The cellar stairs creaked.

Someone was on them.

Wild-eyed now, Barry went back to the cellar door and slammed it shut. He grabbed a kitchen chair and wedged it under the knob, as if that would slow down one of those things; then, racing to her, he took her hand. "We are *leaving*," he said, pulling her out of the kitchen, half-dragging her across the living room.

Behind them, she heard the cellar door splinter. She chanced a look back as they ran out the front door, and saw a dark shape emerging into the kitchen, kicking pieces of wood out of the way; then they were in the driveway and she couldn't see into the house anymore. She hadn't gotten a view of his face, but she didn't need to. She knew who it was.

Twilight had arrived, was gathering strength. Already the snow was blue, and the stars burned coldly in the sky.

"Wait a minute," Barry said. He kicked the window of Jerome's prowl car, once, twice, three times, and then it broke. Reaching around the shattered glass, he opened the door from within and climbed inside.

Roxanne got into her car, unlocked the passenger side, started the engine. Barry emerged from the patrol car, carrying a shotgun in one hand and a box of shells in the other. He looked her way and his eyes grew wide.

She heard her passenger side door open. "Hey babe," Chris said. His face had a couple of bullet holes in it, black like cigarette burns, including a nice neat one right between the eyes that leaked dribbles of blood, war paint down both his cheeks. "Wanna come to a party?"

Barry leveled the shotgun but didn't fire, perhaps afraid he would hit her. Chris leaned into the car, reached for her, then saw the crucifix, which she had indeed left there, lying on the passenger seat.

His eyes widened and he pulled back. "You've never been fucked the way I'm going to fuck you," he hissed; then he was gone, vanishing among the trees, his legs taking inhumanly long strides. Even though he pumped his legs like a runner, he was flying, leaving no tracks behind.

The explosion of the shotgun shattered the air. A tree near Christian's head erupted in a shower of bark and wood. "Damn it," Barry said as he came up next to the Honda. The gun shook in his hands. "My aim is fucked. Get out of the car."

"What?"

"We'll take mine. It's a piece of shit but they know yours too well. Come on, Annie!"

She turned off the car and stumbled out of it, shoving her keys into her purse. He was already in his ancient Chevy, which refused to turn over the first time he tried it. It caught the second time and sputtered to life. She climbed inside, he slammed it into reverse, and then they were gone in a cloud of snow.

"Damn damn damn damn damn," Barry said, as they bounced along the snow-crusted road into town.

"What happened down there?"

He glanced at her. "There were two of them. Chris, and some woman wearing a shirt with all these cute little puppies on it. *Puppies.*"

Jesus, that sounded like her dog-sitter; Chris must have grabbed her when she came to check on Bernice. Her puppy had been upstairs in the oven, like a roast. Had Chris done that, or the dog-sitter?

"I only got away because it took the both of them to ... to rip ..." He trailed off. Roxanne could barely imagine what that must have been like, watching a couple of chortling vampires tear your friend apart as if he was some sort of New Year's party favor. "I wasn't expecting ... them. I wasn't expecting anything. Even when I saw Chris, I thought he was just, you know, an asshole. You should have told me sooner that he hit you. I saw him down there, all I could think was, *this dirtbag slapped Roxanne.* I wasn't paying enough attention."

"I'm sorry, Barry."

"Jerry has ... had ... a grown-up daughter in Binghamton. They don't talk much. And a niece, on the force. Her father, Jerry's brother, was on the force too. He was beaten to death on a domestic violence call nine years ago. Her mother killed herself a month later. Antifreeze in her tea." He drew a deep breath. "At least *they* do it because they're monsters. Alive, Chris was a creep, but ... monsters. Ha. So stupid, going down there with just guns. I didn't think—"

"Even if we knew Chris was ... It's not like Officer ... Jerry would've let you load him up with garlic and holy water."

"I think we could've handled one," he said, as if he hadn't even heard her. "Not two. She surprised us, hiding under the stairs. Chris was right there, sitting on your old couch, just hanging out. We even talked to him for a minute before she jumped us."

"And if I had come home after dark, they would've been upstairs waiting for me." What nasty delights had Chris dreamed up for her? "Jerry saved me." She put her hand on his shoulder. "*You* saved me."

"We can't take anything for granted anymore," Barry said. "We have to assume anyone could be one of ... them." His fingers worked on the wheel, clenching, unclenching. "I shot Chris in the face three times. He was a person, a couple days ago. Where are we going?"

"The Sleepytime Motel."

"Why?"

"Ken Fletcher is there."

He glanced at her. "You're still hoping for Van Helsing."

"Yeah, I guess I am."

"He could be one of *them*."

"He called me in the daytime."

"They can't dial a phone in the daytime?"

"We should at least find out." She put her hand on his knee and squeezed it tight. "We have to get help from *somebody*. We can't go on like this. We keep losing friends, and there's more of *them* every night."

"Yeah," Barry said. "Every night. Okay, we'll give this Fletcher guy a chance. But if he kills us, I'll be forced to say I told you so."

"I'll take that risk," she said.

"Room 116," the little man behind the desk said. He was about five feet tall, with huge round spectacles that made his eyes enormous. It was disconcertingly similar to talking to a pair of magnifying glasses.

Barry noticed the little man's gaze flicking to the raw scrapes on his cheek, but no words were exchanged on the matter. It was that sort of place.

The motel consisted of one long building, rooms on each side, with a frost-heaved sidewalk onto which the doors opened. Barry asked for and got a room around back; he didn't want his vehicle to be visible from the road. The vampires probably wouldn't be looking for his car yet, but his fellow police officers might be. He hadn't quite figured out what to do about that.

The exterior of the motel was studded with feeble yellow lights, barely enough to illuminate the sidewalk; darkness took hold from the parking lot to the black pines that surrounded the building. They walked quickly from the car to the room, with every step fearing a cold hand on their shoulders, feeling eyes crawling over them, as if the night itself were sizing them up for tenderness and flavor.

Barry unlocked the door that said *116* and they ducked inside like Arctic explorers returning to warmth after a week on the ice. Barry shut the door, leaned against it, set the chain, turned the bolt. "There," he said, deadpan. "That'll keep them out."

Roxanne sank onto the bed, fingers to her temples.

"Are you all right?"

"I've got such a headache."

Alarmed, Barry said: "Any of the other symptoms from that sheet? Nausea, anything?"

"No, no, I'm fine," she said. "Just stress."

"Stress. Yeah, plenty of that to go around." Barry lifted a corner of the curtain and peeked outside. "I could go get you something. Advil, Tylenol, aspirin?"

"You're not going anywhere." She rummaged in her purse. "Maybe I have something."

Barry sat down next to her, peering into the chaos that was the interior of her handbag. "Found it," she said, lifting out a little white pill bottle. She stood, patted Barry's shoulder, and headed into the bathroom.

Barry sprawled out on the bed and looked at the popcorn ceiling. Cracked, dirty, water-stained in more than one spot, it was the sort of ceiling under which you might expect to find a dead junkie, a meth lab, a low-class prostitution ring.

"Why don't you call Fletcher?" Roxanne said. "Room 112."

Barry thought: Help me, Obi-Wan Kenobi; you're my only hope. But still, he rolled over, picked up the phone, and dialed the number.

In answer to a soft knock at the door, Barry peered through the peephole. Outside, a man stood several paces back, far enough away from the door to give Barry a good look. Although he appeared to be almost six feet tall he was rather narrow, his posture slightly stooped. His left arm hung a little strangely, the hand at its end clutching a little paper bag.

Leaving the chain on—as if that would help—Barry opened the door a crack. "Don Mitchell?"

"No," the man said. "Sorry, is this the wrong room?"

"Not if you're Ken Fletcher."

"I am."

Barry looked at Roxanne, nodded, slid off the chain, and opened the door. Ken had his hand in the bag, and before Barry uttered a word the man pulled out a little ball and tossed it to him. Startled, Barry snatched it out of the air. A garlic clove, peeled and notched to let out the smell. He held it up to his nose and inhaled deeply.

"Okay," Ken said, entering. "Now her."

"Heads up," Barry said, tossing the clove to Roxanne. She caught it with one hand, held it a second, then dropped it. Barry closed the door. Ken stayed near the window, giving Roxanne a narrow look that didn't change much when she reached under the pillow and pulled out the shotgun they'd taken from Jerome's car. "Have a seat," Barry said.

He settled into the threadbare chair next to the window. Keeping his gaze on Roxanne, he fished another clove out of the bag and began absently playing with it, rolling it around in his palm. There was a long silence. Finally he held the garlic up between his thumb and forefinger and said: "You don't like this stuff much."

"I used to."

"How many bites?"

She grimaced. "I don't really know. Does it matter?"

"Not really," Ken said. "As long as you're still alive when we kill Martel, you'll recover." He frowned. "At least, I *think* you'll recover. It's something one of them said, once. We never actually tested the hypothesis."

"That's not very reassuring."

"Sorry. Careful that thing doesn't go off by accident"

"If it goes off," she told him, "it won't be an accident."

"Fair enough." He yawned. "Okay, I reckon that's enough tough talk for one evening. So. It wasn't news when I told you about the creature, was it?"

"No," Barry said.

"I've seen this pattern before. The incident is centered on you, Miss Carmichael. Martel has bitten you and left you alive. To him, you're a game animal. He gets off on the thrill of the chase." Ken squeezed the garlic clove, then took a bite out of the end and swallowed it. "He's having a bit of fun with you."

"Fun? He thinks this is fun?"

"Well," Ken said, "it's not supposed to be fun for *you*."

"What can you tell us about this guy? You said his name was Martel? What kind of name is that?"

"He adopted it somewhere along the line. It's not his real name. I think he borrowed it from Martel of Anjou, or possibly Charles Martel, the Hammer."

Roxanne said: "Who's that, a wrestler?"

Ken stared at her for a moment. "No. He was an eighth century king. Martel is hundreds and hundreds of years old, Miss Carmichael; I doubt he even knows professional wrestling exists."

"Okay, fine, it's a made-up name," Barry said. "It says nothing about him, so it's useless to us. What about these vampires? What's the easiest way to kill them?"

"Well, first off, they're not vampires the way you probably think of them. We're not dealing with Dracula. No bats, no spooky castles, no coffins filled with dirt from the motherland. I don't think I've ever even heard the word *vampire* spoken by one of them. They seem to think the whole stereotype is pretty quaint, actually."

"I'm not interested in how they think," Barry said, "I just want to kill them. Can you help us or not? How'd you get involved? What's your story?"

Ken sighed. "This is going to take a while."

"We're not going anywhere until dawn."

"Prudent." He drew a breath, held it, let it out. "Well, let's see.

I've been after Martel for about two years. No, three. God, has it been that long? Anyway, it started in Georgia with my friend, George Follett, and his daughter Elspeth. She disappeared one night on her way home from work. She'd just gotten her license, it was the first time she'd been able to drive alone at night. The police never found a trace of her, just her car, abandoned in a gas station parking lot. Then one day George thought he saw her at the local airport lounge, where he was waiting to catch a red-eye. He skipped his flight and followed her when she left with some guy she met there. They went to the airport motel. George waited outside for a few hours, until she came out again, alone this time.

"It was Elspeth, all right. He confronted her. At first she pretended not to know him; then she admitted who she was, but told him to get back in his car, drive away, and forget about her. Obviously he wasn't going to do that; understand, at this point, he's thinking she ran away from home. She finally got in the car, and promptly attacked him. George being a religious man, he had a rosary hanging off his rear-view mirror. Rosaries, as you may or may not know, have a cross on them. He used the cross to—"

"I tried to use a cross on Martel," Roxanne said. "It did squat. He just took it away from me."

"Mmm, yeah, that's a problem. My theory is that the effect of holy symbols is more psychological than anything else. It reminds them of what they believed when they were alive, what they're cut off from now. Guilt in overdrive. In some cases, the effect seems to be so strong that it can actually kill them. But not Martel. He just doesn't care about any of that.

"Anyway, using the rosary, George managed to drive Elspeth away. He came and told us about it—"

"Who's *us*? You and the mouse in your pocket?"

"Me and … my wife. Lauren."

Barry made a show of looking around the room. "I don't see a wife anywhere. Or a friend George, for that matter."

Ken didn't say anything; his lower jaw worked, the muscles tightening and loosening, as if he was trying to compose himself. "Martel took her," he said at last. "The last time we caught up with him, things didn't go so well."

Roxanne said: "Your wife … is she … blonde?"

"Yes."

"About my height?"

"Yes."

Barry said: "You've seen her?"

"She was at Brown Bear," Roxanne said. "I met her on the slopes. She crashed into me. We rode up the chair lift together, and then at the top she attacked me. She said she was going to turn me, so Martel would lose interest. Martel showed up and chased her away, but then he bit me himself." She massaged the two tiny marks on her neck. "I remember now."

"They fought?" Ken asked.

"Yes."

After a moment, he said: "Interesting."

"Do you have a picture of her?" Barry asked. "I'd like to know who we're dealing with."

Ken fished out his wallet and tossed it onto the bed. Barry took it and opened it, and there was a wedding picture of Ken and a pretty blonde woman. "That's her," Roxanne said, studying it. "How could I have forgotten? She acted like she was making a pass at me."

"You forgot because they wanted you to forget," Ken said.

Barry returned the wallet to Ken. "What happened to your arm?"

"You noticed that? Well, like I was saying, the last time we tangled with Martel was the last time *we* tangled with Martel. George died. Elspeth died. Lauren ... didn't die. Neither did I, even though I was supposed to."

"When Martel came to Roxanne's house, she tried to let him in. Why would she do that?"

"Because he wanted her to."

"Are you saying they can do mind control?"

"I wouldn't say that. It's not mind control, it's ... influence. Some people are more resistant than others, I reckon. Roxanne, here, is remembering things that they didn't want her to. That's a good sign."

"Yay me," Roxanne said, without enthusiasm.

"I've learned a lot about them over the years, some from books—the old legends have a few useful things to say—but mostly from personal experience. Learned it the hard way, like you did, that crosses don't do squat against Martel. You wanted me to separate the bullshit from the real stuff for you? Here goes. They *do* cast reflections; they *can* cross running water; they *don't* sleep in coffins; they *don't* turn into bats or wolves; they *can*, and do, come into your house without being invited."

"Yeah, we found that one out already," Roxanne said.

"Other things: They can't stand garlic; they can turn into something that looks like mist; they can fly; they're five times stronger than a regular human."

"Okay," Barry said, "but how do we *kill* them?"

"Burn them. Cut off their heads. Put a stake through their hearts. Blow them to pieces. Drag them into the sunlight."

"Anything else?"

"Those are the only ways that have ever worked for me."

"How many have you killed?" Barry asked.

"Seven," he said, "including Elspeth. All of them Martel's by-blows. Towards the end, I think, he was making them just to string us along, keep us going, until he got us where he wanted us. Another thing: They're not all the same. Some of them can't turn into mist, or can't fly, or have more tolerance for sunlight. Some are more proficient than others. It's not just how old they are; it seems to depend on the person they were, before. Hell, for all I know, somewhere out there, there really are vampires who turn into bats and don't cast reflections. But I haven't met them."

Barry said: "So all this stuff you're telling us … it could only apply to Martel's line, right?"

"I never thought about that, but it's an interesting idea."

"That thing in the Adirondacks. I don't think Martel did it."

"Yeah. Neither do I. I think it was my wife."

"Why?"

"Too showy. Martel knows his best asset is that people think things like him don't exist. He's got a free ride and he doesn't want to blow it. Also he subscribes to a sort of *more vampires, less blood* philosophy. But Lauren … she was an actress once. Theatrical. She was sort of in awe of Martel, always wondering why he didn't make himself an army and take over the world, that sort of thing." He rubbed his eyes with a clenched fist. "So that killing … it's just what she would do. A big splashy murder, drama for the papers. And it was also, I think, a way for her to throw off Martel's control. Therapeutic, in a way, doing something her Master would never dream of. See, the transformation … it *changes* you. I've seen it, what people become, once they cross that through that door. It's not just that you grow big fangs and start sucking blood; your personality twists, the darker side of your nature comes out." He fell silent, then added, "I reckon it'd have to."

"Ken," Roxanne said, "do you think your wife is planning to make an army of vampires?"

After a moment, Ken said: "Oh my God."

That night, while Martel was out hunting for her, Lauren introduced Krone to a variety of pleasures and positions.

Of them, he liked doggy-style the best.

11

7:15 AM

Roxanne and her home were famous.

There it was, right on the morning news: Video of the house, shot from the street, the place looming burned-out and smoldering in the background. Standing in front of it, wearing a brown parka to ward off the cold, a reporter held a microphone to his mouth while staring hard-eyed into the camera. Nearby, the flashing lights of police cars and fire trucks spun blue and red across the landscape, through the columns of steam and the drifting wisps of smoke, lighting up the scene with oddly festive colors.

She couldn't quite believe they had actually burned down her house; it seemed like such a petty, vindictive, *human* thing to do.

"Foul play is suspected in the disappearance of Roxanne Carmichael, a 27-year-old Mapledale woman whose house stood in a secluded spot in the woods," the reporter said, while a picture of Roxanne appeared in the upper right corner. It looked like her driver's license photo, which, of course, meant it didn't resemble her in the slightest.

"Foul play," she said, "is *suspected?*"

"They're hedging," Barry said. "They always hedge."

"A body believed to be that of a police officer who responded to a 911 call was found by firefighters inside the home; sources say the body was mutilated. Police refuse to speculate on whether or not this crime is related to the death last week of Ronald Dinkins, or to the

189

gruesome mass murder in the Adirondack park, or to the recent rash of disappearances and killings in the area. Police reports indicate that six people have vanished and three have been murdered in the last week; now the numbers are seven and four. Could it be the work of a serial killer? If so, it would be the area's first. Tom?"

The scene flipped back to the NewsChannel 3 studio, where anchorman Tom Bailey wore his eternal anchorman's smile, which never varied no matter the gravity of the story. "Thanks Brad. If you have any information about this or any other disappearance, the police would like to hear from you—"

Barry pressed the mute button and looked at Ken. "Six disappearances," he said, "and that doesn't even include what went on in Brown Bear. How often does a vampire have to eat?"

"Not *that* often."

"So what's going on?"

"For my money, some of them are actual disappearances, people who skipped for whatever reason. Of the murders, anybody who was shot or stabbed was shot or stabbed, but if the heads or hearts are gone, they were vampire food."

"So we have half a dozen people unaccounted for."

"Yep. And those are just the ones that've been reported."

"So, what, are they all vampires?"

"Lord," Ken said, "I certainly hope not. All this notoriety is going to make it tough for you to get around, Roxanne. Does this change our plans in any way?"

"No," Roxanne said. "No, we have to go ahead. We can't fight him until we find him, and I can't think of any other way to do it. We'll just have to be more careful."

"*You* need to stay out of sight, though," Barry said. "At least change your appearance. Cut your hair, dye it black."

"Cut my hair?" She fingered her curls. "Do you know how long it took me to grow this out?" Barry started to answer, but she held up her hand to stop him. "Kidding."

"What makes you think this boy knows more than you do?"

"I don't know. A feeling. We have to find them, or else we're just sitting here waiting to get picked off." She looked at Ken. "You're the big vampire hunter. What do you think? How did you used to find them?"

"Luck. Detective work. Sometimes we managed to track him to where he lived, but usually we just made things too hot for him and he moved on. We don't have that luxury now though. With my wife going around mowing people down, and you already bitten, we're running out of time fast. If you think this kid might have information, I say we try and get it."

"And if he doesn't?"

"We bait a trap."

"A trap?" Barry asked.

Ken nodded. "A trap."

"I take it I'm the bait?" Roxanne said.

"Afraid so."

"And if we find Martel, we'll find Lauren?"

"No. No, I don't think we will. That will require a separate effort. But we have zero to go on when it comes to her, so we might as well try to get Martel first."

"And if we can't?"

Ken shrugged. "Well, then, collect the insurance money on your house now, because property values in the area are going to start falling pretty rapidly."

9:30 AM

As he stood with the receiver to his ear listening to the phone ring, Barry prepared his best, most authoritarian Cop Voice. Usually he used it on children, but sometimes it worked on adults. He only got an answering machine, though, and the Cop Voice didn't impress those at all, so he hung up. "Nobody home," he told the others.

"Call the kid's school," Ken suggested.

"I don't know what school he's in."

"Try calling his doctor," Roxanne said. "The claim said he was going to continue his therapy on an outpatient basis."

"Worth a try," Ken said.

"Psychologists are very bad about sharing patient information," Barry said; but he dutifully picked up the phone and dialed the number. It rang once, and suddenly Roxanne grabbed the phone away from him.

"I'm an idiot," she said. "They might not share information with you, but they will with insurance companies."

"Of course," Barry said. "You guys pay them."

The phone rang, and rang, and rang, and then a harried voice came on. "Dr. Kinney's office, Scott Gerber speaking."

"Hello, Mr. Gerber," Roxanne said, in her most brisk, businesslike voice, sharp and bright as a razor blade. She knew immediately who she was dealing with: The doctor's graduate student assistant-cum-slave. "This is Ann Michaels, from the CNY Insurance Company. We insure one of Dr. Kinney's patients, a Jeff Tracey. As part of our efforts to control expenses, we are encouraging our members to seek out lower-cost alternative therapies. Tell me, Mr. Gerber, has Dr. Kinney recommended hypnosis for Jeff?"

"Well, I don't really—"

"We attempted to contact the Traceys at their home but were unsuccessful," Roxanne said. "Is Jeff seeing Dr. Kinney now?"

"I can't tell you—"

"Based on Dr. Kinney's diagnosis and the transcripts of his sessions, we believe Jeff would potentially benefit from hypnosis therapy. Is there a hypnotherapist on staff at your facility?"

"Yes, but—"

"Excellent. I'm glad to see you're open to alternative therapies." She winked at Barry, who was goggling at her. "Mr. Gerber, as a condition of future payment on Jeff's account, we would like him to undergo at least one session with your hypnotherapist. As a quality-control measure, we will be sending someone down to sit in on the session and, of course, we'll require a tape or transcript of the treatment."

"Wait, wait, you're sending someone over *today*?"

"Not necessarily. Of course, payment for Jeff's therapy will be held pending completion of this hypnosis session, so the sooner it's done, the sooner we can release the assignment to the provider. Can you schedule Jeff today, or is there a problem?"

"No, no, um, we can probably squeeze him in today," Scott said, sounding rather dazed. "I'll talk to Dr. Kinney about it and—"

"Excellent. We'll send our observer right over. He's a police officer who does some investigative work for us part-time."

"Police ... investigative ... listen, we don't—"

"Don't worry, Mr. Gerber, we aren't alleging any sort of fraud, waste, or abuse. This is strictly routine."

There was a long pause, and then Scott said: "Um, okay, I think we can get this done. Where can I reach you if we need to reschedule?"

Roxanne read the number off the dial, changing the last number, then said, "Extension 116."

"Okay." Scott didn't repeat it back to her. "Goodbye."

"You have a nice day, Mr. Gerber," she said, hanging up. Giving Ken her sweetest smile, she said: "Social engineering."

"That was some of the fastest-flowing bullshit I've heard in a long time," Barry said, "and I've heard a lot."

"I learned to talk like that by listening to Ryan badger doctors on the phone. If she were here, she would've had them reading the kid's entire chart to her by now."

"And isn't *that* a scary thought," Barry said.

"Whoever has the gold, makes the rules," Roxanne said.

Barry had gone to Kinney's office for the hypnosis session; Ken had gone to a nearby fast food joint to get something for them to eat. Lying on the bed, looking around the empty room, it came to Roxanne just how *alone* she really was. To the others this was a fight, sure, a tough one, but to her, the one who had been bitten, it was a matter of life and … and what?

She remembered Martel's long white fingers wrapping around the crosspiece of the crucifix, and she thought: God is dead. If there were demons (and vampires were, she thought, nothing more or less than a particularly *human* variety of demon), what else might there be? The dark places of the earth could be crawling with horrors, invulnerable to entreaties to mercy, to reason, to religion. She crawled under the covers, knotted them in her hands, and sobbed into her pillow. She thought of her little dog, of her parents in the cold earth, of Ryan and Irving. Were they dead? Alive? In between? She thought of Ken and his lost wife, of George Follett and his lost daughter, of Jerome Klein's head hitting Barry in the back, of Chris with thick dark blood oozing from neat little holes in his head.

She wasn't sure how long she'd kept her face buried in the pillow; the rough fabric had grown hot and wet against her cheeks when there was a knock at the door. She sat up, her eyes red and swollen;

but it was daylight, she should be safe. She went and looked through the peephole and saw that it was only the maid, moving from room to room like a beetle scuttling from one piece of bark to another, pushing one of those massive multi-functional carts typical of the profession, a cart big enough for … for a vampire to sleep in, sheltered from the sun by canvas and towels. Roxanne opened the door a crack and said, "Not right now, thanks." Then she closed it again and leaned up against it, her head on the cold painted wood, trying to pull herself together. Sobbing and moping wouldn't bring back any of the dead or help them stop Martel and Lauren. After a few minutes, she opened the door. Cold air stung her face and nose. She hung the *Do Not Disturb* sign from the knob, closed the door, and collapsed onto the bed again.

She was still there when Ken returned bearing two fast-food bags. He paused upon entering, looking at Roxanne; then he put the bags on the table, went to the bed, and sat down next to her. "You okay?" he said.

"Do I *look* okay?"

"In my experience, there's no correct answer when a woman asks that question," he said. He put his hand on her shoulder. "Listen, I know it's tough. Believe me, I know. It changes everything. Once you know they're out there, you see them everywhere. You pass a big sewer pipe and say, I wonder if one of them is hiding in there. You see an abandoned building and think, a whole mess of them could live in there and no one would even know. And then you start to wonder, if these things exist, what else might be running around? Werewolves? Zombies? Ghosts? The night takes on a whole new character. You start to think that it was primitive man, who stoked up his fire and hid in his cave, who knew what he was doing. Not us. We think we've conquered the night, with our electric lights and our technology, but it's just a conceit. But remember, if there are devils, then there must be gods."

"How can you believe that, when Martel just threw my crucifix away?"

"I have to believe it." He took her hand and squeezed. "You probably feel like you'll never be safe again, but consider this: Whether you know it or not, they're out there. And it's better, I think, to know it. Forewarned is forearmed, right?"

"Forearmed? I feel so helpless. They're so powerful, and we're so weak."

"No," Ken said. "No, we're not weak. *They're* weak. They can't stand out in the sun. They can't dip their foot in a stream. They can't eat a nice Italian dinner." She smiled at that, knowing it was exactly the reaction he'd intended. "Their powers come with a big ticket. We can beat them. We have to be smarter than them, slicker than them. Stronger. We can do it."

"How can you be so sure?"

He stood up. "I have to be. So do you. If you're not, you can't go on." He went to the table and fished a couple of wrapped burgers out of the bag. He tossed one to her; she caught it and looked at it. Even unwrapping a cheeseburger seemed like too much right now.

"This morning you were ready to take them all on," Ken said. "What happened?"

"I don't know," she said. "I guess I just realized exactly what we're up against. It makes me want to run and hide."

"Do you want to run? I mean, *really* want to run?" He was working at the greasy paper as if it were Christmas wrapping. "Because if you do, go. You can't face them if what you really want to do is run." He took a bite of burger, then said: "But I don't think you do."

"Didn't your mother ever tell you not to talk with your mouth full?"

"My mother told me lots of things," he said. "Listen, this is as much a psychological battle as it is a physical one, maybe even more so. The weaker your resolve, the easier it is for him to grab your will and twist it to suit himself."

"Is that what happened to Lauren?" Then, seeing his expression: "I'm sorry. I shouldn't have asked that."

"No, no. It's okay, it's a valid question. I don't know what happened to Lauren, how he got his hooks into her. Maybe he'd been slowly planting them all along; maybe she was just vulnerable that day, didn't get enough sleep, was starting to come down with the flu. I don't know." He looked at his burger as if it might be able to tell him the answer. "Doesn't matter. I'll kill him for it. And then I'll kill her."

He put down the burger, lifted the curtain, stared out the window at the sunlit lot, the sparkling snow. Roxanne watched his back, watched his neck muscles tighten and loosen, tighten and loosen. He was biting back an attack similar to the one she was having, she realized. He seemed like a good person, she thought; certainly he didn't deserve the hand he'd been dealt, any more than she did, or Lauren, or Christian, or even Martel. The thought surprised her, but it must be true. Martel had once been human. What had *he* lost, in the transition from man to monster?

Well, it was too late for any of them to cast back their cards, to walk away from the table. She felt her neck, felt the tiny bumps where Martel's teeth had once pierced her flesh. There was no way she could quit the game now.

He turned away from the window. "I finally understand what drove George. He was obsessed. Almost never talked about anything else." He sighed. "I guess I'm the same way now. I doubt I've said two sentences that don't concern them. But what else can I do, knowing they're out there—knowing *she's* out there? How can I go on with my life? How can I run away? Tell me how and I will. I should have done it when I had the chance, should have taken Lauren and just run. She almost begged me to, once, early on ... Martel warned us to back off, before he realized we were an actual threat ... should we have done it? We always thought it would end with us killing Martel, then going back to our lives, sharing a little secret that only we knew, but there's no happy ending here. The story isn't over until everyone's dead."

She stared at him. The tears he had been fighting had come anyway, rolling down his cheeks, reddening his eyes. Seeing him cry brought a fresh burst of tears from her, but they were different this time, born of anger, not of fear. However smooth his words, whatever his self-justification, whatever he once had been, Martel was a killer. Ultimately, he was responsible for everything that had happened; *he* was responsible for the murders, the disappearances, the deaths. All those deaths, including her own, looming dark before her. And she knew, with utter clarity, that even were she able to run, she wouldn't. She was one of the few who *believed*, and she was obligated as a *believer* to fight Martel and those like him with all her strength. "If not us, who?" she whispered.

"Yes," Ken said. "The Gipper had it right. Act we must and act we will, be it out of revenge or duty or self-preservation."

"So I'm self-preservation," she said.

"I reckon you are. I'm revenge."

"I guess that leaves duty for Barry."

Ken shrugged. "Or love," he said, and picked up his burger.

They ate a while in silence, Ken over at the table, Roxanne on the bed. Outside the wind gusted, whistling along the patio. Ken cocked his head, listening. "You folks get some seriously bad weather up this way."

"What, this? This is like spring. You haven't seen anything."

"Oh, I wouldn't say that."

"Ken, what did you do … before?"

He looked up. "Before what?"

"You know … before."

"Oh. Before." He smiled wanly. "Trying to get me to talk about something other than vampires?"

She nodded.

"I was a chemical engineer."

"Really? I have a friend who's a chemical engineer," Roxanne said, thinking of Abby. "She says she's a glorified plumber."

"I was into research, not applications," Ken said. "Mix and match chemicals and see what happens. For instance, I know how to make explosives with fertilizer and pool supplies."

"If you can do that, why didn't you just blow him up?"

"See? It all comes back to *them* in the end." He sighed. "We would never have been able to set enough charges. Ever since Oklahoma City, the authorities keep a close eye on large purchases of fertilizer. No, only a small bomb would be feasible, and if you valued your life, you'd never be able to plant it and get away and be sure it would do the job."

"I bet you're a good cook, at least."

"I'm a terrible cook. Unless I'm using a Bunsen burner."

"You can make bombs, but you can't cook food." Roxanne shook her head. "Typical male."

Ken grinned. "I wouldn't say that either."

Ken dozed in the chair by the window and Roxanne vegetated on the bed, looking at but not watching a daytime talk show, checking her watch every five minutes, wondering where Barry was. When he finally showed up, rapping at the door in a prearranged signal, she vaulted out of bed to let him in without even looking through the peephole.

"Barry!" she cried, hugging him tight, then bodily dragging him inside. "I was so worried!"

"I'm okay," he said. "Easy, easy. I'm okay."

"Why are you so *late*?"

"It's not even three-thirty."

"You know how time flies when you're having fun? Well, when you're holed up in a motel room, it slows way, way down."

"There were delays in getting Jeff to the hypnotist. That doctor of his, Kinney, gave me a lecture about forcing him to subject his patient to mystic mumbo-jumbo. I had to falsify about a dozen forms. I met your Mr. Gerber; he practically jumps out of his skin every time Kinney says *boo*. The man's a tyrant."

"So what did you find out?"

"Well, I heard some interesting shit," Barry said. "Let's wake Ken and then we'll talk."

Waking Ken proved difficult. He didn't respond to taps, pinches, or shakes. Finally Roxanne yelled, directly into his ear, "Wake up!"

That did the trick. He almost fell out of his chair.

"Now that we're all awake," Barry said, "here's what happened. A gentleman named John Kendrick put the kid under hypnosis and regressed him to the thing that triggered his dreams. It wasn't his father's death and it wasn't his friend's murder. It was something that happened to him in an old railroad tunnel up in the hills. Apparently, every once in a while he would go there to play. The last time he went, the tunnel was occupied."

"Martel," Ken said.

"And your wife," Barry said. "Kendrick had the kid retrace his steps. Seems that a few paces into the tunnel there's a wall of fog, and beyond that it's dark."

"A wall of fog," Ken said. "That's a new one."

"You learn something new every day. So anyway he went on in, and ran into a naked woman there. From the description she sounds like Lauren. She was going to bite him, Martel intervened, they argued, and Jeff slipped away. Martel caught him shy of the entrance and used some kind of hypnotic suggestion to make him forget."

"What did Kendrick say about this story?" Roxanne asked.

"Kendrick didn't do any analysis." Barry rattled a sheaf of paper. "They prepared a transcript for me. Gerber's girlfriend transcribed it while I waited. She types like seven thousand words a minute. While that was going on, Kinney basically said he knew the session would be a waste of time, asked if I wanted to explore Jeff's past lives, told me if I wanted a vampire story I should read *Dracula*, and had Gerber show me the door."

"Their greatest asset is their nonexistence," Ken said.

"Yeah," Barry said.

"So are we going to check out the tunnel?" Roxanne asked.

"Hell no," Barry said. "It's three-thirty. The sun'll be down in an hour. We'll go tomorrow, early, when we have lots of time."

Ken said: "Did the boy mention Krone?"

"Who's that?"

"Martel's guardian. I assume he's human; he can go out in the daylight, anyway. I've never seen him sleep. He's huge and weird, like a mutant weight-lifter. You can't miss him."

"Evidently the kid could."

"That sounds like the creep who was following me."

Ken said: "Oh?"

"Yeah. He was driving a big silver Lincoln. Followed me all the way here from Pennsylvania."

"That's Martel's car," Ken said.

"Well, whoever or whatever, the kid didn't mention any weight-lifting mutants. Just vampires."

"What day did this happen?" Roxanne asked.

"Tuesday. The twelfth."

Roxanne thought a minute. "That was the day Krone was following me. Remember? I told the police, and they called you and you came and drove me home. Remember?" She patted him on the knee.

"Yeah," he said, smiling at her. The two of them exchanged glances for a long moment, until Ken cleared his throat conspicuously.

"Uh, sorry," Barry said.

"Don't be sorry. It's nice. Did you say Krone was out and about in the car that day?"

"Yes."

"Well, that's just strange," Ken said. "Krone usually stays very close to Martel."

"Maybe Martel sent him on an errand."

"It's not like Martel needs to return videos or pick up dry cleaning," Ken said. "Well, hell. I don't know what it means, but it can't be good. Anyway, if you two want to be able to keep making goo-goo eyes in the future, we better get ourselves ready to shoot it out with Martel tomorrow.

"What do we need?"

"Wooden stakes, wooden mallets, more garlic, holy symbols from whatever religions we can find, gasoline, matches, and a gun for Krone. If he's taken to wandering around in the daytime he might not be there, but if he is he could kill all of us unless we have a large-caliber weapon to use against him."

Barry reached under the bed and pulled out the shotgun he'd taken from Jerome's car. "We already have a gun for Krone."

"Oh, right. So we do. That should take him down if you aim for his head." Ken stood and stretched. "I'm going to my room and get cleaned up, and then I'll go do some shopping if you point me in the right direction. Okay?"

"Okay," Barry said.

Ken exited. Barry stared at the door for a minute, then looked at the shotgun, then turned to Roxanne. "It *should* take him down?" he said. "If I aim for his *head?*"

Roxanne shrugged. "He was a really big guy," she said.

Ken returned from shopping not long after the sun went down. Barry had the television on, watching the news, the sound way down low so as not to wake Roxanne, who slept curled up in a ball beside him. No updates had been released yet on the hunt for the missing Miss Carmichael or the killers of Officer Klein, but the news wasn't over yet. Muting it, Barry joined Ken at the table, looking over the supplies he'd bought. A cross, a Star of David, a little figure of the Buddha, and a stylized sun medallion of the sun (purchased, Ken explained, in the hope that Martel might have been a sun worshiper) all went into the side pocket of a shiny new black valise. He loaded up the large middle compartment with a set of wooden stakes and three mallets, garlic in net-like bags, and a tall plastic bottle, certainly not approved by the fire marshal, containing what looked like gasoline.

"Damn," Barry said. "You look like you're going on the world's weirdest weekend getaway."

"Yeah," Ken said. "Why don't you test those?" He indicated three new metal flashlights. As Ken arranged everything in the case, Barry loaded the flashlights with batteries and clicked each one on, shining them at the ceiling, illuminating the water stains and the cracks. Next he picked up a large box of matches, the light-anywhere kind, wooden sticks with white-tipped red heads. He struck one against the wall and it flared into life. He blew it out and laid it in the ashtray on the table just as Ken closed up the valise.

"I guess we're all set," Barry said.

"Yep, I reckon we are. Ready as can be, anyway."

"Great," Barry said. "Then let's go kill us some vampires."

Upstairs after dinner, sitting on his bed, Jeff Tracey thought about his session with the hypnotist. Everything he had forgotten was clear now, bright and shiny, like one of his mother's crystal frogs polished to perfection. He could recall every word of that afternoon, every sound, every call of every bird that braved the New York winter. He remembered the sensation of the fog on his face, the tiny pulling he had felt passing through it, as if a thousand microscopic hands were grabbing at him; he remembered the smell of blood and corpses.

Jeff knew, in a vague sort of way, that there'd been a lot of disappearances lately, a lot of murders besides Ronald's; but until today, he hadn't known why.

Vampires. In New York. In the twentieth century.

Nobody believed him, of course; Dr. Kinney, the hypnotist, the guy from the insurance company. They all thought it was just a kid's crazy story. Afterwards, Kinney had spent an hour discussing it with him, trying to get him to see that it was all symbolism; the male vampire was his father, the female vampire was his mother, the fog was the barrier between childhood and adulthood, some shit like that. In the end he'd started playing along just to get the doctor to stop harping on it already.

It wasn't symbolism that had killed Ronald; it was vampires. But *he* was partly responsible for Ronald's death too. Hadn't he called his friend up and made merciless fun of him for running away from the ravine? And then hadn't Ronald sneaked out and gone back to the tunnel to prove he wasn't chicken? And then hadn't the vampires gotten him?

Yes, yes, and yes.

Screw symbolism. Jeff knew this was no fantasy. He knew that vampire had drunk Ronald's blood and then cut off his head to keep him from rising as one of the undead.

He knew something else, too.

His father's big wooden tent stakes were in a box in the basement.

10:45 PM

"You like this, Krone?"

Krone nodded his head and mumbled something incoherent. Currently she had him between her breasts, squeezing them together while she moved slowly up and down, up and down, and shudders wracked Krone's body.

"Yes, Krone, you like it. You like it *so* much. Don't you?"

He spurted up against her chin, confirming how much he liked it. She waited until he stopped; it took a while. When he had finished she crawled up and kissed him, her teeth brushing his cold lips. Unexpectedly, Krone enfolded her in his arms and squeezed; for a moment she thought he meant to crush her, but no, it was just a hug, tight, but gentle. This surprised her, and she faltered, but only for a second; then she said softly, "Don't you wish we could do this whenever we wanted?"

"Uh-huh," Krone said.

"We could," she said, "if you'd leave Martel."

Krone opened his eyes and looked at her, releasing her from his embrace. She caught his gaze with hers, showing him the slow, smoldering green fires that seethed in the depths of her eyes. "Leave ... the Master?" he said.

"Yes. Leave him and come to the marsh with me."

"But he would kill me," Krone whispered.

"I'll protect you," she said. "I have friends. They'll protect you too. Some of them are women. They'll do things for you, too. They'll do anything I tell them to."

"No," he said, closing his eyes, shaking his head. "I can't leave the Master."

"Why not? What does he give you? Come and guard our sleep, and I'll reward you in ways Martel never did, or could."

The big fool was still shaking his head back and forth. "I can't. I can't."

"I haven't been coming here just to have you turn me down," she said, letting her teeth sharpen. Krone couldn't be turned into one of her kind, but he could certainly be killed. "If you won't serve me, then you won't serve any—"

A powerful hand grabbed her long blonde hair, jerked her out of the car. Martel's snarling visage greeted her, his face twisted and demonic in a way she had never seen before, even in the years when she and the others had been his most persistent foes. His fangs had grown like the tusks of some wild and fearsome beast; his flesh no longer glowed pale, but instead looked dusky and swollen and mottled, eyes spitting fire, ears sharp and pointed. The knuckles of his long fingers had swollen with fluid, grown into knots, the skin of his hands taut over deformed bones ending in long sharp nails, reddish-black, the color of an old, crusted clot. Steam drizzled from the corners of his mouth. "Enough!" he roared. "Presumptuous child! You think you are mightier than Martel, eh? You think you can seduce away my guardian?"

"Yes," she said, and faded to mist in his grasp.

"I'm sorry, Master!" Krone cried, sobbing. Ignoring him, Martel tried to gather up the mist with his spidery fingers. It slipped through his grasp, thick and oily smoke all around, sliding away, reforming up against the ceiling of the tunnel, until it turned back into Lauren, clinging there upside-down like some sort of scuttling land crab.

"Bitch!" Martel sent his mind at her through the connection they shared, hoping to use the force of his will to submerge her own, return her to obedience. It didn't work; he found the way blocked, like a bricked-up tunnel. The conduit was still there, he could see the outline, but he could not make use of it.

Fine. She was lost to him; if he could not bend her to his will, then he would destroy her instead.

"I suppose you wonder how I got this strong," she said. "It's simple, but your silly *code* prevents you from doing it. I've created ten so far. Mine. My servants. My *soldiers*."

Martel let her babble. Keep talking, he thought; keep telling yourself how strong you are, how fearsome, and perhaps it will become true. He gathered his strength, charging himself up, readying an attack that would smash through her defenses, overwhelm her, obliterate what was left of her mind.

"Their strength is my strength. They drink the blood of the living, and I drink from them. They are my source."

This was so astonishing that he simply had to respond. "Others have tried that, Mrs. Fletcher. Eventually your pets will turn on you. They'll see you for the parasite you are, and rise up and destroy you."

"Not likely. *This is not our way*, you say. Ha! You're weak, Martel, because you're afraid to *use* your power. You are only concerned with survival, when you *should* be concerned with strength." Her expression hardened into something he recognized as hate. "You shouldn't have cast me aside, Martel. We could have ruled the world, you and I."

"Only fools think they can rule the world," he said, unleashing his attack, "and only maniacs want to."

She shrieked as the assault struck her; he saw her let go of the ceiling, turning in midair as she fell toward the old rail bed. Then the tunnel fell silent, except for Krone's quiet sobbing.

Martel swayed on his feet, and collapsed.

When Martel awoke, he found himself lying in the back seat of the car, Krone hovering just outside the door. "Master!" he said. "Are you okay? Master?"

"I am all right," Martel said. "Just ... weak. I need to rest. Where is ... the bitch's body? You must remove her head before she recovers."

"She left," Krone said.

"*What?*" Martel grabbed Krone's shoulder and pulled himself upright. He looked outside the car, looked all around, but she was not there; and, he saw, she had even had the strength to tear down his cocoon as she departed. Ruptured, it was already collapsing into ooze, joining the oily muck of the tunnel.

Martel collapsed back onto the seat. What had he done? What had he unleashed? His attack had worked, it had breached her defenses, he had felt it; why hadn't she fallen? "Krone," he said. "Oh, Krone, you have betrayed me. How long has she been coming to you?"

"Three days." Krone whimpered. "I'm sorry, Master."

"Three days." Martel shook his head. "I understand, Krone. She is lovely. And I had … forgotten the man you once were. Evidently she brought him out."

Silence.

"I had forgotten the man *I* was as well. It's so easy to forget, in the darkness, isn't it, Krone?"

"I don't understand, Master."

"I know you don't."

"You're not going to … to punish me?"

"No. You've served me well these many years. I thank you for that, although you had little choice in the matter."

"Master, why are you talking like this?" Krone licked his lips. "Are you afraid? Do you think she might … kill you?"

"Sleep, Krone," Martel said. "We'll be leaving before dawn."

12

WEDNESDAY, JANUARY 20

7:00 AM

The morning broke pale and cold, with a hard wind that whipped the snow into stinging curtains sweeping across the ground. The sun was up; it tried to pierce the freezing shroud of billowing ice, but from where Roxanne sat looking out the frost-encrusted window it was just a pale ghost, a round white spot surrounded by a gauzy halo.

"Nice morning, huh?" Barry said, appearing at her elbow. "Good day to go vampire hunting."

"You're kidding, right?" she said.

Not far away, Jeff Tracey sat on the edge of his bed, the radio on, playing a song he hated. He was waiting to hear the list of school closures, which he hoped would include his own. From the scene outside his window, he didn't think school was going to happen today.

The song ended. The deejay came on with the list of closures. His school wasn't on it.

Well, he would just have to cut, then.

Jeff jumped out of bed and headed for the shower. He had a vampire to kill, and he had to be home in time for dinner.

Ken's car rolled to a halt partway up the hill. The road continued on from here, curving off to the right through the barren trees. Obviously this street, if it could be called that, was somewhere near the bottom of the town's plowing priority; the space between the high, dirt-streaked snowbanks lay obscured beneath thick drifts of dry, hard powder, which provided plenty of ammunition for the wind that howled down the slope. Frozen pellets pinged and clattered off the doors and windows as the vehicle rocked and groaned in the gusts. To their left, the cutting opened up, decorated with a broken-down fence and unreadable red and white signs.

Roxanne tightened her scarf around her neck, glad that her ski coat had never made it home from Barry's apartment. "All things considered, I'd rather be sitting in front of a fire with a mug of cocoa and a good cop book," she said. "Or a good cop." She squeezed Barry's shoulder.

"What's that noise?" he asked.

"What noise?"

"Listen. Do you hear it?"

She listened, and she heard it.

Ken was humming *Amazing Grace*.

Jeff slogged up the road toward the tunnel. As far as his mother knew, he was walking to school as per usual; he'd just taken a few different turns once he was out of sight of home, cutting through backyards, stealing along behind snow-laden hedges, like a pilot shot down behind enemy lines.

His backpack was lighter than usual, with three stakes and the hammer from his father's toolbox inside it, rather then the usual assortment of schoolbooks. Around his neck, cold against his chest, was the crucifix from the wall in his mother's bedroom. He'd looped a length of yarn through the nail hook and turned it into a crude sort of pendant.

He braced himself against the wind. It gusted every now and again, pelting him with bits of ice, but he stayed warm in his coat and hood and ski mask. His heart raced ahead of the wind, adrenaline flooded him and made him tremble. He thought of Ronald and wondered who had bitten him, the man or the lady.

"I'll get them, Ronald," he muttered, as he pushed on, a small dark shape lost in the blowing snow. "I'll get them both."

Ken flicked on a flashlight and shined it down the ravine. It did nothing but illuminate the oncoming flakes of snow. "Ugh," he said.

"This isn't going to be helpful."

"Come on," Roxanne said, pushing forward. "Let's get this over with." Her neck tingled where Martel had bitten it; it was not an unpleasant feeling, but sensual, as might come from a lover's lips and tongue. She wanted to be rid of it, and of *him*. Barry caught up with her, passed her, and fell into step in front of her. Ken brought up the rear, lugging his valise full of vampire-killing crap. The wind shrieked past, intensified by the confines of the cutting; the crusty snow crunched underfoot. Roxanne's foot turned on the buried, icy surface of an old railroad tie and she slipped, going down on one knee. Barry helped her up and they continued on to the turn, rounded it. The wind lessened; it was coming down the face of the hill, and now they were turned at a cross-angle to it. The mouth of the tunnel loomed ahead of them, startlingly black and empty compared to the whiteness that framed it.

They advanced slowly now, wary of what they might find. Passing into the shadow of the tunnel felt like stepping into a mausoleum full of unquiet dead. This was it, Roxanne knew, no doubt at all anymore; this was where *he* had hidden these past several days. She could smell him on the air, could feel him in the invisible mouth that gnawed at her neck. She'd dreamed about this place, she remembered, and being here in real life was almost as unpleasant as it had been in the nightmare.

"There's no wall of fog," Ken said.

"Yeah," Roxanne said. Then, because Barry had gotten too far ahead, she hurried to catch up. Ken shuffled along behind.

They continued into the tunnel, moving their lights here and there, three spots of brilliance playing tag in the darkness. It didn't take long to find tire tracks in the frozen, churned mud. "Somebody had a big car here," Barry said, kneeling to examine the impressions.

"Martel drives an old Lincoln sedan," Ken said.

Barry stood up, brushed ice crystals off his knees. "How would you get a Lincoln in here?"

"Very carefully," Ken said.

There was a car parked on the road, just outside the fence.

Jeff looked it over carefully. It had North Carolina plates. A newspaper was open on the back seat, but someone had spilled coffee all over it and it was unreadable. Most of the back seat was, in fact, covered with papers and garbage, as if someone had been living there for some time; enough space had been cleared on one side for a person. A head of garlic was wedged between the seat and the back.

Garlic?

He tried the door. Unlocked. He reached in and took the garlic. Then he closed the door gently and turned to face the blowing snow. Apparently someone else was here on a vampire hunt. Maybe the bloodsucking freaks were already dead.

Or maybe they had gotten the vampire hunters instead.

He looked at the piece of garlic in his hand. He hadn't thought to bring any, but considered himself safe enough with the crucifix and the stakes. He'd seen a movie once where the vampire had told the hero he had to have faith for the cross to protect him; and Jeff was pretty sure he had faith. Was pretty sure good enough?

The piece of garlic was cold. He put it in his pocket. It wasn't stealing, because he was going in after the vampire hunters. They might need his help. And if not, he would give it back.

Turning to face the wind, he walked into the cutting.

"Face it," Roxanne said, leaning against the wall, her arms folded and cupped at the elbows. "He's gone."

"Why would he *leave*?" Ken said, as if it were a personal affront to him that there was no vampire here waiting to be staked.

"Maybe he found out we knew where he was."

"How? Who would've told him?"

"Maybe nobody needed to tell him," Roxanne said. "Maybe he just ... *knew*. Because I knew."

Ken raised an eyebrow. "Care to explain?"

"Maybe we're linked. Telepathically."

"They're not telepathic."

"How do you know? They obviously have *some* kind of mental powers."

"If they were reading minds, I think I would know about it."

"You keep saying their nonexistence is their greatest asset; well, maybe they have secrets even from you."

"No. There's another reason he left. Something not to do with us."

"Like … ?"

"Maybe he just found someplace better."

"Maybe Lauren drove him away," Barry said, even though he was only half-listening to their conversation. Most of his attention was going into scouring the tunnel, looking for a clue to what had happened, where Martel had gone. Now his flashlight beam fell on something dark sticking out of a powdery drift against the wall. He knelt down and brushed the snow away from the object. It was too regular to be a rock; in fact, it looked like plastic.

"Lauren drove him away … now that's an interesting idea," Ken said. "What are you digging at?"

"Not sure yet." Barry crouched down, brushed away the obscuring snow. It was a camera, frozen, emptied of film, crushed as if someone had stomped on it. He held it up and shined his flashlight on it, turning it over, looking at it from all angles. On the bottom, one of those label strips was stuck, red plastic with white embossed letters. He picked up the object, stood, shining his flashlight on it so they could see. "It belonged to the Dinkins boy."

A small voice said: "That's Ronald's camera."

"What were you *doing* up there, kid?" Mr. Fletcher asked. They were in the car, on their way back to civilization. The junk had been cleared (or at least swept onto the floor) to allow room for Jeff to sit in the back with the lady, Miss Carmichael.

"I was gonna kill the vampires."

"Not all by yourself you weren't," Mr. Fletcher said. "If they were there, they would have taken you apart. And that little cross wouldn't have done you much good either. The boss vampire doesn't believe in God."

Jeff looked at his crucifix, surprised. "That matters?"

"Yeah. That matters."

Jeff glanced at Miss Carmichael again, and looked away quickly when he caught her glancing back, only to steal another look. She smiled at him.

He said: "You have bite marks on your neck."

Her smile faded and she turned away.

"Are you going to turn into a vampire?"

The big man, Mr. Brennan—Jeff remembered him from the

hypnosis session; he was smart enough to realize that there were implications to his presence here, although he hadn't had time to think through them yet—leaned into the back seat. "Not if we get Martel in time," Mr. Brennan said.

"Who's Martel?"

Mr. Fletcher said, "He's the boss vampire."

"What's the lady vampire's name?"

"Her name's Lauren. She used to be my wife."

"Your ... wife?" Suddenly afraid that Mr. Fletcher might have found what she had done to him, and was angry about it, Jeff said: "I didn't know—"

"Don't think about either one of them too much," Mr. Fletcher said. "If you do, they might know, and come looking for you. You don't want that, do you?"

"No," Jeff said, even though a tiny part of him wasn't quite sure it was true; the lady vampire was so pretty. Then, looking out the window, he exclaimed: "Hey, this is my house!"

Mr. Fletcher stopped the car in front of the driveway. Twisting in his seat, he looked Jeff in the eyes. "Do yourself a favor, kid. Stay well out of this from now on."

"But—"

"No buts! I know you want revenge for your friend, but let us handle it. You don't know what you're getting into here. This eats up your whole life if you let it. You end up going from one town to the next, always looking for clues, always hunting. Maybe it seems like an adventure now, but it's not some ... some video game that you can just turn off or reboot. Eventually you realize it's just luck that's keeping you alive and you lose your nerve, or you get overconfident and make mistakes, like I did. Either way, in the end, you lose. Your luck runs out, you make the mistake that's fatal. You understand me?"

Jeff stared at him, offering nothing.

"Look. You're too young to throw your future away. I've been hunting Martel for three years. It's cost me my job, my home, my friends, my wife. You could say Martel took them, or you could say I gave them to him, and both would be true." He put his hand on Jeff's shoulder. "*Do you understand?*"

"Yes."

"Okay. Good. Go on, go home. Read a comic book. Watch a movie. Forget about Martel and Lauren and everything else. And—" Mr. Fletcher's expression softened. "Be careful."

"I will," Jeff said. Then he bounced out of the car and ran up the driveway, kicking up little clouds of snow as he went. They waited until he was inside—he paused to wave goodbye from his door, and they waved back—and then they drove off.

"Do you think he'll listen to you?" Barry asked as they left the waving kid behind.

"I hope to God he does, for his sake."

"So now what do we do now?" Roxanne rubbed her neck. The tingle had died away, and she was glad of that, at least; but she knew it would be back.

"We go with our only alternative: Lay a trap for Martel. We dangle Roxanne in front of his nose as bait. When he comes for her, we nail him."

"So, what, do we tie her to a helicopter and fly around town? How does this scheme of yours work?"

"Well, I haven't quite figured that part out yet."

"Martel isn't stupid, right? He knows if Roxanne had any sense she'd be hiding where he can't find her. Any trap we lay is going to look like exactly what it is."

"Don't underestimate Martel's ego."

"But—"

"Damn it, Barry! Would you rather let him escape again? When Roxanne dies, she goes to him, unless you're prepared to cut off her head or drive a stake through her heart. Are you?"

Barry looked at the floor.

"I didn't think so."

"I don't just dislike this idea," Barry muttered. "I *hate* it."

"Ken's right, Barry. There's nothing else we can do."

"Okay." Barry drew a deep breath and held it, letting it out in a sigh. "So what if it works? That leaves Lauren running around out there. What do we do about her?"

"I've been thinking about that," Ken said. "I think maybe we lay a different trap for her."

"Using who as bait?"

Ken said nothing.

"Not the kid?"

"No, of course not." Ken tapped himself on the leg. "Me."

The wind had died down somewhat when they got back to the motel, and the newly-blown snow glimmered in the sunlight. Ken excused himself to his room for a nap and, he said, to think; Barry and Roxanne went to their own room. Barry unlocked the door, stepped inside, and found himself facing the barrel of a gun. Behind the gun was a cop in blue, and behind that cop was another cop; and suddenly the parking lot was full of police cars, coming seemingly out of nowhere, sirens wailing.

Barry said: "Max?"

Max Ramirez lowered the gun. "The captain said you two would be together, but I didn't quite believe it," he said. "You got Miss Carmichael there? Bring her on in."

"Um." Barry stepped inside, trying and failing to think of a way to take control of the situation. Roxanne entered and looked, with wide eyes, at the two officers, then at Barry.

"Hello, Miss Carmichael," Max said. "We'd like you to come down to the station and answer a few questions."

1:00 PM

"Why'd you hide her at a motel?" Captain Lee Donovan sat behind his desk, feet on top of it, cigar steaming; the department's no-smoking policy ended at the door to his office. Barry sat opposite him, in the hard, uncomfortable chair reserved for people who were in trouble. At the moment, he found himself strongly identifying with a splotch of gum on the heel of the captain's left shoe. "Why didn't you bring her in? We would've kept her safe."

Barry stared at the end of the cigar, glowing red as Lee inhaled, fading again to black as it cooled. The small room was redolent of smoke; an ionizer at the corner of Lee's desk did nothing to cut the smell of tobacco. The captain blew a big puff of exhaust at Barry and said: "Sorry, does this bother you?"

"It's—"

"Like I care. Listen, do you know how much trouble you caused us? We're doing all kinds of analyses on the unknown tire tracks at

Roxanne's house and now we find out they're yours. We've got people looking all over the place for her and she was with you the whole time. So let me ask you again, why did you take her to a motel instead of bringing her in?"

"We had … things to do."

"*Things to do?*" Lee shouted. "This is a *murder investigation*, Officer Brennan! And not just that, it's a *cop* who's been murdered! A cop who if memory serves was a *friend* of yours! *What* the *hell* could be more important than *that?*" Then he raised his hands. "Don't tell me. I don't wanna know what it is. I have enough to worry about already."

"We know where Ronald Dinkins was killed."

"Who?"

"You know. The Dinkins kid."

"*Who?* Oh—him." Lee eyed Barry as if trying to decide whether or not to just beat the information out of him. Finally he said: "Where?"

"An old railroad tunnel up in the hills."

"And how do you know this?"

"We found his camera there."

Lee considered this, then said, "You know as well as I do that doesn't prove squat. He could've lost his camera six weeks ago. What were you doing in a railroad tunnel, anyway? Trying out the hobo lifestyle?"

"I have a transcript of a hypnosis session with Ronald's friend, Jeff Tracey. It led us up there."

"And why," Lee said, "have I not been informed about this document?"

"I'm informing you now."

"Don't get smart with me, *Officer* Brennan, or you'll be wearing your badge as a nipple piercing."

"Sorry."

"What made you think that checking out this tunnel required your immediate and undivided attention? And this had better be damn good."

"Well …" Shit, what was he supposed to say? The captain would be reading the transcript at some point anyhow. "The Tracey kid was talking about vampires. In the tunnel."

After a moment, Lee said: "Vampires."

"Yeah."

"And you took this seriously."

"Well, I—we—went to check out the kid's story."

"And you found the camera."

Barry nodded.

"But no vampires."

Barry shook his head.

"Of course you didn't. You know why? Because there's no such fucking thing! And what exactly does this bullshit have to do with Jerry getting his head removed? Why does it take precedence over coming here to chat with us, your friends and coworkers?" Lee stabbed out the cigar in his ashtray—it was one of those vacuum models, supposed to suck the smoke through a filter and emit clean air from the other side, but it didn't seem to be running—then took another cigar out of his desk drawer, stuck it in his mouth, lit it, and glared at Barry. "Well?"

"Okay," Barry said. "Maybe I showed poor judgment."

"Mighty big of you to admit it."

"But listen—" Barry said.

"No, *you* listen. You don't get to talk for at least another hour." Lee checked his watch. "Two-thirty. You will not open your mouth until at least two-thirty. Understood?"

Barry started to say yes, then thought better of it and nodded instead.

"Good," Lee said. "Maybe you've got half a brain after all."

"You want a cup of coffee?"

"Sure, thanks."

The detective, Jack Davidson, whom she remembered from the traffic incident the week before, signaled to a flunky lingering in the corner of his area. The guy vanished into the hallway. Then Davidson offered Roxanne a pack of spearmint gum, one silvery stick protruding. "No thanks," she said. "Doesn't go with coffee."

"Everything goes with coffee." He took the stick himself, then crumpled up the wrapper and tossed it at the wastebasket, missing by a wide margin. He didn't make any move to pick up the litter. "Okay," he said, tucking the gum into his mouth, "let's go over it again. You came home, found your house a mess, and called the police."

"Yes," she said.

"Then what?"

"Then Officer Klein came out and looked around. He checked out the rooms upstairs, then he went downstairs. A few minutes later I heard shots and I ran outside. That was just when Barry came."

"And what did Officer Brennan do?"

"He took the shotgun out of Officer Klein's car. We saw somebody running into the woods. Barry shot at him but missed. And then we —"

"Fled the scene."

"Yes." Roxanne glanced over the detectives shoulder, out through the mesh of thick wire that blocked the window. The sky was deepening, turning from pale white to a moody grey. "It'll be dark soon," she said.

Davidson twisted his neck around. "So it will. And I'll be getting overtime in forty minutes. Won't it be glorious?" He turned back to Roxanne. "So Officer Brennan shot at someone who was running away?"

"It looked like the guy had a gun."

"Was he pointing it at you?"

"Well—"

"Did Officer Brennan command this person to stop?"

"Yes, but he didn't."

"How well do you know Ken Fletcher?"

"What?"

"Ken Fletcher. He a friend of yours?"

"Um, I guess so."

"You guess so?"

"I only just met him the other day."

"Did you know he's wanted for arson and murder?"

"No."

"Yeah, he burned down an old warehouse in North Carolina. Left a couple of bodies inside, and his car in the parking lot. For a while he was listed as a victim, until they ascertained that neither corpse was his."

Roxanne thought quickly. An old warehouse ... that was where

Ken and Martel had had their last confrontation, where Ken was supposed to have died.

"Coincidentally, *your* house burned down too, after you left. Also with a body inside."

She said nothing.

"Officer Klein's shotgun happened to end up in Mr. Fletcher's car. Me, I'd have to be pretty good friends with somebody to give him a loaded shotgun, but I'm not so much the trusting type."

"Is Ken here?" she said.

"Yes," Davidson said. "Ken is here. Why would Officer Brennan feel he needed to take Officer Klein's shotgun and flee the scene of a fellow officer's murder?"

She didn't answer.

"And, having fled the scene, why would he then give said shotgun to someone you only just met the other day?"

After a moment, Roxanne said: "Shouldn't I have a lawyer or something, Detective Davidson?"

"A lawyer? Please, we're all friends here. Just friends having a chat. And call me Davidson, everyone else does." He looked over at the flunky, who had reentered and was lurking near the door. "Well don't just stand there! Bring Miss Carmichael her coffee!" The flunky bustled over and put the coffee mugs on the desk. Roxanne's was plain white, while Davidson's said *Cops Do It With Handcuffs*. She took a sip and nearly spit it out again. It was lukewarm, bitter, strong as battery acid; Davidson drank it like it was champagne. For a second she thought he had swallowed his gum, but after he put the mug down, he started chewing again.

"Are we done?" Roxanne asked.

"Hardly." Davidson leaned back and traced a slow circle on the desk with one long finger. "You're not being straight with me."

She tried another sip of the coffee. It still tasted like it had been simmering for a year in a rusty pot. "Of course I am. Ask Barry, he'll tell you the same things."

Davidson laughed. "Of course he will," he said. "You two have had plenty of time to cook this story up." He shook his head and smiled sadly, then put down the coffee and motioned the flunky over. "Joe here will take you to a room. You'll stay there tonight. Tomorrow we'll talk some more. Now, I want you to think things over very carefully, and in the morning I hope you'll be ready to tell me the truth. Good night."

"You can't make me stay here."

"Oh yes I can. I can march down to the judge and tell her that I've got an uncooperative material witness on my hands. You walk out of this building, I'll have them haul you back in an hour. Save us both the trouble, cookie."

She stared at Davidson. His eyes, dark as the inside of a pipe bowl, stared right back; and after a moment she rose from her seat and allowed Joe to lead her away.

From the detectives' area, Joe the flunky took her down several flights of stairs, and along a blank corridor to an unmarked door. The door was heavy, without a window, and had to be unlocked with a key. Roxanne entered and turned on the light as Joe closed and locked the door behind her. Roxanne looked around. It was a small room, and like the hallway and door, it had no windows. Perhaps they were underground. That made her feel a little safer.

What the place lacked in windows it made up for in paintings. Each wall boasted no fewer than six of them, framed prints on poster board; most of them seemed to be of European locations: Castles and outdoor cafes and grey rain-soaked streets and small, funny-looking livestock grazing on rolling green hills. A desk stood in the far left corner, flanked by a couple of hard, straight-backed chairs; the pale white linoleum of the floor was broken up by cheap, tatty throw rugs here and there, the patterns mostly Oriental. Against the right wall, next to the floor lamp, was a huge couch covered with virgin vinyl that someone somewhere might have thought was leather had he never seen the real thing.

Barry sat on the couch, blinking at her.

She was there in two steps, and had him in a bear hug a second later. He yawned and apologized, and said he'd been dozing. She didn't care. She just kept squeezing him.

"Are you okay?" Barry asked.

"Better now," she said.

"That picture of a street," Barry whispered, his lips brushing her ear, "is transparent. Odds are there's a detective behind it. They think it's their big secret. So no talk about vampires, okay?"

She nodded, kissed him on the forehead. "I'm really glad you're here," she said. He didn't seem to know what to do with his hands; the fingers squeezed her arms, the thumbs traced circles. He leaned forward and, very gently, kissed her on her left eye and the bridge of her nose, and kept his head there against hers for several seconds.

When they separated, she said: "They told me Ken was wanted for arson and murder."

"So I heard. I just spent the last hour and a half getting reamed out by the captain about my judgment and my taste in friends. I think the only reason they haven't fired me already is so they can dangle the possibility of *not* firing me, if I cooperate to their satisfaction."

"They said he was here. Ken, I mean."

"Yeah, he's under arrest. They probably already have North Carolina on the phone making extradition arrangements. Did you tell them what happened at your house?"

"Yes. They didn't believe me."

"Of course they didn't."

"They can't just make us stay here, can they?"

"They sure can."

"This is all wrong. This isn't what's supposed to happen."

"We don't have much choice in the matter. We try to leave, they'll get a judge to order us to return, and then they'll lock us up someplace with bars." Barry sighed. "Don't think they won't, Annie; they're royally pissed off right now."

"But it'll be dark soon."

"We can't stop the world from turning," Barry said. "Whatever's going to happen tonight will happen without us."

"What *is* going to happen, Barry?"

"If I knew that," he said, "I'd let them keep my badge and make a fortune in the stock market."

Behind the painting of a street, in a space roughly the size of a filing cabinet, Jack Davidson sat on a stool peering into the room beyond. The walls of the tiny observation booth pressed close to his shoulders, the ceiling was scarcely two feet above his head when he stood up, and the only light—other than what filtered in from the room on the other side of the one-way picture—came from a series of tiny bulbs set along the baseboard.

The other detectives affectionately referred to this room as *The Crypt*, which, he supposed, made him the crypt-keeper.

Waiting for the subjects to incriminate somebody, Davidson sat through the hugs and kisses, the nattering conversation, munching his gum as if it had done him some grievous wrong and this was his revenge. A tape recorder whirred on a shelf nearby; he held a notebook, pen poised to write, the point not moving over the paper until Roxanne mentioned that it was going to be dark soon. Then he stopped chewing and took his gum out of his mouth and stuck it to the wall, next to a dozen other wads in varying states of petrifaction.

He scribbled *dark—why?* in his notebook.

Still watching them through the picture, he fished around in his pocket for another piece of gum; after a moment he pulled out a fresh foil-wrapped stick. Somehow his fingers had also closed on a lone cigarette, bent and deformed like an old man, lint clinging to the white paper. How had that gotten in there?

Davidson stared at the cigarette for a long moment, then sighed and ground it between his thumb and forefinger. Tobacco and crumpled paper fell quietly to the floor. Then he tucked the gum into his mouth and started chewing, tossing the wrapper over his shoulder.

Why were they so concerned about nightfall? Were they supposed to be somewhere, do something? What had Barry meant by *whatever's going to happen tonight*? Was something going down out there in the dark? Was he warning her about something? Too many questions, damn it.

Davidson checked his watch. It was nearly twenty after five; it would be dark out already. What was supposed to happen tonight? He sighed and unfolded himself from the stool, then turned and checked the ancient reel-to-reel to make sure it was picking up sound at the proper levels. Everything looked fine.

He left the Crypt and headed upstairs to talk to the captain.

"So what did you get out of her?"

"Well, let's just call it not the truth, the whole truth, and nothing but the truth, so help her God," Davidson said. "And that's being charitable."

Lee grunted and ground his cigar into the ashtray, over and over again, until it looked like one of Davidson's gum wads. "I have something for you to read." He slid a slim stack of papers over to the detective.

"What's this?"

"It's a transcript of a hypnosis session, courtesy of Officer Brennan's fine off-hours investigative work."

"Okay." Davidson picked it up and leafed through it. After a few minutes, he looked up and said: "Vampires?"

Lee shrugged.

"Not a vampire cult, but actual *supernatural* vampires?"

Lee shrugged again.

Davidson continued reading. "Man, this is real fantasy stuff. Vampires living in the hills. Run away and hide the women!" He put the report face-down on the captain's desk. "This horse shit is not helpful."

"I didn't write the goddamn thing. What was that about a vampire cult?"

"You know, like those clowns in Kentucky. Drinking each others' blood and having group gropes and oh, yeah, crossing state lines to beat people to death."

"You think Barry and his little friend are in a vampire cult?"

"No," Davidson said, "but Fletcher might be. Hell, he might be the ringleader, given his track record and all the crazy shit they found in his car. Stakes, crosses, garlic."

"Sounds more like he's a wanna-be vampire hunter than a wanna-be vampire."

"Maybe he uses that stuff to keep the other vampires in line. So let's say he's got a cult, and for whatever reason, they decide to target the lovely Miss Carmichael. Hence the phone calls, the stalking, the vandalism, culminating in the murder and arson. Maybe they were hiding out in the tunnel and this kid ran into them there."

Lee leaned back in his chair, showing Davidson his skeptical face. "This is some crazy-ass theory."

"Well, it wouldn't hold up in a court of law, that's for sure, but at the moment wild speculation is all I have."

"If they're afraid of this cult, why don't they spill it, now that they're here and they're safe?"

"Maybe they don't think they're safe."

"Or maybe Fletcher has hostages. The other witnesses to that incident up north, maybe. What's their name, Stone?"

"Sloane." Davidson nodded. "Irving and Ryan Sloane. They were reported missing today after both of them failed to show up for work, again. Has Morse gotten anything from Fletcher yet?"

"No. Fletcher won't talk, just keeps saying we're making a terrible mistake."

"Don't they all say that," Davidson said.

"Yes they do," Lee said. "And gosh darn if it doesn't make me all watery inside every time I hear it."

"Okay, let's assume there's some sort of conspiracy going on here— we don't have to call it a vampire cult, that would get the media all frothy anyway—and they've got the Sloanes hostage or are otherwise exerting influence over our two guests downstairs. We'll have to produce the hostages or roll up the conspirators before Barry and Roxanne will stop talking nonsense."

"Before we go any farther, let me call Gary in here." Lee picked up the phone and punched a few buttons, then said: "Detective Morse. Step into my parlor. Bring Fletcher's crap."

"Morse the Mouse," Davidson murmured.

Lee raised an eyebrow. "Watch it," he said.

A few minutes later, Detective Morse shuffled in, carrying a glossy black valise and a battered-looking wallet. He set the bag on the floor and tossed the billfold onto Lee's desk. As Lee rifled through it, Davidson said: "Fletcher still not talking?"

"Yep."

"Has he asked for an attorney?"

"Nope." Gary pointed at the valise. "Just keeps wanting his garlic back."

"Look at this," Lee said, cradling a snapshot between his thumb and forefinger. He showed it to Gary, then to Davidson; it was a wedding picture, Ken Fletcher and a woman, standing in a park, young and happy and smiling as if life were grand, while overhead the sun beat down on them. The back of it had writing on it, *Ken and Lauren*, and a year.

"Could be the woman described in the session," Davidson said. "Tall, blonde, good-looking. If you've got a cult, you'd want your wife in it, of course."

"Of course."

Gary said: "Cult?"

"Your colleague here has a theory," Lee said. "He can explain it to you in the car."

"The car?"

"On the way to the stakeout."

"What are we staking out?"

"We're going to turn Barry and Roxanne loose, and you two are going to stick to them like a lawyer to an emergency room."

"But what about Fletcher?"

"He's not talking. You can finish up with him later."

"But—"

"Go. Sit in car. Pretend to be detectives." Lee leaned back, lit up another cigar. "Oh, and watch out for vampires."

It was dark when Barry and Roxanne stepped out of the police station and descended the six cement steps to the sidewalk. The lot was mostly empty, except for a few cruisers here and there, several unmarked cars, and a few personal vehicles, including Ken's rented Ford and Barry's little Chevy. He unlocked the passenger side door of his car and held it open for Roxanne before getting in himself. Muttering, he adjusted the seat and the mirror.

"What'd you say?" Roxanne asked, checking the back seat for stowaways, then checking that the doors were locked, then checking the back seat again.

"I said whoever drove this here has tiny little legs."

The puny engine coughed and sputtered in the cold as Barry tried to start it. His car was such a piece of shit, she was worried that at some point it wouldn't start at all when they really needed it to; but, her own vehicle was now a burned-out husk in her driveway, so they were stuck with his. It finally turned over on the fourth try, and then Barry guided it out of the lot and onto the main drag. She looked over her shoulder at the receding police station. "Why are they letting us leave?"

"They want to see where we go, what we do, who we meet with," Barry said. "We're certainly under surveillance."

"Makes me feel like a criminal."

"Well, look what we've done the last few days. Leaving the scene of a murder. Consorting with Ken the killer arsonist."

"Ken the killer arsonist." It sounded almost funny, like the title of a black comedy or the name of a comical super-villain.

"Too bad he didn't get the bastard back in North Carolina," Barry said. "God knows how many people would still be alive now. Ronald. Jerome. Chris." After a moment Barry glanced sidelong at her. "About Chris. He's not going to stop."

She thought about this for a moment, remembering what Ken had said, how becoming a vampire amplified the darker parts of a person's personality. "Yeah," she said. "I know."

"In a twisted way, he wants you back."

"I don't date vampires. The big teeth are a major turn-off."

"Oh, I don't know about that," Barry said. "You know what they say. Big teeth, big …" He trailed off. "Sorry."

She knew what he'd meant to say, a variation on the old saw. *Big feet, big teeth, big cock.* Roxanne flashed back to Martel's appearance in Barry's apartment. His body, his hands, his mouth. She shuddered, and not from the chill.

"Are you okay? Did I freak you out?"

"I'm fine." She put her hand on his knee, squeezing it. Poor Barry. He had no idea what it was like for her. She hated what Martel had done to her; and yet thinking about him, about *it*, still initiated a certain sequence of fantasies in her mind, ending in an uncomfortably erotic sensation that seemed to flicker throughout her entire body. The way it had felt, his tongue flicking between her legs … Martel had known what he was doing. She needed something to supplant that memory.

She looked at Barry and smiled.

He was going to be a very happy man once they got back to his apartment.

Lauren Fletcher, hair pulled back into a ponytail, sipped her amaretto sour and looked at the bar as the man next to her said, "Hi."

She glanced over, met his gaze fleetingly, smiled a little, said nothing.

"Do you live around here?"

They always asked her that; she must seem exotic, or perhaps transient, always on her way somewhere else. Which, she supposed, she was. "Depends what you mean by *live*."

He smiled, uncertain. Not a smooth operator; she could hardly imagine how he'd worked up the courage to talk to her. "I don't live here either," he said. "I'm just here for the game. My name's Bob."

"Hi, Bob," she said. "I'm Lauren."

"Nice to meet you." He wanted to shake her hand; she indulged him this bit of contact. Introductions out of the way, Lauren looked at the bar and took another sip of her drink. It used to be her favorite, but it didn't taste like anything special anymore. It wasn't that the bartender had made it wrong; to her mouth, everything was the same now, be it coffee or amaretto or orange juice or whatever. Only one thing still had a flavor, and it was flowing through Bob's veins. She could smell it.

"So what game are you going to?"

Bob was astonished. "You don't know?"

"I don't pay much attention to games that I'm not playing."

"This isn't just any game. It's *hockey*."

"Mmm." Hockey. Didn't they play that in Canada?

"White Bluff and Westlake are the only undefeated teams left in the league, and they're playing tomorrow night. Against each other. Everyone will be there. I've never missed a game, not in ten years." He raised his fist. "Go Warriors!"

From the crowd, someone yelled, "Fuck you, go back to Westlake!"

The anonymous retort made him cringe and he quickly lowered his hand. God, what a bore. He was hardly even worth biting. "*Everyone*. Really." Sip. "It must be a huge stadium."

"Well, you play hockey in an arena, not a stadium, and it's really not *that* big ..." He trailed off, belatedly recognizing her sarcasm. Lauren stifled a yawn; she didn't actually need to breathe, so this was mostly for show. She scanned the room, looking for a more promising victim. Bob plowed on, oblivious to her lack of interest, or perhaps hoping he would say something to get it back if he just said enough stuff. "Hundreds of people will be there. I'm thinking about painting my face."

That would be an improvement, she thought. Still, he *had* managed to capture her interest. "Hundreds of people, huh?"

"Sure. It's a really important game."

Men. Always thinking a *game* could be important. But that many people, jammed into an enclosed space, raised intriguing possibilities. "What time is this game?" she said.

"Six-thirty. Why? Do you want to go?"

"No," she said. "Just wondering."

"Oh." Disappointed, he took solace in his drink.

She studied him sidelong, noticed him fidget with an empty spot on his ring finger. "Are you married, Bob?"

"What?"

"Are you married?"

"No, of course not," he said. "If I were married, I wouldn't be here talking to you."

"You're such a liar." Sip. "Does your wife know what you do when you're away at hockey games?"

"I told you, I'm not—"

"But maybe she does the same thing while you're gone. Maybe she takes off the ring, heads out to the bar, tries to pick up strangers."

"She does not!" Bob said. Then, turning bright red, he stood up, drink in hand. Lauren reached out before he could leave, hooked her fingers into his belt, and pulled him back onto his stool.

"I didn't say I *cared* that you were married. Sit down." He stared at her, as astonished as if she'd suddenly whipped out a penis and started urinating on him. "Where are you staying?"

"At the Madison," he said.

"Oh," she said. "Nice place." She'd been there once, with a young woman she'd picked up at the gay bar. "Got a balcony?"

"Yeah," he said. "Yeah, a great view of the city."

If he thought any aspect of the White Bluff skyline presented a great view, he was even more pathetic than she'd thought. Still, a meal was a meal. She leaned over and said softly, "Did you ever fuck on a balcony, Bob?"

"No. Have you?"

Lauren leaned back and stretched. She felt Bob's gaze crawling all over her. "Not yet," she said.

"Roxanne—"

She kissed him to shut him up.

"Rmm-mmm," Barry said, trying to close the front door. "Mmm!" He managed to hook his foot around the edge and slam it closed before Roxanne bore him to the floor, kissing him almost desperately, the way a drowning person would gasp for air or a starving one would gobble a loaf of bread.

"Roxanne, you—" Barry managed to get a few words out while her mouth was on his neck, and she kissed him to shut him up again. She slid off of him and found his belt, undid it quickly, slid her hand inside his loosened pants. Barry made noises as she stroked him, but she kept his lips firmly occupied and eventually the noises stopped. His hands groped at her shirt and began undoing buttons. Her bra snapped in front and he popped it off with a finger. Roxanne leaned forward and smothered him with her breasts as his hands slid down to the zipper of her jeans.

The beat-up old car parked outside Barry's apartment house smelled like a combination of coffee, cigarette smoke, chewing gum, and deli sandwiches. Detectives Morse and Davidson sat inside the car, the former licking salami grease off his fingers, the latter peering up at the lighted windows of Barry's apartment.

"You really think there's some kind of cult thing going on here, Davidson?" Gary said, wiping his hands on the dashboard.

"Who the fuck knows? I'm open to any theory right now."

"Maybe we'd know by now, if Lee had let me keep the heat on Fletcher."

"Oh, yeah. He was almost ready to crack." In a falsetto: "*Gimme back my garlic, I need it for the vampires.*"

"This stakeout is bullshit. Does Lee really think Fletcher's, um, followers, are gonna show up here, knowing we arrested their so-called leader this morning? Doubtful." Gary leaned over and stuffed his napkin into the takeout bag. "They're probably busy worshiping a baked potato or something."

"Whoa." The shades weren't drawn yet, and Roxanne, topless, jeans halfway off, had just appeared in one of the windows. She had Barry in tow; he was grinning like he'd just won two state lotteries and a free ticket to heaven. Davidson elbowed Gary. "Hey, check it out!"

"What?" Gary peered at the apartment, but Roxanne had gone from the window; now Barry's forearm came into view to pull down the shade.

"Too late, you missed it."

"Missed what?"

"If I tell you," Davidson said, "it'll only make you grumpier."

Ken Fletcher lay on the bunk in his cell, staring at the ceiling. It was green, like everything else around here, with a single light bulb to illuminate it. The light was recessed into the ceiling, behind a translucent panel secured by a steel ring screwed into the cement. Must be a pain in the ass to change, but it was one of those new compact fluorescents, so it would probably still be burning long after he was gone.

His cell had no window, of course, although there were skylights in the hallway outside, barred and no doubt rigged with alarms. From where he lay, if he craned his neck, he could just see out through the nearest one. The night sky here was featureless, any trace of the heavens completely washed out by the glare of the floodlights that kept the grounds in a constant state of illumination. The sense of aloneness was complete; not even the moon could reach him here.

But *they* could, if they wanted to.

What would Martel do if he caught a whiff of Ken's presence? Would he attack, and risk exposure, to rid himself once and for all of a persistent nuisance? Ken didn't think so. Martel would be content to let the human justice system send Ken away for a long, long time.

Lauren, on the other hand … Lauren would come for him. And if she caught him, what would she do? What would *he* do?

He didn't know.

Sighing, he rolled onto his side, turning his back on the night. He might as well try to sleep.

In his dreams, maybe his life wouldn't be such a wreck.

Binoculars out, Gary stared up at Barry's apartment. After lengthy cajoling, Davidson had described what he'd seen, and Gary was hoping for a repeat performance. Instead, he saw something moving along the peak of the roof. It paused long enough for him to register what looked like a face, eyes, mouth, looking his way; then it vanished as if plucked away by an unseen hand.

What the hell?

He lowered the binoculars, studied the building in the moonlight.

It was a standard regular house roof, roughly triangular, three or four chimneys suggestive of fireplaces, a couple of antennae, plus all the usual small outlets for venting the plumbing. Nothing special about it, just one of dozens of old, big houses that had been divided into apartments as families shrank and fortunes dwindled.

"Davidson, did you see that?"

"Did I see what?"

"Someone on the roof."

"On the *roof*?" Davidson sounded skeptical. "Look at that slope. Even in summer you'd probably fall off if you weren't tied to it."

"Well, I saw someone up there."

"Was it our blondie?"

"I don't think so."

"Or our giant monkey chauffeur?"

"I didn't get a good look at him."

"Maybe it was Peter Pan."

"Damn it, Jack, I saw something!"

"Where'd it go, then?"

"I don't know."

"Well, unless our perps can fly, I really don't think they're creeping around on Barry's roof in the middle of the night," Davidson said. "Try to relax, and keep an eye on the house. Maybe she'll show her tits again and make the night worthwhile."

Gary grunted and raised the binoculars back to his eyes; but he wasn't looking at the windows anymore.

He was looking at the roof.

Chris sat in a tree near the car, watching the occupants. They looked like bright blobs, the heat of their bodies diffused by the vehicle's metal frame. The engine, which was probably still warm, didn't show up at all, which Chris found interesting; somehow his night-sight could distinguish between artificial heat and the warmth of a living human body. A useful adaptation, since he didn't need to suck oil out of a crankcase.

To Chris, who had an eye for such things, the beat-up Buick fairly screamed *unmarked police car*. Cops loved to ticket Corvettes, even Corvettes that had been inherited from your dead father, even if you told them you were honoring your father's memory by driving fast.

In fact, if he recalled correctly, that statement often seemed to piss cops off. No sense of humanity, those guys. Anyway, when you were constantly in danger of receiving unfair traffic citations, you developed a certain sense of what cars had cops in them and what cars didn't. This one did.

Evidently Roxanne and her new *boyfriend* were under surveillance. He'd seen mention of their capture in the evening paper—some wino had been using it as a blanket, before Chris had relieved him of the necessity of such things—and so he had hung around on top of the police station for a while, then followed them here when they had been released. He wanted to finish what he'd started back at Roxanne's place, but he could hardly do it with a couple of cops watching. Couldn't give away The Secret, not yet, not until Lauren said it was okay.

Lauren ... sure, she was a great fuck, she was the big boss; but he wanted Roxanne. Roxanne had rejected him. Roxanne had *humiliated* him. He could imagine her on the phone with her girlfriends, making fun of him, saying how stupid he was, saying he was a lousy lay. Laughing at him. She would be the one to be humiliated, the next time he got hold of her. She would be the one to beg.

But first ... what to do about these cops?

Lauren stood on the balcony, feeling the wind whip her dress and hair. Bob lay on the concrete at her feet, his pants down around his knees, his dick still hard, blood oozing out of the holes in his neck. Amazing, what idiots men turned into when they got stiff. All the blood that normally went to their brains must go to their crotches instead.

Well ... she licked her lips and decided that wasn't true. Bob still had plenty of the red stuff pumping through his jugular. She nudged him with her foot; he groaned and stirred a little. Waking up, right on schedule. Lauren stretched, then brushed the snow off one of the outdoor chairs and sat down, waiting patiently, a girl who had all the time in the world.

"I don't like this," Gary said, holding his hands over the vent; Davidson had started the car to defrost the windshield and re-heat the interior. "Somebody's watching us."

"Would you cut it out?" Davidson tapped himself on the chest with three fingers. "We're the police. *We* do the watching."

"Not tonight."

"You don't even believe the cult theory, for God's sake."

"So? Neither do you, and you made it up. That doesn't mean he hasn't got accomplices." Gary shook his head. "We're made; we might as well just pack it in."

"You wanna call the captain and tell him that, be my guest."

"Maybe I will," Gary said, reaching for the radio.

"Tell them to send out the heebie-jeebie squad. Christ." Davidson noticed a pack of cigarettes crushed on the seat where Gary's fanny had recently been. The fucking things were following him around. Maybe it was a sign from God. He grabbed the pack and fumbled a bent cigarette out of it, then leaned over and punched the lighter.

Tonight, gum just wasn't going to cut it.

Chris landed lightly on top of the car. He still hadn't decided what to do. He knew the prudent course of action would be to leave quietly, but prudence had never been his strong point. He hated Roxanne, hated her boyfriend, hated these cops in their beater car; since his rebirth, all the anger he'd ever felt seemed to have been magnified a hundred times, distilled into something raw and powerful like concentrated acid. He had the power to act on his rage. And it felt *good*.

He got down on his knees and began feeling around the roof of the car, closing his eyes to better sense the people within. Yes, he could *feel* them, feel the warmth of their blood-filled bodies. He stopped when his hands were directly over their heads, hovering them there, palms down, like he was playing with one of those glass plasma globes. Would he be able to do them both before they had time to react? He didn't think they could kill him, but they could shoot him full of holes and wake up the neighborhood. Then he'd have to murder everyone in a two-block radius. Fun, but time-consuming.

They were moving now, drawing closer together, maybe having a little chat. Deciding to chance it, Chris drew back his arms and punched through the roof with both fists. The metal skin ruptured beneath his pile-driver blow; his fists connected with the pair of skulls almost simultaneously. The one on the right shattered under the impact, and Chris dug his fingers through the bone as if it were a thick eggshell. The man's brains were hot, slick, and squishy, floating in fluid like tuna packed in oil. The other skull didn't pop open like that, but Chris heard a sharp *crack* that he thought sounded like bones snapping; maybe he'd broken the cop's neck.

Chris pulled his arms out of the holes, bringing a handful of brains along. The jagged edges of the broken steel gashed him; thick blood began to ooze from long, deep cuts in his forearms. Well, that didn't matter; they'd heal. After all, his head had, right? Maybe his face wasn't so handsome anymore, but who needed to be handsome when you had power like this?

He held up the brains and sniffed them. The smell of oxygen-rich blood overpowered whatever odor the organ had. He licked the squishy mix of gray and white and found it tasty, so he ate it.

Well, that was that. No more surveillance. But he seemed to have severed something important in his left arm; it had no feeling below the elbow and his fingers refused to move. He could probably still deal with Roxanne and her new boyfriend, but he didn't want to give her the satisfaction of seeing him in less than perfect condition. He'd give it a day of rest to knit back together, and it would be good as new.

Then he'd be back.

Chris flew up and away, his arms sluggishly dripping other people's blood into the snow.

Consciousness returned slowly to Jack Davidson. The first thing he became aware of was a pain in his forehead that radiated over the top of his head, down his spine, and into the small of his back. The car was still running, the heat blowing full-blast onto his face. He didn't smell coffee and cigarettes anymore; now he smelled blood. His fingers drifted in a puddle of something warm and sticky. A shudder shook his body and his hand, the one in the warm stuff, reflexively formed into a fist, then opened again. The pain seemed to be focusing now, localized in his forehead, like the headaches he would get when he didn't drink enough coffee.

Somewhere nearby, a voice said: "Gary? Jack? What the hell's going on? Over."

Dispatch, talking through the radio. Groaning, he pushed himself up and opened his eyes. Moonlight showed him Gary's head. It had been shattered as if struck by a sledgehammer; everything above his nose was a pulpy mess. One eye, its socket destroyed, rested in a jumbled pile of broken bone and gore that had once been Gary's left temple. Its green iris was aimed right at Davidson.

Jack Davidson had once worked the Bronx. Then he'd taken a bullet in his leg and another in his hip, and he'd decided that was enough of the big city. So he'd transferred up here, to the middle of nowhere, where life didn't come at you with such ferocity. He'd gotten used to it over the past few years; he'd done a good job of pretending to forget all the shit he'd seen down there in the city. Now it all came rushing back, and for the first time ever, the sight of a corpse made Davidson puke; he found himself heaving up the contents of his stomach onto the bloody floor mats, befouling the interior even more thoroughly than it had been. The only way to sanitize this vehicle would be to incinerate it, he thought, wiping his mouth on his sleeve.

He fumbled the radio microphone into his hand and pressed the button. "Davidson here," he said. Why was the damn mike shaking so much? "Officer down. We're outside Barry Brennan's apartment. Send an ambulance. Send backup. Send the fucking Marines." He dropped the mike, looked at the shattered face next to him, and whispered: "Jesus Christ, Gary."

A snowflake landed on Davidson's nose. He looked up, and saw two holes punched through the roof of the car, the metal bent down in jagged teeth, the vinyl covering on the inside torn and hanging in tatters.

What the *fuck*?

Roxanne, her body hot and sweaty, lay against Barry's side, her head on his shoulder. "That was nice," she said, snuggling up against him.

"It'll do for now."

"Barry?"

"What?"

"I think I love you."

"You think so, huh?"

"Yeah."

"That's good. Let me know when you're sure."

"Okay," she said, sounding like she was already asleep.

Barry lay there quietly for a little while, feeling pretty content; then he noticed a blue light flashing against the shade, faint, but getting brighter fast. He disentangled himself from Roxanne, who mumbled a protest, and went to the window. He lifted the shade and looked out. A police car raced down the road, lights on, siren off. He saw what was obviously an unmarked police car across the street, not far from a snowy tree, and ... were those *holes* in the roof of the car? He wiped at the window with his palm, clearing the fog his breath had left. Yes, they were holes; and the patrol car was stopping behind the unmarked one, and an ambulance was coming from the opposite direction, its siren wailing, more patrol cars following it. Jesus, it looked like every cop car in White Bluff was converging on the damaged vehicle.

Barry turned away from the window. Roxanne was sitting up now, looking at him. The blue lights flowed across her body.

"Better get dressed," he said. "We'll be having company."

For once, sleep had come easily to Ken, as if eager to deliver a fresh load of bad dreams to torment him. Now showing: Ken, chained and shackled, while Martel and Lauren fucked on the floor in front of him, and Lauren let Martel do things to her that Ken never would have even considered suggesting, while Krone whipped him repeatedly across the ass with the antenna from that big old Lincoln. When two guards came and roused him by banging their nightsticks against the bars, it was such a relief that he almost thanked them.

They marched him out of the cell block and out of the building. Night was fully engaged and in firm control. "Where are you taking me?" he asked, as they stuffed him into a waiting police car.

"Shut up, asshole."

The car whisked him back to the station where he'd been held and questioned earlier, where he was picked up by two more guards who were no more communicative than the first pair. They took him to a room in the basement, shoved him through the door, and closed it behind him.

"Sit down, Mr. Fletcher."

This was somebody he hadn't seen before; he had a gun on the table in front of him, just lying there, a threat veiled about as effectively as a stripper at the end of her show. Ken looked around. There was a couch in here, and several chairs; the place looked almost like a living room from a seventies television sitcom. Ken selected a chair, sat in it, and waited for the man to start talking. But he didn't. He just sat there, his face giving the impression he had just swallowed a frog and was trying to keep it down.

After a while, Ken said: "What's going on?"

"Wait and see, asshole." They all thought his name was *asshole*. Tiresome, really.

About ten more minutes passed, then the door opened and three more people came in: A pale, bedraggled plainclothes police officer with a bandaged head, and Barry and Roxanne. "Are we having a meeting?" Ken asked, as the detective flopped into another chair and Barry and Roxanne took the couch, sitting close together and holding hands.

"You might say that," the man with the gun said. "Ken Fletcher, meet Jack Davidson. I'm Lee Donovan, the captain of this precinct." He jerked his thumb at Barry and Roxanne. "You already know these two. Davidson, how's your head?"

"Hurts like hell."

"I'll bet it does. Lucky you got a thick skull." Lee looked around the room as if verifying that everyone was awake and paying attention, then said: "Okay, Fletcher. Tell us just what the fuck is going on."

"Beg pardon?"

"Detectives Davidson and Morse were on a stakeout at Officer Brennan's apartment when they spotted someone on the roof of the building. A few minutes later, somebody punched holes in the roof of their unmarked car. Morse's skull was crushed; he's dead. Davidson's head hit the dashboard and broke it and he was knocked unconscious. Jack says they didn't hear anyone climb onto their car, or see anyone approaching."

Ken glanced over at Barry and Roxanne. Both of them looked haggard and exhausted; in fact, Roxanne seemed to have fallen asleep. Obviously they hadn't told Lee about the vampires; if they had, he'd reacted in the predictable fashion.

"Fletcher," Lee said. "Hello? I'm running the show here. Not them."

Ken turned his gaze back to the captain.

"Thank you," Lee said. "Davidson assures me that Officer Brennan and Miss Carmichael did not leave the apartment until we went and got them, at least, not while he was conscious. I want to know who your accomplice is and how he did what he did to my men."

"I don't have an accomplice," Ken said.

"God damn it!" Lee shouted, gripping the edges of his desk. "Another one of my men is *dead*! I saw the body! The top of his head was reduced to a pulp! Jerry Klein had his head *torn off*! You tell me everything you know, *everything*, or so help me God I will shoot you myself right now."

"What, in front of all these witnesses?"

"Don't push me, Fletcher. I swear to God, you do not want to piss me off any further right now."

"You really want to know what's happening?"

"I think I've made that pretty clear."

"You *really* want to know?"

"Yes, God damn it!"

The room silent.

"Okay then," Ken said.

Jeff Tracey dreamed about Lauren Fletcher.

In his dream, he had returned to the tunnel, but it was no longer empty; *she* was there, as she had been that first day, waiting for him, naked and predatory. Ken Fletcher had told him to forget about her, warned him that even thinking about her could bring her to him; but in this dream Jeff didn't care. So she and her Master had killed Ronald; so what? She was a goddess, and a goddess could do whatever she wanted—to Ronald, and to him. It was her right. It was his honor.

It was just a dream.

Lauren was on her way back to her lair when she felt a gentle tug on her psyche. She paused in mid-flight; Bob continued on for several more yards before realizing she had stopped.

"Is something wrong, Master?" he asked.

"No," she answered. Bob had started calling her *Master* without any prompting, and she found it annoying. How could one of her minions be such a weenie? "Shut up."

"Yes, Master," Bob said.

Lauren concentrated. Where had that sensation come from? Was it Martel, probing for her? No, the signature was wrong. For one thing, it was far weaker than Martel would be, unless he'd expended so much energy trying to kill her that this was all he had left to muster. She floated in place, her body defying the laws of gravity, waiting, waiting … there it was again! A little pull, a psychic nudge. And it came from … that way. From up in the hills. From near the tunnel.

Maybe this *was* Martel's feeble attempt to pull her in. She said, without turning, "You go on to the place I told you about. Make sure you find it before dawn. If you don't, the sun will take you, and nobody will miss you very much."

"Okay, Master." Bob resumed his silent, wingless flight, drifting out across the houses and streets toward the marsh at the edge of town. Lauren headed up into the hills, following the thoughts of her.

Was it her *Master* calling her? He was a fool. He was weak. She would destroy him. He should never have tried to cast her aside like a newspaper from last year, like a book that hadn't held his interest. He didn't appreciate her potential. She would show him a thing or two about power.

Wait. She was closing in on the tunnel, and in her reverie she had inadvertently passed the source of the emanation. It wasn't coming from their old lair after all. So where was it?

She turned around and drifted back down the hill, this time concentrating on the thoughts that she was tracking. They led her to a small, two-story house with a white picket fence that needed painting and a roof that needed patching. She circled around and homed in on a second-story bedroom. She peered through the window, and almost laughed.

It was the boy, the one Martel had not let her kill.

But Martel wasn't here now, was he?

13

THURSDAY, JANUARY 21

MIDNIGHT

Jeff awoke with a start, feeling suddenly cold. There was a chill breeze blowing through his room. He sat up in bed and looked around, and saw a pale, luminescent mist pouring in through the tiny gaps around his window. The pane itself was cracked, and a trickle of fog was even coming in that way, forcing itself between the sections of glass and dribbling like spittle to join the main mass on the floor.

Was he still dreaming?

Jeff watched as the mist swirled around, forming itself first into a roiling column, then stretching out tendrils like arms. The lower half of the column divided into legs, and gradually the vapor coalesced into a human form. The whole process took maybe fifteen seconds. When it had finished, *she* was there, naked, her body pale and shimmering in the moonlight. She put a hand on her hip and looked at him as he lay in bed, huddled under the covers.

"Well well well," she said. "Look what we have here. It's the little explorer."

Jeff swallowed air, tried to speak but failed. He was trembling all over with equal measures of fear and excitement. He hated her; he feared her; he wanted her.

"I think you've been having impure thoughts," she said, "about me."

He closed his eyes. He was only thirteen, too young for this, too young to die. He had the piece of garlic, the one he'd taken from Ken Fletcher's car, on the table next to his bed; could he use that? He started reaching toward it, sliding his hand under the covers, but then the blanket began sliding away. He couldn't look, couldn't, mustn't—but he did. She was naked and beautiful. Her hands were on the sheets, pulling them off the bed.

She wadded up the bedding and dropped it on the floor by her feet. The air was cold. Then she knelt down and started sucking his toes. "I could bite your feet and suck you dry," she whispered, brushing her teeth against the bottoms of his toes.

If she bit him, he could go with her, and he would live forever.

No, that was a stupid thought. Stupid! She was a vampire, vicious and wicked; he would be her slave, and he had no doubt that she would be a cruel Master.

He couldn't quite reach the garlic without moving. Lauren Fletcher was pulling off his pajama bottoms. The air was freezing. Jeff kicked at her, tried to get away. He rolled over onto his stomach. Now he could just barely reach the garlic. He got it between his index and middle fingers, tried to lift it, but it turned between his digits and skittered away, falling off the table. "Oh, so you want it that way?" Lauren said. He glanced at her. She stuck her finger in her mouth, pulled it out again. It came bloody from her lips.

Oh God. Oh God. His hand groped for the garlic, found it, pinched it between his thumb and forefinger. This time he had a better grip on it. He rolled over onto his back.

Lauren said, crossly: "Make up your mind."

He lunged forward and pushed the garlic into her face.

She shrieked and hurled him away. The garlic slipped from his fingers, bouncing on the mattress. She jumped off the bed. She had a little black smudge in the middle of her forehead, as if she'd just come back from church on Ash Wednesday. "You little fuck!" She wiped frantically at it with the back of her hand, but it didn't come off. Her eyes flared like green embers; her nails stretched and sharpened into jagged knives. "I'll gut you like a fish!"

She flew at him. Jeff grabbed the garlic and scrambled off the mattress before she reached him. She shredded his pillow with her claws. Bits of foam rubber flew like gobbets of flesh.

He ran for the door, but suddenly his guts turned to water, his legs to jelly. Too frightened to scream, too frightened to run, he collapsed to the floor just inside the doorway, wearing only his pajama top, the clove of garlic clutched in his useless hand.

"You fool," Lauren said as she approached him. "You would have *loved* what I did to you. Now you'll suffer." She stopped right in front of him. "You think the fear is bad? Just wait for the *pain*."

"Vampires?" Lee said. "You expect me to believe—"

"It's true," Barry said.

"Shut up," Lee said. "I don't want to hear this garbage, I want to hear the truth!"

"This *is* the truth!" Barry said. "You remember that murder in the Adirondacks?"

"I think we're all familiar with it," Lee said.

"The body we found ... *it* found *us*. It was waiting for us. It jumped in front of the car and attacked us. It tried to kill me."

"Bullshit!"

"Why do you think the Sloanes cleared out? They were running away from the vampires!"

"But you two stuck around?"

"We didn't have any choice. He bit Roxanne."

"What?" she said, waking up a little.

"Oh yes," Lee said. "The vampire stalks the beautiful victim, and the hero must kill the beast to save her soul. Where I have I heard that before? Oh, I know: *Every fucking vampire movie ever made!*"

"In this instance you have two vampire factions," Ken said. "On the one hand you have Martel and his servant Krone. On the other you have my wife Lauren and her spawn. We don't know how many of them there are."

Lee gave him a long, critical look. "Your *wife*?"

"Ex-wife, I guess," Ken said. "'Til death do us part."

"What?"

"Martel turned her, the last time we met, in that warehouse in North Carolina. The one I burned down."

"Turned her." Lee stared at him. "Okay. Let's say, for the sake of argument, that this Martel clown really is a vampire, and he really bit your wife. Shouldn't she be his little bitch now? Fetching his beer, sucking his cock? Isn't that the way it's supposed to work?"

After a moment, Ken said: "I think that's the way Martel *expected* it to work."

Awake now, Roxanne said: "You shit. She was his *wife*."

"Sorry, honey, did I offend your feminist sensibilities?"

"You owe Ken an apology, not me," she said.

"They were fighting over Roxanne," Barry said. "Martel wanted her, so Lauren tried to kill her. We think that's when they split up. In the Adirondacks."

"You really believe this shit, Officer Brennan?"

"I've seen it with my own eyes."

"You gotta be fucking kidding me." He swiveled his gaze to Davidson. "Davidson, are you listening to this horse-puckey?"

Davidson said nothing.

"Jack?"

Davidson just sat there, the tip of his tongue running back and forth over his thin, pale lips.

"Jack, come *on*."

"The Dinkins kid was found down by the old canal with his head cut off," Davidson said. "No blood in the surrounding snow. No footprints. No nothing."

"So the perp covered his tracks. All you need is a broom. Hell, even branches will work in a pinch. You know that."

"I read the report on the bodies up in the Adirondacks. No murder weapon was found. I looked at the pictures. The snow around them was undisturbed. No footprints. Not even any drag marks. How do you kill that many people, move that many bodies, and not leave any traces?"

"Jesus Christ, Jack."

Davidson jerked his thumb at Roxanne. "They trashed her house, burned it down. No footprints. No evidence. Gary insisted he saw somebody on the roof of Brennan's apartment building. Somebody punched right through the roof of our car. I never heard a thing. How do you climb onto the roof of a car and nobody notices?"

"Christ," Lee said. "Next you'll be telling me we've got werewolves running around, too."

"I've never seen one," Ken said, "but I *have* heard stories."

"Go away, please go away!" Jeff cried, skittering across the floor like a crab. Lauren watched him, her cold eyes amused; then her gaze flicked to the bedroom door as it opened to reveal his mother, clad in a tatty pink bathrobe, eyes bleary with just-departed sleep.

"What in God's name is going on in ... here ..." She trailed off at the sight of the shredded pillows, Jeff half-naked on the floor, and the nude woman with wicked nails, fangs, and glowing eyes standing a few yards away.

"Mommy," Jeff said. Lauren took a step toward him.

His mother crossed herself.

Lauren saw the gesture and stopped.

"Get out of my house!" she screamed. "Whatever you are, get out of my house! Leave my boy alone!"

Lauren Fletcher smiled and started walking again, this time approaching Annette. Her eyes flashed and glinted. His mother started to speak, then stopped, as if mesmerized by the vampire's eyes. Lauren stopped right in front of her, reached out, and slowly undid the belt of her robe. Annette was a statue. Lauren glanced at Jeff, smirking and triumphant.

"Mommy," Jeff said, a choked, incoherent sob.

Lauren turned back to his mother. Their gazes locked as she slid the robe off his mother's body. It fell softly to the floor. Jeff's mother closed her eyes as Lauren's fingers went up the back of her head and into the wild tangle of her hair. Slowly, she drew Annette Tracey's head back, stretching out her neck, turning it slightly for a better angle ... then, instead of biting, she leaned forward and kissed her on the lips, open-mouthed like in the movies, darting her long tongue into his mother's mouth. She was *making* his mother do this, to punish him for what he'd done. She would kill them both now; kill them, or worse.

He had to stop her.

But he was so afraid, afraid of Lauren, afraid of undying darkness, afraid of everything ...

She was doing it, somehow. She was *making* him afraid.

Lauren leaned in close. Her fangs pricked the flesh of his mother's throat. Jeff lay there, weak and shivering, just *watching*, as his mother fell under the vampire's spell, as she accepted the vampire's kiss.

She was *making* him afraid. Just like she was making his mother stand there and kiss her. The fear wasn't real. It wasn't coming from inside him.

He could ignore it. He *must* ignore it!

Jeff crawled slowly forward as Lauren's lower jaw unhinged and dropped three inches. Her fangs grew larger still. Blood trickled as they pierced his mother's skin, but they were not at the vein, not yet ...

"Beg for it," Lauren murmured. "Beg for the bite."

His mother said: "Please ..."

Mustering the tatters of his courage, Jeff crammed the garlic clove into Lauren Fletcher's ass.

Lauren shoved Jeff's mother aside and leapt straight up, screaming, clinging to the ceiling as she scrabbled one-handed at her backside, trying to dislodge the garlic. Annette fell down and pressed one hand against her forehead, the other against her neck.

"Bastard!" Lauren shrieked. "Filthy little monster!" Then her features melted to mist, like wax vaporizing. The garlic clattered to the floor, blackened, oozing wisps of thick smoke that sank into the carpet and stank of burned flesh. Lauren retreated the way she had entered, as soupy fog flowing out the cracks in his window.

Jeff collapsed, his pajama top drenched in sweat, quivering with released tension. He was alive; and so was his mother. Even now she was fumbling with her robe, trying to cover herself.

But they weren't safe. Not hardly. He'd gotten Lauren Fletcher royally pissed off. If she came back tomorrow night, if she brought some friends, they would both die horribly.

He crawled to his bed, found his pajama bottoms, and put them on. His mother had regained her feet and stood in the doorway, watching him. "Jeffrey?" she asked, her voice shaky with barely-controlled panic.

"Yeah?"

"You're all right?"

"Uh-huh."

"What ... what just happened?"

"You don't remember?"

His mother made fists, rubbed her eyes. "I think I hit my head." She hadn't, but maybe it felt like she had. "Somebody was in your room? Tried to take you away?"

Close enough. He nodded.

"Get dressed," she said. "We're going to the police."

"I don't believe it, man, I don't *fucking* believe it." Lee paced back and forth, puffing heavily on a cigar, blowing huge clouds of smoke at the exhaust fan in the ceiling. He wasn't even supposed to smoke in his office, let alone in the break room, but fuck it; he needed to think, and he couldn't think properly without a cigar. He flicked the ashes on the floor and stepped on them, grinding them into the tile.

Vampires. It was bullshit. He knew it was bullshit. And yet, it made a freaky kind of sense. How could all these things have happened without any evidence left behind? How could so many people simply vanish without a trace, leaving behind abandoned cars, windows open to the winter night, dogs on leashes whining and scratching at the door?

Christ. *He* walked the dog at night, sometimes. So did his wife. It could've been either of them.

He threw the remains of his cigar into the disposal, stomped up the hallway to his office. He fell heavily into his chair; it creaked feebly, protesting years of abuse. He stared at the picture of his wife and kids that he kept on his desk. He should be home, asleep, not here at the station being told Dracula was in town. He remembered the phone call he'd gotten that had rousted him from his bed in the middle of the night: *You'd better come down here, Captain.* That's what they said. Then, when he got in, they showed him Gary's body. Just what you wanted to see in the middle of the night, one of your guys looking like he had stuck his head into a machine press.

Our refusal to accept their existence is their greatest asset. Fletcher had said that during their session downstairs, one of the smug bastard's many pithy pearls. If that was true, why would they throw that nonexistence away by these blatant acts?

It was ridiculous.

It was impossible.

And, God help him, he was starting to believe it.

Martel awakened to, as usual, darkness; but that was the only thing usual about this morning. He had spent the night in the back of the car, something he rarely did, except when he was on the run. After dealing with Fletcher's little band, he hadn't expected to be put in such a position so soon, and certainly not by one of his own. How had she gotten so strong so fast? How had he lost control of her so completely? He'd been a fool to take her, and more of a fool to stalk another woman while Lauren was so obviously jealous. But he'd never considered the possibility that she would rebel; and even when she had, he'd never guessed that she would try to steal Krone away from him. He'd underestimated her at every turn, and now she was more dangerous than an entire legion of humans armed with stakes and garlic.

Leaning toward the grate, he said: "Krone, where are we?"

There were some grunts from the front of the car as Krone woke up. Then his small, high-pitched voice came through the barrier: "We're on a back road in the woods, Master. I don't remember its name."

Martel shifted in his seat. "Is it light yet?"

"No, Master. It's ... twenty after two."

Martel grunted. That meant about four and a half hours of darkness left. Enough time to find food? He doubted it. The sidewalks in this area rolled up at dusk; nobody would be out this late except for the odd derelict or streetwalker, the occasional motorist. He wasn't feeling strong enough to scour the city looking for prey; the risk of encountering Lauren or her spawn was too high. Tomorrow night, he would feed, renew his strength, and then resume his hunt for Lauren Fletcher.

And if he found her? What then? Fight her? Fight the others she claimed to command? If there were more than two or three, he could not hope to prevail. If only he could hunt her down while she slept, as the humans did ... perhaps he could send Krone? No, that would never work. Krone was too slow-witted; they would tear him to shreds, assuming their whorish leader didn't merely seduce him to her side.

Damn Lauren Fletcher to hell, anyway.

He could flee, go somewhere far away, like Alaska. He understood that in winter, it was dark for six months at a time in Alaska. But no, he couldn't do that. He had created her, and she had betrayed him. She had tried to suborn Krone; she had attacked him and forced him from his lair. He had to face her, or word of his cowardice would spread throughout the twilit underworld where his kind dwelled.

He'd made enemies aplenty in his long existence; if they heard he had run from his own, they would be … emboldened.

Martel shook his head. Such doubts were useless. He would think of something; he always had before. For now, he would rest. He closed his eyes.

And for the first time in decades, he dreamed.

He dreamed of daylight.

He dreamed of the sun he had not seen since before the time of Shakespeare, since before Columbus had sailed.

He dreamed of a road through the woods, and a herd of restive goats, and of one goat in particular that ran off into the woods and vanished down a dark hole. He dreamed of a woman, a peasant woman, rail-thin, knees and elbows red from hours spent down on them, fingers raw from cold water and harsh soap. He dreamed of children, children laughing and running as he swung them around by the hands, carried them on his back; and then he dreamed of the same children, dead, butchered, turning slowly on a spit over a low fire, leaking juices into the earth. And then from the earth rose the same thin peasant woman, bursting up like a tree eager to be born, flesh hanging off her bones in strips like leaves, eyes gnawed by pale white beetles, teeth stark white, maggots falling from her mouth; and she grasped his hands with hers. He felt the sharp bones of her fingers dig into his flesh as she squeezed him and tried to speak but only spit putrid larvae into his face.

Martel awoke, screaming like a mortal.

"Master!" Krone cried. "Master! What's wrong?"

Martel shook with dry sobs. He'd thought the nightmares long since gone, but suddenly they had returned, as bad as they had ever been. He dragged his fingers across his eyes, but his cheeks were cool and dry; his kind had no use for tears.

"Master!" Krone said again.

"All is well, Krone," Martel said, his voice raw. "Sleep."

7:15 AM

Dawn broke over the quiet city. Steam billowed from chimneys. Cars chugged out of driveways, carrying people to their jobs. The snow glowed orange in the early light.

"That little shit," Lauren muttered, rubbing her backside. It still burned as if someone had shoved a torch up there; she wondered how long it would last. Here she was, one of the mightiest creatures in the world, and some prepubescent punk had the balls to stuff *garlic* up her ass! She'd rip him limb from limb … later; tonight she would be busy.

Tonight, she was finishing her army.

She shoved her way into her cocoon. It seemed to alleviate the pain somewhat and she scrunched down into it as if she were nestling into the coolness of a featherbed. Oh, yeah, that was better.

Better …

Surrounded by the reassuring presence of her followers, she drifted into an untroubled sleep.

"All right," Lee said, once again presiding over the basement room. All the participants looked better for several hours of sleep, except for Davidson, who looked worse. "Suppose—just suppose, for the sake of argument—that you're telling the truth, and there are … vampires running around. What do we do about it?"

"Well, for starters, your guns are pretty much useless," Ken said. "Unless you blow their heads clean off, they'll keep coming no matter how many bullets you put into them."

"Yeah, Barry shot Chris in the face three times," Roxanne added. "Didn't do a thing."

"Marvelous," Lee said. "What *will* work?"

"Garlic. It burns them like acid."

"You're telling me I gotta load my men up with garlic?"

"And stakes. Wooden stakes in the heart will kill them. Any other material won't do. Or you could cut off their heads."

Lee grunted. "Unfortunately, swords are in short supply."

"What about crosses?" Davidson asked.

"Useless, unless the vampire is … *was* a Christian," Ken said. "You have to show them a symbol of their old religion from when they were alive."

"Anything else?"

"Well, there's always burning. And sunlight, of course."

"All right," Lee said. "Let me tell you my predicament. I cannot do a single one of the things that you're suggesting. I cannot issue my officers garlic. I cannot issue my officers wooden stakes. I cannot issue my officers holy symbols. Do you know why?"

After a moment, Ken said: "Because—"

"Because as soon as I do any of those things, word is going to get out that I'm arming my officers to hunt vampires, and then I will be removed from my position and replaced with someone who *isn't* crazy."

"So what's the plan, then?" Barry said.

"The plan?" Lee laughed. "Who said anything about a plan? There's no fucking *plan*!" Then, in what passed for a normal tone of voice: "I could assign some men to go around checking places they might be hiding. They sleep during the day, right, Fletcher?"

"They sleep, but they wake up easy. Martel has a guardian named Krone who could flip a prowl car with his bare hands. If your officers stumble across a sleeping vampire unprepared, they're more than likely going to wind up dead, or worse."

"We have to do it ourselves," Roxanne said.

"Just the five of us? Davidson here can hardly stand up. I can't go gallivanting around because I gotta stay here and pretend to run things and get yelled at by the mayor and the chief and the city council and anybody else with a title who wanders by. That leaves you three, and Fletcher's a wanted man." Lee sighed. "Why couldn't it just be gang warfare?"

The intercom on the wall buzzed. Cursing, Lee got up and went over to it. "*What?*" he shouted.

"The chief's on line one. He wants to know what the hell is going on and why the hell he shouldn't fire you." The female voice sounded totally unruffled by the captain's tone. "Also, there was another disappearance last night, and we've got a report of an attempted kidnapping. They're sending the mother here to talk to you."

"Shit," Lee said. "Okay, thanks, Connie."

"Always a pleasure," Connie said.

"So?" Davidson said. "Are we letting Fletcher go?"

"No, goddamn it, we are not letting him go. Fletcher is wanted in North Carolina for arson and murder. If I let him walk out of here, my ass is toast." He jerked his thumb at Barry and Roxanne. "And every time we let these two out of our sight, people die."

"We can't keep them here much longer without charging them with something, or at least talking to the judge."

"Who's on the bench right now?"

"Coulter, I think."

"Fuck. Coulter would find a reason to make me let Charles Manson go." Lee ran his fingers hard through his rapidly-greying hair. "Okay. Okay. I need a little more time to think. Barry, you and the cookie are free to go. Fletcher ..."

"Yes?"

"You have to stay here a little while longer. I need to make some phone calls before you get to walk."

"Okay. Can you at least get my stuff back from the jail?"

"Yeah, yeah, I know, you want your garlic and shit. I'll see what I can do."

"While you're at it, can you pick up some things for me? I can write you a list."

Lee stared at him. "Do I *look* like a concierge to you?"

"Well, if you want me to do my own shopping, I can—"

"Christ. Fine. Give me your list, I'll see what I can do." He turned to Barry and Roxanne. "Why are *you* two still here?"

With nowhere else to go, Barry and Roxanne returned to his apartment. The answering machine blinked a message, and while Roxanne collapsed onto the couch, Barry played it back.

"Hi, Barry, Roxanne, if you're there ..." Ryan's voice, in a loud whisper. "I'm calling from ... well, I can't tell you where, but it's not in New York. We're hiding out. Irving said not to call you, but he's in the bathroom right now. He doesn't want to get caught up in whatever is going on. He thinks the government is testing out a new drug or something. I tried Roxanne's house but the machine didn't pick up. I'm not sure what that means, but—oh, I have to go, Irving just flushed the toilet. Good luck."

"Thanks for nothing," Roxanne told the machine.

"You okay?" Barry said, sitting on the floor beside her feet. He took them in his lap and gently rubbed them, massaging with his fingers and thumbs.

"I'm tired," she said. "That feels good."

"You go to sleep," Barry said. "I'll stand guard."

"Okay," she mumbled. Two minutes later she was asleep.

Three minutes after that, so was Barry.

"Good morning. You're Annette Tracey?"

"Yes," she said, taking his offered hand. They shook, and then Lee went and sat down behind his desk. He rubbed his eyes, red and raw, and reached for his coffee.

"So tell me your story," he said, weighing in his mind whether to put creamer in the coffee or not. Looking around and finding no creamer, he decided he didn't want it anyway. He took a long drink from the mug. He noticed she was watching him appraisingly. "I'm sorry," he said. "Would you like a cup of coffee?"

"No, thank you. I don't think I've ever seen a cup quite that big before."

"What, this?" He looked at the mug; it was rather large, actually; he could dunk doughnuts in it without breaking them in half first. "It's a long way to the coffee machine."

"Well, I hope your heart can take the caffeine." She sniffed the air. "And the nicotine."

What was this, his annual physical? "So, I understand that you're reporting an attempted abduction."

"Yes. Someone came into my house, tried to take my boy."

Lee paused, pencil poised over notepad. A computer sat on the corner of his, but he only turned it on when somebody from the mayor's office was coming over. Otherwise, he preferred to write notes longhand; paper never crashed or ran out of memory or gave him a Blue Screen of Death. "Someone known to the family?"

"Not directly. My son says she's a new substitute teacher at his school."

At least it wasn't another fucking vampire, thank Christ. Teachers molesting students, that was something he could understand. "What's her name?"

"Lauren Fletcher."

Lee broke his pencil point against the paper.

Annette Tracey said: "Is something wrong?"

"No," Lee said, reaching for another pencil. "Please, go on."

Out in the waiting room, Jeff Tracey sat under the watchful eye of a young female officer whose name tag identified her as Monica. The room had smudged yellowish walls ringed with plastic chairs bolted to the floor. They were of various dreary colors: Muddy orange, turd brown, puke green, death black. The floor was old tile worn dull and stained by years of shuffling feet. The place stank of tobacco smoke, although a large red sign on the wall proclaimed that smoking was prohibited.

Jeff fidgeted. He was anxious to get out of here. He'd tried to tell his mother not to come to the police, but she wouldn't listen; now they'd think both of them were crazy. Maybe they'd put them in the same cell at the loony bin, at least.

"You hungry?" Monica said, pointing at a dilapidated vending machine in the corner. "You want something?"

"I don't have any money," he said.

Monica smiled. "I don't think it'll bust our budget to give you a candy bar on the house," she said. He watched her go to the machine and do something to it that didn't involve paying it; then she tossed him the promised snack. Being, in fact, starving, he quickly devoured it.

While he was licking chocolate off his fingers, a tall, skinny guy entered the room. His head was bandaged. At first Jeff thought he was coming to complain that somebody beat him up, but then he noticed that the man had a gun under his jacket. He must be another cop. Monica looked up from her magazine and said: "Yo, Davidson."

The man she called Davidson glanced over, his eyes bleary, change gleaming in his palm. Jeff figured he must not know the secret of getting candy without paying. "Monica. Babysitting?"

"His mom's in Lee's office filing a report," she said. "Listen, I heard—"

"Ken!" Jeff cried.

Ken Fletcher, who had entered just behind Davidson, was startled to see the boy. For a moment he struggled with the kid's name, and then it came to him. "Jeff," he said. "What are you doing here?"

Jeff began to cry. "It was Lauren," he said. "She came ... she tried ... she was going to—"

"Shush," Ken said. He nudged Davidson.

"She came into my room," Jeff said.

"Why don't you clear out, Monica?" Davidson said. "I'll keep an eye on Junior here."

"I'm supposed to watch him," she said.

"No problem. I'll take over."

"What's going on? Why all the big secret meetings today? It's something to do with my uncle, isn't it?" She glared at Ken. "*He's* involved, isn't he? I saw him with Barry and that girl. What'd you do to him, you son of a bitch?"

"Monica, calm down. All I can tell you is, we're working on it." Her hand seemed to be inching toward her gun.

"Listen, Miss—"

"Fletcher, be quiet," Davidson snapped. "Nothing you can say is going to improve this situation." Then, to Monica: "And *you*, don't even think about touching your side arm."

"I wasn't." Her hands went into her pockets instead.

"I'll fill you in later, okay, Monica?" Davidson said. "I've got no information for you right now."

She continued to stare bullets at Ken.

"*Goodbye*, Monica," Davidson said.

Muttering, she left. Ken wiped his forehead with the back of his hand. "Jesus, I thought she was going to pistol-whip me."

"You should be so lucky," Davidson said. He got a package of M&Ms and went over to slouch in the doorway, watching the corridor outside. Ken plopped down beside Jeff, who was shivering like he was about to burst.

"So what happened?" Ken asked.

"She came in through the window," he said. "She … she turned into fog … and she came through the cracks … and she was gonna kill me and my mom! Except I used that garlic I got from you."

"Jesus H. Christ!" They both looked at Davidson and he said: "Sorry. Fog? She turned into *fog*?"

"Did she say anything?" Ken asked, ignoring Davidson's outburst. It would probably take the detective a few minutes to get his mind around the idea of a perp who turned into mist when you tried to cuff her. "Give you any idea where she was hiding, what she was up to?"

"No," Jeff said. "But she said she'd come back and kill me."

"They always say that. Don't worry, we'll get her first."

"Yeah, we're doing a bang-up job so far," Davidson muttered.

"But you don't even know where she is!"

"No," Ken said. "No, we don't. Okay, let me tell you what you should do. You and your mom should get a hotel room somewhere and stay put until this is all over. Don't think about Lauren. Remember what I told you would happen if you think about her too much?"

Jeff nodded.

"Okay, well, now you know it's true, right? Don't think about her. Stay up all night watching TV and playing video games if you have to. Tell your mom it's on the orders of the police department." He reached out with his good arm and patted the boy on the shoulder. "I'm sorry you got involved in this. If we'd done the job down in North Carolina, none of this would've happened. But I'm gonna put things right. This time, we're gonna stop them."

"Monica said your mom's filing a report," Davidson said. "She planning to mention vampires?"

"I don't know," Jeff said. "She doesn't remember it that good. After it happened, she just … forgot everything. So then I told her Mrs. Fletcher was a new sub. At school." He looked at Ken. "Do the police know about the vampires?"

"A few do. Not too many. I wouldn't go around advertising it, about the vampires I mean." He spiraled his finger at his temple and made a soft cuckoo noise.

"Right," Jeff said. "Crazy."

"Ain't we all," Davidson said.

Monica reappeared in the doorway. "The captain wants you, Davidson. He says to bring the prisoner and the kid."

They followed Monica down the hall and filed into the captain's office. Ken felt her glare on the back of his head as he passed her and entered, like she was trying to melt his skull with laser vision. He was relieved when Davidson shut the door, leaving her on the other side. She hung around for a little while, a shadow visible through the pebbled glass.

Lee sat behind the desk, chewing on a pencil, tearing the pink eraser to shreds with his teeth. Evidently he was out of cigars. "So, I just had an interesting chat with Jeff Tracey's mother," he said, gesturing for them to sit. "Last night, a woman matching Lauren

Fletcher's description entered the Tracey house and attempted to molest our little friend, here."

"Yeah, we got the story from Jeff," Davidson said.

"Mrs. Tracey's recollection is a bit fuzzy," Lee said. He looked at Ken. "Her testimony amounts to hearsay, but she identified your … wife … as the assailant."

"*I* remember it just fine," Jeff said. "It was Mrs. Fletcher. turned into mist and came in through the window and she was going to bite me and then I—"

Lee raised his hand and Jeff stopped talking. "Okay, okay. She's a vampire, I get it. Your mother, however, does not, and we're not going to inform her otherwise. Did you tell her Mrs. Fletcher worked at your school?"

Jeff nodded.

"Great. Now I'll have to deal with the board of education." Lee sighed. "Anyway, you'll be taken into protective custody until we get this … issue settled."

"You mean until you kill the vampires."

"Yes," Lee said, sounding like someone was under the table, twisting his toes with pliers. "Until we kill the vampires. Davidson, take the kid to the holding area. His mom will be there. Try to make up a convincing reason that they need our protection. Hang out with them until their accommodations are ready. Fletcher, you stay here."

Davidson stood, put his hand on Jeff's shoulder, and guided him out of the office, closing the door behind him.

"Jesus!" Lee exploded, throwing his pencil at the wall. "*Until we kill the vampires. Did I really just say that shit? I can't believe this is for real."

"This is as real as it gets."

"Do you think you can bring these bastards down?"

"Maybe. I can't do anything while I'm in custody here."

"If only there was some way to mobilize the police department," Lee said. "But there *isn't*. You know what I mean, Fletcher? I can't tell them what precautions to take without telling them *why* they have to take them. And if I tell them that …"

"I know," Ken said. "I've lived with it for years."

"Well I haven't and I sure as Christ didn't need to start. Why did they come here, of all places? There's *nothing here*!"

"You have people, you have plenty of places to hide, you have a widely dispersed and isolated population. It's perfect for them."

"Maybe so, but we can't absorb all these disappearances. This isn't fucking New York City where they got eight million other clowns for every one who disappears. The Feds are threatening to get involved! We've been on the cable news channels! Have you seen it?"

"No. I've been in a cell with no television."

"Well, the mayor has seen it, believe you me." Lee closed his eyes. "All right, Fletcher, you win. I'm letting you go. Collect your shit, it's waiting for you at the front desk. Gather your merry band and put these meatballs out of business. Do it fast. Get whatever evidence you can, because God knows we're gonna need it. If we can prove they're real ..." He trailed off. "Shit. I just want them gone. I don't care what we can prove, at this point."

Ken said: "How long can you give us?"

"How long can I *give* you? Hell, in another month the area will be depopulated and we'll *all* be goddamn vampires." He waved his hand dismissively. "Take all the time you need."

Roxanne woke up to a buzzing in her head. No, not in her head; it was coming from Barry's intercom. She got up, pulled her feet out of Barry's relaxed grip, and shambled to the apartment door. Pushing the button, she mumbled: "Yeah?"

"It's Ken."

Ken? Roxanne buzzed him in, then waited until he knocked at the door. She peered through the peephole. Yep, Ken. She turned the deadbolt and opened the door to let him in. "You're out," she said. Then: "You didn't *escape*, did you?"

"Hardly." Ken went to Barry's eat-in kitchen table, set the black valise down onto it, and sat down in one of his chairs.

"Hey, Ken," Barry said, awake now, but sounding sleepy.

"Morning. So, you remember that kid from the tunnel?"

"Yeah, sure."

"Well, Lauren took another shot at him. Lee has the kid and his mother in protective custody. He wants us to stop the vampires. So here I am."

"Great. Now what?"

"What we discussed yesterday," Ken said. "Bait and grab." He looked at Roxanne. "Are you ready?"

"No, but don't let that stop you."

"I won't," Ken said.

5:30 PM

People began arriving at the hockey rink well ahead of time, devoted fans willing to brave the chill air of the arena for the chance to watch men skate around and beat each other up. When Scott Gerber and Melinda Robinson arrived, the undersized main lot was already jammed with cars. A bored-looking arena employee with a flashlight waved them on by, sending them around back to the auxiliary lot, which was also starting to get pretty full. They found a spot at the end, right next to a large Dumpster full of cardboard boxes.

"I hope we get to see some blood," Scott said, as they began the long walk to the building.

"You want blood?" Melinda said. "I'll punch you in the nose."

On the roof of the arena, Lauren Fletcher crouched on her hands and knees, watching the lot fill up with fresh meat. Bob should be arriving any minute. Most of her servants were here, hiding, waiting for her command to descend upon the rink and transform those within. But first, they would have to make sure no one could get out. Once Bob was inside, that would be his job, getting the place's security to lock all the doors but this one. Then they'd cut the phone lines; she'd already had her pets scout the area and disable the only nearby cell phone tower. She checked Bob's cell phone again, just to be safe. No signal.

She smiled, then crushed the phone in her hand.

Before anybody could figure out what was happening, it would be too late, and she would have her army.

Ken and Barry sat in Ken's rented car, parked in the darkness, peering out into the darkness, the murmuring of the radio the only sound, until Barry said: "Here she comes again." Roxanne walked down the sidewalk, quickly, but not *too* quickly, hands in pockets, looking at the night sky. "Still no sign of Martel."

Ken shrugged. "There's no guarantee this will work. He might not show up at all."

"I don't like using her as bait."

"Yes, you made that pretty clear. But I reckon this is our best shot to find him right now."

Barry sighed. "I know."

Roxanne passed by, not looking their way, and stopped beneath a street light near the corner. "She'll be coming 'round the mountain when she comes," Ken said. "Hey, your team just scored a goal."

"Go Devils," Barry said, turning the radio up a little louder. The crowd was roaring its approval of the score, sounding more like static than applause through the car's shitty speakers. As the adulation subsided, the announcer's breathless description of the action suddenly gave way to an equally breathless description of a strange event. "A spectator has jumped onto the ice," he said. "Now another one, and another. It looks like we might have the beginnings of a melee!"

The other commentator said: "We haven't had a good fight here in nearly three months."

"It looks like the fans are wearing fake pointy teeth," the first voice said. "They must be Devils supporters. Hey, mister, hands off the equip—"

The radio fell silent.

Barry and Ken looked at each other.

"Do your hockey fans usually wear fake pointy teeth?"

"Yeah, they do, actually."

"Do they usually trash the radio?"

"Um, no."

They were silent a moment, and then Ken said: "This fishing trip is over." Ken started the car. "Call Roxanne."

Barry looked out the window.

She was gone.

Roxanne was flying.

She was in Martel's grasp, cradled in his arms like a baby, clinging to him with her own arms wrapped tightly around his neck. She had been too shocked to scream when, a few minutes earlier, he had grabbed her from behind and lifted her off the ground; and now, screaming would be useless. Rescue was out of earshot, and out of the question.

"You were thinking about me," Martel said. "I felt it."

"I was." No point in denial.

"I regret that our business the other day went unconcluded," Martel said. "Since then I have been … busy. Troubled. But perhaps we shall further our relationship now, eh? Tonight you will join me in the darkness."

"No," Roxanne said.

"No?" Martel gently nibbled her ear. "You do not want this?"

"No. I want Barry."

"The policeman? An ineffectual fool."

"No," she said, feeling a sudden flash of anger. "He's good and nice and kind! Not like you, you … monster!"

"Such a sharp tone! But what bland adjectives you choose for your white knight, my dear. He is not *exciting*. He is not *thrilling*. He is *good* and *nice* and *kind*, like a doddering uncle. Why were you thinking of me, if you desire him?"

When she didn't answer, Martel's confident smile faltered. "It is true," he said. "You *do* desire him instead of me." He frowned. "You were thinking of me … to draw me to you. A trap?" He chuckled. "I would not have thought your good, nice, kind policeman capable of concocting such a ploy. He risked you, and now he has lost you. Apparently he considers you … expendable."

"It wasn't his idea! Ken—" She broke off.

"Ken." Martel's eyes narrowed. "Ken. Ken *Fletcher*?"

She said nothing.

"You need not answer. It can only be him. This was *his* trap. I thought him dead!" He gave Roxanne a little shake, making her gasp; how far above the ground were they? "He is supposed to be *dead!* And how did he find me, eh?" Another shake, stronger this time. "*How?* Tell me!"

"That family Lauren murdered. He read about it in the paper. He knew it couldn't have been done by a … a human."

Martel made a growling noise deep in his throat like a wild, dangerous dog. "*Lauren Fletcher!* I curse the day I took her."

Roxanne thought: Join the club. She looked back into the darkness, back the way they'd come; the lights of the city were retreating into the distance as they passed over undeveloped forest land, where the trees grew thick and tall, broken only by streams and the occasional road to nowhere. "Where are you taking me?"

"To my car. We are almost there." They began descending through the chill night. Roxanne looked below them. The road, a winding gap in the canopy of trees, came into view as they descended.

"How do you fly?" she asked.

"What?" He seemed startled. "What did you say?"

"I asked how you fly."

"How do I fly?" Martel was murmuring, as if distracted, or deep in thought. "I don't know. I will it, and it is."

They landed gently on the pavement. Martel led her to his car, which idled not far away.

"You will it and it is?" she said. "Is that the way you think everything should be? You will that I should be yours, and so that's the way it has to be?"

"I grow tired of these analyses," Martel said. "I did not bring you here for conversation."

Krone, the turnip-headed gorilla, emerged from the vehicle. He seemed agitated, shaking, as if he'd just survived some terribly close brush with death and hadn't recovered yet.

"You will it and it is," Roxanne said. "You think you can *will* anything and it will be. You think it's your right. But it's not. It's *not*. I'm a human being. I have thoughts, feelings, hopes. You don't have the right to steal those from me. No one does."

Krone said, "Master—"

"Silence, Krone." To Roxanne: "I have the curse, and the power that comes with it. Your God, if you believe in him, gave me this power. Should I not use it?"

"Oh, yes, you have the power," she said, watching him, his face. She seemed to be striking a chord. Jesus, she thought, all it takes is *conversation*? No stakes, no crosses, no fighting, no blood. Just *talk* to the beast and reveal … what? That inside the beast is a man? "I know you've lived a long time. I know that if you don't drink blood, you'll die. But—"

"Not die," he said. "I cannot die, not that way. But I can fade. My spirit will go to a place of hellish non-being, until someone comes near, someone whose blood flows warm. Then I will awaken, attack, drink the blood, eat the flesh, like an animal. It has happened to me before. I do what I do to avoid that. I do what I do to survive, and to keep my mind intact."

"Master—"

"You say that. I think it's a lie. I think you *enjoy* it. You *enjoy* causing misery. You *enjoy* haunting us. Tormenting me and Barry, turning Ken's wife into a vampire. You think it's fun, don't you? It's a big game to you. Well, it's not a game to *us*."

"No, Roxanne Carmichael. It is not just a game. I do it to survive. I am not the monster you think I am."

"You can tell yourself that," she said. "You can believe it. You can even *will* it." She licked her lips. "That doesn't make it true."

"Master," Krone said. "Master, listen to me, please!"

Martel stared at Roxanne. The green glow of his eyes burned low. "What is it, Krone?" he said, not turning.

"Master, on the police scanner. They're sending a police car to a hockey arena. They said it was a riot."

"Riots do not concern me."

"But Master, other things are happening too. Alarms going off all around the city, and the shopping mall is on fire, and so are the oil tanks."

Martel did turn then. His long, delicate hands clenched into fists. "This is the night, then. She is making good on her threat, waging war on the humans."

Roxanne looked at her abductor. In the light of the moon, his pale skin glowed, and she could see the expression on his face, fear and bafflement and consternation all jumbled together. Fear. He was afraid, actually afraid, of Lauren Fletcher.

Could she use that against him?

"You say you're not a monster?" Roxanne said. "Prove it."

"Roxanne!" Barry bellowed. "Roxanne!" He looked around desperately, at the glittering stars, at the uncaring moon.

"It's no use!" Ken said, sticking his head out of the window. "She's gone. Get back in the car!"

"Roxanne!"

"He must've grabbed her while we were distracted. Come *on*, Barry! There's nothing we can do here! We have to get to the arena

—it'll be a slaughter! *Barry!*"

Barry slowly turned to look at Ken. His feet moved jerkily, and when he reached the car he practically fell into it. Ken stepped on the gas and they shot away from the curb.

"I don't know how to get to the arena," Ken said, staring at the falling snow. Barry said nothing. "*Barry!* Listen to me. How do we get to the arena?" He said it slowly and distinctly, and Barry stared at him as if hearing him for the first time.

"The arena?"

"Yes, God damn it!"

Barry looked around. "Turn right here," he said, pointing to an intersection they had just entered. Ken swung the wheel hard around and the car's rear end whipped sideways on the snowy street. It kept on spinning, nearly doing a three-sixty before the wheels found some purchase. Ken pulled the wheel hard to the left and they fishtailed back into the intersection. An oncoming driver leaned on his horn and swerved to avoid them. Ken's car plowed a furrow through the snow and finally returned to his control. The driver of the other car stopped, rolled down his window, and hurled curses and gestures at them as they raced down the street at sixty miles per hour.

The arena was dark and quiet when they pulled up outside. Nothing strange, nothing unusual, except that all the lights were out within, leaving only the pale glow of emergency lighting spilling out the window. A single police stood in the circular driveway near the entrance, locked up and empty.

Barry said: "Maybe we're overreacting."

"No such thing."

They got out and headed for the front entrance, where they stopped, finding Lee Donovan rocking back and forth on a nearby bench, knees drawn up to his chin, heels against his thighs. A shotgun lay across his lap.

"Lee?" Barry said.

The captain gasped and looked up at Barry, hands fumbling for the shotgun; then the tension ran out of his face and he sagged again. "Oh," he said. "It's you."

"Lee, what are you doing here?"

Lee looked up, and there were tears in his eyes, running down his face to drip off his chin into his lap. "They're here," he whispered.

"Inside."

"You sure?"

"I *heard* them."

"What about the police?" Ken said. "I see the car. Where are the cops?"

"It was already there when I got here. They must have gone inside and those bastards killed them."

"Where are the *rest* of the cops?"

"The fuckers are blitzing us," Lee said. "Alarms going off everywhere. Banks, jewelry stores, gun shops. Both malls on fire and so is the fuel depot along the canal. There's nobody to spare on a riot." He laughed, sounding a little crazed. "Arena security will have to deal with it."

"Come on, Lee," Barry said. "Get up. Let's go in there and get our boys."

"They're *laughing.* People are screaming and the bastards are cackling like they're watching a goddamn sitcom. I … I couldn't go inside." He looked at them, as if hoping they could make it all go away. "I didn't know I was such a fucking *coward.*"

"He's snapped, Barry," Ken said. "Leave him."

"You can't go in there!" Lee said, grabbing Barry's wrist. "They'll eat you alive!"

"Jesus Christ, Lee," Barry said, pulling his hand free. "I didn't know you were such a fucking coward either."

Suddenly a car raced up the driveway, skidding to a stop at the curb. Jesus, now what? The door opened and Monica Klein got out, weapon drawn. She raised it and pointed it at Ken and started up the sidewalk toward the entrance. Barry moved into her line of fire. "Monica—"

"I've been following you two since they let *him* go," she said. "You almost lost me with that crazy driving. Almost. Get out of the way, Barry."

"Monica, listen," Barry said, "you don't want to—"

Behind him, the front doors of the arena erupted in an explosion of shattered glass, followed by a thousand faint whispers as the shards fell to the snow and vanished. Christian Keems flew out of the opening like he'd been fired from a cannon, both arms outstretched, nails like claws glistening in the moonlight, misty blood hanging in the air behind him.

"Officer Aryan!" he shouted.   His clawed hands fastened onto Barry's shoulders, driving him to the sidewalk. Snarling, Chris raised Barry's head and smashed it into the cement, hard enough to make lights explode all across his vision. "I'll chew your fucking heart out!"

Barry heard Monica shout, "Get the fuck off him!"

"Monnnnnnica," Chris said, sing-song. "Don't worry, babe, you can be next."

She started shooting. Barry could feel the vampire's body jerk as the bullets tore into his flesh, but Chris wasn't going anywhere. Then Lee appeared next to him, shotgun held at waist level. Ken shouted: "No no no, go for the head!"

Lee bellowed something incoherent and pulled the trigger. The report echoed like a bomb, rolled away like thunder; the blast tore off half of Christian's backside, carrying it away like a bloody pile of laundry and smearing it across the pavement, blood and sinew and twitching muscle, staining the snow crimson.

Chris, still holding Barry down with one arm, backhanded Lee across the chest. The captain sailed off, smashing through the back of the concrete bench, coming to rest among the leafless, snowy bushes.

Ken's shaking hands finally got the valise open. He grabbed a bottle of something, ripped the cork out with his teeth, and splashed the stuff all over Chris. The stench of burning flesh filled Barry's nostrils; Chris shrieked and flew off, low to the ground, legs flailing as if he were trying to run, trailing smoke and ash as he vanished around the curve of the building.

"What was that?" Barry gasped, as Ken helped him to his feet. "Holy water?"

Ken shook his head.   "Olive oil infused with garlic.   From the supermarket. I gave Lee a shopping list."

Monica stared after Chris. "What ... the ... *fuck?* I *know* that guy."

"Not anymore," Ken said. "Come on, let's get the bastards."

Krone drove fast through the hills, following the directions given him by Roxanne. The Master had ordered this; he had closed his eyes for a little while, then announced that everything else was a diversion. The real attack was at the arena.

The Master meant to confront Lauren Fletcher.

Krone was afraid. He was afraid of the woman, afraid of her power, which was strong enough to defy the Master to his face. And the Master was still weakened from their last encounter.

Krone didn't think they should go, didn't think they should fight, but it was not his place to give advice to the Master. He wasn't good at thinking for himself. Hadn't Martel told him that? Hadn't Lauren Fletcher proved Martel right?

"Turn right," Roxanne said. "No, *right*—that way!" She pointed, and Krone wrenched the wheel in the proper direction, sending Roxanne sliding across the seat and into Martel.

The Master was weak. Why didn't he feed on the live woman, before they reached Lauren? Maybe it would make him a little bit stronger. But probably not enough to make a difference.

As they came out of the hills, Krone felt his cheeks grow wet; it took him a little while to realize what this meant.

He was crying.

Because the Master was going to die.

"We can't wait all night," Ken said. "Every second we're out here, people are getting killed in there!" He pointed at the shattered doors.

Barry looked up from his kneeling position next to Lee's body. The man's breastbone and chest had been caved in by Christian's blow, and smashing through the cement bench hadn't done him much good either. The snow beneath him looked like a cherry Italian ice. Barry stood. He picked up Lee's shotgun from where it had fallen. Monica had one, too; the trunk of her car was open, she must've gotten it from there. Did she always drive around loaded for bear, or was it because she had been following the man she thought was responsible for her uncle's murder? What had she been planning to do?

This wasn't the time to worry about that. "Okay," he said, "let's go." He climbed through the hole Chris had made in the door. Monica and Ken followed, Ken whispering to her in a low, urgent voice. Filling her in on the situation. She would probably think they were both insane, if not for what she'd just seen out front.

The screams and hysterical laughter grew louder as they moved through the deserted lobby toward the entrance to the ice; it was like eavesdropping at a torture chamber where the employees really enjoyed their work. Barry fingered the shotgun. He would surely run out of ammunition before he ran out of targets. Go down fighting, hey? Martel had Roxanne, Lauren had an army, and he had a popgun.

They were doomed.

He didn't realize how far ahead he'd gotten until he heard Ken and Monica hurrying to catch up with him. Ken hissed, "Take this," and handed him a clove of garlic. Barry tucked it into the pocket of his winter coat. What good would one piece of garlic do? Was it Ken's lucky clove or something?

He looked at the others. Ken's face was flushed; Monica's was dead white. "Ready?" he said.

They nodded.

Barry turned and yanked open the door to the rink. The screams burst out with physical force. Just inside, a burly black man stood, his back to them, gazing at the pandemonium like a bouncer coolly surveying the dance floor and finding nothing objectionable. Barry saw vampires swinging from the rafters; saw them capering in the aisles, parodying the messianic gyrations of rapture; everywhere he looked, blood, and bodies, and more blood, and more bodies.

He put his shotgun to the base of the sentry's neck. The thing's head spun around and his hand came up, grabbing the barrel just as Barry squeezed the trigger. The man's head erupted, brains, bone, and blood spraying in an arc and down into the seats, splattering the cackling monsters and their struggling victims.

The vampire, his head gone, tottered and fell.

The shotgun blast echoed throughout the arena, reverberating, fading, vanishing beneath the screams and laughter and the horrible soft, wet sounds of feeding. The monsters didn't even pause to see what had happened. Barry leapt over the fallen vampire and charged into the arena, shotgun in one hand and stake in the other, ready to kill and be killed, because the world had gone to hell and so had they, and Lauren and Martel had paid for the ride.

Martel had removed the barrier that separated the back of the car from the front. He felt an unusual calm, as if he were going to some sort of an ending; and for some reason he felt an urge to speak, to look inward and take stock of what he found. He had not done that in a long, long time, and was surprised at how dusty the memories had gotten, how drab and pathetic, over the centuries.

He said: "Shall I tell you a story, Miss Carmichael?"

"A story?" Suspicious; of course she would be.

"Yes. About a young man, a peasant, taking some skinny goats to market. This peasant, he worked hard, toiled under the sun in the fields, worked every minute of every day for as long as he could remember. He had a wife and young children, you see, and he had to support them."

"Turn left," Roxanne told Krone.

Martel leaned back and closed his eyes. He pictured the sun, that orange-yellow orb, as it had been on the last day that he stood beneath it, shining down on the grass that rippled in the breeze; the green, green grass. And the flowers, the flowers beside the track, blooming through the mud. And the clouds, so white, so soft, drifting aimless in the blue sea of the sky; and the warm summer breeze; and a little bird that bathed in a dirty puddle, splashing water like a happy child. Small, ordinary things, each frozen in his memory for being the last of their kind.

"He was a good man, this peasant," Martel said. "He was kind to his family. He went to church, though he did not believe in its teachings, because it pleased his wife. He wanted always to please his wife." Her image rose in his memory, as from his dreams: Thin, with red knees and elbows, and chapped hands from soap and cold water. Brown hair, always wild. Brown eyes, wild as well. What could she have been, had she been born into a different era? Was it all so long ago?

"So what happened to this peasant?"

"One of the goats broke from the herd, ran off into the woods. The peasant pursued. He plunged into the forest, pushing through the underbrush, following the trail of his goat; they were part of his livelihood, you see.

"He came to a clearing. In the middle of it was a pile of fallen trees, thick and tangled, perhaps felled by a storm long before. A hole black as midnight opened beneath them. He heard the goat bleat, and it seemed to come from the hollow beneath the trees. So he went to investigate, went to the hole, looked inside. He did not find the goat.

"I returned that night to the peasant's hut. I entered, but I was changed. His wife saw that. She made the sign against evil, and cursed me, and bade me be gone. And ..." He pictured the scene; her by the fire, menacing him with a crude wooden spoon; and the children over on the floor watching them with round, frightened eyes. "And a rage took me," he said, "and I slew them all. I poured their blood onto the greedy dirt floor, and roasted the children over the fire as their mother watched. And I drank of them, one by one.

"The peasant had hopes. He had thoughts. He had feelings. *Just like you.* And they were stolen from him when he entered that dark shade beneath the trees. He went in; *I* came out. *His* were the wife, the children, the hut, the sun and the trees and the growing of things; *mine* was darkness and death and pestilence. Thus it has been, for years beyond counting.

"I *am* a monster. I see myself through *his* eyes. Curse you for doing this to me, Roxanne Carmichael! Why could you not just scream and wail, threaten and cajole, like all the others in all the years?"

"You see yourself as you are," she said. "Now you know."

Martel opened his eyes. They had arrived. He saw a single, abandoned police car, another empty vehicle, a shattered concrete bench, blood glowing in the moonlight; and beyond it the arena loomed, round and massive as an ancient keep.

"Yes," he said. "Now I know."

This was insane; they didn't stand a chance. They needed machine guns, artillery, tanks, helicopter gunships.

Ken gasped as a bloodsucker came from nowhere, flashing down out of the sky like Tarzan without a vine, hitting him in the gut and knocking him hard onto his back. An injured spectator next to him squirmed and wriggled as if trying to slither through the cracks in the floor. As the attacking vampire pounced, Ken managed to get his stake into the striking position.

No good. The thing backhanded it and sent it spinning across the auditorium. "This ain't a movie, baby," the vampire hissed, leaning into him, long fingers closing around his throat. It was a guy, tall and skinny, wearing denim overalls and a stained T-shirt. At another time, in another life, the two of them might be discussing what kind of oil to put in the engine of a car. Amazing, the things you thought of when you were about to die.

Suddenly a strong, clear voice rang out: "Stop this insanity!" The authority in the voice was naked and pressing, and all the combatants obeyed without thinking, as the tall, black-garbed form of Martel strode into the arena. Krone came behind him, and Roxanne came last, looking around nervously.

Ken scrambled away from the mechanic-vampire, who stayed in a crouch, staring at Martel as if at the arrival of some god that he'd been told about but had taken for no more than myth.

One, at least, was unimpressed by Martel's entrance. "We don't take commands from you, popinjay!" Lauren cried. She was down on the ice among the hockey players. Most were dead, but many would soon rise. A broken hockey stick lay at her feet, still clutched in the gloved hand of a fallen skater. She stood astride it, a colossus at the gates of death. Ken had been trying without success to fight his way to her, shouting her name, but she hadn't heard; and now he couldn't even find his voice, the vampire had squeezed it out of him. He said her name and it came out as less than a croak.

Martel flew toward the ice. All gazes, even Lauren's, were on him. He landed on the rink a few yards from her and locked her eyes with his own. "I am your *Master!*" he shouted. "You will obey me!"

As the vampires watched the combat between Lauren and Martel, a singular duel waged on some level below the conscious, the humans who were able began scurrying out of the rink, only to find themselves stymied by doors that had been locked or chained shut. Roxanne clambered onto the bleachers to avoid being trampled, waving her arms, directing the flood of escapees at the one functional exit. At least she was smart enough not to shout, which might have attracted attention from Lauren's minions.

Ken wasn't sure about that, though; he suspected they were not merely passive spectators to the fight, but were lending Lauren their strength, helping to fend off Martel's attacks. The air crackled with the energy of their minds. Ken watched, awed by the power of the creature who had once been his wife. She was so beautiful, and so terrible. He loved her so much. So much. And all for nothing; everything wasted, every hour gone and turned to ash.

From the corner of his eye he saw Barry stumbling toward Roxanne, pushing through the fleeing crowd. The gash in his forehead from when the vampire outside had slammed his head into the sidewalk was still bleeding, but it looked like his only injury. Well, Ken was glad the two of them could be together, could get some happiness from each other, for as long as it lasted, here among the ashes. He looked around for Monica, saw her halfway across the arena, bloodied but apparently alive. She caught his gaze, gave him thumbs up. Remarkable.

Suddenly Lauren collapsed. She fell silently, like a puppet with its wires cut, landing with one hand on the hockey stick and the other on the fallen player's ankle. Martel stood over her like a monolith. "Yes," he said. "Down. Down!"

"No," Ken whispered.

With one hand, Lauren grabbed the dead man's foot, wrenching it off his body as if it were no more than a chicken wing. With her other hand she took hold of the broken hockey stick. Then she was back on her feet, driving the jagged end of the stick into Martel's chest. It erupted from his back. Black blood dripped from its edge.

Martel clutched the stick, an astonished look on his face, and staggered back a pace. But the stick wasn't made of wood; it would hurt him, not kill him. Lauren pursued, though, holding the foot with the skate out like an axe blade. She swung it in an arc, putting all the force of her body behind it. The sharp edge of the skate dug into Martel's throat.

Thick, dark blood bounced across the ice.

The Master's head tipped back on his neck. Something like black smoke erupted from the opening, shot screaming into the girders overhead. Martel fell onto his back; his head was knocked loose and bounced away, leaving a trail of crimson dribbles.

Lauren stared at him for a moment, like a shipwreck victim spotting rescue after months adrift; then she shrieked: "I'm free! *Free!* Away, my pets, away!" She rose into the air and vanished among the spidery metalwork of the ceiling. All around them, her minions did likewise; the air became a flurry of movement as the vampires, old and new, took flight.

In moments, they were gone.

Barry held Roxanne tight, over by the exit. Around the rink those left behind slowly stood, surveying the carnage, faces registering shock, revulsion, horror, relief; many seemed to have been playing dead, like frightened opossums. Injured victims, many suffering deep bites and hideous lacerations, continued streaming out of the rink. Future bloodsuckers, each and every one, unless they shut down Lauren's operation.

Krone had vanished; Martel lay where he had fallen, blood still leaking from his severed neck.

Ken stumbled over bodies on his way to Barry, who was stroking Roxanne's hair. "You're all right," he whispered, crying softly. "You're all right."

"We're none of us all right until we stop Lauren," Ken said. "And we have to prevent these poor people from coming back."

"Yeah," Barry said, not releasing Roxanne. "Yeah. I know. Jesus, we'll have to burn the place down or something."

"If it comes to that. Where's Krone?"

Silence answered his question. And then, faintly, they heard sobbing. It was coming from the rink. Ken turned to look down at the ice; there was the big, dark form of Krone, crying over the fallen body of his Master.

"I'll be back momentarily," Ken said, heading for the rink.

"Go with him," Barry told Roxanne. "Make sure he doesn't do anything stupid."

"I can't even imagine what *something stupid* would be in this context," she said. "What are you going to do?"

"Crowd control," he said.

"Krone?"

The big man was on his knees on the ice, cradling Martel's headless body and sobbing. "I'm sorry, Master," Krone said. "I'm sorry."

Ken stopped ten yards away and stood, watching. He wasn't sure exactly what had precipitated Martel's intervention into tonight's events; he was damn glad it had happened, but it sure didn't make everything hunky-dory between him and Krone. So, from the relatively safe distance of the rink wall, he called the man's name again: "Krone."

Krone's knobby, pointed head turned his way. The big vacant eyes were wet with tears. Krone knelt on a field of white ice streaked with red, like a soldier on some wintry battlefield.

"He's dead," Krone said.

"I know," Ken said.

"It's my fault," Krone blubbered.

"Lauren did it," Ken said. "Not you."

"My fault," he repeated. "He told me to tell him if I saw her, but I didn't. I didn't. Because I liked what she did when she came to see me, I didn't tell him."

Ken's jaw requested permission to drop. Denied. "Are you saying …" He swallowed, started over. "Are you saying that Lauren … came to you … while Martel was away?"

"Yes," Krone sobbed.

"And she … she … *did* things with you?"

"Yes. And if I told him he could have caught her, but I didn't tell him, didn't tell him anything until it was too late!"

"Whoa." Ken fell into a sitting position on the bench. He saw Roxanne standing nearby, watching. Had she heard? What must she be thinking? "Okay, I can deal with this. Listen, Krone, did Lauren tell you anything, anything at all, that could help us find her?"

Krone shook his head. Big tears flew.

"Krone," Ken said, "Are you *sure* she never said *anything* that could help us find her? Think hard."

Krone looked at his Master and said nothing.

"Okay, never mind," Ken said. "Listen, Krone—"

"The marsh," Krone said, not looking up.

"What?"

Krone stood. His hands formed fists the size and hardness of landscaping stones.

"Krone, what do you mean about the marsh?"

"She said I could live with her *in the marsh*," Krone said. "I bet she's in that building I saw when we first came here. I told them both about it." He turned and started lumbering toward the nearest exit from the ice.

"Hey, hold up there big guy," Ken said. "You planning to march out there all by your lonesome? She'll eat you for breakfast."

Krone stopped, looked at him dully. "What?"

"*Think*, man! She's got a dozen or more bloodsuckers at her command. They'll open you up like a Christmas goose. But if you tell *us* where she is … if you come with *us* … we'll take care of her.

Together."

Krone looked at where Martel lay. "You tried to kill the Master," he said. "You were his enemy."

"Yeah, but he's gone, and now we've got a common enemy," Ken said. "The thing that used to be my wife. We can stop her by working together. You and us." Ken held out his hand. "Help us stop her, Krone. It's the only way."

As Barry moved through the stands looking for survivors and guiding them toward the exit, he came across a young man and woman in the aisle. The woman lay on the floor, inert as a dead fish; the man knelt next to her, fruitlessly performing what looked like rudimentary CPR. "You're all right, Melinda," he told her. "Please be all right."

He knew these two.

Barry knelt beside the young woman. The side of her throat had been torn open; no pretty little puncture marks, just an animal's vicious, killing bite. "Get out of here, Scott," Barry said. He positioned a stake in the center of Melinda's chest and raised the mallet Ken had given him.

"Stop!" Scott shrieked, jumping on him. The kid was surprisingly strong, fast and wiry; Barry found himself sprawled on his side, with Scott pawing at his hand, trying to make him let go of the stake.

Then he heard the click of a safety. Scott froze as a pistol poked him in the side of the head. Monica. She had lost a handful of hair and part of an ear; crimson slicked the side of her head and all down her shoulder. "You'd better hope you're one of *them*," she said, "because in about two seconds I'm going to blow your brains out, and if you're just a dumb human, that'll pretty much kill you."

"Okay," Scott said. He backed off, raised his hands, watching Monica, who kept the gun trained on him. "Okay." Moving backwards, he tripped over Melinda and fell on his ass beside her.

Her eyes snapped open, as if this had awakened her.

She sat up, turned to Scott, raised her arms as if she needed a hug. Looking delighted, Scott moved to embrace her.

"No!" Barry shouted, lunging, too slow to stop the newborn vampire from sinking her fangs into Scott's neck and tearing open his artery. Blood gushed from the wound into Melinda's greedy mouth.

Then Monica stepped up, put her shotgun to the base of the girl's neck, and blew her head off.

Scott fell over, barely breathing, then not breathing at all. Monica regarded him for a moment. "Poor stupid kid. Took him too long to assimilate new information." She looked at Barry, then at Scott. "I guess this one's going to need staking."

"Uh-huh." Then, shouting: "Ken! They're waking up!"

Ken didn't answer, but Monica did.

"We'll have to burn the place down," she said.

9:45 PM

They had, in the end, set the arena on fire. There were so many bodies scattered over so many places it seemed the only thing to do. The stands were old, and wooden, and very dry; they soaked up the gasoline and burned like kindling, revealing the building's sprinkler system to be wholly inadequate. She prayed no firefighters would be hurt battling the blaze, either by the flames or by a vampire that had escaped them.

Back at Barry's apartment, Roxanne lifted the ice pack to check Ken's hand. "That was the dumbest thing I ever saw," she said, "shaking hands with that ox. You're lucky he didn't pulp your fingers."

"It seemed like a good idea at the time," Ken said.

"So did laying a trap for Martel," she said. "I can't believe she killed him."

"Neither can I."

"At least we stopped her tonight," Roxanne said.

"*We* did jack shit. *Martel* stopped her." Ken shook his head. "After all these years ... anyway, in the morning, we're on our own."

In the morning. When had that become a scary phrase? Roxanne wasn't at all looking forward to tomorrow's festivities. Losing the captain was a blow, but Monica, who wanted to join the fight and would not be deterred, had taken his place. She and Barry had gone to set things up with Detective Davidson. They were moving toward a showdown with Lauren, and Roxanne felt the specter of death as a physical presence lurking in the house. She was free; Martel was dead. She could walk away from it now, like Ryan and Irving, run and hide somewhere, away from all this darkness.

But she wouldn't.

Tonight Lauren Fletcher had attempted something that, as far as Roxanne knew, was unprecedented; but for Martel's intervention, her plan would have succeeded. Tomorrow, who knew? She kept thinking of Martel, of the family he had taken from himself, the wife and children he had killed. Perhaps she was hoping to avenge them, and even, in a way, avenge the man Martel had once been. But she wouldn't tell Ken that; she didn't think he would understand.

As if sensing her thoughts, Ken said: "What happened with you and Martel, anyway? Did you bring him to the arena?"

"No. He brought himself." She sat down opposite Ken, across the small table in Barry's ad hoc kitchen. He looked even more pale and haggard than usual, like a recovering consumptive; the events at the arena seemed to have aged him twenty years. "I just talked to him."

"You *talked* to him?"

"Yes. He told me how he became a vampire. Poor man."

"That never mattered to me." Ken frowned at her. "Are you *sorry* he's gone?"

"No. No, I'm not sorry he's gone. I'm sorry for the man he used to be, for what he became, for his family, for the way things got so twisted." She stood and carried her empty coffee cup to the sink, where she rinsed it under a stream of cold water, her back to him so he couldn't see the tears. "He was evil. He was cruel. I'm *glad* he's gone." She rubbed her neck where he had bitten her. Even the residual scars had faded. "But he didn't have to be that way. There was still a man inside the beast."

"Vampire is as vampire does," Ken said. "I'm gonna get some sleep."

"We have a big day tomorrow."

"Yep," Ken said. She heard him moving around, settling into the blankets on the floor. "The biggest."

She puttered around a bit more in the galley kitchen, rearranging things that didn't need rearranging, then said: "Ken, do we ... do we have a chance tomorrow?"

"Of course we do, honey," Ken said.

"But there are only five of us."

"Six, if you count Krone."

"I'm not sure we can count on him for anything."

"Don't worry," Ken said. "Have faith. Be tough."

"Don't worry. Have faith. You sound like a preacher."

"I'm hardly that," Ken said, and now his voice was starting to slur as he drifted off to sleep, "but I do have a secret weapon."

"You do? What?"

But Ken's only reply was a gentle snore.

14

FRIDAY, JANUARY 22

7:15 AM

That morning they assembled just after dawn at the edge of the road. Down a short drive they could see the ruined factory, its windows boarded up, the driveway leading to it buried in deep white drifts. The leaden sky threatened snow to come, but for now the air was still and calm; the red, swollen sun hung in a clear space near the horizon, a boil getting ready to burst.

"Let's go," Barry said. He plunged into the snow bank, off the road, clearing a path for the others, his legs vanishing up to the knee, then reappearing as he took his next step. They followed behind, silent, grim, staring at the factory. Its broken eyes stared back.

Barry plowed a path wide enough for two. Roxanne and Ken came along behind him, armed with stakes and garlic; Monica, shotgun slung over her shoulder, followed them, Davidson beside her. While the others had battled Lauren's spawn at the arena, he had been home, sleeping. His nightmares, he said, had been incredible, but after hearing what had happened at the hockey game, he'd declared that maybe the dreams weren't so bad after all.

Although the previous night's attacks, blamed on home-grown terrorists, had landed on the front page of papers across the country and on cable news, there seemed to be no witnesses who could say exactly what had happened. By the time more authorities had arrived at the arena, most already exhausted from responding to the half-dozen other incidents, the perpetrators had fled and the building was fully engulfed in flames. The survivors had only fuzzy memories of the event; those who did remember it described the madness and chaos of the scene, the blood, the murder, but none of them mentioned vampires, and no one knew how or why the fire had started.

And so their nonexistence, while tattered, remained intact.

The five of them reached the factory, climbing up the stairs to the large front entrance. The door was boarded shut. Barry and Ken went to work on it, pulling boards with a crowbar. The nails squealed as they came loose, one, two, three, four. Finally the last board came free; there was no door behind it, only a vertical sheet of warped and rotting plywood. It was easily dislodged and fell into the snow, raising a little white puffy cloud. Now the way into darkness gaped open.

Ken turned to those behind. "Remember everything I told you. Stay alert. Stay alive." He looked at Barry. "Let's go."

Ken and Barry vanished into the interior. Roxanne watched them, waiting a few seconds for them to scope out the first room. Then she noticed a shape zooming toward her, a dark missile flying through the air, trailing smoke behind.

She turned, realized what was coming, and screamed.

Barry had only gotten a few paces into the darkness when he heard Roxanne shriek. Turning, he raced back to the doorway, but she was already gone. Monica and Davidson were staring off to the east; Monica had her shotgun pointed in that direction, but hadn't fired it.

Barry said: "What the hell?"

"He grabbed Roxanne and flew away!" Monica said. She lowered her weapon. "I couldn't get a clean shot."

"*Who?* Who grabbed her?"

"I think it was Chris. I mean … what's left of him."

Barry looked at the snow. Dark ash spattered it in a line, going around the corner and vanishing behind the building.

"Keems," he growled.

Krone clambered through the snow like a lost great ape or yeti. He thought Martel would forgive him for making a deal with Ken Fletcher; after all, they were both after Lauren now. But Krone intended to find her first, and kill her for the Master.

He reached the back wall just as a scream became audible. Ash tippled into the snow nearby. Looking up, Krone saw the woman, Roxanne, being carried into a fourth-story window by one of Lauren's spawn. He wondered if that was part of Ken Fletcher's plan. He didn't think so.

Oh well. Not his concern.

Krone grabbed the boards that covered this first-floor window and ripped them loose. They came free easily and he tossed them aside. Then, clearing the remnants of broken glass away with a knotty hand, he climbed through the opening and entered the building.

"Shit," Barry said as he rejoined Ken. The first room beyond the door was a rectangle, with wide, crumbling concrete steps against the left wall leading up and down into darkness. In the wall opposite the entrance, a steel door had rusted half-open. Ken shone his flashlight down the stairs onto a filthy landing, after which the stairway continued, presumably into the basement.

"What happened?" Ken said, not looking up.

"Keems grabbed Annie. Fuck!"

"They're probably down there," Ken said. "Some of them, anyway. I'm going down. You should—"

"Didn't you hear me?"

After a moment, Ken said: "I heard you."

"I'm going to find her."

"Do what you have to do," Ken said, "but remember, we're here for a reason. Don't let them control the situation."

From somewhere above them, a high, trilling cry echoed. Roxanne. Barry looked at the ceiling, shouted Roxanne's name, and dashed up the stairs.

Great. Five minutes in, and things were already falling apart.

Monica and Davidson appeared in the blank opening that had once been the front door, peering into the darkness. Ken said, "You two go that way." He pointed toward the metal door in the back wall. "I'm going down here. Okay?"

"We're on it," Davidson said.

Leaving them behind, Ken descended into the darkness.

Chris, the smoke from his body gradually thinning, carried Roxanne forty feet above the floor, through the big processing room. The back part of the factory formed a huge, tall cavity, with steel crossbeams running across it at various heights, staggered like steps, from the lowest, ten feet above the floor, to the highest, fifty feet up. Below them, in the gloom, Roxanne could see the debris left behind when the place had closed: Defunct machinery, boxes piled high and filled with useless inventory, tools, paperwork, pieces of timber. In addition, people must have been using it as a dumping ground for years, filling it with plastic garbage bags that had been ripped open by animals, stained mattresses, broken furniture, rusting appliances, the castoff things of society that always seemed to wash up in places like this. Even the vampires had washed up here; she was probably flying over some as they lay sleeping in the shadows.

She didn't know what this factory had produced, but the five girders were obviously meant to transport heavy items. They ran from the front of the factory to the rear, where they ended in metal doors. Each formed a track for some sort of car; each car sported a rusty iron hook, sharp at the end like a vampire's tooth. One of the tracks had no car; it had probably fallen off. That was the one closest to her, as Chris carried her along.

"We're gonna have some fun, babe," he whispered in her ear.

The big room ended about fifty feet shy of the front wall, the space between taken up by offices or conference rooms, a separate building-within-a-building with its own wall and windows looking out over the factory floor. Chris seemed to be heading for a fourth-story office. His destination had no glass in its window; a thick, tatty curtain hung limply in the empty socket. As the drapes parted to admit them Chris said: "Welcome to my new bachelor pad."

It was even darker in here than out over the floor. Chris threw her down on something soft and yielding. As she fumbled for her flashlight, a pale glow rose in the corner, and Chris turned, holding a lantern. "For you," he said as he shook out a match. "I know you like to do it with the lights on." He set the lantern on the decaying remains of a desk, then turned the little wheel, bringing up the light level. He turned, revealed in all his naked glory.

She shrieked.

"Yeah," Chris said, leering. "*Scream.*" His once-handsome face had become a shattered mess, pocked with angry red scars where Barry had shot him. His backside looked as if it had been scooped away, and the jellied mass of his internal organs hung down between his legs, greenish-gray and glistening, swaying gently as he moved. Already, she could see thick, tenebrous fibers where his body was rebuilding the lost flesh, his regenerative powers renewing and repairing, lifting and tucking.

His body had been blackened and cracked by his exposure to the sun; he looked like a hot dog that had been overcooked on a grill. Charred, crackling bubbles had arisen across his chest and arms and legs; where his skin had split she could see grey flesh beneath. He was so determined to take revenge on her, he had subjected himself to what had to amount to torture. Did he really hate her so much? He had never made such sacrifices for her when he was alive and they were together. The thought came and went quickly, but left her feeling oddly sad.

That wouldn't stop her from killing him. If she could.

Roxanne fumbled a stake into her hand, but Chris caught her wrist and wrestled the weapon from it, making *tut-tut-tut* noises as if scolding a child. He tossed the stake out the window, then yanked her belt off. Her stakes, her garlic, her cross—all the things Ken had given her—now dangled uselessly in Chris's hand. The belt followed the stake out the window. Having disarmed her, Chris stepped back from Roxanne. He grinned and his lip split a little more, blood welling out.

He had a hard-on all the way up to his navel. As she watched, he began playing with it.

"Yeah," he said. "You're *scared*, aren't you? You should be. You should be. I'm gonna fuck your brains out, babe." He started coming toward her. "And I do mean that literally."

Krone saw Roxanne vanish into the far office, high above, but didn't know what to do about it and wasn't really inclined to intervene anyway. So he did nothing, and instead continued exploring, trying to flush the vampires from their little hiding places. The first thing he came to was a pile of boxes, which had been shifted to create a dark opening beneath them. He looked at it for a moment, thinking of the dark opening Martel had spoken of the night before; and then he screeched in his high voice and pushed the pile over. Boxes tumbled like toy blocks kicked by a bully, spilling their moldering contents onto the cold, slick floor; he saw a gleaming, bulging cocoon in the pile, attached to the boxes. It ripped as the pile toppled and a shape spilled out of it. It staggered to its feet, eyes glowing, looking around, momentarily confused. A blonde woman. Was it Lauren Fletcher?

Krone didn't give the creature a chance to orient itself; he reached forward, grabbed its throat, dragged it near, and tore off its head. The body twitched once or twice and then was still; the glow faded from its eyes as its head swung back and forth like a pendulum, suspended by its hair.

It wasn't Lauren.

He tossed the head aside, let the body slump to the floor, and continued on his way.

Ken heard the others moving around above him; they stumbled and crashed about like neophytes in the woods for the first time. Jesus, how did they think they would ever surprise a sleeping vampire, making all that noise?

Thinking this, Ken came out of the stairwell into a steam tunnel, and tripped over one. The thing lay lengthwise across the threshold after the fashion of a drunk passed out on a doorstep; but his eyes snapped open when Ken kicked him, and his hands shot out to grab Ken's ankle. "My name's Bob," he said. "C'mere and French me. My wife won't do it and I hate her for it."

Ken fumbled in the pocket of his coat, found a clove of garlic, cupped it in his hand. Bob gave a hard pull and Ken was on top of him, smelling his foul breath, looking into his mottled face. Ken shoved the garlic into Bob's yawning mouth. The vampire started to gag and tried to spit out the garlic, but Ken kneed him in the jaw and he swallowed it instead. As Bob writhed and coughed like a cat with a bad hairball, Ken snatched a stake from his bandolier, unlatched his mallet from its holster, planted the spike on Bob's chest, and drove it home with a single blow. Bob's body convulsed; he gurgled like a backed-up garbage disposal, choking on the blood he'd drunk. Drops spit out through his teeth, then clots, then chunks of congealed blood the size of Ken's thumb, before his struggles ceased and he lay still.

That had been much too close; he should've been paying better attention. Bob was a low-level bloodsucker who didn't even rate his own cocoon; Lauren was probably using him as a guard dog. There was no way a creep like that should have come so close to taking Ken out.

He had to be more careful.

Ken shined his flashlight around, but saw no other bloodsuckers nearby. The steam tunnel appeared to run the length of the factory, at least as far as his light could travel. The right wall was festooned with pipes, dials, and gauges; ducts and wiring ran overhead. The wall to his left was bare concrete, punctuated here and there by doors, no doubt leading to custodial closets and the like; dark openings beckoned as well, other corridors leading to unknown hideaways. Not a window to be found. It seemed a likely place to locate Lauren and her crew; but where were they?

George had always said he could *feel* the presence of his daughter, even when she was sleeping. Maybe Ken could *feel* his wife? He closed his eyes, tried to think his way to her. Nothing. All those years living with Lauren, making love to her, fighting alongside her, and he had no more connection with her than he did to some stranger walking down the street.

But then he sensed … something. A little flutter in his stomach, like the way you felt before a first date with someone new, a nervous but excited twinge; an urge pulled him forward as it set his extremities to tingling. Was this the *feeling* George got when Elspeth was near? No wonder he wouldn't talk about it. It was frankly sexual, and no sane man would want to feel such a sensation deriving from his daughter.

But Lauren wasn't Ken's daughter; and besides, he had left sanity behind a long time ago.

He started walking, letting the flutter lead him where it would.

Monica and Davidson moved side by side down the hallway, shining their lights into each office in turn. Monica took the right side, Jack the left. They'd made it halfway down the hall, and had found nothing.

Davidson played his flashlight beam around an office labeled *1B*, the last before a set of double doors leading out into a wide open space. He saw a peeling, graffiti-covered wall, a smashed desk, and a dirty mattress in the corner, a pile of old porno magazines beside it.

No vampires. He pushed open the door and checked the wall beneath the window. Nothing. He took a closer look at the porno magazines. Ten or fifteen years old. He thought he recognized an actress on one of the covers.

From behind him, he heard a muffled, "Whoop!"

Davidson whirled, just as the door to the room opposite him swung closed with a gentle *bang*. Seconds later blood flew up against the glass, splattering and beginning a slow downward track.

"Monica!" He kicked open the other door. Monica was on her back with some guy on top of her, the vampire's teeth buried in her neck, his throat pulsing as he drank her blood. The creature's looked up just in time to catch the point of Davidson's stake in its left eye, with the hammer swinging behind right it.

He hit the stake with all his strength. "Payback, you son of a bitch!" he snarled as the bloodsucker's skull cracked and the stake entered its brain. Gurgling, the creature fell, and Davidson followed the first stake with another to the thing's heart. He pounded it (*Morse!*) and pounded it (*Lee!*) and pounded it (*Klein!*), hammering the stake through the creature's chest, until he heard Monica say, weakly: "Jesus, Jack, nail him to the floor why don't you?"

She was alive! Davidson turned and saw Monica sitting up against the wall, hand pressed to her neck, blood flowing from between her fingers. He pulled her to her feet, but she could hardly stand, leaning heavily against him. "Come on," he said. "Let's get you out of here. Come on." He led Monica out into the hallway and headed for the front exit.

"You saved … my life," Monica said.

"We ain't in the sunlight yet, kiddo," Davidson said.

Barry, breathing hard, checked the last office on the second floor. It, like the others, was empty. Damn it, where had Keems taken her?

He swung around and took the stairs three at a time, going up to the third floor.

Ken stopped. The tingles had led him down a dark side corridor, then down a short, narrow flight of stairs; now he was in front of a metal door that said *Storage* in bright yellow stencil, the paint as yet undimmed by decay.

She was in there, he knew it. His hand trembled on the handle. He closed his eyes, inhaled deeply of the dank air, and then pushed open the door and went in, shining his light around. The room was almost bare; whatever had been stored here had been removed and taken to other buildings, other places, where it would be useful. There was little to prevent him from seeing what he was looking for.

They were here, all right; not all of them, certainly, but enough to make things interesting. He saw eight or nine cocoons, some lying on the floor, some in piles of dirt, some clinging to the walls. And there was Lauren's cocoon; it had to be hers, in the center of the room, nestled inside a sort of altar made of broken cement blocks, timbers, lengths of steel girder. If she was a goddess, then this was her temple. Little tendrils ran from her cocoon to the others, gently pulsing, as if she were feeding off them. A few other tendrils ran out of sight, up through holes in the ceiling, perhaps connecting her to other nests elsewhere in the structure.

Ken had never seen anything like *this* before, and didn't really want to think about what it might mean. He fumbled a stake into his bad hand and then, slowly, with leaden feet, approached Lauren's bier. He stopped beside it, looking down at the cocoon. He dug his hands into it. The congealed blood parted easily before his thrusting fingers, warm and slick and gluey. Repulsive. He pulled it back as if husking an ear of corn, and there she was, Lauren, lying in her nest of blood. The stuff didn't stick to her at all. He looked at her, at her pale skin that seemed to glow in the darkness, her hair that shone like the sun she would never see again; at the lovely curves of her body, her hips, her breasts, her shoulders.

She was so beautiful, and so lost.

Trembling, he laid the flashlight on the edge of her bed, placed the point of his stake between her breasts. Shivering, he raised up his mallet, prepared to drive the final blow.

Her eyes opened. Her head lolled to the side, her eyes looked into his. After a second they widened, and she said: "Ken?"

He hesitated, and in that instant cold strong hands grabbed his wrist, yanked away the mallet, spun him around. His hand swung wildly, knocking over the flashlight, sending it end over end to cast wild, shifting shadows on the walls. The stake flew from his fingers and clattered against the wall.

"Ken!" Lauren shrieked.

Krone punched his massive fist through the side of a wooden packing crate. The wood splintered, clawing at his tough skin, finding no soft spot for its slivers to pierce. He ripped open the side of the crate, looked inside. Moldy fabric, but nothing else.

Then he heard a scrape from above, metal on metal. He looked up. High overhead, he saw a dim shape sitting astride one of the girders. He shook his fist at it; he heard a cackling laugh just as something massive struck him, smashing down with tremendous force. He felt his stomach and chest cave in, felt something sharp enter his back. He heard bones breaking, realized they were his; it sounded like someone eating an exceptionally crisp carrot.

Salty fluid filled his mouth, burst from his nose. It took him a second to realize it was blood. He was tasting blood, *his* blood, forced up and out as he was crushed beneath this thing, whatever it was. But there was no pain, and he was not dead. Or maybe he was dead already.

His head felt light, there was a tickle there, like something had snapped loose and was skittering around and around, marbles inside an empty can. The vampire landed in front of him, still giggling, as if in response to an amusing joke. "Crunch went the big man, hey?"

Krone gurgled and spat blood at the thing's feet.

"Now that's just uncalled for," it said, crushing Krone's head with one well-placed stomp.

Where *was* she?

Barry checked the last office on the third floor, and it was empty, too, like all the others. He turned and started up the stairs again, but something struck him and he flew back down, smashed through the door of the third office like it was balsa wood, landing hard on his back. Then it was upon him, the thing that had struck him, with eyes of fire and muscles of iron. It pinned him down, kneed him in the groin, kneed him again. Barry's stomach turned to jelly but he struck the monster in the side of the head with his flashlight. Again. Again. It pinned his arm. Barry snapped his head up and into its face, attacking with his forehead. Its nose broke and it belched a gout of half-jellied gore into his face, blinding him, choking him, the stench of it filling his nose, the taste filling his mouth.

Snarling, the creature rolled over, pulling Barry with it. As he struggled and shook the goo from his head, it lifted him up and hurled him at the window. He hit it with his back, felt the resistance as the glass broke, and then he was falling, the rubble of the factory wheeling beneath him. By chance, he struck the hook that dangled from the suspended car. It caught his shoulder, dug into it, the rusty point penetrating deeply into his flesh. He screamed, caught hold of the metal with his other hand, pulled himself free, then crooked his arm over it and caught his wrist in a desperate grip; now he dangled by his elbow, thirty or forty feet above the floor.

The vampire appeared in the office window, its eyes shining.

"What's the matter?" it said. "Can't fly?"

Chris had Roxanne pinned against the wall, his hands on her shoulders, slowly forcing his dick into her mouth. It tasted like burned steak, and she was beginning to gag, but she knew he wouldn't stop—no, he wanted her to choke on it. What would he do with her once she passed out? Would she wake up one of *them*? Would she wake up at all?

One option occurred to her, horrific and repulsive, but it was her only chance. Chris was willing to do anything, *anything*, to hurt her; the only way she could possibly beat him was to play the game his way, and stop at nothing.

So she bit down as hard as she could.

Blood filled her mouth, salty and metallic, cold and thick. Chris howled and tried to pull away, but she didn't ease up, and when he tore himself free he left part of his anatomy behind. Repulsed, she spat it into the corner. Chris screamed, "Bitch! Horrible horrible bitch! *I'll rip your fucking lungs out!*" Snarling, he leaped at her, rough fingers splayed. She spun to the side but he caught her left shoulder, his nails piercing her flesh like razor blades. She screamed again, broke free of his dirty claws, retreating toward the desk as he whirled to face her.

Barry, swinging from the hook, heard Roxanne scream. "Annie!" he bellowed. Some rescuer *he* was. The dark shape of the bloodsucker leapt from the window, gliding silently through the air like a night owl, quiet, alert, and deadly to its prey. It landed lightly atop the car and knelt there for a moment looking down at Barry.

"What *do* we have here?" it said. "Meat on a hook." The thing reached down and with its cold, dry hand began plucking Barry's fingers from their grip. First was the pinky. "This little piggy went to market," the vampire sang, snapping the digit like a toothpick. It moved to the next finger, pulled it loose, broke it with a *snap*. "This little piggy stayed home."

Blood streamed down her arm, dripping from her elbow to the old, stained carpet. Chris was up again, licking his fingers. "Tastes good, babe," he said. "Spicy. Just like what I used to get from between your legs."

"You bastard," she said.

He grinned. "You loved me once."

"No I didn't."

The grin vanished. "You're a dirty whore, you know that? You were fucking Officer Aryan before my side of the bed was even cold."

"You pathetic troll. You never even *had* a side of the bed." She edged toward the window. "I was always too much woman for you."

"Oh is that so?"

"Yeah." Blood welled between her fingers where she had her hand pressed to her throbbing shoulder. "Yeah I am. But I'm not too much woman for *Barry*."

Chris growled.

"He's *twice* the man *you* ever were," she said. She was behind the smashed desk now, next to a shattered chair. It dated back to before the days of swivel chairs on wheels, or maybe the owner of the office had been a traditionalist; from the wreckage she could tell it had been a wooden chair, with legs instead of a plastic stalk, and feet instead of rollers. One of the legs was more or less intact, lying there on the floor. She surreptitiously hooked her foot beneath it.

"What are you saying, bitch?"

"*Barry* can satisfy me," she said, "like *you* never could."

Chris howled and leaped at her. She lifted the chair leg with her foot, but the balance was wrong and it slid off her ankle before she could reach it. Then Chris was on her, bearing her down and back, his claws scissoring through her coat and blouse. She caught the tattered curtains as she fell, pulling them free, and they fell down to dangle out of the window like a fluttering ghost.

Barry saw the movement, looked up; saw Chris clambering on top of Roxanne, there in the window for him to watch, a rape for his viewing pleasure. "Annie!" he cried again, desperately, uselessly.

Above him, the vampire said: "Next piggy ate roast beef."

"Should I kill him, Master?" asked the dead woman holding Ken's wrist and arm.

Lauren climbed slowly out of her bed, eyes on her husband. "No!" she said. "Let him go!"

"But—"

"Do as I say!" she shouted. The cold hands released him. Ken looked around. In the dim illumination provided by his flashlight, he saw that they had surrounded him, dark shapes delineated from each other only by their eyes. And in front of him ...

"Lauren," he said. "Oh, Lauren."

"Ken." She reached out, touched his cheek, drew back her hand. "You're warm," she said. "So warm."

His jaw trembled.

"I thought you were dead," she said. "You burned to death in North Carolina. Martel killed you."

"I escaped."

"You're here to kill me?"

"I had to come," he said. "You understand I had to come. You would've done the same."

"So now that you're here, what are you going to do?"

His breath came in choking sobs and he couldn't answer.

"Will you do what you came for?" She put her index finger on her sternum, right between her breasts. "You used to kiss me here. Will you put a stake here now, Ken?"

"No. No, of course not. I can't. I can't. I can't do it. Oh, Lauren, Lauren, I loved you with all my soul, you know that. How did this ever happen?"

"Join me," she said, her voice quickening. "Let me turn you. Be my husband again!"

"Join ... you?"

"Yes. Oh, yes. Join me. We'll live together, forever, the way we were meant to be."

He stared at her, tears falling unheeded from his eyes. Could they really do this? Could vampires really love?

"Come to me," she said; and he came, moving into her enfolding arms. She held him tight, squeezed him, put her lips to his neck. His good arm encircled her.

The other went into his pocket, grabbed something slender and hard and cold. His thumb positioned itself over a button.

Lauren stopped. She moved her lips from his neck, looked up at him, her expression puzzled. Her hands went to the zipper of his coat and ripped it open.

Six metal pipes were strapped to his chest, capped at the ends, attached to wires running into his pocket. The dinner he had made from the ingredients on the shopping list he had given Davidson. A condemned man's last supper.

"I love you, Lauren," he said, "and that's why I'm here."

His thumb came down on the plunger.

Barry swung there, helpless, as the thing's grip closed on his next finger. Up in the window he could see Keems preparing to rip off Annie's pants, rape her right there in the window. Where the hell were the others? Were they all dead? Was this how it would end, him on the floor with a broken back, Roxanne violated by her odious vampire ex-boyfriend?

Then there was a dull *boom*, like the sound of distant artillery; and the building shook from its foundation to its roof. The floor near the back of the factory erupted in a fountain of concrete, carrying boxes and debris and body parts in a volcanic orgasm of destruction. A metallic groan followed, slicing through the echoes of the explosion; the entire back wall of the factory sloughed away, taking a good portion of the roof with it. Debris rained from the sky. The I-beam that Barry hung from, and the others, rotated downward as their back supports crumbled. Their front ends churned the structure of the office walls into putty, and two of the aerial car-tracks broke loose, plunging to the floor below, smashing deep into the concrete, opening more holes into the depths of the building.

Barry felt a jarring impact as the end of his girder hit the floor; he felt the sudden cold of a winter wind blowing over him. And there was the sun, not far above the horizon, shining directly in through the new opening in the back wall.

Christian howled as the light caught him full in the face, and raising his arm over his suddenly bubbling eyes tried to retreat into the office; but now Roxanne grabbed his other arm, and locked her legs around his waist. "What's the matter, *babe*?" she hissed. "Not in the mood anymore?"

He cried, "Let go of me you biiiii—" His curse became a wail; then thick, oily, noisome smoke began pouring from his orifices, nose and mouth and ears and ass. His eyeballs evaporated. He swelled up like a balloon, forcing Roxanne to release her legs, and he took the opportunity to pull his arm free and turn away from the lethal glare. But it was too late; he had not gotten three paces before he burst like a soap bubble on a summer day. His skeleton clattered to the floor, nothing but a bundle of glistening, blackened sticks.

Roxanne approached the pile of bones.

"We are *so* through," she said, kicking it apart.

The creature attacking Barry had, by flattening itself against the front of the car, avoided the sunlight; and it was now delivering a series of vicious kicks to Barry's person. The first one broke his jaw, the second a few ribs; the third was aiming for his nose. But it never landed; the car began to roll down the inclined girder, its long-unused wheels screeching in protest. Barry swung forward and slightly to the side and the creature's foot swished by his left ear. The bloodsucker howled in frustration.

The car picked up speed as it rolled down the length of the girder, stopping with a jarring impact against the rubble of the back wall. Barry swung back when the car hit, his legs smashing into the rubble, and pain shot up his left leg as his ankle shattered against the stones. Then the car went off the track, flipping the vampire out of the shadows, into the sunlight. It screamed like an animal, the high-pitched keening wail of a lost spirit in the face of its ultimate nemesis; then there was a soft *pop* and the screaming stopped.

Barry at last lost his grip on the hook and tumbled down the rubble. He slid to a stop at the edge of a hole leading into the ruins of the boiler room. Down in the shadows, dimly, he saw a few body parts; he thought one of them looked like Ken's head, but he couldn't be sure. The still form of Martel's servant Krone lay nearby, crushed beneath rubble and debris; he lay in a pool of thick yellowish liquid, like caterpillar blood.

Barry had seen enough of such horrors. He closed his eyes and welcomed the darkness.

He was brought back to reality by a hand on his dislocated shoulder, shaking him, sending delicate slivers of pain down his back and up his arm. His ankle throbbed; his chest throbbed; his jaw throbbed. He was a bundle of pains wrapped up in a package.

Barry's first thought was of *them*, and he tried to pull away. He heard rubble shifting beneath him, slid a foot or so before the hand grabbed his wrist and checked his progress. "Easy," said a voice, Roxanne's. "It's me. Careful or you'll slide down into the hole."

Now he looked around; it *was* her, Roxanne, alive! She knelt beside him on the pile of shattered concrete, the sun on her shoulders and her face, her hair shining like a lustrous new penny not yet dulled by countless fingers, countless exchanges. How fortunate she was to wear the sun on her head like a crown, thought Barry; and how fortunate *he* was, to be regarded with such concern, as if his well-being were the most important thing in the world. More important than sunlight; more important than freedom.

Suddenly he saw that her left arm was all blood, drying to a dull, caked brown. She was hurt, too. "I love you, Roxanne," he said, though speaking filled his broken, bloody mouth with pain.

"I know," she said softly. "I love you, too. Can you stand?"

She helped him to his feet. He tested his broken left ankle and it refused to support his weight, so she took his arm over her shoulders to help him remain upright. They slowly made their way down the broken remains of the back wall, skirting the hole in the floor, then picking their way through the rubble and debris that littered the floor in random patterns, thrown this way and that by the explosion.

They passed through the darkness of the office hallway, where blood had begun to freeze on the wall and floor; they entered the front room with the stairs; then they emerged from the front door into the shadow of the building. Davidson came running to meet them.

"What happened? What was that explosion?"

"Ken saying goodbye to his wife, I think," Roxanne said. "Is everything okay?"

"I called an ambulance for Monica," Davidson said. "She got ripped up pretty bad. Fuck, your boy here looks worse though. I don't think we should be moving him."

"I'm getting him away from this place."

"Okay, easy, let me help." He took Barry's other arm and assisted them up the snow-covered driveway.

"At least now people will know about them," Roxanne said, looking over her shoulder at the plume of smoke and dust rising from the ruins.

"Are you kidding?" Davidson said. "The story we're going to tell about this won't have anything to do with vampires."

Suddenly Barry coughed. Bright red blood burst from his mouth, staining the snow a brilliant crimson. Roxanne gasped, horrified.

Davidson said: "Aw, shit."

Barry sank to his knees as Davidson and Roxanne struggled to hold him up. He coughed again, more violently, spewing more blood out onto his shirt, staining the snow. "Don't do this," Roxanne said. "Barry, don't you dare do this!"

"Lay him down," Davidson said. "Gently, gently. Shit! He must be bleeding internally."

Barry heard them but they sounded far-off, as if they were talking in some distant restaurant booth and failing to keep their voices down. "Barry, please," Roxanne said. She was sobbing. He couldn't answer her plea, couldn't obey the implicit, desperate request.

Davidson said: "Where's that goddamn ambulance?"

Barry wanted to say something to Roxanne but he couldn't. His chest felt tight, wet; a swimming pool was forming in his lungs. His mouth was full of blood, he tasted it. Better to keep his lips shut.

"I hear it!" Roxanne said. "Do you hear it, Barry? The ambulance is coming. Just hang on a little longer."

Barry heard the ambulance, but it wasn't coming, it was going away: The siren was getting fainter, not louder, and the world was getting darker, the sky going black, dawn in reverse, Roxanne and Davidson fading into a sepia background, nothing left to see or say.

Davidson's voice murmured something. Barry heard the sounds but they didn't seem like words. Whatever they were they made Roxanne upset, she burst out sobbing even more. She looked at Barry and said *I love you*, or maybe she just mouthed it. His ears had gone to stone and he couldn't tell the difference.

I love you too, he thought.

For Barry, the night came down.

And the sun shone on.

EPILOGUE

SUNDAY, JUNE 6

3:30 PM

The engraving said *Ken Fletcher, Beloved Husband* and, below that, *Lauren Fletcher, Beloved Wife*, but the ashes within the small silver urn only nominally belonged to those named on the outside. What could be scraped together of Ken and Lauren Fletcher and positively identified as them would nearly have fit into the urn even without being cremated; the rest was biological matter of questionable origin indeed. Once the investigation was over, the *material*, as the evidence technicians referred to it, had sat unclaimed for some time, until Davidson pulled some strings and got it released.

"Here we are, Ken," Roxanne said. The stream burbled and splashed as it jumped rocks and vaulted a small, half-submerged tree on its stepped path down from the crest of the hill, slowly wearing its way into the earth in which the dead slept. Already it had sliced a deep, steep ravine, difficult to climb into and, presumably, even harder to climb out of. The cemetery had erected a low wrought iron fence to discourage explorers from descending into the ravine, to little effect.

The wind picked up, rustling her hair. She'd had the length chopped off and was wearing it bobbed. Davidson scratched his new beard and looked uncomfortable. The leaves shifted and whispered. "Can we do this and get out of here already?" Davidson said.

"I brought flowers for you." She knelt and tossed a handful of roses into the water; they spun in an eddy, then began drifting out toward the swift current in the center of the stream. She unscrewed the cap of the urn and poured the ashes out. They spattered and splashed, grey and slightly oily, the occasional chip of unconsumed bone hitting with a soft *bloop* and sinking. Davidson fidgeted, shifting from one foot to the other and back again, his tan raincoat flapping. Roxanne told the ashes, "Don't mind Jack. He doesn't like cemeteries."

"How do we know none of *them* are here?" Davidson said. "Gives me the creeps."

"Jack still hasn't gotten over it," Roxanne said, addressing the ground at their feet. "But he's getting there. He doesn't jump every time something creaks anymore."

"When did I ever do that?" Davidson said.

"Monica's gone," Roxanne said. "She's off hunting vampires. You'd be proud of her. Jeff and his mom are gone too, they moved away. I think they'll be okay. As okay as anyone can be, after what we all went through."

"Okay, okay, kiddo," Davidson said, taking her arm. "Enough talking to the ashes. Let's get out of this hole in the ground."

The sky was full of black-bottomed grey clouds scudding along beneath the sun, high and pale and cold. She could see it through the trees as they neared the lip of the ravine; the cemetery was built on a hill outside the city, a tall and solitary hill, so there was nothing to impede the view. From here, the sky went on forever, an ocean over the low buildings and prolific trees of White Bluff. Beyond the city was the far wall of the valley, green with new spring growth. That was one reason she'd brought Ken's ashes here: So he could have full run of the sky, so he could soar over the hills.

Davidson cleared the ravine first, then turned and helped Roxanne out. "Are we done here?" he said.

"I want to make a side trip," Roxanne said.

Davidson nodded. "I thought you might."

The small tombstone was unremarkable except for the quantity of flowers surrounding it. Davidson stood nearby and watched as Roxanne finished weeding. She had already accumulated a big pile of intrusive greenery; it was amazing how fast noxious plants took advantage of the spring thaw.

Life was unstoppable, even though *lives* could be snuffed out in an instant.

He helped Roxanne haul the weeds to a nearby trash bin and dispose of them. Then she went back to the tombstone by herself and stood there for a little while, head bent. She knelt and ran her fingers over the name engraved in the dark stone, following the curve of the Bs with her nail, as if tracing his name might bring him back the way a needle in a record brought back the sound of music from long ago. Davidson couldn't bear to watch anymore and turned away. It had gotten chilly all of a sudden; the sun couldn't bear to watch either, and had hidden its face behind a screen of clouds.

Then she was back beside him, tears in her eyes.

As if in sympathy, a cold drizzle began to fall.

It was a short walk down the hill to Davidson's car. They made it in silence. Clouds had taken over the sky, the mist growing into an actual rainstorm; the wind kicked up in shivery gusts, whipping the droplets into icy little bullets. Roxanne popped open her umbrella and sheltered beneath it; Davidson tied his coat shut.

There was a little vault near his car. When they'd arrived its black iron door had been closed, but now it hung open, revealing the midnight interior of the sepulcher. They both saw it. Roxanne's hand found Davidson's, and squeezed. She said, "Just somebody visiting relatives."

"Yeah," Davidson said; but still, they hurried to his waiting car and sped away from the open crypt, tires spinning on the wet pavement.

The war never ended.